What Makes It Worthy

What Makes It Worthy

A Novel

David Paul Kuhn

Acclaim for *What Makes It Worthy*

"David Paul Kuhn has achieved something quite impressive with this absorbing novel. The novel does what nonfiction cannot: it allows readers to know what it's like to live Washington politics, warts and all. You are brought inside the blurred lines between politics and journalism with fictional characters who seem all too real. Anyone can gripe about Washington's dysfunction, but Kuhn's novel allows us to feel the dysfunction by taking us on a journey inside America's troubled media and politics."

—**JAMES CARVILLE**, chief strategist for former President Bill Clinton

"*What Makes It Worthy* is a heartfelt page-turner that proves a good novel can both entertain you and inform you. Beautifully written, this important book exposes the forces threatening our media and our politics. Yet it also retains integrity and optimism, and after a gripping journey, you'll walk away from the novel deeply moved and enriched."

—**JENNIFER GRANHOLM**, former governor of Michigan

"Both a love story and an exposé on modern American campaigns, David Paul Kuhn's *What Makes It Worthy* takes readers inside what it takes to run a modern-day campaign and illuminates the personal toll it can take on those who are part of it. In a compelling manner, Kuhn's novel shows the good, the bad, and the ugly of campaigns, from candidates to spin doctors to those whose job it is to cover them. I trust readers will come away with a healthy skepticism of all they read during a campaign and an appreciation for those who survive the process."

—**CHRISTINE TODD WHITMAN**, former governor of New Jersey

"A genuinely tender love story that demonstrates how hope can bloom in even the most inhospitable places. . . . Insightful political commentary that will keep readers immersed."

—***KIRKUS REVIEWS***

"This novel, at the intersection of media and politics, provides a disturbing education in the process by which the virus of half-truth is injected into political discourse and disseminated across a bewildering array of platforms, acquiring by mutation that peculiarly postmodern trait, 'truthiness.' The fever rises until the end is inevitable, but the body that truly suffers, Kuhn suggests, is not one party or the other, but the body politic itself. *What Makes It Worthy* is part case study, part postmortem, and part love letter to political intrigue. Real-life bold-faced names mingle with those of invented characters in a way that evokes Bruce Wagner or Bret Easton Ellis, and the fast-paced, telegraphic prose calls James Ellroy to mind. The fragmented sentences become metonymic for the radically reduced thinking required of political operatives and reporters, and the blinkered present-tense narration heightens the sense of claustrophobia and conspiracy. The epigrammatic dialogue and aggressive exchanges of wit highlight the impossibility of people ever getting close to one another in a world this lupine. This portrait of the cynical side of political wars fought in the theater of the media is not a comfortable place to dwell in, but then again the truth is so often uncomfortable. The outlook for the republic may be dark, but the journey into the night, in David Paul Kuhn's hands, is a captivating one."

—**MATTHEW THOMAS**, author of the *New York Times* best-selling novel *We Are Not Ourselves*

"Despite conventional wisdom to the contrary, *What Makes It Worthy* is a welcome reminder that fiction can still deliver the news. With an astute and probing eye, David Paul Kuhn provides a devastating insider's look at the bloody intersection of media and politics. Full of surprising twists and inventive plotting, Kuhn's writing is at once lyrical and realistic. And despite his vision of a corrupt, dysfunctional world, he still manages to evoke both tenderness and hope. Especially rare, he breathes life into three-dimensional female characters. The book's depiction of the current political landscape and those who cover it make it a *Primary Colors* for this generation."

—**LYNN LAUBER**, author of *White Girls, 21 Sugar Street,* and *Listen to Me*

"This novel about the American political process, *What Makes It Worthy,* could not come at a better time. At a point in American history where houses are divided, sentiments run high, and alliances between press and political figures are at an unprecedented peak, along comes a novel to nail all these actions and place them in perspective. . . .

As readers move through a vivid, personal story, it's the people interactions that are striking. One would expect the novel to be replete with political exchanges (and it is), but not necessarily the depth of personal relationships explored here—which, after all, are the foundation of any decision or belief system's evolution. Under Kuhn's hand, the realities of conflicts that become landslides, relationships that become matters of political convenience or manipulation, and cultural and social settings that separate D.C. from the rest of America make sense. Under his pen, politics lives and breathes in the form of human interaction as much as political process. . . .

Wrap it all up in a novel that delves into these circles and reveals their underlying motivations and influences and you have a story that truly explores the American system not just from an insider's viewpoint, but from the very real experiences of human beings just like you and me: people that tend to ask too little or too much of life, but rarely get it right—even in love. And yes, add a dose of romance to the political cocktail: it's just what this drink needs to make it perfect!"

—**D. DONOVAN**, *Midwest Book Review,* Senior Book Reviewer

"Kuhn does a stellar job in cast development, especially with the money-and-fame-driven characters, such as Luke Brennen. Kuhn also keeps his debut novel fluid by alternating character scenes throughout each chapter and throwing in unexpected twists and turns along the way. *What Makes It Worthy* is indeed riveting and eye opening from beginning to end."

—**ANITA LOCK**, who rated the novel "Recommended" in *The US Review of Books*

"*What Makes It Worthy* by David Paul Kuhn is a one of a kind political thriller that portrays the extent to which the media influences and shapes politics . . . It is an incredibly well written story and fans of political drama with a touch of romance will have a thrilling reading experience."

—**FARIDAH NASSOZI**, who rated the novel Five Stars for *Readers' Favorite*

What Makes It Worthy is a work of fiction. Although portions of this novel are derived from real events, all characters, incidents, dialogue, and locations, as well as appearances by public figures, are from the author's imagination or composites and are not to be construed as real. Where real-life events, institutions, agencies, organizations, or public figures appear, they are utilized fictitiously and do not depict actual events or change the fictional nature of this work. In all other respects, any resemblance to groups as well as persons living or dead is entirely coincidental.

See DavidPaulKuhn.com for details on author. He can be reached at DPK4Media@Gmail.com.

Publisher, CLM.

ISBN: 9780692379141

Library of Congress Control Number: 2015909235

Cover design by Jim Tierney.

for Jessie

PART ONE

–

General Election

I

August
New York City

"It's time to start failing."

"What are you talking about?" Gabriel asks.

"I need to go after something worth failing at," Taylor Solomon replies. He stares at a vast blue canvas. Small blotchy black circles float beside a splash of red. The shapes appear frozen and small within the vibrant blue space. "This guy came from nothing. He was an accountant. One day he just quit. His early work was trashed. I think he had a nervous breakdown. But he kept at it."

"And what? He went on to convince people to pay ridiculous amounts for something a child could paint?"

Taylor sips his vodka rocks. "It takes guts."

"Eh." Gabriel shrugs. "He risked less. He didn't have to afford this city."

Taylor nods. "You ever feel like as you get older, the big things seem farther away instead of closer?"

"It's called getting older."

"You sound like my father."

"Damn, I do. Sorry, man. It's the hangover talking." Gabriel finishes the last drops of his vodka. He shakes his drink. Ice cubes ricochet off glass. "I hear you," he continues. "I wouldn't mind having this place someday." They glance down the town house's immense foyer. The cocktail-clad stream in over Persian rugs, past trophy art, beneath imposing chandeliers, handing off coats, greeting friends, feigning friends, goldfish kissing cheek to cheek, eyeing the inferior, the superior, the interior. "It'd be a solid starter house," Gabriel deadpans.

Taylor hints at a smile.

"Give me time," Gabriel says.

"But that's just it. This is our time. Maybe it's just me. But if I don't make a play now, when will I? I don't have children. I'm not married. I have an apartment. Stuff. I don't really need any of it."

"You need to pay your mortgage."

"I could sell."

"What are you getting at?"

Taylor finishes his drink. "It's time for a grand gesture."

Gabriel hits him on the shoulder. "It's time for another drink."

Bar bound. Zigzagging. Pardon me. Excuse me. Soft touches on shoulders, mid back. The cocktailers keep coming. Almost five hundred now, bunching and buzzing, here to book party for *Banana Republic USA: How the Super Rich Thrive Off American Decline.* Billionaire media mogul Mort Zuckerman chats with Al Franken and producer Harvey Weinstein. Zuckerman is storytelling in his understated and confident way, a man accustomed to winning rooms. Franken puffs out his doughy cheeks and gives his Joker grin. Weinstein bends back chuckling.

At the other end of the floor, the kitchen doors swing open. The hors d'oeuvre hawks swoop. Servers dodge. Silver trays soar, float atop fingertips, and sink into the crowd. Empty trays emerge quickly. For cocktailers never do tire of this appetizer movement. Miniature Wagyu burgers dripping with foie gras. Truffle mac and cheese. Tiny haute dogs, dressed with clean parallel lines of condiments.

Taylor nears the woman of the hour. A half dozen guests encircle her, adore her, adorn her. "Darrr-ling, how are you," Sofia purrs to Taylor. "Wonderful to see you," she adds with a touch to his wrist. He says hello. She smiles like an old friend. Rapid-fire chitchat. "Always the belle of the ball." "I try. Love the linen suit." "Thank you." "No, thank you for coming." "Never would miss it." The adorers pile up. Traffic jam. Move along. Move along. Sofia must greet on. "Have fun. Have fun." "Always."

Number 237. Calling guest 237. Sofia's ready to receive you.

Taylor and Gabriel carve through the crowd. "How do you know this woman, anyway?" Gabriel asks.

"I'm one of her thousand closest friends."

"I thought you were all about sincerity."

"Oddly, she is sincere. I think she simply loves people."

"So she's the opposite of me?"

"Precisely."

"She does get a crowd for August," Gabriel says. "It's more my mother's scene. But it's a crowd."

"We can escape downtown soon."

"Cool."

"Meet Liam at Soho House by eleven."

"Done."

Joe Scarborough and Mika Brzezinski arrive. The room's gravity shifts. Paper clips to the magnetic. Regular guests, wannabe guests surround this social center of the Acela elite. Joe stands boxy, gesticulating, splaying his fingers, opining before onlookers. Mika smiles politely. Eyes peek between suits. Stares follow them. People feel they know them. It's the pundit rom-com in real life. The conservative hubby. The liberal wifey. Joe and Mika greet along. Cohosting here too.

Taylor and Gabriel settle barside. The framed cocktail menu describes three designer drinks and details their Okamoto ice cubes. They order. "When you were a kid," Taylor asks, "could you ever have imagined that 'made in Queens' and 'artisanal' would be in the same sentence?"

Using metal tongs, the bartender drops large cubes into the glass and drowns the ice with long pours of vodka.

"I'm sick of that word," Gabriel says. "What does artisanal even mean?"

"It means traditional. For example, you're an artisanal drunk."

"I knew I was something," Gabriel says, as they weave their way out.

Taylor walks as if he has a destination in mind. He pushes his black hair away from his blue eyes. They ascend a flight of stairs and pass the elevator. Alexandra Kerry, the daughter of John Kerry, stands svelte in black. The young man next to her pushes the elevator button. She hesitates. "Can we take the stairs?" she asks. "I once got stuck in an elevator in Mexico." Gabriel is nearest to them. The man says to him, "Tell her, elevators never really fall." "Well," Gabriel replies, "there's a first time for everything."

They enter the library. Red velvet couches. Matching drapes. A fireplace. Antique books. Brittle bindings. A flake falls off one binding, drifts downward, and disappears in the air.

"What's this guy's racket, anyway?" Gabriel asks.

"Hollywood."

A woman turns to them. "This was once Andy Warhol's home," she explains. "He did his Campbell's Soup cans here."

"Seems a bit conformist for him," Taylor says.

"That's only because you don't know about the trapdoor in the bedroom," she says with the rise of her eyebrows. She adjusts her footing. Her skin is red around the rim of her black high heels.

Introductions follow. Taylor and Gabriel meet Saundra Winston. A hefty man walks over, smacks Taylor's back, and exclaims, "Hey man," as he spills a few drops from his glass.

"Oh, Thomas," Saundra says.

"Sorry," Thomas Fuller says. "It's only vodka."

"This is why they only serve whites at these parties," she says.

"What?" Gabriel asks.

"White liquors," Taylor explains. "That's why there's no whiskey."

"Oh," Gabriel mutters.

Taylor turns back to Thomas. "It's been a while."

"It has. Since the last Sofia event, I bet," Thomas says. "I see you still haven't decided whether you want to grow a beard or be clean shaven."

"I rather like the five o'clock shadow on men your age," Saundra says to Taylor. She steps to Thomas and air kisses him hello. "Did you fly in for this?" she asks him.

"I had business."

"Isn't this business for you?"

"It's never business to speak to important progressives like yourself."

" 'Important' is a pleasant euphemism."

"Republicans have their mega-donors. We have our committed Democrats. But I'm here for the party. Sofia's events are always worth attending."

"Particularly when they honor Sofia," Saundra says. She surveys the room. "I wonder if any of these people actually read her books."

"They sure as hell never miss her parties," Thomas replies. "By the way, Taylor, you ever receive my card?"

"I did. Thank you. You're the only person I know who still sends handwritten notes after a good conversation."

"That's one reason Thomas basically runs the California Democrats," Saundra says. "People remember such things."

"They do. So"—Taylor turns toward Thomas—"I saw that you officially endorsed Girona a few weeks ago. Did they offer you any carrots?"

"More like an implicit stick," Thomas says. "Although technically, it's not official for superdelegates until the day the candidate is nominated. But sure. Girona's staff micromanages everything. They'd have tried to block me otherwise."

"Oh, no one can block you, Thomas," Saundra says. "They need Hollywood's means far more than its stars."

"What Girona needs is someone who can manage him," Thomas says.

"Oh please," Saundra says.

"Well, there's chatter."

"There are always silly rumors. Not every candidate is like that."

Taylor drinks.

"Listen, I'm old enough to remember what it was like," Thomas says. "In so many elections, as we used to say, Democrats would wrestle defeat from the jaws of victory. We're the ascendant party now. I cannot abide another careless pol risking any of that."

"He's *not* just another pol," Saundra responds. "For God's sake. I know you supported Miles Riley in the primary. But Joe Girona won. The convention is around the corner. You need to get on board. Our party loves him."

"Not as much as your husband's business must love him," Thomas says.

"How many of those have you had?" she asks, eyeing his drink.

"Shoot, you're too serious, Saundra."

"I wish sometimes you were more serious. Perhaps you should get some air."

"I could use a smoke," he says.

"You can smoke on the rooftop," she replies. "The view of the park is lovely up there. By the way, did anyone see the sky during that tornado warning the other day? I went out to my terrace. There were these gigantic gloomy clouds over the city."

"I saw it," Gabriel says. "I was actually in the park at the time. It only lasted about ten or twenty minutes, I think. It was like that scene when the alien ships fly over the city in *Independence Day*."

"Jesus." Taylor's eyes reach across the room to a silver-haired woman in the hallway. "Is that—"

"Barbara Walters," Thomas says.

"No, the woman she's talking to."

"Oh, her," Saundra says. "I've met her. Barbara and Sofia revere her. She was a war correspondent. Something of that sort." Saundra flicks her right hand. Her diamonds reflect the chandelier. "One of those jobs that makes for a delightful dinner guest. I recently saw her somewhere . . . yes, yes, at the Guild Hall gala in East Hampton."

Taylor takes a long drink and looks at Gabriel.

"What's up?" Gabriel asks. "You know her?"

"That's Caitriona's mother."

"Who?"

"Caitriona. *The* reporter from the campaign."

"Oh shit, really? You going to say hello?"

The silver-haired woman notices Taylor. "Now I should," he says. "Excuse me."

Taylor steps away. He pulls out his phone and emails his colleague, Luke Brennan. "Need a favor. Pls look up what Saundra Winston's husband's biz is, the Dem mega-donor. Any relationship to gov? Lets discuss tmrw. Thx."

The woman's silver hair falls over one shoulder and ends beside the V-neckline of her green satin wrap dress. Taylor recognizes Cait in her, the same pale complexion, the large hazel eyes, the smile that lengthens but does not heighten. "Ms. Ellis," Taylor says to her.

"Taylor."

"Yes," he replies with a pang of surprise.

"Cait once showed me a picture of you two beneath a streetlamp. In Charleston, no?"

"Yes . . . Charleston."

"Barbara, this is Taylor Solomon," Erin Ellis says. "He's one of the *Washington Current*'s young stars."

"Oh, aren't you guys on fire," Barbara says.

"That's what they say."

"Is that what you say?" Barbara asks.

"It's not for me to say."

"Well said," Erin responds.

"Indeed," Barbara says. "Now I must run. I'm tasked with toasting Sofia. If you'll excuse me."

"Oh, I'm sorry, Barbara," Erin says. "You didn't get to finish your story."

"Not at all. To be continued over dinner next week." Barbara looks at Taylor. "Nice to meet you."

"The pleasure's mine."

Barbara navigates the crowd. Chitchatters' eyes track her.

"You remind me of your daughter," Taylor says to Erin. "You have her smile."

"Cait would get a kick out of someone saying I have her smile, instead of her having mine."

"That she would."

"Does she still refer to me by that nickname?"

"Nickname?" Taylor clears his throat. "How do you like being back in the city?"

"Now I know you've heard it. You must work on that poker face, reporter . . . but yes, I like being home, very much. Barbara saves me when I overdose on the cocktail circuit. I forgot the way people here try to outwit each other."

"Ah, the city vice of verbal one-upmanship. My friend was just competing for the best view of bad weather."

Erin gives a small laugh, a long look. She pinches the stem of her wineglass and sips and studies him. "Bellow has a good line on that. That conquered people tend to be witty."

"Or sarcastic. But yeah, I agree. Passive-aggressive wit tends to betray weakness."

"So you favor candor?"

"I'm just not into anyone who has a more precise sense of irony than of their own principles."

"Good luck with that in this city."

"Yeah, it's a problem in certain circles."

"I imagine it is. Cynicism and irony are so fashionable these days. Rather, these decades. Especially around here. Though . . ." She hesitates, gazes off at Saundra gabbing, diamond fingers fluttering, amid the chortling drinkers bumping about as the orators and oglers cycle and flaunt throughout, stories of summering here and what-do-you-do there, as hands lazily hang off wrists and CAT-scanning eyes peer over shoulders, perpetually probing for more clout. ". . . it's perhaps a stretch to call this crowd conquered."

"I don't know," Taylor says. "People who have something, but not their idea of everything, often fixate on what they don't have. They have the most to prove."

"The perils of comfort."

"A far cry from the correspondent life?" Taylor asks.

"Very far."

"Do you miss it?"

She brings the glass near her lips but does not drink. "Some of it. The camaraderie. The spontaneity. The way everything felt more . . . critical. But I think I was ready to return to the city. It's wonderful to spend so much time with Cait again, when she's off the trail. It's easy to take the normal things for granted. Seeing old friends. That sort of thing."

"It's the best sort of thing."

"It is," she replies. Their eyes meet. "I'm glad Cait met you."

Taylor drinks.

"So how do you like covering the campaign?" she asks.

He begins to speak but balks. He drinks again. The air thickens with the unsaid. "Earlier, I was looking at a Miró and thinking about how he was once an accountant."

Her eyes pull inward. She sips her wine and looks at him again. "In my mid-twenties, an editor tried to place me on the society beat. It was a secure beat. Rather popular. It was considered a woman's beat," she adds, with a roll of her eyes.

"And?"

"I quit. A few weeks later, I flew to South Asia and freelanced."

"I love that. And it clearly worked out for you."

"I worked it out."

Taylor nods. "Everyone always focuses on the leap, the quitting. But perhaps the hardest part about leaving anything is working out where you're going next."

"That's true. But first you must leap."

Barbara taps a glass before the microphone. Cocktailers hush.

"So you think," Taylor whispers, "covering presidential politics is like covering the society set?"

"I'm not the one to say," she whispers. Barbara begins her toast. Erin looks back at Taylor. "You must be the judge of that."

II

Washington, D.C.

Peter Miller hunches over his keyboard like a houseplant that gets too little light. The stem is too long, too thin. His head appears too heavy for his wiry torso. Glasses cling to the edge of his pasty nose. His phone is lodged between his right shoulder and right cheek. He's calling the Democratic nominee's spokeswoman. He's responding to emails. His fingers burst. Click. Sent. He moves the mouse. Next email. Click. Sent. Next . . . He can type 202 words a minute. He once timed himself. For fun.

The only window is behind him. Gray sky, gray office towers, gray pavement, gray partition walls. There is one framed picture on his desk. In it, Peter and his two sisters wear Santa hats. Six empty Diet Coke cans litter his desk. He chugs them, forgets them, grips them unconsciously, squeezing the crackling aluminum as he thinks. He's Washington's most influential reporter. He's the factory owner's ideal: a man perpetually caffeinated, with no place to go, unless it enhances his work, unless it makes news. He's preparing to interview the Republican nominee for president. Peter needs bait. Reel the candidate in. Splash.

"How are you?" asks the Democratic spokeswoman.

"Super! Is your mother feeling better?" Peter asks.

The spokeswoman's mom broke her hip two weeks earlier. She flew home to be with her. It was her first weekend off in five months. She told only a few colleagues. Peter should not know.

Yet Peter knows. That's what he does. He learns enough about people to treat them like people. He asks at least one personal question in every conversation. He collects individual trivia the way other men collect baseball statistics. It disarms DCland. Sources notice. He cares about people for more than their usefulness. It makes them more useful.

"Thank you, Peter, she's recovering. So, you're interviewing the ice queen tomorrow?"

"Yup. You have any great questions?"

"You didn't get this idea from us," the spokeswoman says. "So off the record?"

"Course."

"Ask her how many yachts she owns."

Peter hands a bouquet of yellow tulips to Constance Abigail Huntington Wallace. Her husband, Ted, deadeyes Peter. "Flowers, huh?" Ted asks. "Would you give these to a male candidate?"

"I'm sorry," Peter replies. "I meant no offense."

"Hell, I'm surprised a reporter would give a candidate flowers at all. Where I come from, that's called—"

"They're lovely, thank you," Wallace interjects. Her lips purse. Her eyes shift sideways. And with that, her husband knows to let it go. She waves her maid over. "Maria will put these in water."

Wallace's hair is chalk white and swept back. Her eyes are large and dark amber and, in the sunlight, carry a golden-orange hue. Her skin is porous and displays faint lines that swirl at her chin, gather in her cheeks, cross laterally at her forehead, and branch outward beneath her eyes.

They are a short drive east of Savannah, on the back porch of the antebellum mansion that has been in Wallace's family for generations. The garden is a maze of pruned hedges. A stone pathway splits the green and leads to a pine walkway that stretches across the sand dunes to the Atlantic.

Ted scans his phone, rubs his short gray hair with his fingertips. He whispers to his wife, outside Peter's earshot, "I need to talk to you for a minute."

"Now?" she asks.

He nods and the Wallaces excuse themselves.

"Vince just emailed me," Ted whispers to her as they walk away. "He spoke to this reporter, this Miller guy, earlier today. Vince has a bad feeling. He thinks Miller has some dirt."

"On what?"

"I don't know. But Vince is uneasy. Is there any chance he knows about the . . . the law school thing?"

"Jesus, no." She winces. "Vince doesn't even know about that. No one does but us."

"What else could it be?"

She shakes her head. "He couldn't know about that."

"You're probably right. But just in case, watch yourself."

"Of course."

Ted walks inside the house. She returns to Peter. "I'm sorry," she says. "Campaign logistics."

"No problem," he replies.

She asks about his flight. Peter small talks back. He points to the wicker chairs that encircle an outdoor stone fire pit. "Ever make s'mores back here?"

"No," she says, "but I'm sure that would be lovely." Wallace sits first. "Shall we begin?"

Peter sets his tape recorder on the arm of Wallace's chair. He asks about her search for a vice presidential nominee, her convention theme, whether she sees herself as a role model for young women. Mild questions. Lure the politician in. Get the pol off guard. She expects an attack. But Peter remains placid. Until she settles. Then he asks, as if it's a passing thought, a curiosity, "How many boats do you and Mr. Wallace own?"

"I think, ah—" Wallace stammers. "I'll have my staff get back to you."

Peter's eyes widen with adrenaline.

Wallace's gravity amasses. She does not blink. Anger blasts through her glare. "I don't want to say anything further," she seethes. "I'll have them get back to you."

Peter writes the lede in his head. He asks more questions. But he has his headline.

Nineteen minutes later, he's driving away, dialing the Democratic spokeswoman, blurting, "Wallace didn't know how many!"

"When are you reporting?" she asks.

"Tomorrow morning."

Peter scurries to his hotel room. The plastic card fails to open the door. He groans and shakes the door handle and mumbles "doggonit." He realizes the card is upside down, enters, and plugs in his work phone, his personal phone, his camera. There are no more outlets for his laptop. He unplugs the desk lamp. Darkness. He places his computer on the desk, opens it, wakes it, turns on the television news, presses the mute button, and sits, bending forward, coiling his torso, his fingers tensing over the keyboard like claws, until he bursts and straightens up and his fingers mechanically spring into the keys, as he types in the dark room, half lit by the flicker of television light.

Fourteen minutes pass. He submits the story. *The Washington Current*'s second-highest-ranking editor, Rick Ergaleio, calls him. "This is so good," Ergaleio says. "It went just like that?"

"Just like that. I'll file another story later, on the rest of the interview. We can post that tomorrow afternoon."

"Yeah, yeah. But this is the money quote, right?"

"It is."

"Wow. So good. We'll have this teed up for dawn. This deserves a siren."

III

5:58 a.m. *Current*'s publicity director sends the story to Matt Drudge. Subject line: "*Current* exclusive!! Wallace does NOT know how many yachts she owns."

6:04 a.m. The story is live at WashingtonCurrent.com. The headline: WALLACE UNSURE HOW MANY YACHTS SHE OWNS.

6:05 a.m. *Drudge Report*'s top-left headline: WALLACE UNSURE HOW MANY YACHTS SHE OWNS . . .

6:07 a.m. A publicity subordinate blasts the story to The List, hundreds of top-shelf influencers, from social media to radio to television. Cable news remains a primary target. It has more time to fill than content. So *Current* serves up the content. It writes the story pitch for assistant producers to present to senior producers. The "drivers," those newsmakers who steer America's conversation, get their pitch with a personal note. For products require marketing. Marketing enhances profits. And profits affirm products. The faster a product sells, the more that story sells, the more the company values the producer.

6:11 a.m. The Democratic spokeswoman tweets the headline and asks, "How can Wallace understand average Americans' lives?" Democratic operatives retweet.

6:16 a.m. *The New York Times* political editor wakes, stumbles to his desktop computer, and bleary-eyed, before coffee, habitually skims Drudge.com. He sees the headline and forwards the story to his campaign reporters.

6:17 a.m. A *Morning Joe* producer tells Mika Brzezinski, via her earpiece, to check out *Drudge*. He emails her the link. She peeks at her phone. Mika reads the story's headline out loud, on air: "*Drudge* has a story up. I guess Wallace didn't know how many yachts she owns. Really?" She laughs and shakes her head. "I'm just saying, how can you not see that question coming? I mean, seriously."

6:29 a.m. Peter emails *Scorecard* to tens of thousands. *Scorecard* is DCland's must-read morning newsletter, a summary of the morning's hottest political news. It's neo-concise for the A.D.D. Age. Talking heads are given talking points. Birth, birthday, and wedding announcements are listed. Inside-media morsels are dished. And there's the tattling, how titillating, about the politician eating here or the bold-faced names at the soiree there.

Peter notes: "FLASH: Wallace unsure how many yachts she owns. Wallace said she would have her staff get back to us on the number. How will Dems respond? Will Wallace's shop push back? Stay tuned."

Readers will. Peter is the mainline to the hive mind. And the hive is hooked.

6:34 a.m. *New York Times* reporter Cait Ellis yawns. She reaches blindly for the bedside table at her Gramercy Park apartment. Her fingers pat the surface. She locates her phone. She awoke without an alarm, again. Her mind races. She had problems sleeping last year. But it's worse this time. She recalls when she last slept well. Even her sleeplessness is a road back to him.

Cait's powder-white skin emphasizes her large hazel eyes, her pronounced cheekbones, her tiny nose, her small pink lips, her narrow chin. Her pixie hair is auburn with blond highlights. It's brushed forward. The boyish length contrasts with the curves of her petite hourglass figure. Her textured bangs fall to her lashes and are longer at the edges of her eyes. Her haircut accentuates the symmetry of her face but also, now, highlights last night, the mascara that's smudged, the thin black eyeliner that's dried out.

Cait leans up, braless in a sleeveless white undershirt. She reads her phone. There's the usual clutter of press releases, travel itineraries, *Scorecard*, hate mail, subject lines beginning with such DCland acronyms as ICYMI (in case you missed it). She sees her editor's first email to campaign reporters. She sees his second email above it, sent a few minutes later, to her. Subject line: "Find the second day lede." She opens the message. Clicks the link. Reads the yacht story. *Second day lede,* she thinks. *I'll have to file something by nine, well before the morning speech. Damn old man. This is why* Current*'s killing us.* And she detests that *this* is what "killing us" means. She falls back into bed, never letting her phone go, dreading it, watching the emails pile up with the morning, taunted by the blinking red light.

6:47 a.m. In red font, *Huffington Post* banners: WALLACE DOESN'T REMEMBER HOW MANY YACHTS SHE OWNS.

7:13 a.m. The Democratic chairman appears on CNN and mocks Wallace: "She couldn't count high enough."

7:20 a.m. On air and online, *Fox News* headlines: DEMOCRATS ATTACK WALLACE FOR OWNING BOATS.

At half past seven, the head of *Current*'s trending team sends out a staff alert:

```
Hi all,

We'll likely work at least a dozen sto-
ries related to Peter's scoop. Based on our
research, below are terms that people will
probably use when they search for this story
or related topics. Please use these phrases
as often as possible, especially in head-
lines and ledes. It will help harvest traffic
from Google News, Facebook, Twitter, etc.

Words/Phrases/Ideas that connect stories:
- Rich, richest president, millionaire, one
  percent.
- Yacht, yachting, sailing.
- How many yachts does Wallace own? How rich
  is Wallace?
- $200,000 per speech.
- Ted Wallace consulting (outsourcing),
  polo, gambling.
- Wallace inherited (inheritance), born
  rich (privileged, wealthy).

Ping me with questions.

Thx,
Darrel
```

7:51 a.m. *Current* posts the clip of the Democratic chairman's comments. CNN has not yet placed the video online. *Current* sends the link to *Drudge*. *Drudge* adds a headline: Too

Many Yachts to Count. The video is CNN's product. But looters get the link. *Drudge* often brings hundreds of thousands of hits per link. Hits are readers. Traffic. Ad revenue. The spoils of new-media wars.

8:02 a.m. *Good Morning America* leads with the yacht story. NBC's *Today* reports it.

9:03 a.m. Cait's small *Times* story is live on the campaign blog. She summarized *Current*'s story and added context. In it, she writes, "Democrats have already seized upon the news to further portray Ms. Wallace as a 'detached plutocrat,' to quote one Democratic operative."

9:05 a.m. *Time* magazine runs an old file photo of Wallace yachting. A Democratic spokesman sees the image. He sends it to key media contacts. The image spreads across Twitter, Instagram, online. Copy. Paste. The creator is lost. The photographer's credit is ignored. The plundering is too vast. Copyright law too anachronistic. Readers do not go to *Time*'s website. The photo comes to them. An NBC producer sees the image on *Drudge*. The *Today* show displays the picture. The news is discussed on air. NBC credits the story to *Current* and the image to *Drudge*.

Republicans rue the photo. It's the elder Bush baffled by a grocery store checkout scanner all over again, though he never really was. How quickly reality is irrelevant. Public perceptions might form slowly, but they affirm easily. So history rhymes. Again. The stereotype is substantiated, and context proves difficult after the gaffe. The picture reinforces the perception. Never mind the date. It's apropos. The way she reclines on the ivory yacht. Her honey hair blowing in the wind. Her youthful, teasing smile. The preppy collared blouse. Caught on camera: rich white lady!

10:00 a.m. Democrats post an ad online titled "Four." It consists of everyman interviews. The spokeswoman doesn't want to burn Peter. So she made sure the ad looked like a rush job, as if they first saw the story this morning.

In the ad, interviewer asks archetypal American: "Do you own a yacht?"

"No."

"How many yachts do you think Wallace owns?"

Everyman guesses: "One?"

The interviewer says: "Four."

Everyman replies: "Four! I can't even pay my credit card."

Huffington Post headlines the ad. Mainstream news outlets follow. And the media-made drama ensues, as campaigns for the most powerful job in the world duel over yachts.

IV

Columbus, Ohio

His gray-blue eyes contain it all, the promise and the gravitas, the preacher and the populist. He is a serious man. The small, creased bags beneath his eyes underscore his urgency. His silver hair is mildly wavy and thick for a man north of fifty. He's broad in the shoulders and trim in the waist, middle-age trim, from dawns of kettlebells and crunches. There is a reassuring quality to him. He has that smile that's big and buoyant and winning. He does disarm people this way. Oh yes, Joseph Esperanza Girona is a handsome political animal. Lyndon Johnson wrapped in Javier Bardem.

He somehow bridges the disconnected like that, gliding between combative populist and sanguine patriot—all too easily for his opposition. But he only makes it look easy. He thinks like a poet who writes in iambic pentameter, emotive yet calculating. And it's brought him here so fast. Several pundits have already referred to him as the first Hispanic president. He has this effect on them. He even looks like the new American flag. Nuevo Americano wears creased navy slacks, a crisp white shirt, and a red tie. The almost-presidency suits him. No one can own a stage like him. Girona prefers to stand alone on the dais, as he does now, backlit above the massive crowd, daring America to believe again.

Top advisers are side stage, clicking through their phones. The traveling press fills three rows of metal folding chairs. The reporters are quartered off from the real people by rope. Their heads tilt fifteen degrees downward toward glowing monitors. They're working. They have his stump speech memorized. They hear it every . . . single . . . day.

But the two thousand in attendance tilt forward. They hear of the diplomat who became a populist and the populist who became a politician and the politician who became something more. Because great candidates must become more, to reawaken the public's imagination all over again, to preach of little people and big dreams, as if it had never been dreamed before.

Girona circles back to the beginning. He talks about his immigrant grandfather, Jose, from Spain. He tells of his own traumatic birth, when he almost died, and how his mother named him hope, named him Esperanza. So he travels, city by city, speaking of "new beginnings." And when the fire returns, with all the populism that made his name, he'll be sure, these days, to finish with that easy smile and say, "Our country, like each of us, far exceeds the sum of our failures." He'll speak of a nation that began with an idea. Of an idea that can restore a people. And a people who can revive a nation. So they hear of a second American century. Of renewed factories, rising wages, and lowering tides. Of a city on a hill that shines once more. "Because I believe in a woman who holds a torch and a torch that lights our way. I believe in that immigrant dream, in our forefathers' dream. It can be true again, if we can only believe again, if we can only dream again."

And thousands rumble with their faith. Countless white Democrats chant, "Viva Esperanza! Viva Esperanza! Viva Esperanza!"

For Girona strikes hope. And fire consumes the land.

Hope's sleeves are rolled up. An aide advised him before the event, "Bill Clinton would roll up his sleeves. It's very Ohio."

Girona can do very Ohio. He's been Medio Joe-ing all morning. "Now, not everyone cares about an America where we all rise as one nation. They say a high tide lifts all boats. My Republican opponent seems to campaign for a nation where the tide lifts only the yachts, and everyone else sinks. You know what, somebody actually asked Constance Wallace yesterday about yachts."

Reporters look up from their monitors. It's like hearing a new line in the national anthem. You notice.

"She was asked how many yachts she owned. She said, 'I'm not sure. I'll have to check with my staff.' True quote: 'I'm not sure. I'll have to check with my staff.' So she asked her staff, and they said, at least four. At least four yachts! Not fishing boats. Yachts. For the record, I don't have a yacht. Could anyone who has a yacht raise your hand?"

No Ohioans raise their hands. The shepherd knows his flock.

Fresh strain. The story mutates. Post it. Tweet it. Retweet it. Germ warfare. Reporters spread the quote in seconds on their phones. Four tweets ripple to three hundred. Six blog posts become seventeen; seventeen becomes ninety-three. And the news contagion multiplies. *Current* posts the quote on its home page. *Drudge* links. *Huffington Post* leads with it. The old media follow. *Current* cuts a clip of the video from C-Span and broadcasts it on its home page, its YouTube channel, its social media feeds from Twitter to Instagram to Facebook. The clip soon tops websites from Reddit to Yahoo. *Huffington* cuts its link to *Current*, clips the comment from

MSNBC, posts it, attaches a thirty second ad, and profits off MSNBC's footage. Seven minutes after the comment, Girona ends his speech. Cable news channels replay the sound bite. They will loop the line all day. Networks will broadcast the segment this evening. Tomorrow's printed newspapers will quote it. But virtual DCland is already infected by it, living with it, fighting over it.

It's midday, and liberals smell blood. They report Wallace's gaffe beside facts about her wealth. Some retell Wallace's controversial remarks. During the primary, at a private fund-raiser, Wallace told supporters, "Those who preoccupy themselves with the earnings of successful people by stressing the income gap, frankly, usually envy others' success. They want to lower the top to make the bottom seem better. It's socialism by any other name." So liberals pound her as a plutocrat. Conservatives rush to stop the contagion. They ask, who reminisced to Minnesota farmers about buying kale? Yup, it was Girona. That cultural elitist. That grocery elitist. Real Americans eat iceberg lettuce.

Peter Miller skims *Drudge* from his hotel room. He watches the headlines stack and smiles his victorious smile.

Conflict clicks. Reporters dream of exposing wrong. But that's so hard. So rare. Who has the time today? Sensationalism is simpler. There are many ways to nail a politician. People forget the reasons. But they'll recall the fall. The fall means the story mattered. Somebody is destroyed. Or the campaign's sick. An aide fired. A candidate knocked down in the polls. News.

And news means the reporter matters. The quickest way to matter is to make news. Cause the cancer. Sunder a campaign. End a pol's career. And people will remember you.

As the hour nears one, Girona's campaign posts a professional ad on YouTube. It's the banner headline on *Drudge*: Girona Ad Slams Wallace for Owning 4 Yachts. Campaign reporters receive the ad in their email inboxes. More than a million people will view the ad today. *Current* posts a follow-up story that afternoon. One of its reporters found a fifth yacht. *Drudge* links. Moneyyyy.

And marketing. At half past noon, BBC reports the story. Credits *Current*. Tokyo's *Yomiuri Shimbun* covers it. Credits *Current*. German television calls Peter Miller for an interview. *Current*'s brand goes global with a gaffe.

The new gossip site, *Redline*, posts an ad offering "significant compensation" for "juicy" images of Wallace "living large, especially yachting."

Not that they're really Constance Wallace's yachts. They're her husband's. Some collect coins. He collects yachts. Constance Wallace has sailed on only two of them. She rarely sails. She finds it slow. She's a pilot. She made her name in the U.S. Air Force with a hero's tale that won her the governorship—a tale that still fuels her star.

Wallace's husband, Ted, has sailed his entire life. Four of his yachts are docked in Savannah. Two of them are dry-docked, including the prized century-old yacht constructed by the estimable British builders Cox & King. He purchased it after he sold his interest in his consulting firm. Ted Wallace's flagship is *Scarlett*. She's a four-cabin, 169-footer, with a flame mahogany interior and an understated dining room that, if only because of the woods and humidity controls, has the warmth of a humidor. The fifth yacht is a 30-footer docked near their Virgin Islands beach house. There are docking taxes. The expenses are listed on campaign finance reports.

Yet Wallace's staff, like the candidate, did not foresee the question.

Democrats have sought, all year, to turn the first female nominee into an old story, another rich white Republican, to use her class to smother the change she represents. But Wallace is surprising most. Polls show her within the margin of error. Thus little margin for error. It's either pol's presidency. The media has its quadrennial hype. Let the sports metaphors sing! Reporters cover it as if the two pols are entering the ring. Herald the contest. Instigate the fight. Exaggerate the stakes. Polarize the pugilists before those klieg lights. It's blue versus red, browning of America versus white-bread America, male versus female, State Department versus Pentagon, diplomat versus warrior, populist versus plutocrat. America's two political tribes rally to their chosen pugilist. Let's get ready to ruuuummmmmble.

Ladies brunch in Manhattan's Upper West Side. "This race is too close," Saundra Winston says.

"None of my friends are voting for Wallace," a bony woman adds. "Why is Joe not further ahead?"

Saundra's childhood friend leans forward, looks left, looks right, and whispers, "Because he's Mexican."

Saundra scowls. Her friends nod knowingly. "You do realize he's of Spanish descent, not Mexican?" Saundra asks.

"That's not the point, Saundra," the bony woman answers.

Saundra relents and nibbles her brioche. She glances at her phone, if only to avoid extending the topic. She sees a missed call. And there's the story in her inbox. "News Alert: Wallace Does Not Know How Many Yachts She Owns."

Saundra's husband, Clayton, sails competitively. Four summers ago, off the Vineyard with friends, the Winstons sailed with the Wallaces. That day, Mr. Wallace and Mr. Winston realized they had attended boarding school together. This is what endures of the governing class. The Winstons are not a First Family named Kennedy, Adams, Bush, or Roosevelt. But Mr. Winston's grandfather knew FDR socially. FDR shares a bloodline with Ulysses Grant and Zachary Taylor. And Zachary Taylor's father fought beside Saundra's paternal forefather in the Revolution. Saundra's husband is the fourth Clayton Winston. The second Clayton Winston worked alongside Prescott Bush at the private bank Brown Brothers Harriman & Co. And it goes on. The bridesmaids of Howard Dean's grandmother included the grandmothers of George W. Bush and Saundra. Thus the Wallaces and Winstons understand each other. From afar.

Saundra's twinge of sympathy ends at afar. She recognizes that this is a nightmare for Constance Wallace. Both women believe conspicuous consumption is crass. But Saundra cannot forgive Wallace for being a Republican, for opposing abortion rights, for not contributing to her fund-raiser to fight climate change. She passes her phone to her childhood friend and says, "Such poor form. Look at this." Plucked eyebrows arch.

In Arlington, Virginia, Girona's national office is abuzz. Girona's communications director checks Twitter and glances at *Drudge* for the ninth time that day. He counts the *Drudge* headlines about the yachts. "Now seven," he mumbles. "Wow." He oozes a smirk. He kicks his feet up and places them on his desk. "A helluva gift," he tells his deputy. His deputy knows it's no gift. Democratic aide feeds question to political reporter. Reporter asks question of Republican candidate. Candidate bites. Reporter notifies the Democratic aide. The Democratic headquarters produces the ads. Reporter pops the story the next morning. The story spreads for a few hours before the first ad is posted. It's processed food, labeled organic. But it's still red meat. And we are all carnivores.

V

Earlier That Day
New York City

Sunlight bounces off the black tower. The white room brightens. The light cracks this corner of the cityscape at midday. Taylor Solomon considers that fact—the bedroom is no longer dark. He realizes he's missed his train. "Fuuuuck," he groans, closing his eyes. He's been in town since Sofia's book party. Last night: the Standard rooftop until two, a dozen people partying at Liam's after, Ava strip teasing, standing over him on the bed, her bra straps gliding past her shoulders. That was fourish. Thinking hurts. He rubs his eyes and looks at Ava. She sleeps as though the world shuts off with her.

Taylor rises, traces their trail of clothes, and finds his phone. He scrolls through the emails. There are more press releases than usual. He reaches the source of the buzz and feels relief. The yacht story will dominate the news. It has nothing to do with him. His editors are less likely to need him today. He returns to bed, kisses Ava. Her lips waken. She pushes her hips upward.

"I've gotta run," he whispers.

"Babeee . . . stay."

"I missed my train by four hours," he says, lying on his back beside her, yawning.

She looks over at him, rises on top of him. Her lips tease their way down the lines of his stomach. "Go tomorrow," she says. "We can play all day."

"I can't stay, Ava. But Liam won't care if you crash here longer."

"Baby," she replies. "You never used to say no to me. What's happened to you?"

"Nothing. I just lost track of time."

"Baby?"

"What?"

She rests against his chest and looks at him. "I don't know, last night—" she says. "You were not your usual self."

"We had our fun."

"I'm not talking about that. That's always fun with you. God, you're such a guy. But last night, lately I guess, you sound . . . I don't know . . . disappointed. That's not like you. I mean, what happened to the guy who used to always declare how much he loved life, who read poetry to me drunk and always made all those ridiculous but adorable toasts. Remember that time after . . . wait, what was Eugene's old spot?"

"Level V."

"Yeah, Level V. You wanted us to see the sunrise. You remember? It was after that party, the one where that Russian rented out the Statue of Liberty's island and we were escorted there by that gunship. The eighties band, Duran something, played. You were dating one of those runway mannequins—"

"I remember the party."

"I remember, much better, the weekend after at Level V. You were saying how we're all running on treadmills, moving too fast, but not getting anywhere or appreciating anything."

Taylor gazes at the ceiling and recalls the night, but says nothing.

"You remember? You wanted us to watch the sunrise. But my feet hurt. So you carried me a few blocks to the river. Remember that dawn? God, Jersey never looked so beautiful

. . . What's happened to that guy? It's like you're becoming a bitter old man."

Taylor lifts her off him. *Bitter old man.* Her words reverberate in his head. "I've gotta go, Ava. But I'll see you again soon."

"When?"

"I don't know. Soon."

Taylor puts on last night's clothes and packs his garment bag. He calls Amtrak, changes his ticket, kisses Ava goodbye, and closes the door behind him. There's a girl in a short dress, with pink toenails, passed out on one of the loft's four sofas. Liam's door remains closed. Taylor sets his bags down. He remembers the book party, the email to his colleague. He checks his phone again and notices Luke's reply: "The Winston thing is interesting. There's something there. When r u getting in?" Taylor replies that he'll arrive in the late afternoon. He goes to the bathroom. There's a small television over the toilet. It's tuned to CNN. *Current*'s Peter Miller is commenting on the yacht story. Taylor shuts it off, cups cold water with his hands, and splashes his face. He looks at himself. His eyes are shadowed dark. He hears Ava in his head. *You're becoming a bitter old man.* "Fuck that," he mutters. He walks to the elevator. *Bitter old man.* Pushes the button. Ding.

Beeeep. The barman pulls the chicken teriyaki rice bowl from the microwave. He places it in a cardboard tray beside the coffee and Gatorade. Taylor drops a few dollars in the tip cup. He walks to his booth. The train is bumpy. His hangover is worsening. He sets down the tray, slides into the booth, and tilts his head back, wishing for ibuprofen. He chugs his Gatorade and takes out his phone and catches up on the news. There is an email from Jason, a Republican National Committee operative. Subject line: "Hey dude, got a sec?"

Jason feeds dirt off the record for a living. The GOP cannot be caught pushing volatile material. So Jason uses his personal account to email reporters' personal accounts, including Taylor's. This keeps it off the RNC and *Current* servers. Taylor replies via email: "Shoot me a call."

Jason's calling. Taylor answers.

"Hold on," Jason says. Taylor hears him close the door. "Taylor, how are you?"

"Good," Taylor replies. "What's up?"

"Let's begin off the record. Okay?"

"I guess. What is it?"

"You know how Girona was living in Brussels twelve years ago. It was well within the last fourteen years—"

"Oh."

"Oh what?"

"I see where you're going."

"Where?"

"Article Two."

"Exactly. The Constitution says the president must have, and I quote, 'been fourteen Years a resident within the United States.' It capitalizes 'Years' for a reason."

"Jason, did you even think about this? It's not fourteen contiguous years. Eisenhower was in Europe in the mid-forties during World War II. Hell, even John Adams was in England, I think, until 1788, and he became president not even a decade later. Girona's eligible."

"But maybe no one ever contested the point before. You should look into it."

"You're reaching here." Taylor laughs. "Is this the only reason you wanted to talk?"

Jason hesitates. "No," he says. "But hold on. Unspool it for a minute. The founders were obviously worried about allegiance. Girona, on several occasions, spoke in Europe about being 'a citizen of the world.' Spanish was his first language. And—"

"Jason, sorry to interrupt, but I think you know this goes nowhere. Girona's Hispanic. Martin Van Buren grew up speaking Dutch."

"What-the-fuck-ever. This call is a favor. I wanted to give you a heads-up. One of your competitors is about to publish a story on this."

"Okay."

"Don't you care?"

"Frankly, this seems like the RNC pushing conspiracies."

"That's bull. Don't forget, we're off the record."

"I know. I'm only fucking with you. Anyway, I have to run. Have a good day."

"Yeah, okay. You too."

Taylor knows how Jason wants this to go. RNC official feeds sensational material to reporter. *Current* publishes speculative story while protecting the source. GOP's hands remain clean. The rumor becomes legitimate. Is the Democratic candidate eligible to be president? Is he fully American? Can he be othered? Repeat lies enough, raise a false premise enough, and a lie can feel true. "Truthiness," as satirist Stephen Colbert coined it. Perception becomes reality. And politics is perception. The more outrageous the story, the more attention it receives. The rumor develops like Lyme disease, lodging itself, intangibly distorting the American mind. Didn't Al Gore claim he invented the Internet?

VI

Washington, D.C.

Taylor cannot recall the last time he spent a morning offline. Then New Hampshire comes to mind, and with it, a weekend and her. He shakes his head, as if forgetting is ever easier than remembering.

He stashes his bags in the corner of his office and, having avoided his editors' notice, feels relief. He listens to his voice mail for the first time in days and ignores the pile of mail. Sunlight reflects off his desk's lamination. He closes the blinds. The light is directed upward, highlighting the mineral fibers of the white ceiling tiles. He sits back against the mesh of his office chair, staring upward, yawning, and remembers his work. He IMs Luke that he's back.

"Didn't c u," Luke replies.

"Took the back elevator."

"Ha. How'd u ever get an office outside the newsroom?"

"They had no space when I started."

"Don't they push u to move?"

"I just say don't worry about it, like I'm doing them the favor."

"Well played."

Taylor receives the edit of his story and cringes. "Hold on. Call u in a min. I have to deal with Rick's edits."

"K."

When Taylor calls, Luke asks what he's working on.

"Just an analysis," Taylor replies. "They want to know whether some whites won't vote for Girona because he's Hispanic."

"What about white Hispanics?"

"You know what Rick and company want."

"So are the pundits right? Will whitey not vote brown?"

"Same old story. Those who never vote for any Dem largely won't vote for this Dem. In fact, he's attracting more whites than Dems usually do. He's also at historic levels with Hispanics. But at the end of the story, I also explained why there remains some valid concern, like all presidential firsts."

"Then why are you pissed?"

"Rick switched it around, to lead with the racial hype."

"Of course. Better click-bait."

"Yeah."

"You going to ask them to switch it back?"

Taylor glances at the two dozen press IDs that he accumulated over the years, from party conventions to the UN to the NYPD. They dangle off his desk lamp and cover a picture of him with some close friends, taken at dawn in Barcelona when he was twenty-two. He shakes his head. "Probably not. You got to pick your battles, right?"

"Right."

"Anyway, I'll come by soon to talk about Girona."

"Cool."

Taylor walks to the Cave, a conference room gone new-media darkroom, where zombie-eyed twenty-somethings search for viral content, mine reader data, create rapid-fire video segments, and scan the news for sensational clips. *Current* saw that the news aggregators, from *Gawker* to *Huffington Post,* thrived amid the barren media-scape. So it scavenged on the side, too. Locate the protein in another website's story. Rewrite. Add flashy headline. Post. Attract readers. Cha-ching!

Taylor stops at the doorway. He asks whether an editor requested video for his story. If yes, they intend to feature the story. The young man's eyes remain on his massive silver monitor. He takes the two-liter Mountain Dew bottle out of his mouth, gulps, and says, "Uh huh. Did it twenty minutes ago."

"Damn," Taylor mumbles. He walks on, past Philip Larson and Rick Ergaleio, the founders of *Current*, who are talking inside Philip's office. Washington knows the two men by their amalgamation, P&R.

Taylor enters the fluorescent-lit newsroom. The aisle splits eighty cubicles. The air is stuffy. Poor circulation mixes with bottled desperation. A dozen reporters hunch over and type hurriedly. A copy editor tells a producer, "It's ready to go live." Luke sits before the newsroom camera. He buttons his navy jacket. A publicist dabs powder on his forehead. She dials in. A Fox producer gives the cue. He's live. Overhead, on the newsroom's televisions, Luke's broadcasted. The TVs are muted. Taylor hears a computer printer warming up.

Taylor has worked for newspapers that energized as evening neared, where metal radiators rumbled with the printing presses. *Current* has a print newspaper that covers Capitol Hill. It is printed off-site and circulates where politicos work and live. *Current* is already a new-media icon. But the print edition remains a major source of revenue. *Current* began with the understanding that the online world cannot sustain the vast news operations of old. But you seize the gold while there's gold. *Current* earns that gold, those print dollars, largely from lobbyist ads. The ads urge Congress to fund this fighter jet, end that environmental policy, or pass this tax exemption. Sometimes the ads are mere brand maintenance. Spend money to make money. Spend money to win policy. The pig is fat. Get your slice. Providing quid pro quo remains possible, money finds lobbyists and lobbyists advertise and D.C. media profits along the way. There are innumerable ways to feed a pig, cook a pig, dress a pig. But it's still a pig.

And what's wrong with the other white meat? It also feeds the beast. It funds *Current* online and, sometimes, good journalism. A reporter's campaign travels can cost outlets thousands of dollars a day. Presidential campaigns charge media for the plane tickets, the sandwiches, the chocolate on reporters' pillows, if they can.

Congressional reporters, lifestyle writers, churn out copy to fill the print edition. Those pages provide space for the ads. And those ads fund *Current*'s stars, as stars go in little DCland. The stars lead the website, cover presidential politics, appear on television. It's grunts versus flyboys. The grunts subsidize the flyboys. They resent the flyboys. The flyboys rarely bother to look down.

Luke is a news grunt flirting with flyboy status. He's thirty-four, short, with feathery blond hair. He races from the newsroom camera to his desk, quickly for someone so pudgy, as he grimaces before deadlines and sits between his towers of stacked manila folders.

Taylor walks to Luke's partition. They exchange hellos. Luke adds, "Gimme a sec, I never got to finish up this other shit." Taylor offers to come back later. "No," he replies. "It's fine." Luke stabs the enter key with his index finger, looks up, and rubs his head with his fingertips, as if he has lice. "They're just fucking grinding me, man."

Current's publicity director speed walks within earshot. "Stop bitching, guys," she says. "Remember, *Current*'s about the cause. It's not work."

"Did you really just say that?" Taylor asks with a small laugh.

She's already two cubicles away, speeding onward.

"Man, I wish I could laugh that off," Luke says. "I haven't had a good night's sleep in a year because of that shit." His eyes dart to his inbox and back to Taylor. "But so it fucking goes." He pops a Xanax and washes it down with sugar-free Red Bull.

"Good thing that Red Bull is sugar free," Taylor quips.

"Dude, don't dis the '*Current* cocktail.' It works. By the way, I meant to ask you earlier, did you read that *Times* front-page story three days ago, on Wallace's husband's love of polo?"

"I heard about it."

"Read it. Now that's bait. It painted him as Thurston Howell and shit."

"It can't be worse than the *Times* profile last year."

"You mean that sentence?"

"Yeah, where it claimed he gambled hundreds of thousands."

"No, no. They provided evidence this time," Luke says with a trace of sarcasm. "They ran a picture of him on a horse, all polo-ed out. Dems are loving it."

"And now Peter writes this yacht story. Wallace's staff must be furious."

"Shit, that reminds me. I've gotta get back to Peter."

"In a minute. I came all the way to the newsroom."

"You trooper."

Taylor smirks. "So what'd you find on Saundra Winston?"

"Right, yeah. She's Girona's sixth-largest bundler. I checked past campaigns. She's never bundled this kinda cash before. Her husband is a different story. He's a lot older and he's been a big Dem donor for years."

"Who's her husband?"

"A Wall Street player named Clayton Winston. Now, it gets interesting with him. Outside what they've bundled, he has separately given at least one point one million dollars to groups aligned with Girona."

"That's enthusiastic backing for a financier, considering Girona's rhetoric during the primary."

"Exactly. They've also helped host several lavish gatherings since those totals were reported. But here's what got me more intrigued. You know how FEC filings list donors' employers?"

Taylor nods.

"Well, the number two at Winston's outfit has personally given almost seven hundred thousand to some of the same groups. And this dude has contributed to GOP candidates in every other election since at least '92. Then I searched his name with Girona. He's on the damn steering committee of Girona's national security policy group."

"What's a Republican venture capitalist doing on Girona's military policy group?"

"Precisely."

"We need details on this outfit's big investments."

"Already compiled that." Luke double-clicks on a file. They scan an Excel spreadsheet. Minutes pass. They stop and research a business. There's nothing abnormal. A name strikes Luke. It leads to nothing. Luke keeps tapping the downward arrow on his keyboard. Another company comes to naught. About ten minutes later, they read the name "NxtGen." Taylor tells Luke to stop. It's one of the largest investments. And to Taylor, the name rings of an environmental start-up. They discover it is indeed a renewable fuel company. Last year, the firm moved from Silicon Valley to Virginia. And they read on. Taylor swipes his index finger over his phone. Luke scrolls and skims websites. "Here's something," Luke says. "They developed some new fuel or additive. It didn't meet expectations."

"Seems too obvious. But maybe."

"What?" Luke asks, swiveling around in his chair.

Taylor looks at Luke. "You know how biofuels are still far more expensive than fossil fuels?"

"So?"

"Well, where do you go if you want a lot of capital for a product that's much more costly than the alternative?"

"Uncle Sam."

"Specifically?"

"The Pentagon."

"Exactly. Maybe it's another company trying to spin their project as the next microchip or Internet. You know, the next breakthrough for government to fund."

"But this doesn't seem like an R and D thing."

Taylor nods.

"It may be just another company cozying up to a candidate," Luke adds.

"Yeah. I need evidence of a horse trade for this to be a story, if it's a story."

"It's almost impossible to prove this shit. Also, it's not like the president can declare how to invest tax revenue. There are congressional appropriations. Although, it could still be creatively inserted into a bill."

"These days, you wouldn't gamble this much on any representative's ability to barter, let alone fund a major project. This is Congress we're talking about."

Luke grins. “Okay then, what if it is an executive thing?”

“NxtGen would have to get a serious Pentagon contract.”

“But like you said, the trade must be provable. Otherwise it’s just more pork.”

Taylor hesitates. “It felt like something. The Winston woman reacted, in that way.”

“I know the way. I felt the same around New Year’s,” Luke says resentfully.

“I know. I just couldn’t do that story. You didn’t need me anyway.”

“You don’t need me on this story, either.”

“I could use your help with this. But it’s your call.”

Luke hesitates. Then he juts his head upward and nods.

“Cool,” Taylor says. “And listen, I’m sorry I couldn’t be more helpful on New Year’s. Whatever happened with that story?”

“The hunt continues. But never mind that now. I need to deal with this shit with Peter. You’d think he’d chill after his yacht story.”

“What’s Peter on you about?”

“Just this heavyweight mess. I should get back to him, though, before it gets outta hand.”

The wooden windows are large and arched, and when fully opened outward, as they are now, it’s as if there are no windows. Spears of rain fall outside. The building’s half-moon driveway shimmers in the darkness. The rain is visible on the pavement, the cobblestones, where the building’s iron lampposts and streetlights capture dancing drops, as the clean smell pushes away the August humidity and fills the apartment.

Taylor is listening to the rain, reading a stack of papers, as he lies across his brown, cracked leather couch. He's digesting details on the alternative fuel industry with a pen in his hand and a lowball glass on his chest of Lagavulin 16, his favorite. He reaches for the silver bucket beside him and retrieves a fresh cube. Ice cracks.

His phone buzzes. Christian Ulster, Girona's longtime adviser, wants to meet him for a drink. "Need to run something by you," his email reads. Taylor wonders what. Christian's someone you plan lunch with at Charlie Palmer's weeks in advance, a man who shakes four hands before he sits down. Taylor suggests the Hilton hotel bar. Christian replies: "Be there in a half hour."

VII

New York City

Cait Ellis spent the day covering the yacht story from inside her cubicle. She shuts off her computer, stares at the black monitor, thinks about the journalism her mother did, and sighs.

She exits the thousand-foot tower of steel and glass and horizontal ceramic rods. A pigeon flies overhead and soars upward. She tilts her head back. Billowy clouds burn magenta and pink against a grape-soda sky.

Cait weaves through the thickening crowd. She nears a man sitting on the gum-spotted cement. His face is sweaty and sallow and his fingernails are lined with dirt. He holds a cardboard sign that reads I'M YOU, WITHOUT MONEY. Cait places a dollar in his paper coffee cup. She smiles. He says, "God bless you." She likes that he said it after the smile and not the dollar.

Her black-leather briefcase hangs off her inner elbow and sways with her walk. She places white headphones in her ears. Her silk blouse is off-white, sleeveless, and tucked into a red skirt, which begins above her navel and is tight to her knees. Men turn back as she passes.

The sidewalk is jammed with tourists who have stopped in the middle of the pavement, seemingly unaware that this is where New Yorkers commute. Cait steps off the curb and navigates the street's narrow shoulder. Times Square seems to open up to her. Cars stream past. A traffic cop whistles. Neon bathes the streets. She listens to Coldplay's "Viva la

Vida" on her headphones and feels present in the city but removed from it, as if she is in a film and listening to her own soundtrack.

She enters the dense, windowless Russian Vodka Room and looks for her mother. She sees her at the bar's front corner table. *Of course the great woman got that table,* Cait thinks. Erin Ellis sees her daughter, smiles, and waves. Cait makes her way through the crowd. Erin kisses her on the cheek and pulls back, holding her shoulders, examining her.

"A little formfitting for work, no?"

"Jesus, Mom, you baby boomers are so conservative."

"That's an interesting theory for the generation that ushered in civil rights, women's rights, and gay rights."

"Yeah—and as if nothing's changed, like any conservative, you're stuck on the issues of your time."

Erin begins to reply but balks. She considers the point as they sit.

"Hon," Erin says, "all I meant was, do women show their shoulders in the *Times* office now? And isn't that a little too couture?"

"It's not the eighties. I don't have to hide being a woman to succeed as a woman. And I don't recall you ever dressing so proletariat or conservative."

Erin smiles. Cait reaches for the small carafe on the table. "Allow me," Erin says, pouring the raspberry vodka into a tall shot glass. "Sip it, Cait, it's deceptively strong."

Cait shoots the vodka down, finishes the glass, sets it on the table, and brushes her bangs away from her eyes. She looks at her mother with a stiff glare, a flat, defiant smile, her eyebrows inching up with an undertone of irritation. "Oh well," Cait says.

"Don't be that way, Caitriona. We're finally able to spend time together."

"Fine, you're right. I still can't get used to you living here again."

Cait sets her briefcase between them. It's zipped half shut.

Erin sees the book inside. "What are you reading?" she asks.

"It's nothing."

Erin reaches in and winces. "Who's Jane Green?"

"I'm also reading *Nixonland.*"

"I didn't think you read chick lit."

"Yes, it's a boy-meets-girl tale of Richard Nixon finding love."

"You know what I'm referring to."

"Sure. But I don't like that term. People don't call Tom Clancy books guy lit. 'Chick lit' sounds so condescending."

"Fair enough. But it does tend to be a bit frivolous, no?"

"I don't know." Cait refills her glass. "Chick lit writers are romantic and favor happy endings, sure. But they're also realistic about people. In many basic respects, I find them less judgmental and more honest than people who think for a living often are."

"Okay . . . I can see that." Erin slides the book inside Cait's bag. "I finally read *The Looming Tower.* You ever read it? There's no better book on what led to 9/11 and shaped our wars after."

"I'm not you. I'm not covering wars."

"I didn't mean it like that."

Cait drinks and gazes around at the crowd. A yuppie couple squeezes beside two thick men dressed in glossy suits. The piano music blends into crisscrossing conversations and the low light glimmers off glass jugs of cranberry and blueberry vodka.

"How's work?" Erin asks.

"Fine. How's not working?"

Cait sees her mother flinch. She doesn't want it to be this way either. She wants her mother here, loves the glow she has these days. She believes the retirement package was good for her. She realizes that her mother wants it to be good for them as well. This is the great woman Cait recalls. Erin's silver hair is pulled back into a loose bun, a few strands spilling out around her forehead. There's an effortless elegance about her. Cait remembers the girlish way she idolized her mother, but also the teen years, when she resented her for being away. And Cait now finds it difficult to take down her defenses, to allow the present to be as she wished the past could have been.

"I'm sorry," Cait says. "Really, how's life after the *Wall Street Journal*?"

"Good."

"Really?"

"Really. You thought I'd be miserable?"

"Sorta, yes."

"It wasn't easy at first. It would've been easier to leave the European political beats. I didn't want to leave Afghanistan, though. It's odd. But I knew I couldn't focus too much on the next stage or wait for that perfect time to retire. If you do that, you'll never retire, unless you are forced to . . . I had done enough." Erin rubs her fingers on the tabletop. Sips her raspberry vodka.

"You must miss it a little?"

Erin's eyes wander off into the crowd. "Aspects, yes. How do I put this . . . it's difficult to get used to life without polar extremes once you've lived that way." She fiddles with a bangle on her left wrist and looks back at her daughter. "Perhaps, in large part, I came to realize that it's just as important to think about what you're leaving behind as what you are running after."

Cait pats her mother's hand. "It's nice to not have to worry anymore about you becoming collateral damage."

"I can worry more about you now. Incidentally, everything okay with all of that—"

"Yes."

"You sure?"

"I am."

Cait can feel her mother's eyes, probing for whether that's true. At the next table, a businessman barks into his phone, "Arrange it. Arrange it. You tell! You don't ask."

Cait recoils.

Erin says across Cait, "Sir." He ignores her. "Excuse me, sir."

He stares at Erin. "Hold on," he says into the phone. "Yes?"

"Would you mind, please, speaking more softly?" Erin asks.

He waves her off and blares on.

Erin winks at her daughter. She reaches under the table, into her tan shoulder bag, presses a few buttons on a walkie-talkie-like device.

The man barks "hello" twice. He holds the phone three inches from his ear. He stares quizzically at it, groans, and walks outside to locate a signal.

Cait asks, "What did you just do?"

"It's a cell phone jammer, a relic of my former life that's still useful."

"I don't know whether it's scary that you have that with you or brilliant."

"Probably both. There's no phone etiquette anymore. I never thought I'd get sentimental about phone booths."

"What's a phone booth?"

"Very funny." Erin slips the device back into her bag and sets the bag to her side. "Shall we order? You must try the borscht here."

"You took me for borscht, once, as a little girl in Leningrad. I mean St. Petersburg—"

"You don't have to correct yourself around me. It was Leningrad then."

"Anyway. It's just nice to be taken to dinner. I'm so broke."

"That Blake must always take you to dinner."

"It's different. And why do you always say 'that' before his name?"

"I didn't realize I did."

"Well, you do. Most parents would love him."

"I'm sure. By the way, it was a pleasure meeting Taylor the other night."

"I'm still getting my head around the fact that you met him."

"He's very thoughtful. And handsome."

Cait nods. She picks at a cuticle on her right index finger.

"What happened between you two?" her mother asks.

Cait continues to pick at her cuticle.

"You can talk to me."

Cait takes a long breath. "Weren't we about to order food?"

VIII

Washington, D.C.

Christian Ulster is bald, squat thick, with the cheeks of a basset hound. He stuffs fries into his mouth and skims his phone. He's catching up on the yacht story's fallout. He exhales as if at least this much is going as planned. He pushes the fries away, reaches into his pocket, pulls out a plastic container of antacid, swallows two white tablets, washes it down with his ginger ale, and sets the glass down beside a coaster. He notices a half-full beer at a nearby table and glares.

ESPN reflects off the bar polish as Taylor orders a whiskey, nods at Christian, slides an upholstered stool to the side, and sits. Taylor sets his phone down on the table. Christian sets aside his phone and asks about Taylor's book. "Could be worse," Taylor replies. "It feels like ages since I saw you on that panel."

"Damn, that was last summer," Christian says. "You getting enough press for the book?"

"I'm too swallowed by the campaign, like all of us."

"This is obvious, I know, but are you pushing it enough on social media?"

"I'm doing a little. But I'm skeptical about whether it helps that much."

"Sh*iii*t, it can help. I know of one reporter who figured out that his publisher—I guess the house had the option on his book—partly determined advances by counting authors' Twitter followers and Facebook fans. So he bought tens of thousands of fake followers and fans well before he pitched it, and they're like in India, or bots or something."

"That's disturbing on so many levels. Yet it probably worked."

"He said it did. Of course he was drunk at the time."

"So what about you guys?" Taylor asks.

"What?"

"Does your campaign do that?"

"Hell no."

"Don't sound so offended. Hollywood does it. Small-time pols do. You just told me about a reporter who did it. So it's fair to ask."

"We're not small-time. Or crazy."

"What about Wallace?"

"Sh*iii*t, I'm not touching that."

"There before the grace of God go I?"

"No comment."

"Are even half of your zillion Twitter followers active accounts?"

"Off the record: technology changes, politics does not."

"On the record?"

"No comment." Christian smirks.

"On this, no comment?"

"You can use that other line on background."

"I'm not quoting someone on background about Twitter. But let me ask you something else?"

Christian slurps his straw. "Go ahead."

"What does it take to be on the steering committee of one of Girona's policy groups?"

"I've no idea. I'm not managing this goliath."

"You're his closest adviser."

"Not for that. I'm his man for the big picture . . . Where you going with all this?"

Taylor does not want to tip his hand. So he affirms the virtue of the vice he wants detailed. "I'm just working on this 'real Washington piece,' about horse-trading in D.C., or why, as the trading dwindles in Congress, Congress is less efficient."

"Because there are less inducements to compromise?"

"Exactly."

"Well, if there's one word to describe Washington, it's 'transactional.' But everyone knows that. Sure though, the commodities change. If it's not an actual vote, it's publicity or fund-raising. But we're hoping to fix that."

"How?" Taylor asks.

"Let's not get into all that. Not tonight, please." Christian's tone stiffens. "I'm the one who asked you here."

"Why did you?"

Christian looks Taylor in the eye. "Why'd you never mention anything to me about that day in Iowa?"

"What day?"

"Before the caucuses."

Taylor tries to read him. "I wasn't sure what I saw."

"You ever mention it to anyone?"

"No. It's not the journalism I do."

"I need to be off the record tonight."

"Ahh. So someone is sure of what I saw."

"Then you did see something?"

"Of course. It wasn't conclusive. But it was suggestive."

"I figured you told Luke Brennan."

"No, why?"

"He's been chasing the story since the primary."

"Really?" Taylor asks, though he knows this much.

"Yeah. I don't think he ever found anything solid. But who the hell knows?" Christian sighs. "These stories don't happen until they do. Then they become a landslide."

"So someone has the story?"

"Someone who can do more with less facts."

"Who?"

"Again, off the record?"

"Yes."

"I think *Redline*." He scratches his nose. "They are either bluffing or maybe bought someone off in our campaign. Goddamn tabloids . . . the reporter won't go into details." Christian tears at a corner of his coaster. "But if this gets out, even if it's unsubstantiated, reporters will be on us like flies on shit."

"Jesus, and you sat here while I went into all that other shit, with this going on?"

"I've got to play chess on five boards right now."

"I've heard chatter. But I thought that was the usual gossip."

"What chatter?"

"There are Dem whispers that he might have a mistress."

"Who said that?"

"The same folks you know, I know."

"Damn." Christian shakes his head. His jowls jiggle. "I can't believe we may live this nightmare. It just can't happen yet fucking again. Not to us . . . I guess I thought it could remain gossip."

"When'd you find this out?"

"This afternoon. Joe's sweating more than a whore in church."

The South knits Christian's cadence and idioms. He was born in Northern Virginia, when Northern Virginia was more Virginia than Washington. He moved to West Texas as a boy, after his father got work as an oil roustabout, and became the first college graduate in his family. He went on to Georgetown Law but never took the bar. Instead, he volunteered for Bobby Kennedy. And, thereafter, ascended on gut instincts.

"Is *Redline* publishing?" Taylor asks.

"In a few days, I think."

"Before the convention? Your campaign must be flipping out."

"Very few know. We were trying to contain it. Now . . . who knows? *Redline*'s delaying. I don't know. They might have it."

"Why would they delay? This is a tabloid's dream story."

Christian rips the corner off his coaster. "I don't know. Just when you think it couldn't get any worse."

"How can it get worse?"

Christian's cheeks balloon, then collapse with an anxious exhale. Taylor's phone buzzes. He glances at it.

"You can check it," Christian says.

Taylor sees two missed calls from Jason, the Republican operative. There's an email. Subject: "More." Body: "You were right. There was more. I wasn't going to give this to you. But it's about Girona. Call me."

Taylor isn't sure what to make of it. But he's too focused on Christian to think about it. He sets his phone on silent. Looks at Christian. "So wait," Taylor says. "Is this about what I saw in Iowa?"

Christian's eyes withdraw. "Well . . . not exactly." He reaches across the table and drinks Taylor's whiskey. It's his first taste of alcohol in three years. "It involves someone," Christian continues, "notable."

"Notable?"

"It's complicated . . . a goddamn complicated mess." Christian holds Taylor's whiskey three inches from his mouth. His dry skin flushes. "Shit," he mutters. "I can't believe I just did that." He sets down the glass. Grabs his ginger ale. Sucks the straw as if he's gasping for air.

"You okay?"

Christian's cheeks inflate and deflate. "Never been better." He bends toward the edge of the booth. "Trent," he calls to the bartender, "another ginger ale. And another whiskey for my friend."

"Do you need a minute?" Taylor asks.

Christian holds his glass. He tilts his drink back. The ice cubes pile against his mouth. He swallows the last drops, chomps the ice, and looks back at Taylor, calmer.

"So what do you mean by complicated?" Taylor asks.

Christian eyeballs Taylor. "This is where I need your help. You know the *Times* reporter Cait Ellis?"

PART TWO

–

PRIMARIES

IX

Eight Months Earlier, December
Manchester, New Hampshire

She steps over slush in red heels, avoids two puddles, and finds a dry patch of cement on the other side of the pack of reporters. She has pixie hair, large eyes, pronounced cheekbones, a small chin, and a tiny nose. Her complexion is doll white. Her cheeks flush cherry in the cold. Her red wool coat has a narrow collar and big black buttons. It's nipped at the waist with a black belt and hints at her figure. She seems to be smoking her pen. The end of it is in her mouth. She pulls it away from her pink lips. Her breath clouds in the frozen air. She wears black leather gloves and holds a notepad against her hips, tapping, tapping, a metronome tapping, as the media swarms the candidate at the edge of the office parking lot. Television cameras rest on shoulders. Reporters elbow, shove voice recorders forward, kneel beneath the cameras. Two middle-aged men scribble shorthand. Pens glide across pads. Shutters click. Flashes pulse. The candidate talks. Taylor does not listen. His notepad is blank. His recorder is off. He feels time like a smoker savoring each drag, as he watches vapor leave her lips.

The media herd moves indoors. Constance Wallace speaks about free market virtues to three dozen suits. She has no free market experience. She believes in that market. Her husband has thrived in it. But she cannot claim his business success. Before she became governor, she earned a few million dollars in speaking fees. Corporate gatherings love a hero. She believes she earned this rate, by her labor and her wounds. But her staff decided that those speeches would highlight her wealth. So she'll talk leadership, talk character. She focuses on the Air Force squadron she led. The candidate seeks The Connect.

Reporters line the wall and hear the same old stories. Taylor glances at the woman in red heels. She sits on a chair with her legs crossed, right leg on top, watching Wallace, moving her right foot back and forth. Her red heel dangles off the tips of her toes and Taylor loves that, the way some women do that. Wallace's daughter sits on a white plastic chair, among the white starched shirts, beneath white fiberboard ceiling tiles. She stares up at her mother, with her chin up, her mouth closed, her legs crossed, portraying the dutiful daughter. And the political theater plays on.

At the hotel bar, red heels chats with two older men. Wallace's closest adviser, Vince, has recessed brown eyes, a ruddy face, and is short, with the barrel chest and fattened broad shoulders of a man who, when half his current age, could bench-press twice his weight. Vince leaves red heels with the young New Hampshire attorney general. He walks to the bar, asks for water, and sees Taylor enter. "I heard you were back with us," Vince says to him. "How are you?"

"Apparently, not as well as you," Taylor replies.

"Naaah. My days of prowling for drink are done. I've got to crash. This is what middle age does to a man."

"Aren't you still in your early forties?"

"My liver is in its seventies. It's a weighted average."

"Was that a polling joke?"

Vince chuckles. "That was god-awful, I know. I'm doing too much shoptalk."

"Vince, who is she?" Taylor asks, looking at the woman in red heels.

"Cait Ellis, from the *Times.* We've given her too much information for the past hour."

"When are you going to give me too much information?"

"When you look like Audrey Hepburn," Vince says. "Watch. She even carries herself regally."

"I saw the regal this morning. But she seems . . . more aware."

"You can insult my boss. But not my first crush."

"I'm sure Hepburn only feigned being flighty because of the time."

"The sixties?" Vince asks.

"Because she was a woman in the early sixties. It's like the *Great Gatsby* line, when Daisy says, 'That's the best thing a girl can be in this world, a beautiful little fool.' "

"I hate that book."

"*Great Gatsby*?"

"Damn right," Vince answers. "It's about a bunch of whiny, spoiled rich kids. It worships the same WASP establishment it pretends to disdain. Fitzgerald has all these little digs at poor whites, blacks, Jews . . . anyone not in the club."

"Vince, your candidate comes from that club."

"The Dems will paint us that way. But it's difficult to portray a war hero as spoiled."

"She doesn't help herself sometimes."

"Meaning what?"

"Well . . . when she said that people concerned about the income gap really just envy others' success."

"Those are meaningless gaffes."

"In my experience, operatives say that gaffes don't matter when they don't want them to matter."

"That one won't mean squat."

"Most don't, sure. But sometimes anecdotes accumulate into an impression. You know that. She did say *Atlas Shrugged* shaped her political worldview." Taylor smiles.

"Why is that funny?"

"It contextualizes the gaffes. *Atlas Shrugged* goes off the deep end."

"In what sense?"

"For one, that climactic train crash. You know, where hundreds died."

"I never actually finished it. It's too damn long."

"It is. But you should know this scene. Rand writes that since the passengers didn't oppose the hyper-socialist state, or were too passive, they deserved to die."

"You like *Great Gatsby,* though some portions of it are prejudiced."

"Small portions. This gets to the core of Rand's worldview."

Vince shrugs.

"Fitzgerald is like Hemingway or T. S. Eliot," Taylor says. "Yes, some of their work is woven with prejudice. *The Sun Also Rises* is bigoted, sure. But their writing is not about that. Hemingway was an incredible writer, regardless of his personal faults. *Waste Land* was brilliant. *Great Gatsby* probably has the best last line in American literature."

"And Rand was smart as hell. But of course, she was no Hemingway."

"You know the funny thing about Hemingway, to me, has always been not his writing about men, which is more nuanced and resonant than I think he gets credit for today. It's his overdone bravado in real life. I mean, in Paris he mostly sparred with an artistic crowd, not trained fighters. And I don't mean to belittle the bravery involved, but he was an ambulance driver for a few months in World War I, not a soldier."

"Wasn't he injured?"

"By shrapnel, distributing chocolate to soldiers."

"Distributing chocolate?" Vince smirks. "Considering how he acted, you would've thought he was at least a soldier. But isn't it often that way?"

"It is."

"Frankly," Vince says, "after a long day, I'd rather read John Grisham over Hemingway or any of them. Though, I know, Grisham's not literature."

"Don't give into that. So much of today's celebrated literature is consumed by inner thoughts, however granular, as long as it's culturally agreeable. I mean, maybe it's just me, but the navel-gazing can drag on, you know."

"I know. It's boring."

"Not always, but often, yes." Taylor says. "It's also the opposite of reality. Most people judge others by their actions and not their intent. Yet in the last few decades, a lot of literature has placed intentions ahead of actions."

"Well, how many culture writers are the Brooklyn overthinking type? It may be that, shit, what's celebrated nowadays reflects the lives of those who celebrate it."

"Which can reduce literary fiction to a search for personal affirmation. And that reduces literature to, ironically, self-help."

Vince smirks. "Some of it, probably . . . It sounds like our business—the way partisans only read what fortifies their outlook. So maybe some critics celebrate what fortifies their choices, or values."

Taylor nods.

"That's what comes with the Internet and cultural fragmentation," Vince continues. "It enhances division and, really, the demand for affirmation. That's certainly true in politics. Neurologists have run tests. They've found that ideologues, liberals and conservatives alike, can only see the hypocrisy in the other party's politicians, but not their own side."

"But this isn't politics," Taylor says.

"You sure this isn't politics, just the cultural variety?"

"Maybe it is. But you can love different books for different reasons. You don't have to choose a side."

"Brother, in everything we say or do, we choose, and our choices betray us."

Taylor thinks about that after the conversation ends, as Vince calls it a night and Taylor sits down at the bar and orders a whiskey. He watches basketball highlights on the overhead television until he notices two young women, network producers, talking beside him. "Why does she dress like that? It's New Hampshire." "Right. Like, why was she wearing high heels in the snow?"

Cait Ellis arrives.

The producers' eyes flee sideways as one changes the subject and the other watches Cait anxiously.

"Grey Goose soda please," Cait orders. She sets down her purse. Glances at the women. They look down and away. She turns to Taylor. "And who are you?" she asks.

"Taylor. And you're Cait Ellis."

Her hazel eyes turn up. "Yes," she says, "you're Taylor Solomon of *Current*." She rolls her eyes.

"Was that directed at me?"

"What?"

"The eye roll."

"Of course not. Sorry. *Current.*"

"Ahh. Well, we can't all work for the *Times.*"

"No, we cannot."

Her confidence pulls him in. "I noticed you earlier, wearing heels in the snow."

"I forgot my boots at the last hotel."

"You showed impressive dexterity." He drinks his whiskey. "For what it's worth."

She hesitates. "That's worth something." And her smile is slow. The bartender places her drink on a black napkin. "Okay," she says. "I have to continue letting this pol talk to me."

"He's looked over a couple times."

"Yeah, he keeps trying to buy me drinks."

"You won't let him?"

"No way."

"Smart move."

"Oh, you've no idea. I mean, either way, he'll get drunk and probably soon offer to leave his wife and kids for me."

"They never offer to do that for me."

She half smiles.

"Is this guy bothering you?" Taylor asks.

"Not especially. It's just indicative."

"Of politicians?"

She nods pensively. "Yeah . . . I just find. Oh, never mind."

"What?"

"Nothing."

"No, I want to know."

"Well, I guess . . . they're usually the type of guy who never got the girl in school. And now, with their power, or proximity to power, they try to make up for an *un*spent youth. I guess it's like Wall Street in that way . . . anyway, I'll let him blab until he says something newsworthy."

"Give them enough rope and they hang themselves."

"Absolutely."

"It's a solid tactic. He probably thinks he's working you, but you're working him."

"Isn't it often that way with men?"

"More than we realize, I suspect." He smiles.

She smiles back and her left index finger traces her left earlobe. "Perhaps I'll see you later," she says as she walks away. Taylor whispers to himself, "I hope so." Cait glances back. And their eyes meet.

The hallway clock blinks 12:09 a.m. in electric red. Taylor is buzzed and hungry. The hotel bar closed at midnight. His colleagues have gone to their rooms. Taylor wants to do something. But there's little to do. He walks to the snack room and surveys the familiar collage of plastic-wrapped microwaveable food. Cait walks by, sees him, and stops. "Oh hey," she says.

He turns to her. A smile escapes him.

"Too many choices to choose?" she asks.

"Huh?"

"The food."

"Someday Domino's Pizza and a hotel chain will team up, and it will be grand."

Cait smiles.

The soda machine hums. Her eyes glance up and down. “I didn’t realize you were so tall,” she says. “I mean, you were sitting before . . . You know who’s surprisingly tall? Chris Matthews.”

“Oh, you did his show on set?”

“Yeah.”

“How’d it go?”

She rolls her eyes. “He told me I was now out of the minor leagues.”

“How’d you respond?”

“I didn’t, really. My first thought was, I work at the *Times*, you jerk. But he’s so gracious in person. You just want to like him. And I realized he’s right, in a way. That’s the gauge of journalism success today.”

Taylor nods. The soda machine continues to hum. Cait’s figure is backlit by the machine’s red Coca-Cola light.

“So what brings you down here?” Taylor asks.

“A glass of wine. But no luck. Who closes a bar at twelve?”

“A New Hampshire hotel. There’s a bar down the street. I could use another drink.”

“Me too. There’s something about sending a story that calls for a drink.”

“And with it, letting the story go. I’m trying to learn to let them go.”

“Yeah,” she says. “I can’t let anything go.”

X

Streetlights capture snowdrifts. A Miller Lite sign glows red and blue in the white haze. Icicles descend from gutters. Inside, Cait sips Shiraz. Lip gloss smudges the wineglass. Her skirt rides up her legs. She pulls her skirt toward her knees. Taylor sits on the edge of his stool. His gray wool blazer is tailored slim. His black scarf loosely wraps around his neck. Cait glances at his eyes. He glances at her silk camisole, how it hints downward.

"The great woman," Cait says of her mother, "thinks campaign journalism isn't real journalism. She looks at me like I'm an entertainment reporter. She's probably right . . . I could write more about serious issues, about policy. Of course, my series on debt was hardly read."

"Yeah, that's the problem with the Internet." Taylor smirks. "Before, we could be in denial about what was read."

"Do you even remember before?"

"Barely. But we can still pine."

"We can."

"Does she read your work?"

"The great woman?"

"Yeah."

"Incessantly. She'll write me little suggestions. She actually rewrites my ledes sometimes, after the story's published. Of course, they're unfailingly better. It kills me."

"I can imagine."

"Sometimes I run into some old school reporter who knew her. If I have to hear, yet again, about how she stole an army Jeep in Vietnam and tried to head into Cambodia, to report on the bombing, I'll snap."

"Well," Taylor says, drinking his whiskey, setting it back down, "she's kind of a rock star."

"I know. That's the problem. I feel very small around her."

"You shouldn't. You're the *Times* reporter on Wallace."

"One of several, right now."

"Still, thousands of reporters would kill for your beat."

"They'd kill for your job too."

"Maybe. But no amount of links from *Drudge* buys you *Times*' respect."

"At least we still have that." She sips her wine. "I guess . . . I mean, these days, I'm always on the coattails of *Current* stories."

The bartender sets down a wooden bowl of pretzels. Behind them, at the back of the bar, a domed light hangs by an interlocked metal chain. The yellow light glows over the green felt of the pool table. A young man leans on his cue. The wood bends, curving slightly outward with his weight. He surveys the table. Beside him, a girl in a green miniskirt and dark sweater sits on a stainless steel stool. Her frizzy hair and slim frame are lit from behind, where a refashioned jukebox hums with blue and red neon light.

"Where do your parents live?" Taylor asks.

"In the city. But they're divorced. The great woman only recently moved back."

"Does she miss being in the action?"

"I'm not sure. She lives near friends in the Upper East Side and seems to enjoy being a fabulous Manhattanite."

"Oh, she's of the bygone Elaine's crowd?"

"Yeah, with all the creative geriatrics. She even goes to Equinox now. I bumped into her at one of their midtown gyms, running on the treadmill, in Lululemon for God's sake. She never exercised when I was growing up. She smoked." Cait laughs and sips her wine. She reaches for a pretzel, breaks off the end of one, eats it, and looks at Taylor. Her thin fingers trace the bar. She wears no rings.

"So you're from the city?" she asks.

"How'd you guess?"

"One can tell."

"I moved to D.C. for the campaign."

"You think it helps?"

"Not really. The campaign is out here."

"But you grew up in the city?"

"Yeah. I spent most of my twenties there too, in the West Village. But I lived in Moscow, Idaho, for my middle school years. My mom's a geologist. She worked in the Rockies there, taught at the University of Idaho for a while. My dad took a break from his work, taught me to climb, make a one-match fire, stuff like that. It was . . . a wonderful time. I didn't know it then. But that's how it goes, right? We often only know the great times in retrospect."

Her eyes stray left and up, briefly, until she says, "I think so."

And their eyes meet once more. Neither turns away.

"So what brought you back to the city?" she asks.

"My dad got some offer they couldn't turn down. He was in finance, started a firm with old colleagues."

"Ah . . . So we both have parents to live up to. And your mother?"

"She landed well. It took a few years. Manhattan is not ideal for a geologist. But she got a good gig at the Natural History Museum."

"They're still together then?"

"Yeah, almost thirty-five years."

"Does your dad work crazy hours?" Cait asks.

"He did. He's sixty-seven. Younger partners are pushing him to retire. He's going to sell his stake in the firm, I guess. I think it's hard for him. He's going to miss being an important man, though he'd never admit that to me. What about your dad?"

"He's a prof at Columbia. Classics."

"Classic."

"Right. We're city stereotypes."

"You must've grown up partly abroad? Your mom being a correspondent and all."

"A bit. I lived in Paris for a while."

"Do you speak French?"

"*Un peu.* It fades."

"You notice how everything sounds better in French?"

"Most things, sure."

"How do you say journalist in French?"

"Journaliste."

"There you go. French makes even journalist sound nice."

She smiles.

"You should move back after the campaign," Taylor suggests. "Relearn the language. Just live there."

"God," Cait replies with a slight sigh. "After the campaign, I'd love that."

"Then you must do that."

She brushes her bangs to the side. The bartender announces last call. Taylor orders them another round. Cait's phone vibrates. "Sorry, let me check this," she says. She scrolls through her emails and sets down her phone.

"Is everything okay?" Taylor asks.

"Yeah, it's just my itinerary. I've got to wake up early for a flight to Iowa to interview Girona. I only found out today."

"Why so last minute?"

"Who knows? I'll take it, whatever the reason."

"So you're not embedded with Wallace?"

"It's fluid until the caucuses, I think. I was embedded with Girona until he became a superstar and I got replaced."

"It's cool you're interviewing Girona."

"It sorta is. I mean, I spent three months with Girona's campaign. I never got to speak to him once in that time. He's that insulated. So tomorrow's my chance."

"I don't want to keep you up. You want to head back to the hotel?"

"No . . . I'm prepared. Let's enjoy our drinks." Her knees point at Taylor. She uncrosses and recrosses her legs.

"What's Cait short for?" he asks.

"Caitriona."

"The Irish Cathleen. Does anyone ever call you Caitriona?"

"The great woman, when she's annoyed with me."

"Do you mind if I do, even if I'm not annoyed with you?"

"Why?"

"It's a really nice name. It suits you."

"Sure . . . okay." She glances away and back, conspicuously choosing to change the subject. "So you wrote a book?"

"Yeah."

"*From Roosevelt to Reagan.* On the changing roles of government, no?"

Taylor nods. "It was nothing."

"It's something. I've caught you on TV. Why do you never plug it?"

"I don't know." He scratches under his chin. She looks at him patiently. "A lot went wrong. But that's common with first books . . . What matters is the next one."

"What's that going to be about?"

"I don't know yet. But something more—"

"More what?"

He catches himself and gives a guarded shrug.

"Tell me."

"I don't know. But there will be more."

And Cait understands the space after his words.

"Well," she says, her hand nudging his shoulder, "you should be proud of having a book published at your age."

He nods.

"I see. You're the type who's perpetually hard on himself . . . You know, it's important to also enjoy the things along the way to more. Otherwise, life becomes only about what's next."

"I do believe that."

"There must be something Taylor Solomon is proud of?"

Taylor looks at her. "There is." He brushes her bangs off her forehead and half smiles. "I'm proud that you want to drink with me, even though you have to wake up early."

"Well, you should be," she says, biting her lower lip.

XI

The Next Day
Southeastern Iowa

It's like walking on the prairie at night, when lightning strikes and the darkness flashes white, and you startle, turn to your friend, and ask, did you see that? Onstage, Joe Girona can be as elemental as that. He speaks without notes. A small microphone is clipped beneath his notched lapel. He walks the stage like that lazy summer night, standing in one corner for a few minutes, ebbing center stage, and, in time, flowing across the stage. He's this way until the air between his words electrifies and the lightning comes and his arms dart and his face reddens with fire. But then his voice calms and his tan skin cools. His arms become limber. And water seems to wash over his words.

"What's the essence of the American dream?" he asks with a pregnant pause. "Here's what I think it is: where we start out in life is *not* supposed to dictate where we end up. That's the America I believe in. But unlike in the past, today when researchers compare Americans' income to that of their parents, they consistently find that we are earning *less money* for the same work. They find that we are more likely to remain in the economic class we were born into, unlike other big national economies. That means—and this kills me every time I consider it—the American dream is becoming truer outside of America. Is that right? Is that the way it should be?"

Nooo, the crowd yells.

"Heck no." His voice quiets. "See, I came from a small town like this, from real America. I spent my early years in rural New Mexico. My dad lost our shop to a big retailer. By high school, after some moving around, we settled in Louisiana. My dad finally got work on a commercial fishing boat. He did that for the rest of his life. He kept us going with his will, with his hands. Gosh, I still remember his hands." Girona glances at his smooth palms. "My dad's hands were swollen and had these thick, coarse calluses that were always peeling away. He shed skin daily for his work. And, if I may say so, I think that so many of you do this every day. You shed part of yourself for your family. My dad is gone now. But I see him in you. He was the sort of man Washington forgets. And that's why I'm running for president, to represent him, to represent you. I want to stand up for you, for the invisible America, the folks who sometimes struggle to get by, who seek no favors but are sick of feeling put down by the left and placated by the right. You see, I know that the politicians from all sides have forgotten about you. But I never have. I never will. Because I'm one of you."

So they hear his story in minutes—of the young man born with little, who earned a Georgetown J.D. and Ph.D., who became a State Department wunderkind, and rose to the heights of diplomatic USA. And then he gave it all up. Here they hush, as they are told of the ambitious man who went home to keep his family together, to take care of his sick father. He tells the story with a confessional tone. How he grew distant from his wife—with his work, with her corporate practice. So they decided to return to the world he fled as a young man. They had their first child and worked side by side and found their marriage again. And he smiles that charming smile as he tells it. He says how he fell back on his law degree and began representing the salt of the earth, as he often puts it, quoting Gospel. So he adds, "I came to realize I never really left this America, not in my heart. How could I? When it has carried me this far. When it has carried me to this cause."

Cait Ellis enters the gym with her black luggage. She knows that politics is a performance. But she never gets over this sight. More than five hundred people are crammed inside. They hail from little cities and three-block towns and places too small to be named, yet care so much for a country so vast and beyond them, a country molded by coastal cities and rich men, and yet they choose to come and hear this man who says the nation is really for them. So instead of resting after a full day's work, instead of television and supper, they drove here, as the weather worsened and headlights streamed into snowdrifts, all to vet this candidate, to see this man outpacing expectations, this man who, to so many of them, feels raw and real, a man worth believing in. Overhead, dim aluminum tubs glaze the gymnasium in uniform fluorescent light. But he's aglow. A spotlight follows him as he flows to the front of the stage and stands before an immense American flag, as big Iowans stuff narrow bleachers and heat saturates the air.

"I realize power brokers and pundits criticize me for calling our campaign a cause. But they are not living paycheck to paycheck. You see, I don't think they see what's going on in America, in the *real* America. Well, I do. Why do corporations like General Electric and ExxonMobil earn tens of billions of dollars in profit but often pay no income taxes? Why do our tax dollars insure the big banks' risky investments? Why are hedge fund managers taxed at a lower rate than you? Here's why: the fat cats have their lobbyists. It's time the president was *your* lobbyist. Oh, it's time. It's time the elite met its match. Oh yes, the powerful take and take and take. They take more than your taxes. They can make you work more, often without increasing your pay. They can take your vacation days. They can hurt your pride, take your job, and ruin your ability to support your family. But they can't take all of you. They cannot take that part of you that knows something's not right. They can't take away your dreams. I'm here to make sure that much stays true. See, I think real change begins there. It begins with saying America deserves better. That you deserve better. That you'll fight for better. Because your vote counts as much as their vote. Yes, you, ma'am, you count as much as them."

Girona looks at a plump middle-aged woman in a red marshmallow coat. She realizes he means her. Her eyes drop to the floor. She turns her head down. Her chubby cheeks begin to match her coat. She glances left and right, looks back at him shyly. He sees her and knows.

"And you too, sir. You count as much as them."

Girona points to a man wearing a snowmobile jacket with green racing stripes. His mouth maintains a stiff line. He deadeyes Girona. There's no hint that Girona has him. But Girona knows he does.

"Don't all of you deserve better leaders?"

Yesss.

"A better Washington?"

Yesssss.

"A better America?"

Yesssss!

He gazes outward and adds, "And we really can achieve it. God, I'm so proud of all of you, for your willingness to believe again. I'm proud to see real Americans speak out. *Me encanta cómo luchan.* I love how you all fight. "So he lets his Latino out. And the white crowd cheers.

Ethnic pride threads his populism. Yesterday, on his way to a formal lunch, he entered the restaurant through the kitchen. He often does that. He visits more with the help than with the chefs. He talks sports and salaries with the dishwashers. He notices that they are so often Mexican, Central American, even in lily-white Iowa. He is taller than they are and not as brown. Yet he feels like one of them. It's a good photo op. But he believes this too. He is a pragmatist. But this gets to him. He sees them, so many descendants of indigenous populations, and he wonders what it must feel like to be in the back of the restaurant, to earn less, to be the labor, to even be smaller in stature. He finds himself thinking of lots in life and prescribed destinies. He wants to make them proud. Most Hispanic Americans do see themselves in him. He looks like a tan Anglo. But so do many soap opera stars in Mexico. He is still one of them. And America feels more real to them, part of them, possible for them, because of him. And Girona prizes that most.

"You see," he tells the crowd, "I don't just want to be president to be president. I already earned my big white house. I want to be president to do right by you. For once, for it to be about *you.* Because I'm sick of letting all that's wrong continue one day longer. I'm so darn sick of it. I think we all are. We're sick of the ruse that the GDP or the stock market reflect how America is doing. They show how the elite is doing. We're sick of it being legal to fleece the poor—from payday loan sharks who charge four hundred percent interest, to mortgage loan sharks who take advantage of the dream of homeownership. Because I'm here to say, keep your scam away from *our* American dream."

The crowd cheers and hollers and a woman screams, "Speak it, brother."

"Oh, I will." He smiles and eases and then fire builds once more. "I'm only getting started."

They cheer louder.

And his voice rises with their applause. "Oh yes, we are sick of it. We're sick of politicians who are more concerned with their reelection than with what's right. We're sick of government wasting our tax dollars. But we're also sick of politicians who protect rich folks' tax loopholes while proposing to cut health care for our seniors, as if the elderly should suffer first. We're sick of companies penalizing workingwomen for motherhood. We're sick of a justice system that is *not* blind. We believe some wars must be fought. But we're sick of wars of choice, of risking our children's blood, risking their honor, to secure an elite's fortune. We're sick of them calling rich people 'job creators.' If that's true, how come the rich keep getting richer, but there are far fewer good jobs? Because it's *not* true. It's a ruse. And I'm here to call them out. I'm here to say we've had enough. We've. Had. Enough! Have you had enough of their lies, of our lawmakers selling out, of our great republic being sold to the highest bidder?"

Yesssss.

"Listen," he says as his voice soothes, "I know politicians visit you every four years. I know they praise you and promise you change, even as they let Middle America rust. I hear them too. And while they talk, I ask myself, Where are the better jobs they have pledged? Where are the better schools they promised? Why do I keep working harder for less? Why must we accept this disappointment? Well, I'm tired of being disappointed by our leaders. We have waited long enough. We've heard enough talk. We want action. As you know, I worked as a diplomat. And there is a time for negotiations. But this is not that time. This is *not* that time. It's time someone fights for you and refuses to settle for their scraps. It's time we take the fight to them. It's time to stand up and fight! Will you join me?"

Yesssss.

"Will you march with me?"

Yesssss!

"When it gets hard, will you fight harder?"

YESssss!

"You hear that, Washington? We're not going to be silent any longer. We're not going to settle for your empty talk any longer. We're not going to be pacified any longer. We mean business, and we will not back down. We will never back down! We *are* coming! We will fight! And this time, the people will win!"

He claps his hands once and thunder blasts through the speakers.

Screams and cheers ricochet off the rafters. Tom Petty's "I Won't Back Down" blares out of the gym's sound system. Girona punches his fist upward. They cheer louder. He waves once. Exits on the high note. Punctuate. Leave them wanting more.

The showman steps off the stage. Girona hears the lyrics "I'll stand my ground." And this man who promises to speak for the invisible, to take the fat cats down and lift the people up, he feels it in his bones. He does believe it's all possible. For here is a man in his arena, preaching town by town, aching to reawaken an old populist creed and create his own fire.

The song plays on, "Well, I know what's right," as Girona walks down the steps and winks at Christian Ulster. And Christian smiles with pride. A few beads of perspiration glisten off Girona's forehead. He wipes them away with his sleeve as if they were raindrops, cool as that. He feels more overheated than people know. Sweat has soaked through the back of his shirt and under his armpits. But Girona will keep his jacket on.

Cait leaves her bags against the wall and walks to the front of the gym. She watches Girona lope into the crowd. Hands shake, hands clasp, small conversations. People want to touch him, speak to him. A pretty twenty-something hands him a note. He stuffs it into his pocket. A middle-aged man tries to tell his story. The candidate has only six minutes for glad-handing. Still, Girona stops and nods and gives this man his entire attention. Twenty-two seconds later, Girona points to his bodyman, the personal aide who trails him. Bodyman records the man's information. Girona glides on. He smiles his trademark smile. The people push closer. They affirm the candidate's belief in himself. Girona feels destined, a leader, the leader. But he greets them as if he's one of them. He pauses a split second longer than powerful men often do. He periodically adds a shoulder pat, a jocular tap with his fist, nodding agreeably, looking each in the eye, reaching over people, shaking on, clasping on, smiling all the way. He finds his way to the other end of the front row. He darts his right hand up one last time and waves to the people. This man of the people.

Girona walks side stage. He tells the bodyman to take a break. An aide holds a door open and Girona exits with Christian in tow.

"Shit, they love me," Girona says as they pass red lockers, as fluorescent light reflects off the white-tiled floor.

"They sure do," Christian replies. "And it was chugged full."

"Hell yes, it was. We're coming on strong. I feel it. I really feel it. I shook thirty-eight hands in there."

"I've never gotten over the fact that you count them."

"I shake at least one hand for every minute I speak."

"You should try fewer handshakes and more TV hits. Remember, these days, retail politics only matters if it can be seen wholesale."

"No shit."

"But man oh man, you were good. I think you're making up for all those years you guarded your words as a diplomat."

"Maybe I am, maybe I am. All I know is, I was born for this."

"It's like watching a bird fly. But it's still game time. We've got a twenty minute meet-and-greet now, closed to press."

"Jesus," Girona groans.

"They're contributors, small-time. But we need it all right now."

"Shit then, let's go." He pushes out his chest and cracks his knuckles.

"Then one quick stop at a diner."

"Great. Another diner. Is the press at least coming along?"

"Of course."

"See, Chris, I'm always thinking wholesale." Girona smirks.

"I guess so. Also, the media folks keep harping on me to get you to sign off on their new campaign. They want to increase targeted impressions on key websites. You should talk to them."

"I will."

Christian stares at him. "Soon."

"I will tomorrow," Girona says.

"Good. So after the diner your staff set aside thirty minutes for call time. We need to step that up too. I heard you were only doing three hours daily. That's subpar. Donors need to feel closer to you. And that brings me to tonight. After your calls, we have the big dog dinner. We flew in ten of our largest donors. It's a day around Iowa thing. We're bringing them inside the campaign to make them feel special. It's the usual blowjob."

"Yeah, I know."

"Also, don't forget, at the hotel, you have that quick remote with CNN. The *Times* interview too, afterward."

"What about after that, you arrange it?"

"You sure you want to do that?"

Girona nods.

"I'm not your scheduler, Joe."

"I know. Just please keep handling this one thing," Girona says, patting his shoulder. "Give me a two-hour buffer after the *Times* interview."

"I think it's a bad move."

"Stop worrying."

Girona and Christian enter the teachers' lounge. Three dozen Iowans applaud him. Girona thanks them. The card table has coffee and doughnuts. Girona campaign mugs are set out on the table. They feature only his face. A forty-something redheaded woman scurries to him and gives a toothy smile. "Sir, gosh, please allow me to say, well . . . that was such a great speech. I've been waiting my whole life for a Democrat like you." She taps his hand impulsively, like a schoolgirl meeting a boy-band star.

"I appreciate that, ma'am."

"And I so love your wife. She's such a strong woman, a real woman. I knew you were a good man because of her."

"Bless your heart. She is my better half."

"Wives always are."

"Ain't that the Lord's truth. What's your name, ma'am?"

"Lisa Erickson."

"What do you do, Ms. Erickson?"

"I actually work at a bank—for some of the men you were talking about."

Girona's eyes take on a patient focus.

"Well, they're not that bad," she adds with a sturdy countenance.

"But they could be better?"

"They could."

"Do you think they pay you what you deserve?"

"Well . . . I don't. No, sir."

"You need to ask for what you deserve."

"I don't want to, you know—"

"Risk losing your job?"

"Pretty much."

"I understand." He folds his hands in front and leans toward her. "But you must believe in yourself," he adds. "I can already tell you are a businesswoman who gets the job done. I see that in two minutes. You must as well."

Her cheeks and ears blush. She glows from his glow. The sun shines only on her. She looks up at him. He smiles back at her. And she feels like a woman seen for the first time.

XII

The bags under Christian's eyes are bloated and dark. His skin tints yellow. Cait thinks about the way the election corrodes these men. They greet each other. She enters Joe Girona's suite. The sitting room has a navy blue muslin couch, a large TV, a dark cherry coffee table, a black single-serve coffeemaker, a metallic kitchenette, everything familiar yet generic, like so many nights in so many hotels. The faucet drips. The drapes are open. Outside, building lights sprinkle the darkness.

"Joe needs a few minutes," Christian says. "He had to make a couple of calls after the CNN hit."

"No problem." Cait hears the candidate grumbling in the other room. She can't make out his words.

The bodyman offers to take her coat. She hands it to him and sets down her bag.

"You can have a seat there." Christian points to the couch.

"Thank you," Cait replies in a cool voice, sitting. She's in all black, a blazer that's buttoned, with a fitted sheath dress and heels, save the strand of pinkish pearls with matching studs. She pulls out a notepad and a slim white digital recorder from her briefcase and sets the recorder on the coffee table.

"Are you okay waiting here?" Christian asks. "We were going to grab a bite across the street. He's expecting you. It shouldn't be long."

"No problem. I have plenty to read." Cait prefers to do interviews without aides present to censor candidates, to ruin what little remains candid in politics. Christian and the bodyman excuse themselves. She waits. Crosses her legs. She should be tired. She flew here that morning and had to transfer through Chicago. But she's wired. This is a major interview. The Iowa caucuses are a few days off. Girona could win the first election of the presidential campaign. He could have the momentum. She thinks of *Current*'s success. She decides to focus on the horse race. She wants the story to be widely read. She focused on policy when she interviewed Constance Wallace. And her story was ignored in the Twittersphere and cable news. She thinks about Girona's appeal. She finds his populism intriguing. She wonders whether this works. She wishes she knew more political history. She was a crime reporter, who became a city political reporter, and this year, a national political reporter. She's learning presidential politics along the way. Most campaign reporters do. And it occurs to her, Girona could win Iowa. He could win. This might be her last chance to interview him.

The Girona campaign selected her for the interview. She didn't have to fight for it. It felt like a statement of faith in her. She recalls what Chris Matthews told her. *Now I've arrived.* It's the first major interview handed to her. This may not be war reporting. But Girona could be the man who begins and ends wars. Cait, for the first time, feels a serene absence of inferiority. She thinks of her mother but does not feel small.

Girona opens two sliding doors. His face brightens. He smiles that famous smile.

"I'm sorry about the wait."

She rises to greet him. Her handshake is firm. His gentle. The smile.

"Pleased to meet you."

"And you, Senator."

She realizes the chair is against the wall. It's not near the couch.

"Senator, should I get the chair?"

"No need. We'll use the couch. After you," he says, splaying his open palm toward the couch. She hesitates, then sits in one corner. He chooses the opposite corner.

"Do you mind if I record this, Senator?"

"Of course not. And you can call me Joe. And you're Cait?"

"Yes, Senator," she says flatly.

"May I offer you some water? Something else perhaps?"

"No, thank you."

"How long have you been with the *Times*?"

"Four years. Sir, may we begin?"

"Of course."

"Senator, you're the only populist in the race. Will stressing inequality work? Don't Americans admire the rich because they believe they can be rich someday?"

"Many do, sure. And Americans will accept inequality providing there's mobility. But mobility is lessening. Birth is becoming destiny more and more, in class terms. The news always headlines GDP. But the wealth of the nation is increasingly defined by the wealth of a few. Corporate profits no longer equate to jobs. Meanwhile, the middle class is disappearing. Tens of millions live in poverty. This is supposed to be the land of opportunity for all. But it's becoming a fat-cat nation."

"Sir, aren't you a fat cat?"

"That's Republican spin."

"Sir, no it's not. Fat cat is your line."

"Your implied criticism is Republican spin. Conservatives expect that once someone like me makes it, I should become selfish and forget how hard it is out there. Our safety nets are already wearing thin. This nation's wealth gap is larger than many third world nations. The top one percent own forty percent of the nation's wealth. The average man's income has *not* increased since the early 1970s. You know what's happened in America since the 1970s? The really rich got richer and everyone else got credit cards."

She nods. *The really rich got richer and everyone else got credit cards.* She worries that she might betray her regard for the quote and stiffens her back.

"I've noticed that your accent shifts," she says. "You sound a tad Southern with these audiences. But I've heard you roll your *r*'s in front of urban audiences. Today you used only one line of Spanish but generally sounded conventionally Southern or rural. Critics say you choose your accent for your audience."

The smile. "Listen, as a child, the only speeches I heard were from southern preachers. It comes out when I speak in front of rural crowds. I'm not ashamed of how my faith has shaped me."

Political jujitsu. The pol shifts the attack's momentum to an advantageous position. Girona defends his variable accents by defending churchgoers.

"Sir, some wonder whether you'll make Washington even more partisan."

"Hold on. It's hot in here. Maybe it's your questions."

Must not roll eyes.

"You mind if I take off my coat?" he asks.

"No, of course not."

He stands up and removes his jacket. "Can I take your jacket?"

"I'm fine."

"Want a glass of water?"

"No. But thank you."

"All right." He hangs up his coat, returns to the couch, and loosens his burgundy tie. "Go on."

"What I'm getting at is, aren't people sick of partisanship? Some call you a partisan pit bull."

"Sometimes diplomacy can only get you so far."

"That's ironic coming from you, no?"

"No. I would know. There are times for words and times to fight."

"And you think we've had enough words?"

"Some good has been accomplished in recent decades. But not nearly enough. It sometimes takes a fight to break gridlock. I'm trying to get real Americans in the fight. Change will only happen if we push lawmakers. After all, you can't hope your way to change."

"But beginning with your middle name, your campaign emphasizes 'hope' foremost."

"Listen, the first obstacle is low expectations. These days, cynicism is understandable. I first have to restore the belief that we can do more." He pushes his fluffy hair back, focuses his blue eyes on hers, and turns toward her.

She moves her knees slightly away and fixates on her notepad. "But, well, could your words give the impression that change in Washington happens in grand waves rather than small steps? And doesn't Washington work only if there's give-and-take? Are you instilling false expectations that could ultimately enhance cynicism?"

"I don't know. Anyone who seeks significant change takes risks. But such is life. The reward is worth the risk. And leadership requires the willingness to risk worse for better, if you believe the status quo is intolerable. And for most Americans, it is." Girona places his right arm on top of the couch and looks at her. She continues to focus on her notepad.

"You speak for regular people, but it took time for you to catch on. Do you think Iowans came to you slowly because you're Hispanic?"

"Listen, people have to get to know new candidates. Iowans care about my cause, not about my ethnicity or race. If I win, they know I'll make the income gap a colossal issue. I'll enact policies that get Americans out of poverty. There are many ways to make history."

She nods.

"Can we speak off the record for a moment?" he asks.

"Of course." Cait turns off her recorder.

"Do the *Times* editors think I'm going to win Iowa?"

"People are not sure, sir. It's very close."

"What do you think?"

"I don't like to talk about what I think to candidates."

"I admire that."

"What?"

"How professional you are."

"Sir, I know you have little time. Can we go back on the record and continue the interview?"

He swats the thought like a fly. "Oh, no rush. I never get to talk to a smart young reporter like yourself. I thought you were going to be another one of those trolls."

"So you think we're trolls, do you?"

"Not you. Certainly not someone as lovely as you."

Girona scoots to the middle of the couch. He places his left hand on her right thigh. His right arm reaches around her. She freezes. She looks down. Sees his hand. On her. Her eyes are fixed on his hand. She's frozen. She stares at his hand. She hears his breathing. Feels his breath.

She hears the faucet drip.

"Do you mind if I kiss you? You're a very beautiful woman."

What? This is Joe Girona. It feels unreal to her, as if she's watching herself. He dips his head and kisses her. Her lips are motionless. She's still staring at his hand. It's now on her upper thigh. *Do something.*

The faucet drips.

Girona moves his hand higher. He cups her inner thigh. No boss has ever done this to her. Editors have asked her out. Young pols, campaign staff, have made moves. But at bars. No one has ever kissed her mid-interview. Faces sprint through her head. Guys at work. Guys in bars. Guys across tables. No reference point. Girona kisses her again. His hand starts to caress her inner thigh, moves farther up. *This is happening.* He kisses her neck. Her eyes shift to his face. She sees his silver hairline. The lines in his forehead. The creased bags under his eyes. She feels his breath, his hand. Her shock becomes an overriding sense of violation. He tries to kiss her again. She jerks back.

She's leaning against the arm of the couch. There's space between them. His eyes blast open with shock.

"I'm sorry," he blurts. "I couldn't help myself."

She stands. He does not move.

"You *must* help yourself. Jesus Christ." She straightens her jacket. Her eyes fall back cold. She's trying to compose herself. Tears gather at the corners of her eyes.

"I'm sorry. Forgive me. I've never done that before."

She glares down at him.

"I'm truly sorry. I forgot myself. Can we please act like this never happened? I'll make it up to you. I'll do a long professional interview and give you news."

"I should go."

"Please don't."

She places her recorder and notebook in her bag and zips it.

He stands. "I'm sorry," he continues. "But that was off the record. Remember?"

Her eyes narrow.

He realizes, shrinks. His shoulders tilt forward. "Ms. Ellis, please forgive me. Perhaps we should call it a night . . . I hope we can continue on professionally. I won't tell a soul. I know you won't. I forgot myself. It's just that you are very beaut—"

"Please, I must go." Cait turns around. Opens the door.

He's flustered. His eyes follow her out.

The door closes behind her. The hallway's empty. *My coat.* She looks back at the door. *Not worth it.* She walks to the elevator. Her hazel eyes flush red. She has trouble breathing. Her stomach feels knotted. Confusion collects, compounds. Pressure builds within her. The long hallway closes in. She's inside an accordion. Closing. Deafening noise. No noise. It's like after an explosion. She feels as if she's falling backward in slow motion, as if the hallway tipped on its axis and she can't pull herself back. Moments flash. She sees herself on the couch. Frozen. Letting him kiss her. Letting him touch her. Letting it get that far. *How could I!* She sets down her bag and leans against the wall. She needs to stand still for a moment. She's still gasping, crying. *Someone could see me.*

Breathe. She begins to compose herself. *My mascara.* She blinks and tilts her head back. She breathes. She hears the buzz of overhead lights. She sniffles and blots below her eyelashes with her sleeve. Her hands tremble. She closes them. Her body starts to obey. She begins to feel steadied. *Breathe.* She respires. *I can't let anyone see me this way. Breathe.* Deep breath. Blinking. Her hands calm.

She picks up her bag and walks briskly to the elevator. She presses the button. Ding. The elevator doors open. And there's Luke Brennan from *Current.* Her eyes drop. He says hello. She nods, steps in, turns around, and stands in the opposite corner. She pushes the lobby button. Pushes it again. Again. There's a mirror across from the elevator. She glances up, sees her reflection. Her blotchy skin. Her puffy, bloodshot eyes. And Luke behind her. *How could I let this happen?* The doors close.

XIII

Elevator doors open to Constance Wallace. *Madame President.* She could hear it all year. The words have grown fainter. But she still believes she'll win it. There have been other female candidates, though none had her hero's tale. Wallace walks through the New Hampshire hotel lobby minding that tale. Her white hair is pulled back. Her countenance is disciplined. Her eyes are carved with exhaustion. Her chin is level. She shakes strangers' hands, nodding, giving that pro forma smile. Her teeth are clenched behind her smile. She bites down on her concern. She was the prohibitive front-runner. She's now losing in Iowa. Wally Reynolds, the Texas governor, a former Southern Baptist pastor, has surged ahead. An outside group, Americans for Families, is attacking her. The most recent advertisement alleges that Wallace "supports abortion." She opposes legal abortion. Yet she supports exceptions in cases of rape, incest, or life of the mother. The group never actually paid to air this ad. It posted the ad online, sent the URL to reporters, and cable news bit that bait. News channels replayed the ad all day. So it goes. Drama wins attention. The Big Show has a new scene. Broadcast. Ratings rise. The media becomes mouthpiece. And a political organization sends its message out for free.

Wallace understands that political advertising is a peripheral factor. Her moderation is an issue, however. The wartime hero is mired in the trenches of partisan politics. She's too moderate for some social conservatives and too socially conservative for some libertarians. She had her eye on the general election. She now wonders if it could all fall apart.

Reynolds is overtaking her on the right flank. He describes himself as a "constitutional conservative," while he terms Wallace "the lukewarm Republican." He frequently speaks of Ulysses Grant. Historians had redeemed much of Grant's reputation. But Reynolds stuck with the slight. Good soldiers, he suggests, don't always make good presidents. Because of this, some pundits accused him of offering a "coded appeal" to Southern bigots who, as one CNN commentator put it, "are still fighting General Lee's war." So he argued with the mainstream media, which won him more right-wing supporters. Near the close of every speech he swore, "I'll never *go Washington.* I'll never place party above principle. I may not be the media's conservative, but I'll always be *your* conservative." And the more pugnacious he became, the more conservatives donated. So he became more pugnacious. The harder he hammered Wallace, the more the media covered him. So he hammered harder. Reynolds began repeating, across Iowa, that the veteran is "weak on gun rights."

About twenty years earlier, as the lore goes, Wallace demonstrated her affinity for gun rights. She was on leave for Christmas, at her parents' ski house in Sun Valley, Idaho. Her daughter was playing in the snow. Wallace was waiting for the babysitter. A grizzly bear wandered into the yard. Wallace was dressed for a party, wearing her mother's pearls. She grabbed her shotgun, opened the sliding door, and shot the grizzly dead. Some say it was a black bear. Regardless, Republicans love the tale. She is still known as the woman in pearls who shot the beast dead.

But the NRA rallied to Reynolds. And the reasons were foreseeable. Wallace believes there should be a limit on the number of bullets in a civilian firearm magazine. She supports mandating background checks for purchases of firearms online and at gun shows. The proposals are popular writ large but not among GOP activists. Thus a few months earlier, Vince asked her to back off. He knows that partisans are the protein of primaries. But she said she would stick with her stance. "Otherwise, what's it all for?" she asked Vince. And he replied, "It's all for nothing, if you don't win."

Yet principles come easy in good times. Wallace thought she could remain above wedge issues. She was the front-runner. She felt protected by the aura of myth. But in primaries, even heroes can be grounded.

And as the pilot descended into the partisan swamp, her image was sullied, and soon her support softened with it. Reynolds spoke rarely of abortion. Yet surveys showed he made inroads with married conservative women on the issue. Reynolds's wife, Betty Anne, helped. As Joe Scarborough defended Wallace on *Morning Joe*, the Reynoldses refused invitations to rebut on MSNBC. Instead, Betty Anne, as she was commonly called, appeared on *Fox & Friends* as often as possible. She traveled Iowa and South Carolina, barnstorming events from fund-raisers to church gatherings. And whenever she can, she deems Wallace: "Another compromising, country club elitist, a RINO (Republican in Name Only) who does *not* respect the Tenth Amendment, who loves big government, who wants more abortions and less guns." Betty Anne will even talk children. Liberals dote over their few children. Wallace raised only one child just like *those* liberals. Betty birthed a hockey team. Betty says she's the real mom without saying it. She strikes the female candidate as only a woman can.

Wallace believes she can lose Iowa and recover in New Hampshire. What choice does she have? She sees the surveys. Already, she's thinking comeback. She'll climb back. Constituency by constituency. The media is one more camp to court.

She walks over to a long pine table inside the hotel dining room. Fourteen reporters, including Taylor, await her. There are no recording devices. The occasion is off the record.

"I'm glad we could do this," Wallace says, resting her hands on her lap. "I've been traveling with most of you for almost a year. I feel like some of you are my children."

They know she does not feel this way.

"I wanted to sit down with all of you before Christmas."

They know she's here because she's losing.

The waiter arrives. He's scrawny, flat-faced. His ears protrude outward. He asks about drinks. Wallace recalls her adviser's advice: *Be Air Force, not austere.* She orders Miller Lite. She takes the wheel of the conversation. She has objectives. Evoke executive. Appear presidential. Play to your strengths. A war story follows. They all know *the* story that made her a hero. She speaks instead of breaking barriers. "The media is a sucker for talk about breaking barriers," her chief strategist, Vince, told her. "You've got to remind them that you also represent change." So she will exhibit change while stressing her strength.

Her big break, she tells them, came in 1990. She joined with several female pilots and confronted her commanding officer. They requested deployment in Operation Desert Storm. She flew 162 hours during the Gulf War. "We were not allowed then, even in 1990, to fly strictly combat missions. But I was still being shot at, for goodness' sake." That changed for her in the late nineties, when she made a little history. She was among the first women to officially fly combat missions. She excelled at destroying Yugoslav artillery and tanks. She doesn't get into the details now. She only says that, of this period in her life, she sometimes wonders if it could have gone another way. "But such is life. Great reward requires great risk. But, with those rewards, it's important to remember how easily these risks can go wrong." She hesitates, watches them watching her. "Don't get me wrong, I believe the cream usually rises to the top. But . . . not everything is in our control." Wallace places her hand around her beer. "I suspect most soldiers don't think their fate is entirely their own." She drinks.

The *Los Angeles Times* reporter is quick with her question, "You've broken historic barriers as a woman. Do you think that if abortion were illegal, fewer women would accomplish similar feats?"

Wallace purses her lips. Her thin torso stiffens. "First, I want to say that unplanned pregnancy can be terribly heart wrenching. It does sometimes get in the way of one's dreams. I understand that. All I can say, however, is that I don't think it justifies ending a baby's life."

Reporter continues. "You oppose abortion, yet you believe it should be legal in cases of rape or incest. But if it's murder, how can you ever support it?"

"Certainly, murder is the greatest moral wrong. But those terrible circumstances, rape and incest, constitute a very small share of abortions. Listen, many Americans struggle with this. I've never met a liberal woman who wants to be pregnant, suffers a miscarriage, and is not deeply hurt by the experience. What does that tell me? Liberal women see a *wanted* fetus as a baby. But I bet you would never challenge a liberal female candidate that way, would you?"

After the words are said, Wallace's eyes do not stray from the reporter's eyes. The reporter is speechless. "I thought not," Wallace adds. Wallace cannot believe that leading media outlets claim objectivity, yet describe liberal women's groups as synonymous with "women's groups." The majority of white women and a quarter of Hispanic women vote Republican. They favor more limits on abortion. These women constitute the majority of all social conservatives. Yet, she asks herself, don't they count as women to the liberal media? But she believes that argument will win few allies among reporters. So she sips her beer.

Taylor asks her, "I know your belief in meritocracy shapes your worldview. As you just put it, you think the cream usually rises to the top. Yet if that's true, why do you think in this large democratic nation only a few families like yours, or the Kennedys or the Bushes, have wielded astonishing amounts of multigenerational power?"

"Don't all successful people see themselves as proof of meritocracy? That's how we know we deserve our success." She hints at a smirk. They realize she's joking. "On a serious note, I've thought about that. Parents look out for their children. That's instinctual and good. For parents, children incentivize hard work. So democracies are always, I suspect, vulnerable to successful families trying to pass on their success. Dare I say, even off the record, genetics are probably one factor. Though that does not explain some presidents." She teases a smile. "Who knows? Humans had chiefs and monarchs for eons. Perhaps even democratic societies find their way back to that ancestral memory—particularly if they lack a symbolic monarchy, as with this country. The Kennedy mystique may exemplify that."

"So you had advantages in life others did not?"

"Of course. That said, you still must work for it. I entered the military partly to earn my privilege. It should also be said that a lot of difficult pressures come with privilege."

"You campaign on this Eisenhower-esque theme of 'prosperity and peace.' Governor Reynolds suggests that this slogan typifies how you, and I quote, 'hope to rise above hard issues and sail into the presidency as if you're special.' What's your response?"

"That if this is sailing, it's rough waters."

A few reporters smile.

"Why is it rough?" one asks. "Why do you think you're struggling in Iowa?"

She recalls politics 101: answer the question you want asked, not the question you're asked. "I can't say. Wally is an exceptional public speaker. A win in Iowa can propel a candidate to victory. Frankly, Wally is the front-runner in Iowa and beyond. I'll do my best to make it a close race."

She knows presidential politics is an expectations game. If reporters undersell your chances, your accomplishments will seem greater. Jimmy Carter soared after placing second in Iowa. Eugene McCarthy and Bill Clinton did it in New Hampshire. Perhaps she can too.

Wallace goes on. "My problem is getting the eighty-five-year-old woman to come out and vote for me."

"Do you feel women politicians face a different type of scrutiny?"

"I think . . . well, humans are cosmetic by nature. Modernity amplifies that, because there is more distraction. We look for easy ways to assess topics and people. Physical image plays into that. And yes, women face more scrutiny for how they look. But male politicians have been pummeled if they're perceived as effete."

"Is that false equivalence?"

"I'm not so sure anymore. There's something I've long thought is underrated about everyone who runs for president: whatever we've gone through, we've come out on top." Her fingers rub the tabletop. "But most people have not experienced that success, sadly. Women and men. Sometimes they look for something to blame. And sometimes that's right, whether bigotry or sexism or the reverse. But other times it's our fault we fail, or it's bad luck. Yet we still scapegoat. I think the media commonly suggests that working-class whites are always scapegoating, but it wouldn't dare say that about liberal constituencies."

"You think sexism is scapegoating?"

"No. Sexism is very real. But *sometimes* we want to excuse our failure to persevere. I nearly fell into that with my injury. And if we do that, we accept less from our future. The consolation is a psychological asterisk. Oh, she was hurt in war; she's done her best. I find that so patronizing or from some, matronizing—if that's a word. I don't know . . . maybe this is the WASP in me. I think nothing undermines personal agency more than considering yourself a victim. I wish more feminists agreed with me on that."

"Do you consider yourself a feminist?"

"If you mean equal opportunity for women, yes. But most feminists, like liberals in my view, wrongly judge the world by equal outcomes. And heck, I'm not a socialist."

"But don't women still face unique obstacles?"

"Of course. It's far easier today than in my younger days. But my military service likely helps me cross over the commander-in-chief threshold. That could be an obstacle for other women. Of course, Reynolds might complain that my war record—or anytime I act tough, even in a debate—well, that it gets extra praise because I'm a woman. Frankly, he might be right. So sure, there are obstacles. Again, I simply think it's healthier to focus on action instead of obstacles in life. I've never met a successful man who doesn't do that."

"What will you do if you don't succeed at this?"

"Sleep."

Reporters chuckle.

"Do you enjoy campaigning?"

"I enjoy governing."

"But don't you hate government?"

"I dislike bloated and wasteful government. I'm a Burkean conservative."

"But," Taylor asks, "isn't American conservatism un-Burkean, partly because it's culturally populist? You often sound more like a British Tory than a modern GOP leader."

"Institutions *conserve* order." She taps the table with her finger. "I want to cut the fat to save programs like Social Security, not ruin them. But let me also be clear, the other extreme is problematic. Citizens can feel too entitled. The Scandinavian nations may soon wrestle with how their extremely liberal social services deincentivize economic productivity."

"But don't those nations, from their generous parental leave policies to their healthcare systems, have a lot to teach us?" a reporter asks.

"That's a popular comparison in the liberal press. But the Scandinavian nations are tiny, prosperous, and homogeneous. Does ethnic uniformity enhance a sense of common cause in citizens? The Scandinavian model says yes. American liberalism has never come to terms with the fact that two of its chief values—diversity and the social welfare state—are often at odds with one another."

"Are you saying we should reemphasize assimilation?" a reporter asks.

"I'm suggesting one should ask liberals that question, when they praise the Scandinavian model."

"If I may, on a separate matter, why do you speak of 'Islamic extremism' in your speeches?" another reporter asks. "Doesn't that insult Muslims and affirm the radical interpretation of Islam?"

"This is what I'm talking about. Firstly, no historian would discuss the Spanish Inquisition without discussing Christianity. Yet in the modern era, we're told to ignore that a pattern of terrorism and repression stems from a radical but real group of Islamists—one supported by at least one hundred million Muslims worldwide, of the roughly billion and a half Muslims, according to Pew polls. And we must make that minority-majority distinction. But we also must not turn away from the problem. To cure a cancerous idea, you must first diagnose it."

"But is it your place to diagnose it, as a Christian?" the reporter asks.

"I'm diagnosing it as someone who cares about civilization. This is not a battle between civilizations; it's a battle for civilization. Pluralistic Muslims, fighting this fight, know that. Many liberals seem willfully blind, however. That's easier here.

This battle of ideas is more acute in Europe and the Muslim world. But regardless, liberals again seem not to recognize the tension between values. Tolerance is an important value. But some things must never be tolerated. Why does multiculturalism trump the supposedly liberal belief in free speech or empowering women? Why aren't more liberals, especially feminists, on the front lines of this fight?"

And she fences on. She is asked about Medicare vouchers. "I'm open to reasonably restructuring Medicare to get our fiscal house in order. I will work tirelessly to be sure we can afford our promises and our programs." She looks at the reporter who pressed her on abortion. "As you know, we women are used to working twice as hard to succeed." The *LA Times* reporter smiles.

That always works, Wallace thinks. She feels it's working. She goes on. The warrior lets out her wonk. She talks about the details of entitlement reform. *Show I have regular problems.* She mentions that a deer ate the vegetables she was growing behind her house. *Check.*

She spins the oddsmakers one last time. "I think a lot about Mario Cuomo's line—we campaign in poetry and govern in prose. I may not do the poetry so well, like say Joe Girona. But I sure know the prose. I will get things done."

Wallace realizes this is her greatest weakness. People march for missions, not minutia. She sees younger and greener pols catching the wind. *None of the men in the race risked their life for this country. They haven't really sacrificed to get here.* Yet she's seen this before. Two of her old friends, Lamar Alexander and Bob Dole, watched younger men surpass them. She thinks of John Glenn and his inability to campaign. She's come to believe that the presidency also requires the right stuff. But it's different stuff. She wonders if she has it. She can't own a stage the way Girona or her political idol, Ronald Reagan, can. She is campaigning as the experienced and pragmatic choice. But she's worried that this strategy depends on weak competition. She's been thinking about the 1960 Democratic primary. She's not a political animal like LBJ. She knows that a younger, more telegenic candidate overshadowed Johnson, too. She recalls LBJ's line about Kennedy: "Jack was out kissing babies while I was out passing bills." And in the back of her mind, she cannot forget who won that day.

So she'll try harder. She's like a fighter who needs to take a few hits before she gets into the fight. Still, it's difficult for her. She does not love the show. She does not savor pressing the flesh or drinking tasteless beer. And the food. *Oh the food.* At the Iowa State Fair alone, she ate deep-fried pork chops, deep-fried Twinkies, deep-fried bologna. *Why do Americans insist we out-ordinary each other?* And voters' questions. *Those asinine questions.* She must nod, comatose, as they blab. Reporters are worse, to her. The way they stalk each word, seeking to turn any misstatement into a headline.

She questions the integrity of politics. On some long nights, when she wakes from a nightmare and her mind drifts, she wonders, is any profession honorable if it requires you to shake hands with those you disrespect?

But she'll shake those hands. Do what she must. And what galls her, shall remain inside her. She will only say so much. She will not slip. She's too good to be that bad.

Taylor opens his hotel room door. It's 2:12 a.m. He grabs the bottled water, chugs it, and collapses into bed face forward. He reaches to the bed table. Dials reception. Requests a six a.m. wake-up call.

He wonders whether tonight was an act. Either way, the little gleaned from Constance Wallace will remain hidden from the public. On running as a woman, off the record. On the role of luck in life from the social Darwinist, off the record. Candid thought, off the record. He thinks about how the arrangement warms the media to the candidate, even though nothing is reportable. They will return to their positions tomorrow. Witnesses to stagecraft, talking points, like theater critics dissecting the drama, the script, the visuals, the intended audience, and whether the actors rise to their roles. He's aware that this is not new. He recalls the famous line by Donald Regan, President Reagan's chief of staff. That "each presidential action" was scripted "as a one-minute or two-minute spot on the evening network news, or a picture on page one." It's the presidential universe. Reporters are small planets orbiting a star. They can observe from afar. But the planets can never know the star.

Taylor pulls his phone out of his jeans pocket. There's another "memo" from Joe Girona's communications director. Faux memos feed the media's insatiable desire for news. But there is often not much that's new, that's news. So reporters are left with campaign machinations, small ball, inside baseball. Little matters are enlarged to news. Political flacks realize that if they call a press release a "memo" and format it as a strategic campaign document instead of a press release, the media report it as news rather than publicity. Taylor skims the first lines, sees that it's more spin, and deletes the email.

There's a *Current* human resources email that warns: "This is a reminder that all staff will lose any unused vacation days at the end of the year." *Current* editors, however, pressure reporters not to use their vacation days. Taylor anticipates his first vacation and wonders if there will be issues. He has a long weekend planned next month in Playa del Carmen. He notices that the Girona campaign blasted a virtual holiday card to its supporters. The family is pictured with wide smiles. Below, it reads "God bless you this holiday season. We are reminded of what is important, of family, friends, and how we must sacrifice for those less fortunate. With all our love, the Girona family." He sees an email from his editor, who requests that he fly to Iowa tomorrow and cover for Luke on the Girona campaign. Taylor wonders why Luke is returning to Washington. Girona's the hottest candidate. It's the eve of the Iowa caucuses. But Taylor will roll with it. The idea of a morning flight nauseates him. He decides to figure it out after some rest. He tosses his phone onto the carpet and closes his eyes. The sun is a few hours off.

XIV

Cait runs toward the winter sun. Salt pebbles crunch beneath her feet. The scabrous surface is uneven, cracked from ice, from traffic, from time, another country road forgotten.

She couldn't sleep. She doesn't sleep well anymore. But four hours is poor even for her. She relented with dawn. She wanted to gather her thoughts. She needed fresh air.

She runs alone down the plowed two-lane road, past pine needles painted with white powder. High snow banks border the pavement. She races toward the traffic. But the road is now empty except for her. Her arms move rhythmically with her legs. Small white pods are in her ears. She's listening to Cyndi Lauper's "All Through the Night."

She slips on the snow, catches herself with her left hand, and her wrist bends back. A Honda whizzes past. She stands and runs on. She shakes her left hand, turns her wrist. It hurts. She runs uphill. "This precious time. When time is new." She clings to the emotion behind the lyrics. The beat rises. And so does she. More. Harder. Her breathing hastens. The air has a faint hint of pine. *Should I tell anyone?* She thinks of her editors. *I can't tell them. I should. I should write it in first person and ruin the asshole.* Her pace quickens. *But it's not about me. I don't want to be another reporter who makes the story about them. But he made it about me. That story would blow up. Blow him up. I need to call Mom. She'll be so high and mighty . . . But she'll know what to do. Or Taylor.*

No way. We only hung out once. Jesus, I should want to call Blake. He won't understand.

As she runs, the pine trees end and the road rises with the hill. A 1950s pickup truck sits in a ditch, half buried beneath dense powder, abandoned. The rounded hood is maroon and rusty, and ice has collected along the metal grill. Cait ascends faster, harder, and nears the brow of the hill. *How could I let him touch me like that? Kiss me!* She's sprinting. Breathing heavily. The crest is near. Sunlight reflects off the snow and glares bright white. She squints. Runs harder still. Reaches the top of the hill. And America's breadbasket extends like eternity. Victorian houses sprinkle vast patches of farmland. She's alone. Her breath dissipates in the cold air. The wind picks up. She runs on. Snow gusts and twists and builds. And the horizon clouds white.

Steam escapes from the bathroom as Cait opens the door, walks to her bed, and lies back. A towel wraps her hair, another wraps her body. She stares at her phone. The red light blinks. She thinks about calling her mother. The Girona bus leaves in a half hour for another speech. Christian Ulster has emailed her. "You joining us today?" he asked. He's never emailed her before. She closes her eyes and calls her mother. One ring.

"Hon." Erin Ellis is panting. "The treadmill. Hold on."

Who is this woman? Cait thinks.

"Hi, Cait," Erin continues, catching her breath. "How are you?"

"Are you at Equinox again?"

"I am. And I quit smoking. You can't even smoke in parks in this city anymore. So I quit. After thirty-four years. Just like that."

The great woman. "Of course it was easy for you."

"How are you, Cait? How was the Girona interview? It's wonderful that the *Times* chose you to do it."

"That's actually what I'm calling about. I need some advice."

"Sure. What is it?"

"Is there a place you can go that's private?"

"Hold on, let me find a room."

Cait waits. She can hear the shuffle of static over the phone.

"Okay," Erin says. "I'm in the torture room."

"Huh?"

"There are boards and straps everywhere. It looks like something Jordanian intelligence would use."

"Oh. The Pilates room."

"This is Pilates? I've been meaning to try it."

"Mom, I have to talk to you."

"Did something happen, Cait?"

"Yeah."

"With work?"

"Yeah."

"With the Girona interview?"

"Yeah." Cait sniffles. She tells herself, keep it together. But it's hard for her. It's her mother. She wants to let it out. But there's this image on the other line. And she's trying to live up to it.

Cait's breathing is audible.

"What happened?" Erin asks. She hears Cait's exhale. "Did you have the interview?"

"Yeah."

"Where was it?"

"His hotel room."

"Was it just you two?"

"Not at first. But then his aides left. So yes, for the interview, just us."

"Did he make a pass at you?"

Cait inhales.

"How did he make a move?"

"He . . . well . . . he kissed me—and—you know."

"What do you mean he kissed you? Did you kiss him back?"

Cait hears a young woman in the background, asking if she can use the room. Erin says "hold on" to Cait and tells the woman, "I'm sorry, you have to leave. Right. Now."

"Sorry, Cait. I was interrupted. Did you kiss him back?"

"Of course not."

"But he kissed you?"

"Yeah."

"You let him kiss you?"

Cait closes her eyes. Her mother's words ping her deepest regret. "He blindsided me. I didn't expect it. We were sitting on the couch—"

"Wait. You were side by side with him, on the same couch, for an interview?"

"Yeah, I know. It just happened that way. The chairs were moved out of the sitting area."

"He probably moved them away before you came in. So you had to sit that way."

Cait never thought of that. She feels naïve.

"What happened exactly?"

"He put his hand on my thigh—"

"Wait, you mean you were interviewing him, and he all of a sudden put his hand on your leg?"

"Not really. He asked to speak off the record."

"So you shut off your tape recorder?"

"Yeah."

"And he made a pass at you then?"

"Well, we chatted for a minute, and then he put his hand on my thigh." Cait shudders. "Then he kissed me. At first, I froze."

"Then what?"

"He moved his hand up my thigh . . . all the way up. He kissed me again. I got a hold of myself. I jumped up and left right away."

"You walked out?"

"Yeah."

"Good. Nothing else happened?"

"No."

"Good."

"But I mean—"

"Cait. You were alone in a presidential candidate's hotel room. And of all guys—I hear women talk about how handsome he is. He's obviously full of shit. They're all car salesmen. What did you expect would happen?"

Cait is sniffling.

"I'm sorry," Erin goes on. "I mean, that must've been shocking for you. I forget how protected your generation is from this stuff."

"Whatever, Mom. Candidates conduct interviews from their rooms all the time. Politicians don't regularly do this stuff. It happens, sure. But not at his level."

"I'll grant you that. They're not going around patting women on the ass anymore. But these men do feel entitled to women. Trust me. And, frankly, countless women feed that. We love men with power and influence."

"Anyway."

"Don't be glib. If you had listened to me in the past, this wouldn't have happened."

"That's not fair."

"I'm sorry. I'm only trying to say . . . you must be on your guard. You're a young, attractive woman. It can help and hurt you."

"I know. I just didn't see it coming. Not like that."

"You should expect worse. When you're working sources, even good men can get the wrong idea—because it can feel intimate—to say nothing of the jerks. That's why you must watch your manner, tone, all that. At least, handle it when things go wrong."

"I did. I can. I feel like you're blaming me."

"Hon, this is not about blame. It's about recognizing reality."

Cait sighs. "I get it."

"Then follow it. You can't just meet a man anywhere because you say it's an interview. I mean, Christ, alone in a hotel room with a damn car salesman—"

"He's a senator, actually."

"They're all car salesmen! Don't stand up for him."

"I'm not. And for God's sake, he should change his behavior."

"Enough with the 'should.' This is not about how the world *should* be. You are not one of those intellectuals who mistake ideas for reality, who spend their days only on what reinforces their worldview. You were raised to navigate the world *as it is.* My God, how could you put yourself in that position?"

"Mom, I'm sorry!" Cait blurts. She begins to cry.

Erin quiets. "I'm sorry." Her voice warms. "I'm really sorry. I just worry about you."

Cait sniffles, collects herself.

Erin calms too. "Well, I'm glad nothing really bad happened. I'm glad you got out of there. You should be proud of that . . . one sec, that girl's coming back."

"What's going on?"

"This princess wants to use the room. I locked the door. She's flipping out. Anyway."

"Mom, what do you think I should do?"

"What do you mean, what should you do?"

"I think I want to write about what happened."

"Caitriona Elizabeth. You cannot do that."

"Why?"

"Listen to me. He's a jerk. He was way out of line. But I've come to realize over the years that, well, the right move is not always the *right* move."

"What does that mean?"

"Think about it, hon. You are morally right to expose him. But if you do, you will always be that woman. You'll become part of the gossip machine. The media will eat you up. Most of your colleagues will choose the story over you. You'll be treated as ammunition in the culture wars by both sides, not as a person. You'll also become the woman who sunk Girona. But it won't be for a great story. It'll be because he kissed you. And don't forget, it will be your word versus his. He might say it was consensual."

"He would never." *Would he?* Cait wonders.

"Listen. However events transpire, it will follow your career forever. And regardless, you stopped it before it went too far."

Cait wonders if she's overreacting. *No. It went too far. It's not okay. But . . . maybe she's right. Maybe I should let it go.*

"Cait," Erin says, "if you tell the story, the piece will get great readership. But you'll have gotten far by playing the victim. And your career will never move past it."

"Mom, I think women will support me for coming forward."

"Maybe. But you also could become Anita Hill. Trust me, you lose either way."

"Maybe they'll just assign me to Wallace for good. I've covered her a lot."

"This is why we need more women in power. You should cover her. She's a better story, regardless. She seems like a good woman."

"I thought they were all car salesmen?"

"Well, she's been tested. She's not like these people I meet in the city who talk about 'putting out fires' at work or think of themselves as tough because they excel in a boardroom. They don't know what true bravery is, what—"

"Mom, do we always have to get into societal crap?"

Erin exhales. "Sorry. So they haven't permanently assigned you to a candidate?"

"No."

"Good. If they push for Girona, make something up. You should request Wallace. That's a good idea. You just can*not* report this incident."

"I don't know."

"Hon, I know how you feel. Sometime I'll tell you my stories."

Her stories?

Her mother goes on, "But for now, you have to play this like a guy would if a candidate humiliated him or took advantage of him and made him feel powerless. I don't know, like if they were off the record and they got into an argument and Girona shoved the guy against a wall."

"Many would report that—"

"In your D.C. media world, maybe. But not most. Listen, tough it out. Stiff upper lip. All that stuff."

"Okay."

"You going to be okay?"

"Yeah."

"You sure?"

"Yeah, Mom."

"Damn right. You're *my* daughter."

XV

The afternoon sun slices through the hotel window blinds. The white tile floor is lined by stripes of shadow and light. Cait enters the lobby with her luggage. She searches for her sunglasses inside her black satchel handbag. Her phone rings. It's her boyfriend, Blake. She clicks it to voicemail. She skims her phone inbox. Her editor emailed her. She doesn't open it. Her mind wanders to her mother's advice. She drops her phone in her handbag and puts on her Jackie O sunglasses.

"Ms. Ellis?" an attendant asks.

"Yes."

"Ms. Ellis, one of Mr. Girona's aides said you left your coat in the office. He left you a note. Here you go." He hands over an envelope with her coat.

She reads the note: "Cait, you forgot this. Please call me when you can. I want to see if I can be of any assistance, on any matter. Please call. Christian."

"I need to check out," she tells the attendant.

"Of course. You can right over there. I'll look after your bags."

She walks to the front desk. Cait hands over the plastic key card, says the room number, and waits for her bill.

Taylor enters the lobby and sees her and smiles. He asks a bellhop to watch his bags. And he quietly walks over to her. "Caitriona," he says, standing behind her, surprising her.

She turns around. "Taylor!" And she smiles as if she's known him for years.

"How are you?" he asks.

"Okay."

"How'd the interview go?"

"Fine."

He notices her reserved tone. "You sure?"

"Yeah. I just didn't get enough sleep . . . it's really good to see you, Taylor."

"It's really good to see you too. Where you going?"

"Des Moines, to catch a flight. I'm returning to the city for a few days. What are you doing here?"

"They asked me to cover Girona today and tonight. Luke had to head back to D.C."

"What . . . why?"

Taylor shrugs. "You have time to get lunch?"

"Don't you have to catch up with Girona?"

"I can catch his speech this evening. That's probably enough." Taylor pauses. He's covered hundreds of these stump speeches. News rarely breaks. It's his third presidential campaign. He's never skipped a speech. It's how he justifies his late nights. He still does his job. But he doesn't see why there need to be dozens of reporters covering the same speech. The fuck-it door opens. "Let's get lunch." And Taylor walks through.

"But not here," Cait says. "I'm craving grilled cheese."

"Then grilled cheese it is."

"You sure your editors won't kill you? I mean, isn't that partly why you guys are rocking all of us? Or were, at first."

"Is that the rap on my employer?"

"There are so many."

Taylor smiles.

"I mean, yeah," she adds. "They say *Current*'s a Maoist sweatshop for political reporters."

"That's not entirely true."

"What part?"

"We're not Maoists."

XVI

The Washington Current wanted to cover the contest in politics and keep score. Political mavens scoffed at the mission. But DCland already followed politics as if it were sports. *Current* simply redoubled indigenous behavior. It made minor-league politics critical to the big game. It was like a 24/7 cable network. There's too little news and too much airtime. Thus more news must become newsworthy. *Current*-worthy. Cable news pundits already covered political events as if they were ballgames. *Current* intended to report the everyday that way. Pre-game the speech. Cover the speech. Postgame news and analysis. It was ESPN. It was also E! Washington was already called Hollywood for ugly people. Why not make it Page Six worthy? The ugly people were pretty too, in their political way, at least to those obsessed with politics. Newsmakers were news. Gossip about them could be too. Most campaign news might not *really* matter, but it mattered to political junkies. Finally, someone would cover Washington for all that Washington meant to itself.

New York Times Washington editor, Philip Larson, and chief White House reporter, Rick Ergaleio, conceived *Current.* From D.C. to Silicon Valley, select individuals were outshining their institutions. P&R decided they could matter more and make more by having their own outlet. So they found funding and resigned from the *Times,* paving an entrepreneurial road online that other big bylines followed. P&R had no ownership stake. But their baby would be born. Soon they recruited a half dozen journalism stars. The talent was offered more money and more visibility via a publicity machine designed to turn reporters into pundits and pundits into brands. And in the beginning, that meant courting one man.

Not long before *Current* was first published, P&R flew to Miami. Philip and Rick sat down with Matt Drudge at Forge, a Miami steak house. As they ate red meat and drank red wine, P&R won over this steward of the news gods. An understanding was reached. And mass marketing followed. From day one, *Current*'s reporters were urged to provide the sensational stories that won over the prime hosts of viral news, *Drudge* foremost. But it also relied on its relationship with Matt Drudge, as well as his assistant, to assure enough links. Peter Miller regularly fed Drudge over IM. P&R preserved the dynamic. They attended a Cubs' game with Drudge's assistant. They passed along privileged media passes for political events. They were like any sales firm dependent on one rainmaker. Whatever needed doing, they'd do. Because it paid. *Current* received at least forty *Drudge* links a month in those critical early months. *Drudge* was not the only game in town. There were challengers, from *Huffington Post* to the Twittersphere. But since the late nineties, no figure was more influential than Matt Drudge in shaping American news—a fact many journos rued, but few contested.

Current relied on its stars for those links—to spread viral news, to garner millions of readers, to earn broadcast publicity. It relied on a supporting cast to cover the rest of DCland. A caste system developed. The stars earned 100 to 245 grand, annually. They had contracts securing their jobs. *Current* saw the contracts as good for it as well. Once it made someone a star, that star was contractually obligated to remain with

Current for at least a few years. The lower caste was paid standard salaries, 40 to 85 grand, for perhaps fifty to ninety hours of work weekly. They worked without contracts or job security. Rick liked it that way. Insecure reporters meant productive reporters. They were afraid to say no to work. They say the Japanese are more German than the Germans. *Current* was more German than the Japanese.

Reporters, across the media, felt only as valuable as their last story. They counted the comments about their story. They searched for Twitter handles and blog posts about their story. They checked the "trending" and "most read" boxes. Did their story earn traffic? Did it matter? Did they matter? The volume of readers increasingly defined a reporter's value.

Reporters accepted the terms. It was a matter of worse alternatives. Journos also believed in the relationship's potential. *Current* magnified the publisher's con: cultural currency. Modern reporters are suckers for recognition. *Current* fed the insecurity. Affirmation became more valuable. Reporters want to impact the world. No one enters journalism for the money. The boss can underpay, considering the hours and the anxiety. Publishers can prosper from journalists' idealism. The idealism may fade. But there are other rewards. You're on television.

In the wider editorial world, the news business worried about its viability as a business. Networks were bleeding viewers. The traditional business model overloaded newspapers. Classified revenue once comprised about 40 percent of all American newspaper revenue. But classified earnings fell 70 percent in a decade. Websites such as Craigslist won that money. Commercial advertising migrated online. Print ads are costly. Web ads are cheaper, more efficient, but also far less lucrative for publishers. Newspapers lost as much as ten dollars in print revenue for every dollar they earned online. And unlike with the print magazine spread of old, companies could see what ads readers actually viewed.

So ad teams tried everything. *Current* joined the rush to video ads because they commanded higher rates than banner ads. It invested in targeted advertising, offering different ads based on a reader's online history. News outlets were like desperate mining firms digging deeper, searching for a massive trove of gold that would never be found; and as time went on, they only seemed more panicked, more in need of an answer that would not come. New-media companies thought they changed the question. They lacked print's legacy costs. But once they grew large enough, most found it difficult to find the revenue to meet their ambitions. So, like many, *Current* pushed the ethical envelope. Soon major news websites, *Current* included, began publishing ad copy that read like news and was posted beside news, with a subtle note that the content was "sponsored." Media insiders debated the propriety, but the industry could not ignore anything that helped sustain its business. Yet not even looser ethics could revive the revenue of old.

Big media companies began shedding their print assets. Most small dailies were thinning or disappearing. Hence, already, there were fewer watchdogs covering municipal governments across America. Many newspapers shrunk and found a diet that sustained them. They could, as the *LA Times* did, localize and survive, by monopolizing a smaller news market that remained profitable—albeit less profitable online. Most magazines could not. In this era, *Newsweek* acquired so much debt that it was sold for one dollar. Meanwhile, search engines, from Google to Yahoo, gleaned ad dollars from newspaper content while newspapers paid the costs to create the content. Subscription revenue became critical. Yet the news business initially decided that free products were good for business. But someone had to pay. So media paid. Some outlets began erecting paywalls. The walls had to be low, however, because the industry had conditioned consumers to not paying. Meanwhile, as overall profits dwindled, digital subscriptions increasingly accounted for earnings. Therefore, newspapers depended more on their subscriber count. And advertising depended on padding that count. Some national newspapers offered their apps for free to the subscribers of smaller city newspapers. More readers meant higher ad rates. But nothing new could restore the old.

Yet publications continued to look backward to see a way forward. Newspapers artificially inflated their print subscription numbers. Many effectively gave away the paper edition for free with an online subscription. Publishers desperately sought to preserve the illusion that print ads were still worth the cost. While they could. Because the advertising reckoning was underway. Print was becoming a niche product. And with that, the great cash flows were drying up. No one knew how to recover yesterday. Newsrooms began wasting away. In one generation, almost a third of all American newspaper jobs were eliminated. And insiders knew that the bad news had only begun.

The day of the writer had passed. Newshounds will chase news. People will write. Some will remain influential. There will be the unique author who woos the masses or the literati. The uncommon screenwriter who makes it, and makes it count. The rare reporter who exposes wrong. The rare essayist who can contextualize great events. And periodically, another media star will strike out solo and found the next hot venture online. A handful will even last. After all, there will always be the atypical serious outlet that succeeds. Yet what flourishes online will not come close to offsetting what perishes offline, as far fewer writers prove able to live off their words.

It was odd that way. Decades ago, television depreciated the cultural value of words. Yet the Internet demanded more words than ever before. Content became cheap. Writers were cheapened. Prose became surplus. And words became less profitable. Consequently, quality diminished. There were exceptions. With the new oceans of data, there was a rising expectation that reporters' claims must be provable. Yet those advances, like quality overall, became harder to locate amid the din. As a result, the old infrastructure deteriorated. The editor who could efficiently cut fat, make words sing, or improve a writer's argument, joined the editorial world's growing endangered species list. Without the advertising revenue to fund glossy print pages, even iconic magazines began to cut their staff photographers. In a generation, the normative became luxuries: line editors, fact-checkers, fulltime photographers, essayists, narrative and investigative journalism, as well as foreign news, as the most prominent U.S. papers cut overseas staff. The news industry's future was being devoured by market forces, but also by itself, amid pervasive content cannibalism—where the meat is taken from another's story, rewritten as your own, and published in a brief post on your website. Some cannibalistic websites were shamed. Eventually, many of them hired a small corps of writers to effectively serve as a patina for public relations. But patinas could not compensate for the jobs lost. It did not matter if you were a reporter or a copy editor or a printing press operator. News workers saw a landscape eroding, column inch by column inch.

Old media was internet-ed. The future might not include newspapers. But there would be news. The institutions could live virtually. Most of the jobs could not. Positions were either vanishing or heading down the road that every worker dreads: do more but earn less. Because just as media accepted the transition from print to Web, just as the first quake passed, new tremors were felt. Consumers began reading more news on their phones and tablets. And the media moneymen started realizing how times could worsen. Those ten dollars in print advertising, which translated into a dollar online, became dimes, even pennies, with mobile advertising. Concerns over ethical conflicts seemed quaint beside this new-media world.

Yet the disarray exceeded journalism. The news industry was one story within the great disruption. The laws of bundling once ruled mass media. Buy an album for one good song. Buy the newspaper for one headline. Buy this best seller and subsidize literary fiction. Subscribe to countless cable channels for a few shows. Younger viewers were watching and reading only online. Soon most people would. The disorder was good for a few. But the industries en masse, from publishing to music to Hollywood, the writers and artists writ large, saw that the future was against them. The expectation that media should be free threatened an entire species of livelihood. The movement to make it free, from Google Books to the random online pirate, made good on that threat. The cultural class hoped that the parasites would realize they needed a healthy host. But in the hierarchy of consumer concerns, many preferred cheap and convenient to good. So it went from music to film. The Internet demanded plenty of photography, not premium photography. People favored streaming over HD, ease over excellence. And with words, as quantity trumped quality here too, people forgot what it felt like to experience a great read.

Fewer people were reading books these days. But less money was also being made on those books, amid the publishing price race to the bottom. The music industry faced similar forces. Ninety-nine-cent downloads destroyed the profit margin in albums. Live streaming began, in this period, to undercut the profit margin in songs. Traditional media didn't help itself. It was passive amid new predators. It was too slow to accept the Internet. In those early online years, newspapers notoriously viewed their business as newsprint instead of news. And they were not unique. Most of the old media mistook their product for how it was delivered. Yet not all responded equally. However ineptly, before the rise of streaming, the music industry was relatively quick to challenge pirating. Journalism invited the pirates. Free content meant more readers. More influence. And the siren song wooed on. Top universities increasingly offered lectures for free online because, apparently, even academics could only learn some lessons the hard way. But self-inflicted wounds aside, the creative class had reason to fear that their heyday had passed. As the world entered a post-humanities age, the creators of culture were losing their incentive to create.

There were new safe havens for journalists. A handful of titans were willing to risk millions, sometimes hundreds of millions, because they could lose millions. They wanted to wield the cultural sway of a media institution, produce the news slant they favored, or, in rare cases, support good journalism. Nonprofit news watchdogs were formed, from *ProPublica* to *PolitiFact* to *InsideClimate News.* There was some pushback online for substantial content. A few outlets invested in explanatory, investigative, or empirical journalism. But they amounted to lifeboats surrounded by sinking ships. At best, there were reprieves—the next new venture, where a small share of souls would still get out and even go on to prosper—but in the end, only so many could get out. The smart journos realized it was every man for himself.

Start-ups such as *Current* seemed to show the way to shore. Talking heads used talking points. Why not news by bullet point? Women's magazines used lists. Gossipy websites did too. News could be cut into main points. *Current* popularized the idea of list stories in serious news. And soon the "listicle" littered the news. Yet, above all, *Current* coveted brevity and rapidity. Sure, P&R wanted to offer gravitas for the purists. That's why Taylor and Luke were originally hired, as well as a handful of eminent graybeards. But they also became essential to winning the news cycle.

Then *Current* began winning. Soon dominating. So recently, as *Current* transitioned from upending the political-media establishment to becoming part of it, P&R wanted to show that *Current* was more than empty calories. Accordingly, P&R considered how they could affordably create content that could win respect and not be cannibalized. The new online magazine section followed. In practice, this section included mostly short articles with a few in-depth features. To afford it, *Current* imitated the online business model of elite publications. It farmed out nearly all of those articles to freelancers for low pay, offering cultural exposure to compensate. In other words, ironically, the more substance *Current* began offering online, the less it would pay writers, as more freelancing meant fewer new hires, and fewer new hires meant fewer journalists able to support a family with their work—and that trend, seen throughout the media, would lead to fewer talented people seeking journalism work. Yet P&R hardly sweated such concerns. With success, they worried about retaining success. Therefore, they chose to outsource substance and insource impact—that is, news cycle impact. *Current*'s staff was directed to write the brand and win America's decreasing attention span.

Current made that brand with its signature fare, fast-food journalism—the scooplet. The four-hundred-word story. "We need big dunks," Rick commonly told stars. Those were the quick stories that were spectacular to read and watch. They were replayed on television, looped like sports highlight reels. This copy also rapidly went viral on social media. It was conventional germ warfare. Infect The List, the influential. Because, in the beginning, a successful epidemic depends on the right hosts rather than the number of hosts. At the same time, offer specialized copy that lobbyists will pay to read. Provide political junkies with the news fix they need. And if production slowed, Rick pushed, "We need layups! Get points on the board or get off the court." Few dared leave the court.

Current scored those "points," in part, by freeze-framing the movement of news. Ohio's governor endorses the presidential candidate. Headline. The governor's actual endorsement. Headline. The opposing campaign's response. Blog it. Never mind that endorsements almost never matter. People will follow it if you cover it. What was once one story became a series of smaller stories. A sound bite could be a story. P&R touted Peter Miller as their Olympian reporter. And Peter counseled staff: "Don't go deeper, go forward. News must move the story forward. Inches count."

To encourage Peter's philosophy, P&R considered offering bonuses based on a reporter's readership tallies. Salesmen were paid this way. Why not journos? But the publisher vetoed the decision, for now, he said. These days, he believed the deterrents were severe enough. Labor was abundant enough. And the stars were already paid enough. Why add a bonus? Why offer journos a new lucrative pay structure? Reporters already viewed increased relevance as its own reward.

So the scooplet factory encouraged its staff to define what's relevant and seize control of the news cycle. Thus *Current*'s motto: "Own the hour!" This slogan soon spread across the media. Again, the mavens scoffed. But in the news business, few could afford to ignore the result.

Current sped up Washington's metabolism. It became the snack of choice. Politics with sugar on top. Vegetables transformed into brain candy. Some editors stayed true to their sugar-free diet. A few elite publishers thought they would survive because they should survive. The public will eat vegetables again!

Yet what succeeds somewhere tends to, eventually, succeed everywhere. For sugar does sell. The advice of *Current*'s top editor, Philip, defined the outlet: "Exaggerate—and then walk back."

Media reporters soon wrestled with *Current*'s impact. Many asked how *Current* did it. Fewer asked where it was taking the business. They were interested in any new journalism outlet that succeeded in these times—not as a cannibal of others' work, fielding some reporters for appearance's sake, but as a producer of news. *Current* did aggregate news on the side. But what predators didn't scavenge amid famine? Many media critics scorned *Current*. After all, it accelerated the appetites that were undoing journalism. But even survival was a feat these days. And *Current* was prospering. So countless journos applied. Because perhaps there was one fate that reporters feared more than irrelevance, and that was becoming old news.

Current refused to mistake the past for the future, the medium for the message. It frantically chased tech trends to meet consumers where they consumed. Its rapid-fire video segments confirmed that written media dare not rely on words alone, not anymore. Yet it also realized video's limits. It considered webcasting news, à la cable news, but that proved too costly to do well. Instead, it focused on the mobile consumer.

It understood that for youth, and soon for everyone, the virtual *is* reality. Social media is socialization. And the public is paparazzi, as privacy goes public. So *Current* partnered with social messaging apps to bait "guppies," *Current*'s term for young readers. It encouraged readers to use their gadgets to personally film any moment that might titillate politicos, and then anonymously submit the footage. Most recently, it emulated influential business outlets and began experimenting with an early version of robo-reporting. For deep-pocketed subscribers, *Current*'s techies created an algorithm termed DCbot, designed to produce brief, inhumanly fast news alerts after a congressional vote or an emergency broadcast, to supply professionals who profit from knowing the news first—from K Street lobbyists to Wall Street's automated trading desks. Meanwhile, social messaging apps, Twitter's emergence as the communication utility of the influential, the ongoing atomization of news, all of it amplified the "*Current* Effect," as one media writer coined its impact, although *Current* no longer controlled that effect. Faster fast-food journalism. Ever faster. More means to put cook before cuisine. Follow my feed! *Current* catalyzed this buzz-feeding news breed.

The old giants were initially caught flat-footed. But they wanted to be the future too. Publishers wanted influence too. That's why they owned media outlets. Soon, dons from *The Washington Post* to *The New York Times* to *Bloomberg News* recruited *Current* reporters and, above all, considered the strategy they had to emulate to overtake. *Current* bought its big bylines by offering larger salaries. A few outlets started buying the boldest names in punditry. News power was worth the price. They wanted to keep their long game. Keep their broad coverage, their beat watchdogs, their depth. But they also hoped to replicate *Current*'s short game, to own the hour and drive that news day—as did some online giants, such as Yahoo, who decided to produce on the side as well. The future seemed to be in the short game. So big media sought *Current*'s recipe: speed, hyper-concision, a conversational voice and vision, influencer centralization, ripple marketization, true 24/7-ization, news-genre fixation, scooplet industrialization, flyboy celebritization, grunt exploitation, search engine lubrication, medium homogenization, social news causation, mobile app integration, news incrementalism, list-ism, viral-ism, *Drudge*-ism, and old-fashioned sensationalism.

The *Current* Effect soon mattered more than *Current* itself. The creation dwarfed its creator. Key competitors regained their influence and fresh outlets entered the news race. But the competitors largely did it on *Current*'s terms. In order to beat *Current*, the news media became more like *Current*.

XVII

"You ever think that politics is even more fucked-up than the public thinks?" Taylor asks.

"Absolutely," Cait replies.

"Well, I'm starting to recognize that *Current*, or rather, that *I'm* part of the problem."

"No you're not."

"I'm not so sure anymore. Take today. It didn't make sense that I had to watch the same speech for the thousandth time."

"But that's normal."

"It is. It's the why that gets to me. My editors want some bullshit new gaffe, something new. So I can *make* a story out of nothing. It's my third campaign, and it's only getting worse. Ironically, I was hired to write think pieces."

"But that ship has sailed, no? Even most think pieces have to be sensational now."

"Yeah, I don't know why I'm sweating this." He rubs the back of his head. "I think the longer I do this, the more apparent it is that most of what we cover will not really impact who becomes president. Yet I keep covering it. D.C. gets more dysfunctional, the campaigns get sillier, and I don't know . . . I reward it."

"It's not that simple."

"Maybe it is. You know, I'm not even pitching stories I'm proud of anymore. I'm pitching what will get them traffic."

"That's *Current*'s thing, though."

"I know. I just think the media often talks about what's wrong with Washington as if we're witnesses instead of culprits." Taylor shakes his head. "I should only speak for myself. I'm starting to feel culpable."

"I don't know. It's complicated. It's on the public as well. I mean, you know how they say people get the democracy they deserve, or vote for?"

"Yeah."

"Well, people also get the media they demand, or the media they'll pay for."

"No, I know. That's part of it," Taylor acknowledges.

"So maybe it's a cop-out, but editors are the ones who have to weigh that tension, the whole need-to-know versus want-to-know. It's your job to meet the demand. It's not just you guys anymore, anyway. In one respect—and I hate that I'm about to say this—we're all like *Current* now."

Taylor nods.

"I mean," Cait adds, "my editor's pressuring me to write more daily posts about nonsense and become more visible on Twitter. And that feels so done, or overdone, like more of the silliness. Of course, that's why the great woman looks at me like I'm an entertainment reporter."

"I don't want to make you more cynical about this stuff," Taylor says. "I don't even want to be this way."

"You're not cynical. You're, I think . . . you seem disheartened. And trust me, I get that."

"Of course, big events happen. And after, there are fleeting periods of substantial news. But they always seem to prove, well—"

"Fleeting . . . God"—she sighs—"the great woman is right about this too."

Cait bites into her grilled cheese. She looks at it, as she chews, like the sandwich is exactly right. A waitress rushes down the aisle. She has a coffeepot in each hand. She refills ceramic mugs table by table. Two mothers are at another booth. The younger mother chats while she habitually moves her baby's stroller back and forth with a tidal rhythm. The older mother talks about her daughter's college plans. Taylor leans against the cracked green vinyl cushion. Cait's black sunglasses rest on the top of her head. Her hazel eyes are subtly framed with black eyeliner. Taylor chomps his turkey sandwich. Cait dips her grilled cheese into her soup and bites. Not a drop spills.

She looks at the two mothers and says, "You know, when I was in college, my girlfriends would always talk to their mothers. My roommate talked to her mom almost every day. They'd tell them everything. They just talked. About nothing, really. And everything. I never really had that. You think that's peculiar?"

"That girls talk to their mothers that often, yes."

"You know what I mean."

"I think that comes with success," Taylor replies. "Your mother didn't have as much time to do those things. She was, well, in war zones. Life's a trade-off. No one can have it all, or be it all. We all make choices."

"I guess," she sighs.

Cait dips another corner of her sandwich. She takes a small bite. Taylor watches her. She feels self-conscious. She wonders if there are bits of food around her mouth. She reaches for a napkin and dabs. Taylor finishes his water. Cait watches him and says, "Can I ask you a question? It'll seem out of nowhere."

"Sure."

"If you were hanging out with a candidate, in private, and he shoved you into a wall or something, would you report it?"

"Did something happen to you?"

"No . . . the great woman was just telling me a related story. Anyway, I'm just curious."

"I wouldn't report it, no. You sure something didn't happen?"

"Yes. It's just something the great woman said."

"Did someone shove her into a wall?"

"It's nothing like that. Sorry. I'm all over the place."

"No you're not," Taylor replies. "I see how it can be hard for you."

"What?"

"Your mother's legacy."

Cait picks at a cuticle on her finger and stares off. "I'm probably thrusting all these unfair ideals onto her."

"Was she there for you when it counted?"

"Yeah. I think so. Yeah. She was, mostly."

"Is she now?"

"In her own way. Absolutely." Cait's eyes turn up. "She's certainly always reachable. I never had that before."

"That's nice. You can make up for all those missed conversations."

Cait blinks a few times. "So we all make choices, huh?"

Taylor nods. "I realize, more and more, I'm making choices."

They look at each other and eat. Cait thinks about how nice it is to simply talk to him.

"Do you have a girlfriend?" she asks.

"No."

"Figures. You're a serial dater, aren't you?"

"I have my fun. But D.C. quiets that. It's a conservative city. Socially, I mean."

"That hit me the other week. You know that big coffeehouse in Adams Morgan?"

"Tryst?"

"I was told this was the hipster area. So I go to that coffee shop. It had a sign outside that read 'Battle of the Bands.' But it was for law firms only. I swear, only in D.C."

Taylor laughs. "That's true. But with cities, like with people, your virtues are your vices, right? I think D.C. has the most Ph.D.s per capita in America. It's a smart city."

"Smart can be overrated. The great woman used to warn me, do not trust anyone who lives above the neck. Of course, this advice came after she married and divorced my father, the professor."

Taylor smiles.

"Anyway, it's not like D.C.'s an intellectual's ideal," Cait continues. "People there really do live politics. It even permeates bar talk."

"You must be missing New York?"

"Lately . . . yes."

"You have a boyfriend back there?"

"Kinda."

Really? Taylor thinks.

"I mean, I do. A little over three years."

Three years? He's surprised she never mentioned him before.

She nods. Glances at her cuticle. Looks back at him. "We haven't seen each other much lately. I don't know." She wishes now that Blake was not in her life. She wants Taylor to reach across the table and kiss her. She feels guilty for the thought.

"Have you ever been drawn to someone," Cait asks, "because you feel they are exactly the sort of person you should be with? And then, once you're with them, I don't know . . . you just keep waiting for it to happen, waiting for yourself to fall, to feel that way, but then you just find yourself waiting . . . instead of falling?"

XVIII

Taylor tries to parse spin from sincerity. He sits across from Girona's closest adviser, Christian, in a conference room at an Iowa hotel. In an adjoining space, a half dozen aides labor side by side. The staff is a mishmash of frazzled hair, baggy eyes, pallid skin, untucked shirts, and wrinkled slacks. Caffeinated legs shake underneath the rectangular table. The table is covered with laptops, a printer, half-eaten burgers, aluminum wrappers, open ketchup packets, fries, paper soda cups, gnawed straws. The staff wears headsets hooked into mobile phones. They type frenetically into their computers. Conversations clutter the room like a PBS pledge drive, with more drive.

Christian's phone vibrates on the wooden desk. He glances at it, sets it down, and continues. "Our data profile on voters is unmatched by any Dem shop. I would say only Wallace has a similarly deep microtargeting operation."

"Yeah, but isn't this the latest exaggeration of campaign tactics?" Taylor asks. "You've had this operation for months. But you only took the lead now. Look at Wally Reynolds. He has a small staff, no number crunchers, and he recently soared past Wallace despite her massive data shop."

"It can help a point or two on turnout."

"Sometimes. And sometimes not even that much."

"I would agree with that."

"But big data is often hyped as revolutionary. What if politicians believe the hype and credit their success to it? In that event, won't many laud the industry instead of contemplate the downside, such as protecting people's personal data from abuse?"

"Sh*iii*t, I do strategy. Maybe. I don't know."

"Well, either way, even if data doesn't make presidents, the belief that it can fattens the coffers of a new subsector of consultants."

"You're going there, huh?"

"The media has fixated on microtargeting since George W's reelection. It feels less like news and more like free publicity for your business."

"You can't fault any businessman for plugging his business."

"And what a business it has become, in your lifetime."

"A lot of changes." Christian's eyes trail up. "When I started my shop decades ago, there were few competitors. Political consulting scarcely existed. Today, you can't throw a stone in Washington without hitting a consultant. But the primaries escalate that."

"Because there's more business?"

"Sure. Consultants also help more with the small ball, which can shape primaries."

"Rarely."

"Sure. But they can. This cycle, more on the GOP side, yes. Some might say it's the narcissism of small differences. I'm not saying that. But primaries bring that out. And pros help position candidates amid . . . well, less evident disputes. Often, it's about—off the record—getting portions of the base exercised over the small shit."

"So the money's in sweating the small stuff."

"Ideologues are passionate about smaller differences. And it's the passionate who participate."

"And contribute."

"Sure. No one depends on moderates to raise real cash. That's one reason you heed your flank in politics. But what business doesn't move toward the money?"

"Is there a line, where civil service becomes too much of a business?"

"Jesus." Christian rubs his hairy knuckles and stares at Taylor. "Listen—and again, off the record—I'm no different from most folks who make their living in politics over the long haul. After a few years, you realize it's hard to accomplish anything worth a damn. But if you can't do that much good, you can at least give your family the good life."

"When you lose, you still win."

"You said it."

"Not really. It's a notorious Washington tradition, failing upward, that is."

Christian shrugs. "You're being a real hard-ass today. It's not all bullshit. You raised data mining before. Hell, that impacts a campaign more than ninety percent of what the media covers."

Taylor nods. "I've been thinking a lot about that lately. But okay, let's go back to data. Isn't all that only useful, in the end, to make conventional door knocking more efficient?"

"Sure. But isn't anything that engages voters good?" So Christian carries on, explaining how Republican voters are more likely to be found driving a Land Rover, shopping at Cracker Barrel, and watching the Golf Channel. Democratic voters are more likely to be found driving a hybrid car, shopping at Whole Foods, and watching the Lifetime channel. Campaigns cross-reference this commercial information with demographic data, voting records, voter propensity rankings,

Internet use, and so on. He confides that big data cannot dependably target persuadable voters, but that it helps campaigns turn out their base. "The nation's so damn divided that all that may matter, matters."

"But doesn't this entire industry, from lobbyists to consultants, only exaggerate that divide? The more division, the more contested races, the more business."

"Obviously, competitive campaigns are more lucrative for consultants."

"Thus partisanship pays."

"I didn't say that." Christian's phone vibrates again. He smirks. "Saved by the cell." He reads the number. His mouth straightens. "Taylor, sorry, I need a minute."

Christian answers the call. "Hi. Thanks for getting back to me."

Taylor leans in, but only Christian's voice is audible to him.

"I'm on my way back to New York," Cait tells Christian.

"I heard it didn't go . . . as planned."

"Listen, I don't want to talk about it. I'm not reporting it. But I better not hear of this happening again. If I do, I *will* reconsider."

"Okay." Christian exhales. "I'm sorry this happened. Anything I can do? I owe you."

"You don't owe me. This is not a chit. Just speak to him. Don't let it happen again."

"This has never happened before. It won't again."

"Listen, I have to go. The flight's boarding."

"Thank you for your . . . professionalism," he says.

"Whatever. It's how I'm handling it. Be sure you handle it."

"I understand."

Dial tone. Christian sets down his phone. "Sorry about that," he says to Taylor.

"No problem," Taylor replies. "Let's get to his proposal for executive pay clawbacks—"

A Girona aide enters. He hovers in the doorway. The clean-cut aide's anxious eyes gesture sideways. Taylor sees Christian looking past him and turns around. The aide stiffens.

"What's up?" Christian asks the aide.

"Well, umm . . . something's come up. I need to talk to you for a minute."

Mrs. Girona enters the room as pretty as ever, though fatigue shadows her eyes. She glowers at Christian. "Where's Joe?"

"I don't know."

"What's this?" she storms, holding up an iPhone.

Christian replies coolly, "I don't know."

"This iPhone was left in Joe's hotel this morning. It was given to me, to return to him."

"Okay," Christian says.

"Well, Joe uses a BlackBerry."

"Oh."

"And he always uses the same passcode. What's this about a hotel? And who the hell is this woman?"

Christian's eyes shoot forward. He glances nervously at Taylor. Taylor looks back. And Christian knows that Taylor knows. Instantly. Like that. It's out.

Christian leaps to his feet like a deer before danger. Mrs. Girona sees the reporter's notepad. "Hi," she says calmly to Taylor. "I'm sorry, just thought I saw . . . a staff member get out of line. I need to clearly be," she continues, glaring at

Christian, "more on top of things." She turns back to Taylor and offers the sweetest smile. She too has political skills. She introduces herself. She shakes Taylor's hand with a soft squeeze and blinks maternal warmth.

"Taylor," Christian says, "I'm afraid I must handle some business. Can we continue this another time?"

"Of course." Taylor packs his bag and steps to the door.

Mrs. Girona asks him, "You won't say anything about my little outburst, will you? I'm not myself lately. This pregnancy has been so hard. I'm just so tired all the time."

Taylor nods politely. Mrs. Girona looks at Christian. Christian looks at Taylor. And Taylor looks at the door.

A few hours after dinner, Taylor tries to concentrate on his notes but finds himself staring out of his hotel room window at an empty parking lot. White light glows over scattered cars and bare pavement. Taylor thinks about pitching a series on the business of political polarization. Other thoughts dance in and out of his mind as well. Mostly in. He realizes the gravity of what he saw. That, if he nailed the facts down, it would make his career. *But in the wrong way. This is what's wrong with journalism. The story's a sellout. But if I don't report it, my inaction is also action. It will allow Girona to maintain his image as the perfect family man. But what do I really know? Even if it's an affair, should that undo a candidate? I wouldn't report some candidate's fetish or, I don't know . . . Private life is not news unless it impacts the public sphere, reflects on their job . . . their character. But shit, if infidelity means bad character, is Martin Luther King, Jr., bad? I hate this shit.*

And he spirals on. He thinks journalism has become too much soap opera and too little substance and reminds himself to practice what he preaches. Taylor privately subscribes to many trite maxims. He recognizes the irony. He works for *Current.* But his employer need not define him. Not all of him. He sees a high road. He's always argued that, in JFK's time and before, reporters were right not to report on presidential paramours, barring mitigating factors like national security. And he still believes that the public's right to know does not extend to a politician's family life. Taylor recognizes that it's not his call. He knows that most Americans probably disagree. He sees how fidelity relates to character. But he believes that politicians must fall if they fail to be good for the people, not if they fail to always be good people. Because, in his view, there are many ways to be good.

He thinks that if a politician makes it the people's business, if he pushes policies related to marriage or fidelity, the pol's marriage is newsworthy. In lieu of that, everyone should be entitled to some measure of a private life. But he has the whiff of a scoop. And what a story! Yet he does not want to be the bearer of a sex scandal. He believes the news will get out, either way. He need not peddle dirt. Still, he sweats it. This would be the biggest story of the campaign. He has an out, the public's right to know. *I can report the news. Let Americans decide what to do with it.* But no matter how long he considers it, it feels as if it's the final distinction between him and *Current.* He tells himself these things. That he cannot be a hypocrite. Because he believes in certain things. That we must become what we believe in. His instincts say shun the low road to success. He wants to get there the right way. He believes it's only worth doing the right way. He's old enough to understand the way things are. But young enough to believe he can succeed on his terms. *Damn, though, it would be a helluva story.*

XIX

New Year's Eve
Central Iowa

A blue dusk falls over land that is flat and frozen white. The road is barely visible, as snow gusts in the dark and the bus plows forward, its rubber tires spinning through the slush, its windshield wipers rubbing the cold glass rhythmically. The bus passes long stretches of barren farmland, until it slows because of black ice, only feet from a rotted wooden fence that skims the snow line. Beyond the fence, there is a corroded metal shed that drips with icicles and a large old house with only one light on.

In his seat, Taylor stares through the frosted window at the house, as he listens to the high-pitch whirl outside. His attention soon drifts to his phone. And his life back in New York—what he would be doing tonight—returns to him. There's a text from his former girlfriend, Ava: "R u in the city?!" He is, instead, somewhere between Waterloo and Des Moines, in the state between the Mississippi and Missouri rivers, this small rural place that, in an accident of history, became the epicenter of the American presidential campaign. He stares at street signs coated with powder. And the silver bus pushes on through snowdrifts, along Highway 63.

This morning, after finishing a stint with Girona, Taylor rejoined the Wallace campaign. He reported that Girona already seemed to be pivoting to the general election. Taylor also thought about what he saw that day with Christian. In subsequent days, he didn't notice anything else suspicious.

Still, he realizes, the more Girona means to the presidential race, the more exposing an affair would mean.

In one month, Girona went from long shot to contender to front-runner. Just two days earlier, for the first time, polls placed him ahead in Iowa by more than the margin of error. Iowans are now waiting hours in line to see him. It was the Great Mo that campaigns crave. Here was, here is, the next political superstar.

Taylor recalls the previous day in snippets. Girona had long been atop a wave of momentum. But it was as if the waters shifted suddenly. Taylor blinked. And the wave became a tsunami.

Millions see more myth than man. There is a massive machine behind the man. Girona's operation is corporate. But the man can win without the operation. The operation cannot win without the man.

And Girona is made for that marketplace. Ph.D. and J.D. Well educated? Check. State Department. The Senate. Presidential experience? Check. He resigned from State to save his family. Has a daughter. Another child on the way. A bright and beautiful wife with everywoman appeal. Family man? Check. He clawed his way back as an attorney representing regular people. Man of the people? Check. He was born in the West and weaned in the South. He actually hails from a small town. Americana? Check. And Hispanic. Check! The casting call had its new star.

Yet he had been that mold for a long time. What changed was incalculable. Campaigns are not science. No academic has invented a consistent formula to predict the margins of presidential victories well ahead of time. Presidencies are most often won by tides. Does a candidate fit the time? Is this her party's time? But, as Christian said, some actions matter on the margins because some presidential elections are won on those margins. Can the contender prove presidential? Can he secure his ideological flank *and* convert moderates? Can he seize his time?

Joe Girona has seized his time.

It's a winter night in Des Moines and onstage is the future. Rafters shake. Girona speaks of fights won, of civil rights, of workers' rights, of women's rights, of gay rights. "None of that could've happened without the dream. To fight, you must first desire more. You must first believe that more is possible. You must believe again."

And another era of public disillusionment wanes away. As faith restores. And hope spreads like wildfire.

Girona's not fighting corrupt capitalism. He's fighting cynicism. He is the personification of progress. He is the best of America. Proof that you celebrate the browning of America. Proof that you want America to progress. If you believe. In him. Do not dare stand against him. To be against him is to be against progress. Or, in your heart of hearts, perhaps you're against minority progress. Reporters investigate. For what racism still lurks in the hearts of white men?

Oh, how the media does adore him. Headlines preach his lore, his hope, his esperanza. Most journalists subscribe to the great man idea of history. History does not make men, men make it. They became journos to witness it, to report it. And how it does sell. But this is also a story they live to tell. He could be the first Hispanic president. He preaches that old-time populism. And millions do flock. It sure seems like history. Read all about it: the dream rises again.

So the media cynics recede, all over again. And the romance recycles once more. For America is long on hope and short on memory. "Surely there has never been a campaign in which so many reporters were dying to be players," wrote Timesman Russell Baker of the 1960 race. He watched reporters adore JFK. Baker admonished, the media should keep candidates "at arm's length." But the vice became the norm. Another generation of reporters ignored H. L. Mencken's maxim: "The only way a reporter should look at a politician is down."

Girona looks over his flock and soaks up their belief in him. "The present need not be our future. We decide our fate." He lowers his voice and closes his hands as if he's pulling people toward him with rope. "We can get there together. All we need is a spark. Just one spark. And we can change the world." He is the spark. He shall increase wages, spread equality, and save the climate. So he says. So they believe. So it shall be done.

Bear witness. For it is he. And he has the fire.

The pol has inherited the wind. So the political machine around him, advising and sculpting him, insulating him, is doing right by him. They ensure that the media never get too close to the fire to see the pyrotechnics. So the man can become myth. Even Gospel. And America can know the Good News.

Girona waves his hands in the air, as if his mere gesture summons the masses. And his new chorus follows: "We must win back the American dream. We are a nation that aims for the horizon. But to get there, you must take that first step. You must find the part of you that yearns to believe again. America can be great again. Greater than it ever was. But you must believe it's possible." And he points to the crowd. "You must take that first step and march with me. We must push through the frustration, break the gridlock, and fight for the America we love. I know we can do it. I know we can cross the desert and leave the wilderness. And there we will find the dream. And the dream shall live again."

Bear witness. For it is he. And he has the fire.

Constance Wallace has never known the fire. She has known a hero's love. But she has never stirred the masses with her words. She cannot fathom Girona's monopoly of the historic narrative. She broke barriers in the military, that most masculine of worlds. She could be the first female president. She suspects that Girona might tell her not to fall prey to the hierarchy of the oppressed, not to let them pit brown against women. And it galls her. Yet Girona's never spoken this way to her. She's unsure why he gets to her. She pays excessive attention to him, though she appears less likely to face him. And perhaps that's why. She's worked for it. It comes so easy to him. She feels history moving away from her. The potentially first female president is becoming another Bob Dole. Another marriage of convenience, while Girona wows the party that, as Bill Clinton said, forever wants to fall in love.

But if she cannot be myth, they can love her as a real woman. Americans might not be inspired by her poetry, but they can esteem her prose, her sense of duty, her work ethic. They can respect her. There are many kinds of love. And, Wallace believes, the love she seeks is the love that endures.

So she pursues that love by working harder, by showing up. She flew on her jet midday from Waterloo to Des Moines for her New Year's party, to be with the staff that believes in her on this sentimental night.

The reporters tasked with covering Wallace are here with Taylor, on two media buses somewhere in central Iowa, pushing through the snow.

Current's managing editor rings Taylor. Rick Ergaleio tells Taylor that he spoke with a senator heading to Wallace's party. Rick asks for a quick piece about the party. Taylor's written eight articles in six days. And here's Rick, of all people, asking him to cover a party. Taylor realizes that they need copy because of the holiday. But the request, however innocuous, triggers what has come to bother him about his work. "I have no idea what's happening at her party," Taylor replies. "I'm on the press bus in rural Iowa. She could be in New Hampshire for all I know."

"Ask her spokesmen."

"Since when are you asking me to write about parties? Regardless, I'd need to be there to cover it. If you need copy, I can work tonight. But do you guys really need this?"

"Maybe not. But do you have anything else?"

"The first installment would take a few days. But I've been thinking about a series on the industry invested in partisanship, from campaigns to consultants to cable news."

"Boring. There's no time for chin-wagging. We need a dunk. What about all your contacts? Is there anyone good you can call who'll make headlines?"

"Maybe . . . with the caucuses around the corner, Nader may have something controversial to say—"

"Perfect! Call him."

Taylor calls liberal activist Ralph Nader. Nader lambasts "corporate politicians." Taylor sits wedged in his seat, his headset in his ear, typing notes into his laptop. Nader will not endorse. He says he favors Girona. But he worries about Girona softening his populism. Taylor knows this is not the headline Rick wants.

Taylor presses, "You sure, in the eleventh hour, when your endorsement matters, you don't want to back a candidate?"

Nader says he hopes liberal Iowans will "vote for Girona. He is at least highlighting how this country is being sold to corporations and the superrich."

Current-worthy.

Taylor has his lede. Hangs up with Nader. Writes the story. Files it. Rick rings.

"This is fantastic," Rick blurts.

"Thanks."

"Someone else is going to edit it. We'll headline it: Nader Endorses Girona. *Drudge* and *HuffPo* will be all over it. Twitter too."

"Okay."

"Good work. What's your next story?"

Taylor closes his eyes and reopens them. "I don't know."

"We need you to file something tomorrow."

Taylor runs his fingers through his hair. "Okay."

"Any more ideas?"

"Perhaps something obvious. Iowa is slipping from Wallace's grip. She should probably move to New Hampshire by caucus morning. We'll know more in an hour when the last *Register* poll comes out. I could do the piece replete with the cheesy military analogies. That she should decamp, retreat, and retrench in New Hampshire. It can be packaged as the warrior's last stand."

"Perfect. Just like that. It's a good headline."

"Of course it's not really that dramatic. She probably can lose New Hampshire because of her fund-raising, because she has high name ID, and still come back on Super Tuesday."

"No, the last stand angle will be read more."

"I could also do a demographic story on the Dems. It may be that Girona has Latinos and enough blacks and the vast majority of college-educated liberal whites. If so—barring some earthquake—not even a pol as big as Miles Riley can win enough support to defeat Girona. That, for all the campaigning, the winner of this primary is already decided, because it's fated by demographics."

"That undermines our ongoing coverage of the race. For now, write the Wallace story. Do it exactly as you said. Wallace's last stand. Remember what Philip says, exaggerate—and then walk back."

"Yeah."

"Good. Let's talk tomorrow. For the time being, nice job on the Nader story. You can have the night off."

Taylor is grateful to have New Year's Eve off. But the conversation sits inside him like spoiled food. He's worked two months straight, including weekends, with only Christmas off. *And I'm grateful to have New Year's Eve off?* He thinks about his coming break in three weeks, the long weekend in Playa del Carmen. Taylor usually takes all his vacation time. *Current* reporters do not. Most of this bus does not. His colleagues want to be here. This is supposed to be one of the great journalism beats. He understands that some see poetry. But he does not feel it. He is too aware of the artifice to see art and too close to the candidates to see myth.

Taylor thinks about New Year's Eve. He looks around the bus. And realizes, you must love politics to like this work. He finds politics interesting. But the more he lives it, the less he likes it.

Many reporters do love it. They talk about politics when they're not working. They savor the horse race. They want that unique bite of news. They speak of living out of suitcases as if it's a badge of honor. He recalls the city, listening to those who brag about their hours at work, about how little they see their family. For how normal it comes to feel, in time, when everyone in your world acts one way, even if it's the wrong way.

His conversation with Rick lingers. He offered to dramatize the Wallace story. He forced the Nader story. He knows he's enabling the hype. But he keeps doing it. He's coming to see himself as a prime enabler of what nauseates him. He's one more stagehand constructing the show. It's a human show. It's an all-American show. It's the Big Show. But it's still a show. And worst of all, Taylor knows it.

But this is what it takes to cover the making of the president. This is what he does for a living. This is what most political journalists do with their lives. And what they do is supposed to matter. That's why they do it. Why he does it. This is his work. It's what *Current* does best, and worst. But wasn't it Norman Mailer who said the best move lies closest to the worst? He tells himself he has a mortgage and bills and a career to mind. He considers the dozens of résumés *Current* receives every day from the rusting ships of print: the *LA Times, USA Today, Newsweek, Time, U.S. News.* He thinks of the ranks of unemployed and talented reporters. They ache to be salaried again, to be in the mix again. He reconsiders the poetry. This is the making of the president. It matters. It matters to him. Or, at least, people say it should. But he no longer entirely believes it.

Sincerity surrounds him. Reporters want to objectively inform the people. And most boys and girls on the bus see it differently. They smell bullshit. But the circus is more to them than it is to Taylor. They are among lions and tigers and elephants. People want to know what they think about the circus. Their thoughts are broadcasted.

"Dude, Taylor," Chase says. Chase is a CNN producer, handsome in a frat-tastic sense, with gelled black hair and a short stature. He's sitting with Sherry, an NBC producer. Taylor knows both of them from the campaign trail. Sherry's also small, with a tiny curvy body, and classically pretty, if not also TVed. Her brown hair has a plastic sheen. Her eyebrows have been reduced to penciled arcs. Her skin tone is unnaturally even.

Network executives call them the "kids." Every four years, the networks find twenty-somethings who can dedicate a year or two to the campaign. Their belongings go into storage. Apartments are sublet. It's a fast lane to a producer post. To cover the Big Show. To be part of the show. Mom can brag about you to her friends. My girl is traveling with Constance Wallace—as if she sits next to Wallace on the plane and shares peanuts.

"Taylor," CNN Chase persists.

Taylor turns around. "Hey, what's up?"

"Join us at Centro tonight. We have a table. We reserved it months ago."

"It's okay. But thanks."

"You sure?"

"Yeah."

"Dude, join us."

Taylor does not want to dampen Chase's enthusiasm. There are some two thousand media workers in little Des Moines at the height of caucus season. And Centro is where politicos go to see and be seen.

"I don't think I can take that place tonight," Taylor says.

Sherry says, "So come to the press party with us after. We'll make it fun."

"Sure," Taylor says. "I'll meet you guys there."

Champagne bottles and clear plastic cups are passed back on the bus. Media organizations will be charged later for the bottles. No one is drinking. A bottle is handed to Taylor. He leans across to Wallace's traveling spokesman, who sits catty-corner. The spokesman's fiancée flew in for New Year's. They sit hunched down in the burgundy seats, talking, in their private world, if only for a couple hours. Taylor pours some champagne for them and passes it their way. The spokesman holds it, but does not drink. His eyes drift. This is the first time he has not worked with the challenger. In 2000, he got his start as a student volunteer with John McCain. He wanted to be with a winner this time. He has been working this campaign for seventeen months. He postponed his wedding a year for it. And now, like his candidate, he's considering what he will have to show for it. Wallace is filling halls and gyms. Women press the rope line. She is history to them. But she has not inherited the wind. And the spokesman conceives for the first time, it could all be for naught. Again.

Taylor rests against the threadbare seat and drinks. The window has fogged over. He rubs the glass and stares off.

Whitewashed acreage blurs between fence lines. A strong wind comes and whips up the snow and the sky becomes indistinguishable from the land.

In time, Taylor checks his email and sees a note from Luke: "Hey man, I need advice. I've been chasing a hunch for a few weeks, based on something I saw in Iowa. It's potentially explosive. Are you coming to this media party?"

XX

News. The final *Des Moines Register* poll is published online. It's traditionally predictive. A political event, in a race this competitive. The caucuses are only days away. The *Register* posts the story online. Peter Miller, *Current*'s Olympian reporter, waits for the survey at the downtown Marriott. He sits at his desk, robotically refreshing the page. His tweet and blog post are written. He read the aggregation of previous state polls at RealClearPolitics.com. So he guessed the leader correctly. He punches in the new numbers. Sends the tweet. Eleven seconds pass. The blog post is live. He's ninety-six seconds ahead of the herd. The stampede retweets him. The tail of the tape will show it. He was first. He feels victory, eases a smile, closes his laptop, grabs his coat, and leaves. Outside on the curb, as he walks to Centro, a single snowflake falls in front of him. He reaches out, tries to snatch it, does, smiles a victorious smile, opens his hand, and there's nothing there.

P&R dine at Centro. Crowded conversations reverberate. Rick stares at his phone. "It's out," Rick blurts. "Peter posted."

"So who's ahead?" Philip asks.

At Wallace's party, her traveling spokesman skims the results. His fiancée sees him sigh. She asks, "What's wrong?" He cannot hear her over the band.

Across town, at a Mexican restaurant, Wallace's strategist, Vince, sits with his wife and digests the result. His wife flew in for the holiday. She slurps her giant margarita as Vince shakes his head over enchiladas.

In Manhattan's Tribeca, Cait is at a loft party with Blake. She wears a semi-sheer black couture dress that twirls above her knees as she twirls. Cait takes a break, finds a drink, and feels her phone vibrate inside her black clutch.

Uptown, Democratic bundler Saundra Winston wears a long, elegant black gown. She stands against her oak banister between a gabbing peacock and chuckling hen. She looks over her annual party of bold-faced names, hundreds socializing and oxidizing, none seemingly realizing, or stressing, what could be lost and won. Her husband walks up the steps and mouths to her "we did it," and she flinches. But then her smile comes.

Christian checks his phone anxiously. He stands backstage at a ballroom that was once a World War I rubber factory. Benny Goodman performed where Mrs. Girona stands. She's revving up the crowd, being her vintage self, witty and peppy and beautiful, her cheeks plump and round and as rosy as ever. She looks out at the crowd. She says how proud she is of them. "I know what you've sacrificed for us, for this great endeavor. Your sacrifice will change America."

There are few hints of her backstory onstage. She has regular headaches. She feels nauseous constantly. The IVF treatments, all the hormones have been hard on her. But America knows that much. There was an Oprah interview three months ago. She opened up about her struggle to get pregnant at forty-one. She explained why she waited, spoke of her work as a lawyer, and the choices she made. She refused to give up on having their second child. It was the family she always imagined. She took viewers inside the experience—the doctors, the sterile hospital hallways. She showed the pills and hormone injections, discreetly of course. And, at the end of the program, she announced that she was pregnant. The audience burst with cheers and tears. It was one of Oprah's highest-rated shows, ever. A large *New York Times* feature followed. On television, the women of *The View* discussed it all week. Few eminent women had ever opened up about something so personal. America fell in love with her that night. And there, by her side, holding her hand, was Joe Girona, silver haired, as handsome as ever, his eyes damp with admiration. In the subsequent two weeks, Democratic women's support for Girona ticked up seven percentage points. News events almost never did that. And Girona knew it. He knew whom he owed it to.

"Hell, yes!" Christian pumps his arm back. He shows the result to Girona's communications director. "Go tell the missus the news," Christian says. "I'll tell Joe." The communications director walks onstage and whispers into her ear. She inhales and pushes her short blond hair behind her ear. Three thousand faithful look up at her. Behind her, volunteers hold posters that read JOE FOR PRESIDENT. The posters are painted in primary colors and appear handmade, as if they were totems of the candidate's varied democratic support. They were instead made by the campaign's industrial army of young staff, as election signs generally are. A metallic ball circles overhead. A banner reads "New Dreams for a New Year." And Mrs. Girona looks over at Joe. She nods more than smiles. They have come so far together. And it suddenly all seems worth it. She announces, "Here's why I know your sacrifices, your work, will matter. Here's a reason to believe again. We just received the poll results. We're ahead by five points! We're going to win! A new day is coming!"

Young volunteers scream and lift their beers high. A burly union man tosses his frayed baseball cap in the air. A lanky young woman wears a tight tee reading "Joe Girona is sexy." She shoots a wide smile. Two male volunteers slap hands and knock over a card table. Buttons litter the floor—TEACHERS FOR GIRONA; GIRONANOS! LATINOS FOR GIRONA; WOMEN FOR GIRONA; STEEL WORKERS FOR GIRONA; and buttons with only his handsome face.

Mrs. Girona declares, "By the way, Wallace is losing to Reynolds." The crowd heralds this news too. Democrats prefer to face anyone but the woman warrior. "We're really going to do this!" she yells. "Happy New Year, everyone." And inside the hall, it feels like Times Square after the ball drops.

Taylor blows into his hands. It's twelve degrees outside. He enters Des Moines's restored Masonic Temple, a Greek Revival hall teeming with hundreds of reporters. They drink and chat between faux-marble columns. The buffet table features Iowan cuisine: mini-corn dogs, corn salsa, cob corn, Maid-Rite luncheon meat, Maytag blue cheese. Taylor eats a corn dog. "I love this," he tells an ABC producer. "If we were back in the city, no way the spread would include a good corn dog." They talk, and a circle gathers. The journos debate the importance of the Iowa poll. Taylor excuses himself.

On his way back from the bar, his colleague Brandon intercepts him. In his mid-twenties, clean-cut and crew cut, Brandon's already co-bylining some big articles for *Current.* He's covering his first campaign. He yells over the band, louder than need be, that he can't believe "the primary is a jump ball." That it's "crazy close." His eyes bulge. "God, it's better than basketball, because it matters. You know, my girlfriend complained to me that I was spending all my time at work. Then she found out I'm taking Modafinil. Which, by the way, is fucking awesome."

"Is that the new Adderall?" Taylor asks.

"It's mellower. Narcoleptics take it. It helps you focus. And that's my point. She flipped out when she saw I took it. But she took Ritalin during finals week. At Princeton, lots of our friends did. And this job is like perpetual finals. She just doesn't get that ten-hour days are minor league. I've gotta establish my brand now."

"Not the brand talk."

"Everyone's a brand today."

"God, what hath social media wrought?"

"What? Are you some kind of Luddite?"

"I'm skeptical."

"But you made your name in online media."

"I'm a conflicted skeptic."

"Conflicted about what? I just don't get all the concern. So print dies. There's more news online than ever before. Yes, there will be less conventional reporters. But dinosaurs go extinct. That's the way of the world."

Taylor sips his whiskey.

"Watch," Brandon continues, "in a few years, people will say the media is better than ever."

Taylor drinks more. "You ever read a *Time* magazine from the sixties?"

Brandon shakes his head no.

"It was meant for Middle America, not elites," Taylor adds. "But the writing, the context, it's better than anything we have today. There's a lot more words online, sure, but much of it feels like junk in a superstore."

Brandon shrugs.

"Of course it's not all bad," Taylor continues. "At least with the self-branding, corporations have less control over you. It is easier to strike out on your own."

"Exactly."

"So how's your girlfriend taking everything now?"

"Not well. Last week she asked me, 'What's more important, *Current* or me?' "

"And you said?"

"*Current*, of course."

"How'd she take that?"

"She didn't say anything." Brandon's eyes glide up and back. "I don't know." He drinks more of his Caucus-tini, the signature cocktail of the night. It's a sweet and pallid aqua drink made of vodka, Sprite, and Kool-Aid. "Whatever. It's worth it. I was just on *Morning Joe.* Right before Ben Affleck! I spoke to Ben in the green room. He's cool, lower key than you'd think. And before they went to commercial, the camera shows us live, talking side by side, like we're boyz. With that exposure, *Current*'s going to make my career."

Taylor gulps his whiskey, finishes it, eyes Brandon's glass, and says, "Cool. Just don't drink too much of that Kool-Aid. It can give you an awful hangover."

Brandon looks at his glass. "I don't get hangovers. It's good. You should try it."

Taylor tells Brandon he needs to get another drink. He passes Peter Miller, who's slurping a Diet Coke and speaking with NBC's Chuck Todd. Todd drinks his beer listlessly and fingers his Iowa prosciutto.

Taylor secures another whiskey. He says hello to a CBS executive producer. A willowy woman, with gunmetal hair and a nose that sinks at the tip, she's a former print reporter who moved to television with the advent of CNN. He knows her from the last campaign. With Girona's victory, he is thinking about another front-runner, one felled by an affair. He asks her if she covered Gary Hart in 1987. "Oh, did I," she replies. They talk about the race. "Looking back," she says, "even if Hart won the nomination, George H. W. would've been hard to defeat. He was Reagan's heir. But back in '87, Hart was the top Dem. And he was great to cover. I remember him talking about the internal battle between our Apollonian side and our Dionysian side. Would any candidate speak that candidly to a reporter today, or speak in such literary terms?" And she begins to retell her memories of the scandal and "how it escalated." Her colleague received a phone call, like other reporters, about Hart's affair. "Hart dared the press corps to dig deeper. We worked so hard to get that story. Gosh, it seems old-fashioned now. It isn't like today, or when things changed with *Drudge* exposing Clinton's affair. There was no 24/7 media. No Internet. So the investigation was quiet. Regardless, it didn't work out." She crinkles her lips. "*The Miami Herald* beat everyone to it."

Luke taps Taylor on the shoulder. "What's up, man?" They greet each other more like college friends than colleagues. "Now a good time?" Luke asks.

Taylor nods, excuses himself. "Yeah. What's up?" Taylor asks.

Luke directs him to a corner. "So don't say shit to anyone," he insists, his eyes scanning left and right.

"Sure."

"Really?"

"Really."

Luke leans in and whispers, "I think Girona's having an affair." He closes his chubby right fist and smirks with excitement. "Shit, man, I think I've got the story first!"

Taylor's stone-faced. "Got what?"

"That he's having an affair."

"And?"

"What do you mean 'and?' That'd be huge."

"I mean, what do you have?"

"I can't really get specific. Yet. I know I'm being cagey here . . . but shit, it's like this damn party. You know how incestuous D.C. is. I just don't know who knows who."

"Be vague. What do you have?"

"I saw a woman leaving Girona's floor upset, at a hotel, with that air about her. And I have reason to believe she came from his room based on . . . let's just say, something related to the campaign at that precise time. Other things too. It's all circumstantial, for now."

Taylor wonders what Luke saw. He recalls that Girona's wife mentioned a hotel. "And you won't say who the woman is?"

"Not yet."

"So how can I help?"

"Well, this is my first time on the trail."

Taylor nods.

"I don't know the senior players. I'm having trouble finding anything concrete. You're close to Christian Ulster, right?"

"Somewhat, yeah. But frankly, I don't really like to touch these stories."

"Why?"

"It's not my thing."

"Fuck that, man. This is not some rudimentary *Enquirer* or *Redline* crap. He's likely to be the Dem nominee. The press treats him like . . . I don't know, saint populist, like some untouchable diplomat of Latino America. This would be a massive story. Help me out."

"I get all that."

"Fine. Just answer this: Have you seen anything on the trail to make you think I've got this right?"

"Listen, I don't know. I guess . . . I wouldn't be shocked if you find something."

"Which means?"

"I don't think he's the . . . as you put it, the saint people think."

"You have any reason to say that?"

Taylor hesitates. "Just a hunch. But you're right. You need something concrete."

"Can you speak to Christian and feel around?"

"I'll give you his personal cell phone and stuff. But that's where I have to stop. I don't want you to take this the wrong way, but really, these stories are not for me. I wish you the best of luck, though."

Luke pauses. "Suit yourself. But you realize most reporters would kill for this. Fuck, Peter is right over there. He'd literally, I think, kill for this."

Taylor smiles, takes out his phone, and emails Christian's contact information to Luke. "I just sent you his info."

"Okay. But I'm going to nail Girona on this. You'll wish your name was on that byline."

"Maybe I will." And they leave it at that. Taylor heads back to the bar. He wants to know what Luke saw. But he understands the choice. He's either off the story or on it.

He wonders if Luke bought his ignorance. He's uncertain whether he's doing the right thing. But it feels more right than wrong.

He weaves across the floor, which is now packed with media of all sorts and the spokespeople who work to spin them. Taylor sidles up to the bar. Sherry, the pretty NBC producer from the bus, sees him. She slides up beside him. Her tight black sweater highlights her figure. Her eyes are fixed forward. Waiting. Waiting. For Taylor to say something. To notice her. Taylor notices. "Hi, Sherry."

"Hi, Taylor," she says with pitched upspeak. "Are you glad you came tonight?"

"I am."

Chase, the frat-tastic CNN producer, arrives. "You guys want shots?"

"Sure," Sherry says.

Sherry straightens. Steps closer to Taylor. Her breasts near his lower chest. She looks up at him. "So where's your New Year's date?" she asks, twirling the ends of her hair.

"Alas, I'm solo."

"Me too."

Chase hands out shots. And the hour comes. Countdown. "Happy New Year!" say all. Sherry inches nearer to Taylor and looks up expectantly. Taylor drinks his shot. "Excuse me," he says, walking away from the bar, through the crowd, thinking of Cait.

"Should old acquaintance be forgot . . ."

". . . and never brought to mind . . ."

Blake kisses Cait as "Auld Lang Syne" plays. Revelers embrace. "Happy New Year, babe. I'm glad you came back to the city," he tells her over the song. "You should be with me tonight." Blake kisses her again.

"Do you know what 'Auld Lang Syne' actually means?" Cait asks.

"Happy new year, I imagine." Blake shrugs, tall and sharp in his classic black tuxedo, his blond hair pomaded, textured, longer on top than at the sides. "Who cares?"

"I was just curious," she says under her breath.

Cait's friend asks her, "What are you two doing now?"

Cait opens her mouth. Blake interjects, "Not much. We have to get up early to fly to Newport to visit my parents. Cait's never home anymore. And, of course, I need their approval." He winks.

"That's how your family rolls, huh?" asks Cait's friend.

Blake tilts his head back and sniffs. "My family does not roll. It's an excuse to show her off. But really, we should go. Babe, could you get our coats?"

Cait winces. She sips her champagne and gazes past Blake at the black-tied crowd. Friends toast. Couples kiss. They look so happy. She tries to smile. She listens to the song's last lines. "We'll tak' a cup o' kindness yet, for auld lang syne." And she wishes that someone else had kissed her. That Taylor was across the room. That it could be like the hotel in Iowa. That he would appear again, to take her away. That life could be that way.

XXI

JANUARY
KINGSTON, NEW HAMPSHIRE

Little big-foot Republicans mill around onstage, awaiting Constance Wallace. This will be her second town hall meeting of the day. The New Hampshire primary is in one week. Wallace has barnstormed the state for months. The day before, as Iowans awoke to caucus, she trudged through knee-high snow in a pantsuit tucked into military boots. Before Iowans voted, she helped shovel snow in front of a children's hospital, conducted two town halls, attended a fundraising lunch, and visited a retirement home.

Joe Girona won Iowa. He overtook the Democratic baron of power, six-term California senator Miles Riley, the Senate finance committee chairman who has labored for Democrats since he "got clean for Gene." Riley is another counterculture revolutionary who became the Establishment. He knows the system better than most. But that also means his backstory is set in Washington. And these days, even more than usual, Americans are anti-Washington. He has accepted it. The fire will never be his.

Wally Reynolds, the grassroots conservative star, won the Republican race in Iowa. Wallace saw it coming. She invested her future in New Hampshire. She likes it this way. The lioness is against the wall. Lethargy is abandoned. She's cornered. She must fight.

And as Wallace's audience enlarges, as her staff canvasses the crowd for mobile phone numbers and social media accounts, Vince stands with Cait side stage. He tells her that he wishes Wallace enjoyed "the same ecstatic following as Girona." Cait rolls her eyes. "I've never seen you express a personal opinion about politics," Vince adds.

"I didn't."

"Your eyes did."

"They did?"

"Cait, you're allowed to be human off the clock. You don't have to love Girona like your colleagues."

She intentionally rolls her eyes.

"Well, libs do love him," Vince says. "That's partly because Dems have so few men with balls. I mean guts. Still, off the record, if he wins the primary, and we do as well, I've no idea how we'll slow his momentum and overcome his Hispanic support."

"Your only chance would be to win over some Democratic women, no?"

Vince nods.

"So you still think you'll come back and win this thing, after Iowa?" she asks.

"We'll take it one day at a time."

"Spare me the clichés, Vince. Are you still in it?"

"To win it." Vince smiles crookedly. "On background?"

She nods.

Vince scratches his ruddy cheek. "It's our fault we've fallen behind. We've never transitioned from soldier to candidate, despite her governorship. We should have the same symbolic buzz as the other side. As Girona, I mean. And yes, we must win New Hampshire to win the nomination. Basically, the conventional wisdom is right about us."

"I love how you go on background to confirm conventional wisdom."

"What would you like to use? Tell me. I'll let you know if you can attribute it to me."

"I'm not giving you veto power over what I quote."

"Everyone does that now."

"Not me."

At the front of the audience, TV veterans talk. People watch the living-room faces, as Tom Brokaw chats with Jeff Greenfield and a senior producer with NBC. The veterans toss around trail stories. The producer excuses himself. He directs his cameraman to gather B-roll, to pan around the audience, to set the scene. Focus on the veterans. Ask that old man to stand with his cane. Get a tight shot of it. Now of the flags. Pan out to the audience. Enough, we need more sound.

A woman with pink, slack skin and big blue eyes says that she's with Wallace because "I like folks with conviction." Her husband, whose neck hair escapes his plaid shirt, adds, "She came up the hard way." The producer replies, "You know Wallace was born wealthy?" The man scratches his scalp. "What I mean is, she came back from that injury. That ain't easy." The producer asks, "And it strikes you, regardless?" "Darn right," the man says. "Why?" "I guess," the man replies, "because—I know this sounds funny because she's nice-looking and stuff—but it shows she can take a punch like a man." His wife chimes in, "You're saying she's a tough gal. But not angry or butch or showy. We like that. I love how strong she is. I only wish she were pro-life." The producer explains that Wallace is against legalized abortion, save exceptions such as rape. "She is?" the woman asks. "But I saw somewhere that she wasn't." The producer asks, "Did you see that in a story about an advertisement, or in the ad itself?" She answers, "I don't know. It stuck in my head from somewhere."

A local congressman walks onstage. Veterans sit behind. Wallace's comrades are backdrop. They are there to remind voters. She bled for America, like her family before her. Wallace's forefathers were all Army. A Huntington fought in every major American war since the Revolution. One day, as a girl, she found a *Life* magazine from World War II in her parents' library. A young woman was pictured on the cover. The woman, blond with pigtails, sat on the tail of a military plane. She was a WASP, a member of the Women Airforce Service Pilots. Young Constance told her mother that she wanted to be a WASP. Her mother said, "Dear, that's not an appropriate term, but we are Anglo-Saxon Protestants." Her parents soon understood. As a little girl, she played war in the woods with her older brother and his friends. Her father liked to say, "My girl's rough beneath the edges."

Wallace's father paid for flying lessons in high school providing she maintained an A average. College came and passed. She concluded flying was a girl's dream. And she was always good at school. Thus law school. During her first year at Yale law, at only twenty-three, her brother officially "fell to his death hiking alone" in Cambodia. Unofficially, he was CIA. It crushed her father. She wanted to keep the family legacy alive. She quit Yale. Enrolled in the Air Force Academy. She would earn her last name. Prove worthy of her name. And yet, in the deeper part of her, escape her name. She wanted to prove she could do it her way. She would become a twentieth century knight. Fight alone in the sky. She was almost supernaturally confident in this way. Her family's golden safety net had protected her, empowered her. But no net could save a fighter pilot. She would fly, in part, to prove she did not need the net.

Wallace enters the hall and ascends the stairs. The crowd stands like they're saluting her. There's applause and scattered cheers and a man yells, "Keep fighting, Constance!" Wallace nods thank you. She greets the veterans with hugs and handshakes. She wears a single strand of pearls. Her wool pantsuit is monochromatic black. It's loose but slightly fitted at the waist. Underneath, she has a soft white blouse with ivory buttons. Beneath her blouse are her scars, above her right hip, to the right of her lower spine. But only her husband sees those.

Wallace takes hold of the mic. Her left hand holds her speech. Sharp pain flashes through her back. Long silver nails tap-dance on her spine. She feels this way, off and on. But she grins through it. It's not the smile of a young woman at the peak of her allure. It's not how the flygirl once grinned. She's gnashing her teeth. Bearing it.

Cait sits with reporters at the rear of the hall. She listens to Wallace compliment the local pols and thank the audience for attending. Wallace drones on about "how your vote validates what I fought for." She reiterates her gratitude. She's like a man who, during the date, continually thanks the woman for going out with him. The woman already said yes. It's time to court.

And Wallace finally tries. "I will work every day and every night to achieve prosperity and ensure peace. I will do the hard things. I will reduce our debt and save Social Security. I will save Medicare. I will ensure we can afford these vital programs by cutting waste out of the welfare state. And that includes trimming corporate welfare. We Republicans must be consistent about that." So she lists examples of waste. "Yes, I too want to curtail crony capitalism. Unlike every other presidential candidate, I've never taken a dollar of pork. I owe no one but *you.* I will balance our budget like you balance your checkbook, like an adult. Indeed, it's time we had some adults in Washington. Our government should not be controlled by special interests, but what's in America's best interest. We need leaders who will risk their office for their nation, who *will* make the hard choices. I will. I always have. After all, I didn't get this gray hair for nothing." She speaks on, of the hard things and the hard way. They know she's earned her words. But America knew Bob Dole like that. And the show horse won that day.

She's been thinking about an old saying: *You dance with the man who brought you.* She has campaigned as the workhorse. But she achieved fame as the warhorse. Vince suggested, "Don't campaign as the person they should love; campaign as the person they want to love." So she'll talk war, tastefully. She'll be the hero, if that's what it takes. Constance Wallace does what it takes. She will aim again for that blue sky and keep the race up there—in the thin air, above the ideological trenches that muddied her.

"The terrorists have not suddenly gone away. We are still at war against Islamic extremism." A nation that feels war might elect a warrior. So she will hint the lore. Elizabeth. Valkyrie. She's Athena in the sky. She'll lead men into the darkness. Win the light. End terror in the night. But only if America keeps the fight.

And votes for her. "We can overcome any challenge. Win any war. That's what we do in America. We win." And the audience hears what their forefathers heard. Remember the Alamo. Remember the *Maine.* Remember the *Lusitania.* Remember Pearl Harbor. "Remember 9/11," she says. "We will always defend that sacrifice."

Her war story lingers around her words. And it reaches men deeply. Especially red-blooded Republican men. Some did serve. But few have her heroic story. And those who did not serve feel that strain of male guilt, what comes with staying out of the fight. She proved her mettle. She's owed their respect.

"Behind me are some of the original members of the WASPs. And no, I don't mean Anglo Protestants." Scattered laughter. "These are the women of the Women Airforce Service Pilots. They were the first female military pilots. They were not allowed to serve in combat, but they risked their lives flying during World War II. And I'm ashamed to say, they were not recognized as veterans of the second great war until the 1970s. Please stand and give them a round of applause." And the crowd does. A few veterans baritone "ooh-ahh." "In fact, I ask all women who lived through World War II, who may have managed a family alone during that time, to stand up. These women fought every day, whether in combat or to raise their family. Let's honor them." And women rise. Others applaud. "I'm here for them. I will not always do the popular thing. But I will always work like heck to do the right thing for them, for all of you, for America. So if you want someone who puts love of country above being loved, who doesn't just talk about values, but risked her life for our values, stand with me. God bless you, and God bless America."

Applause. Cheers. Question time. Are you pro-life or not? How come liberals obsess over how popular culture impacts our views of gays, women, and minorities, but act like all the violence and immorality in film and video games has no impact? How do we keep people from feeling entitled to handouts? I'm in construction. How come I'm supposed to accept illegal immigrants taking my job? Shoot, if a bunch of people from India came here and took half of the lawyer jobs, or journalism jobs, would the media be so tolerant, if they lost work or their wages were lowered?

Wallace answers all. She cites position papers. Some attendees check their phones and yawn. But she keeps at it. She'll prove she can answer everything.

Cait watches from the edge of the black media platform. Her feet dangle. She sits with her shoulders back. Her computer rests on her lap. Most of the reporters are in front of her, sitting in metal folding chairs. There's a row of cameras behind her. She's watching, tapping her hand on her thigh, waiting for news.

Taylor arrives at the hall. He catches the last questions. Shuffles up behind Cait. Leans in and whispers, "Hello."

She turns her head. Her thin lips turn up at the ends. Her dimples show as her cheekbones enunciate. Her mouth opens wider than higher. She closes her lips anxiously. But she has already betrayed her excitement. She turns her head downward and looks back up. But as she looks at him, hints of her happiness linger in her blinking eyes.

"Are you stalking me, Mr. Solomon?" she whispers.

"Perhaps," he replies, eyeing her. "Would you have it any other way?"

Her eyes ease down and return to him. "When'd you get here?"

"Just did. I was assigned to Wallace's bus for the rest of New Hampshire."

"Shhh," a cameraman hurtles, while pointing at the microphones.

Taylor bends to her ear. She feels his breath on her neck. She smells his cologne. She inhales, too quietly for him to hear. And he whispers, "I'll find you after."

XXII

Sunlight pierces the haze and flickers in the sky like a fire coal that will not burn out, until the ashy white vanishes and the sun brightens and burns red above the horizon, and the hills seem to flame with crimson light. A small road winds into those hills. A caravan of Black Secret Service Suburbans, white television vans, and silver buses slither along the road, over a hill, and into a valley punctuated by clusters of skinny trees, their icy branches shivering in the wind, their trunks half-buried in the snow. And soon the snow loses the light, as the sun leaves the land and the red glow dissipates into the dusk and the caravan drives on, leaving only a lonely trail of auto lights dotting the darkness.

The caravan nears a sign that reads DINER in red fluorescent and slows and turns into the gravel parking lot. The press races off the bus and inside the restaurant, stuffing the space between red vinyl booths and white tables with chrome bases. Heads turn up and forks are set down and the servers scurry to the kitchen and wait, as if they expected this, are used to this. The candidate and spouse enter with the look of a prom queen and king at a reunion, still on top.

Wallace is familiar to those inside. The husband is unknown. His hair is gray, curly, short. He is in his late sixties and has lines at the outer corners of his green-blue eyes that spread outwards like a symmetrical branch. He skims the room assuredly. The couple walks table by table, greeting, palm pressing. A woman offers Wallace her french fries.

Wallace smiles politely and eats a single fry. Ted does what he does in these situations. "I'll take some." He grins. The woman passes the basket of fries to Ted. Wallace looks back at her husband. A wince escapes her. The presidential candidate is worried about her husband's cholesterol.

Wallace approaches a young man in a Joe Girona T-shirt. It reads "Dream Again" across the chest. Wallace compliments the shirt. The man says, "I'd vote for you, ma'am, if I were a Republican." Wallace replies, "Nobody's perfect. But when you're ready to move from dreams to reality, I'll be here."

The candidate and spouse sit down with the diner's owners, a kind and doughy couple. They talk small business talk. Good Republican talk. Flank steaks and steamed broccoli arrive. The owner tells them that George W. Bush, Joe Biden, Al Gore, Bob Dole, George H. W. Bush, Ed Muskie, and George McGovern have eaten here. But, the owner says, "I didn't dare serve Bush Senior broccoli." Ted Wallace's chest juts forward with a single low Ha. Constance Wallace smiles. H. W. Bush famously hates broccoli. The owner asks Wallace if she's seen the restroom. There are three doors. One for men. One for women. And one that reads POLS. "You should use it. You might be the first female candidate to enter it," he says. "It's real nice." And Wallace thinks, *why is he telling me about a bathroom?* But Ted nods favorably. She feels the urge to shake her head but restrains herself.

Cait and Taylor stand in the back, talking against the dark wooden panels, witnessing none of it. To them, it's one more diner. New scene. Same set. Same script.

Wallace scans the room. She notices the two young reporters not swimming around her. She sees the media as if they were thousands of tiny, curious fish in the sea, that flutter, surround her, unimportant people who nonetheless wield power. She is the shark. They are the pilot fish. They feed off her. But she also believes she needs them. They keep her from the parasites. If they are fluttering around, she still matters.

The other contenders, from both parties, dislike or despise the media. She respects the symbiosis. The little fish must feed off her, fine, providing they know their place. They do give her political life. They're not great people, not to any pol. But she, unlike most, regards the role. Why antagonize them? She periodically sits with them on the plane or the bus. She keeps up her guard but answers every question. Media access spurs goodwill, as much goodwill as they'll offer a Republican, in her view.

She watches the press pool now, shoving and nudging, standing on barstools, big cameras on shoulders, lenses hanging off necks, swinging about, as photogs go low and high, wide-angle, as producers hold small handheld video cameras with one hand, red lights on, and the few patrons who can see her are filming her with their mobiles, as they watch the candidate through their phones. Reporters swim around her, arms reaching out, recorders in hand. Fuzzy boom mics jut overhead. What do they hope to record? She digests. And they encircle her. Even her digestion is newsworthy. Flashes flicker. She blinks and returns to her food. Talking heads do wonder why anyone would want to be confined to this fishbowl? But Wallace prefers her side to theirs. They encircle her. She only provides the crumbs. So she'll feed them. She'll play the everywoman at a diner. She knows many reporters snark privately. They see the stagecraft. But she watches them record and write. She watches them bite.

Wallace's caravan drives ten minutes away. They near a world that weaned her grandfather, father, and brother. Her older brother went to school at Exeter with political VIPs Jay Rockefeller IV, H. John Heinz III, and John Negroponte, as well as Saundra's husband Clayton Winston, who hazed lowerclassman Robert Thurman, the pioneering Buddhist scholar who fathered actress Uma Thurman. Wallace attended Miss Porter's in Farmington, Connecticut, where she did not wish to follow in the footsteps of the most famous alumni, from Jacqueline Kennedy to the women of America's other power clans, from Vanderbilt to Pulitzer to Bush. Today, she recalls a childhood moment, when she visited her brother at Exeter over a long weekend and shared her dreams with him, telling him for the first time that she wanted to become a fighter pilot. He didn't laugh. He threw his arm around her and told her about Amelia Earhart. And in that moment, flying felt attainable. And now destiny has brought her back to where the woman was a girl and the girl dreamed of becoming a great woman.

But the caravan does not stop at the redbrick academy. Or see the white steeple that, on a dare, her brother climbed that weekend. She will not provide Democrats with the plutocratic imagery. So the caravan drives outside town, past large homes, and up along a sinuous driveway to a house that sits on eighteen acres. The land is frozen white. The icy pond reflects the houselights. Glazed trees fade into the ink-blue night.

Inside, donors gather under arched wooden beams and glass skylights the size of small cars. Four large iron chandeliers hang overhead. Each chandelier has two iron hoops and candlelike bulbs. The yellow-white light reflects off wineglasses and wristwatches and shined shoes, as three hundred donors schmooze. The host is the grandson of an early investor in Standard Oil. The investor made a major donation to Exeter academy a century ago and bought this retreat. He wanted to be close to his investment. Close to the happiest days of his life, as if we can buy back the happiest days of our lives.

Reporters are herded through the back door. They enter the kitchen. Silver pots hang and clank. Cooks stand over hot burners. Men carry crates of red and white Bordeaux on their shoulders. Reporters are directed through a swinging door. They enter a massive room. A plush red-velvet rope separates media from donors. Gawk. Watch. Record. But you may not cross.

Wallace stands before a stone fireplace that could heat a ski lodge. Her stump words follow. Prosperity. Peace. Pork. Debt. Protect. Hard calls. She tells of surveys and strategy. She'll assure contributors feel privy to inside information. She is less wary of them than the countless small donors online. Because small donors are more ideological. And she is tired of being pushed ideologically rightward. At least she knows what these people want. So she'll do what pols do. Hint: hand over the money and access shall come. Wallace promises regular follow-up conversations by phone. She thanks them "for fighting the good fight." Donors applaud. And the candidate steps into the crowd and mingles with the money.

"I find this part of the job humiliating," Cait says to Taylor.

"You mean standing behind a rope, watching the GOP moneymen like we're at the zoo?"

"Only we're the animals to them. They're such undeserving snobs."

"Well, people want to feel important everywhere. The only real blue bloods here are the Wallaces."

"Literally," she replies, looking over at Mr. and Mrs. Wallace. Their blue veins are beginning to show beneath their pinkish, thinning skin.

Vince meanders past the little big men. He asks Taylor if he likes Chuck Norris jokes. Taylor replies enthusiastically. Cait says, "God, what's with guys and Chuck Norris jokes?" The guys shrug. "We were talking about how Norris is campaigning up north for Reynolds," Vince says, "and I heard a good one. A cop pulled Chuck Norris over once. The cop was lucky to leave with a warning." "Oh," Taylor says, "I've heard better. Chuck Norris and Superman once bet who could win in a fight. The loser had to wear his underwear on the outside of his pants." Vince chuckles. Taylor says another, "What do ghosts tell around a campfire? Chuck Norris stories."

They soon move to shoptalk. Why is Wallace conducting a fund-raiser so close to primary day? Is her campaign more confident that there will be a future?

"We feel a comeback," Vince answers. "But you can't fight aggression with silence. We need more money to rebut Reynolds's crap about abortion. It's like Napoleon said, an army marches on its stomach. That's true in war and in politics."

And so they chat on. The fund-raiser carries on. Vince sizes up the money. Wallace sizes down the little big men and local hens. She holds her quarter grin and does what it takes. A middle-aged brunette, ponytailed to the last strand, in a sheath dress with long sleeves, stops Wallace and says, "I like you, but I'm worried that if you win, you'll become one of them." "Them?" Wallace asks. "The big spenders," the woman answers, "because it seems like the Republican leadership has gone Washington." "Well," Wallace says, "you can be sure I'll take care of any liberals in conservative clothing." The woman laughs and says, "You're my kinda gal. I look forward to you defeating that socialist. And I bet you thought you were done fighting commies." Wallace's lips tighten. Ted, her husband, runs interference and introduces her to a fat insurance executive. Wallace suffers more strategic advice. She imagines telling the executive how to do his job. She wonders how he would react. She thinks about how certain people who have mastered one thing come to think of themselves as experts on everything. Yet she only nods. Smiles along. Mingles on.

Vince whistles. The room quiets. Wallace cringes. "My apologies, for that," she says. "My staff sometimes thinks that one's ability to hail a taxi applies to other social situations." Polite laughter. "Regrettably, I must leave. But please do stay in touch. There is a tremendous amount of wisdom in this room. I more than welcome your advice. For now, I hope you'll continue to stand up for our great nation, and stand with me. Thank you." Wallace exits on that note. Reporters are herded out the back way, past empty wooden wine crates and brown kitchen help dressed in white. The press walks to the buses. Engines turn on. Tailpipe steam dissipates in the cold night.

XXIII

Reporters retrieve their bags from the belly of the bus. Taylor watches Cait and searches for the right thing to say. It's been a long time since he's been nervous around a woman. He tries to hide it and asks Cait if she wants to grab a drink. "Or many drinks," he adds.

"I would," she says.

They decide to walk to a restaurant near the campus. The sidewalks are glassy with scattered patches of thinning ice that chip and crackle beneath their feet. Snow bunches near the sidewalks, where a fresh coat covers dirty-gray mounds. The temperature has inched above freezing. Brick walls are covered by splashes of frozen powder. Scattered window displays glow yellow. Snow clusters atop the buildings' ridges and stuffs gutters that sag and drip with glossy icicles. Taylor sees something written on the cement. He kicks away salt pebbles. It reads WOOLWORTH's in a slim red font. "Someone should restore that. Of course," he adds, "you could say that about so many of these small towns."

"You really could."

Inside the restaurant, Taylor helps Cait with her coat and hands it to the hostess. Cait rubs her arms and looks at the fireplace. They sit on brown wooden stools before an ornate oak bar, and order shepherd's pie. The bar light saturates their drinks, the rich bronze in his Scotch, the dark cherry in her Malbec. Cait mentions that Blake went to prep school here. Taylor drinks. She realizes he doesn't want to hear about

Blake. "It's just that I don't like his friends from here. They seem, well, unimpressed by everything."

"I took a sailing trip with some guys after I got my book deal. It was a weird mix. But I think two of them went to one of the Phillips. They were good-enough guys."

"Where'd you sail?"

"Around the Croatian islands for a few weeks."

"You sailed the Croatian islands?"

"Yeah."

"Sounds amazing."

"It was . . . it really was."

She rubs her arms.

"You want my coat?" he asks. She hesitates but nods. He takes off his black blazer and places it over her shoulders.

"Thank you," she says.

"You're welcome." And closeness comes with the quiet. "So are Blakes your type?" he asks.

"I don't know . . . there are other types."

"And those are?"

"I'm not answering that. You first. What kind of women does Taylor Solomon like?"

"I'm better at asking the questions."

"It's always easier to ask the questions." She smiles. "Though, I'm curious, what is your type?"

"I don't think there's a type. But . . . perhaps . . . a mix of Elizabeth Bennet and Penélope Cruz in *Vanilla Sky*, or in most any movie."

"Well, other than the heroines of *Vanilla Sky* and Jane Austen's imagination?"

"Okay. Looks are not beside the point, of course."

"Of course."

"But when I say Penélope Cruz, I actually mean her feminine energy."

Cait nods. "So what else is not beside the point?"

Taylor hesitates, looks at her, and replies, "Well, beyond that . . . I like women who can traverse the snow in heels, who are smart but know, indeed, the value of not living too much above the neck, and who appreciate what comes along the way to more in life, partly because they take life seriously but not too seriously."

"I take life far too seriously," Cait deflects. She knows he's not joking. But reason takes hold of her as if she were an older woman hurt one too many times by life. The woman tells her to wake up, to put up her guard, to not let herself fall this easily, to remember who awaits her in New York. Cait thinks about Taylor, about stepping over that old Woolworth's sign. That he can be intense. Yet she too sees a part of America vanishing, cracking in the concrete, as if a way of life can go extinct slowly until one day it's as if it never was. She thinks about how he mentioned Jane Austen. She would laugh if a guy spoke to her this way in a bar. But no man has ever raised Austen to her. And he's not some guy. Her logic finds no anchor below, where all things worth feeling are felt, and found.

Cait is a romantic beneath her rationale. She relishes turning off her mind and losing herself in romance, or in life if she can, as she so rarely can, or has. And she wonders if she ever has, not in books, but in life. She sees Taylor waiting, wondering, as if he tossed the words out there and now watches them grow stale. She wants him to forget about that. She folds her lower lip under and thinks about what it would be like to kiss him. She glances away. But she feels compelled to say more than a joke.

And her eyes turn back to his. "Taylor, things are complicated right now."

"But if they weren't?" Taylor's phone rings. He clicks it to voice mail.

"Weren't what?"

"Weren't complicated. What's your type?"

"I don't know . . ." And her mouth twitches sideways once, with a blend of diffidence and vulnerability. "Although I wouldn't mind a Mr. Darcy with verve . . . I guess, I happen to like guys who are very much alive inside, who are . . . well, after more in life, and who appreciate how difficult it is to traverse the snow in heels." Her words sustain with a slow smile, until color rises to the fore of her cheeks and she looks away and no longer smiles. Her gaze returns to him. She looks at his eyes, his lips, and she wishes it could be easy.

Taylor's phone rings again. "I'm sorry. My editor keeps calling. Give me a moment."

"Sure."

Taylor steps away. Cait skims her phone for news.

"Hi, Rick," Taylor says. "What's up?"

"I've been trying to reach you," Rick says.

"Yeah, I have a bad signal here. What's up?"

"You didn't see any of the alerts or feeds?"

"No."

"Where you been? This happened like a half hour ago."

"What happened?"

"Some video surfaced of Wally Reynolds at a private banquet. Someone brought up immigration and he let loose. He said, 'Listen, Constance Wallace sometimes seems too emotional over issues like illegal immigrant children. I feel for many migrant children, but nations need borders. I'm not going to let feelings color the facts, as Univision's favorite Republican does.' "

"You're kidding?"

"Oh he didn't stop there. He noted that something like two-thirds of American Hispanic television viewers watch Univision. Then he adds, 'Univision is brainwashing Latinos and turning them into 'Girona-bots.' "

"So he alienated women and Latinos in one rant?"

"Yeah."

"GOP strategists must be ramming their heads into walls right now."

"I know."

"I can't believe these idiots still believe anything is safely private. Is the video good?"

"It's good enough for cable and ads. Anyway, eye on the ball. I need any string you have on Wallace's take on immigration. Also, get us any relevant data on the GOP's demographic issues with Hispanics. See if you can crunch something unique, something for the wonkish bloggers. Also, reach out to her senior staff. We need a fiery rebuttal. Something with legs."

Taylor sighs. "Yeah, okay."

"It might be a P&R duet. So send it to us before eleven thirty, in case Philip wants to take a stab at it before he sleeps. I'll work it around four thirty. It'll be our lead story at dawn. No one else will work this hard, not this late on a Friday. So let's move this baby forward. There are some brief posts up, including by us, and people are going berserk on Twitter. But there are no stories that move it forward, that'll be hot in the morning."

"Okay."

"Good man."

"Good night."

"Night."

Taylor hangs up and steps back to the bar. "Sorry. I should call it a night. I have to file something."

"Is this over the Reynolds video?" Cait asks.

"Yeah. How'd you know?"

"Just read about it. He's not your candidate? Why do you have to cover it?"

"They need some string on Wallace, a response, research. To them, even this shit is all hands on deck."

This is all hands on deck? Cait thinks. *He's got to go, now, on a Friday night, just to file string on this cable catnip.* Current*'s ridiculous.* Yet she also knows that recently, she's felt pressured to chase the sensational as well. But not tonight. Tonight was for them. She doesn't want the night to end. She thought Taylor might kiss her. Finally. Nearly. But the moment is lost.

"I'm sorry," he says.

"It's okay."

"Do you mind if I close this out?"

"Of course not."

Taylor lifts two fingers for the bartender. He feels flattened. He let his chance with Cait pass. He wants to do something, well everything, but something would be a beginning. Instead, the hostess retrieves their coats. Cait asks if he wants his blazer back. He says no, to keep her warm. He holds her winter coat for her, as she puts it on. She looks up at him. He sees her disappointment. He puts on his overcoat, pushes the door open, and watches her exit. Outside, icicles continue to melt.

They walk down the quiet street. He feels compelled to explain. But he only says, "This is how *Current* is." She nods.

They pass the shops and see the hotel. He regrets picking up the phone. He glances at her. Her cheeks are flush. The yellow shop-light highlights the hazel in her eyes. They pass a side doorway. Taylor takes her hand. Pulls her into the doorway. And kisses her. At first, she does not move. Then their fingers intertwine. She stands on her toes, energizes, kisses him back. He pulls her close. And she feels the rush of him. And he feels the rush of her. She pulls the front pockets of his coat. His fingers comb through her hair. And they intensify. She tiptoes closer. He pulls her nearer still. And from afar, as gusts of snow rise with the wind, there is only a hint of shop-light to see them, to know they are there, together in the deep blue night.

XXIV

The airplane flies above the white forest. And the great forest looks like frozen moss. The plane meets the cold sky. There is only white. They soon sink through frozen balls of cloud that wane but do not disappear, like steam too frigid to fade. Below, round ice-glazed peaks penetrate the mist until the mist is above them and the mountains are equals. And soon they descend into a valley drenched in snow.

The plane nears the small airstrip. Taylor naps against the window. Cait sits beside him. She notices his physique, the dark stubble that shadows his jawline. His eyelashes flicker. She wonders what he dreams of.

Taylor slept little last night. They entered the hotel as colleagues, said good night, stole one last touch with their fingertips. He worked, thought of her, and finally fell asleep. He awoke five hours later. Rick's story was up. The sun rose. He tried to fall back to sleep. But he thought about Cait instead.

Wallace has not been north for three weeks. Her last trip was a symbolic tour of Dixville Notch, a hamlet cut into a mountain pass in New Hampshire's far north—population seventy-five. Voters have long gathered there at midnight, primary eve, and cast the first ballots of the nation's first primary. They are landing south of the hamlet, in Berlin, a city of ten thousand on the north side of the White Mountains, another small American town withering away.

At the town hall, Taylor and Cait sit side stage with two rows of reporters. He whispers to her, "Do you want to do something tonight?"

"Yes."

"Let's get out of here. Wallace is taking the night off, anyway. We're only about a half hour from the White Mountains. Let's rent a car. Get off the trail for a night."

The road southward winds into small white-tipped mountains. Ahead of them, snow drifts over the concrete. The yellow line fades in the ashen dusk. The car radio plays "Have You Ever Seen the Rain?" Taylor takes a long breath. He glances at Cait and feels lucky.

Cait stares out the window at the ocean of pine. She recalls running in Iowa beside that small pine forest. The Girona incident feels far away. She cracks her window open and the air is saturated with pine. Few cars pass. The wind whistles. Taylor's left hand rests on the top of the wheel. His right hand lays by his side. Cait puts her hand in his and squeezes gently. "This was a wonderful idea," she says.

Cait looks at his hand. She notices the calluses on the knuckles of his index and middle fingers and asks what they're from.

"Just push-ups," he says.

"Why your knuckles?"

He says he does martial arts, and she asks what kind. "A mix of styles over the years. You press your two fore-knuckles into wood or concrete, in the most superficial sense, to strengthen the bones and train you to make a true fist." She asks about the least superficial sense. "You learn to breathe while you exert yourself and that even exertion can be meditative."

Cait thinks about how little they still know each other. Her gaze drifts out the window.

The snow subsides and the air clears and the forest blends into the darkening sky.

The inns are filled to capacity because of ski season. They enter a lodge off a side road. A round man says there's no vacancy. His wife, middle-aged with a white perm, interupts. "Well, there may be another option. I manage a cottage for a girlfriend. At the last minute, the renters canceled. It's ready for occupants and has a stocked kitchen. I normally don't rent it for the night. But we can't have you searching all night. You seem like good people." She explains that it's a few miles away and she'll give it to them for the night for one hundred dollars. "It's in Glen," the man says, "one of those chalets." His wife adds, "You'll feel like you're in Switzerland." Cait gives a big yes with her eyes.

The woman retrieves the keys. Cait thinks about how this is actually happening. She wonders if it's too fast. She feels as if she has waited forever to be alone with him. How odd that is, it strikes her. She tells herself to stop thinking about it. Blake flashes through her mind. Guilt follows. She gulps and tells herself again to, for once, just go with it.

They stop at a small market and buy groceries for dinner. They drive on and ascend a large hill. The road is dark. They pass the house number just as Cait spots it, and reverse. They park in the driveway. The air is cold and crisp. The snow has stopped falling. Taylor grabs their bags and closes the trunk. The car lights shut off. Cait cannot see her hands. She cannot recall the last time that was true. Taylor presses the unlock button on the car keys. The car lights return. Trees surround the chalet. The triangle roof is coated in a foot of snow.

"This is adorable," Cait says as they enter.

"A woodstove. Fantastic," Taylor exclaims. The stove is in the living room. A couch wraps around it. The cabin walls are decorated with fake animal heads and posters of statuesque skiers. Taylor flicks a switch. Track light shines off the lofted ceiling's wood planks.

Cait watches Taylor excitedly examine the woodstove, and she smiles.

The house has no kindling in the woodpile. Taylor retrieves newspaper from a nearby stack and crumples several pages into balls. He takes three pinecones out of a basket on a shelf.

"You can't use those," she says. "They're decorative."

"Pinecones should never be decorative."

He digs out the ash in the center of the stove, places the pinecones in a circle around the ditch, and drops a few newspaper balls in the center. He strips bark off one log and stacks it atop the pinecones. He locates matches in the kitchen and strikes one and places it at the bottom. The newspaper crinkles and burns black and the pinecones flame orange and the fire pops and builds.

"You mind if I open the door a crack? I love the smell of winter air and fire," she says.

"I do too."

Cait opens a sliding glass door. Taylor turns on the porch light. The snow shines bright white. "Just so we can see if a black bear starts rummaging around."

"Black bears?" she asks.

"They're basically harmless. They're not carnivores."

"Were you a Boy Scout or something?"

"No. But I've spent some time outdoors."

"That's right. The city boy who lived in the Rockies. You're not easy to box."

Taylor unpacks the groceries on the tan limestone countertop. He stands beneath a stemware rack made of three old wooden skis that were cut in half and attached to the wall. Cait begins opening a bottle of wine. The cork pops. He pulls down two glasses.

"You sure I can't help cook?" Cait asks.

"Your only job is to relax."

"I don't do that very well. But I'll try."

"Let's turn off our phones tonight," he suggests. "We deserve one night without work getting in the way."

"Absolutely." Cait finds her purse and shuts off her phone. She cannot recall the last time she turned off her phone by choice. She pours the wine. Taylor toasts "to getting away." Her eyes meet his.

Cait relaxes into the worn brown leather couch. Taylor places another log on the fire. She burrows into the leather, pulls a coffee-colored chenille blanket over her legs and hugs a small brown pillow on her lap. She sips her wine and looks at Taylor. He sautés cod with canned pineapple and sweet-and-sour sauce.

"How many girls have you made this for?" she asks.

"You're the first. Of course." He grins.

She rolls her eyes.

"You do that a lot," he says.

"What?"

"Roll your eyes."

"No I don't."

"Often."

She does it again.

"There." He points at her.

"I did that one on purpose."

"I know that."

"Uh huh." She smiles and looks around the interior. "You know what's funny about this place?"

"What?"

"Look at the bear head on the wall. It's a stuffed animal. And look at that." She points to the deer head mounted on the wall nearest him. "It also looks like it's from one of those giant stuffed animals at FAO Schwarz, no? It's a stuffed animal trophy. Even that bear hide, up there." She restrains her laughter and points to a hide that hangs over the lofted banister. "See, it's fake too. The owner of this chalet is either a member of PETA or really hates stuffed animals." And they laugh together.

She watches Taylor cook. The kitchen spotlight shines down on him. She likes how his black hair does not seem to know whether it wants to be curly or straight, and how the edges linger above where the light catches his eyes.

Cait rises and sets the table. She places the plates beside one another at the corner, facing the fire. She sets slim white candles at the center of the rectangular pine table. Match smoke dissipates in the air. "There," she says under her breath, resting her hands on her hips. Taylor carries the food and wine over and they sit. She tastes the flaky fish.

"Don't watch me eat. You make me nervous." She laughs.

"I'm sorry."

Firelight flickers.

"I can't believe this cod was frozen," she says. "It's good. This is really wonderful, Taylor." Cait shivers. Taylor asks if she's cold. She nods. He offers to shut the door. She nods, still swallowing. He closes the door and sits. The fire picks up. It periodically pops. There's a subtle current to it. And it occurs to Taylor that when flames hasten, strengthen, and crackle, fire sounds like rain.

There is comfort in their quiet. Cait wears a loose black blouse that sometimes, when her arms shift, slips off one shoulder.

"You're doing it again," she says.

"What?"

"Staring at me."

"I'll have to work on that."

"Yes, you will," she replies, exaggerating her serious tone, looking back at him, fixing her blouse. Their eyes meet again and they are quiet. She folds her lower lip under. And Taylor notices.

"This really is good, Taylor."

"Thank you, Caitriona."

"I like how you say my name."

"I like saying your name. Is it after someone?"

"Yeah."

"Who?"

"It's a long story."

"We have time."

"God, it's so nice to have time."

"It is. So tell me about your name?"

"Why?"

"Names matter."

"Ugh, okay. My first name is after my father's mother. But his mother was named after a Yeats verse. I guess my great-grandfather read a scene of it to my great-grandmother on their first date. Can you imagine reading verse to me on a first date?"

He smiles.

"Even I," she continues, "and I'm secretly a bit sappy, would think that's a little much. Then again, maybe not." She looks up and rightward and, in a beat of thought, back at him. "It's kind of nice. People don't do that stuff anymore. It's a shame, really."

"What was the verse?"

"*The Countess Cathleen.*"

"Do you know it?"

"A bit."

"Well?"

"I'm not going to recite verse to you."

"Why?" he asks.

"It's embarrassing."

"Please."

"I'll tell you my middle namesake. That's easy."

"Okay."

"I'm named after Queen Elizabeth. Which, come to think of it, is odd for an Irish American girl. But my mother was thinking more about the strong woman part. She was not thinking like a woman whose parents came from Ireland."

"And the first name?"

"This is why I don't date journalists."

He looks at her as if the small space between them is closing.

She twitches her mouth to the side, in consideration. "Okay, but you can't say anything after. And I need a little more wine." He refills her glass and waits. "It's more of a small play. It was based on an old legend, I guess. So I can't recite the entire thing. It's a morality tale, more than a romantic one, and a little too dramatic for my taste. I guess my great-grandfather's father never liked the play because it made English landlords look generous."

"Do you recall any lines—"

"Well, if you would let me finish talking—"

He nods.

"So the little play is about this countess who sells her soul to Satan to save starving tenants. And the countess, who I'm named for, says at one point—" Cait has another sip of her wine, and takes a conscious breath:

> "Come, follow me, for the earth burns my feet;
> Till I have changed my house to such a refuge;
> That the old and ailing, and all weak of heart,
> May escape from beak and claw; all, all, shall come
> Till the walls burst and the roof fall . . ."

She sips her wine and adds, "To me, the loveliest part is not the words or even that he read it to her on the first date. It's why he read it. It wasn't his favorite verse. But he liked the idea of it. If you are going to sell your soul, do it for something righteous."

Taylor says nothing. He sees the dampness of her eyes. It's as if her words carry memories and her memories carry her, a vital part of her that he wishes to know, in every way a woman can be known.

"All right," Cait says, "you can say something now." Her lower lip folds under. Her dimples show. Her eyebrows rise. And she giggles nervously. "Say something, already."

He pulls her chair to him and kisses her. His left hand reaches under her legs, and he carries her to the couch.

He lays her down and moves on top of her. Their bodies press and move with each other. He reaches around her lower back. Pulls her to him. She bends back. They kiss and touch, and their breathing quickens. She wraps her leg around him. Pulls him closer. He takes her body in his hands. She raises her arms. He pulls her blouse over her head and tosses it aside. She lifts off his shirt. He helps and tosses it aside. He reaches around her and unclasps her bra. He slides the straps over her shoulders, down her arms, her narrow wrists, past her fingers. And his lips touch and trace her nipples. She feels chills, and bends her head back. He kisses her collarbone, the slight crevice where it meets her neck, and her lips. He takes her arms and pushes them back and presses them into the couch. She pushes back but he pushes harder. And she wants him more. His lips retrace her long torso, her neck, her nipples, her thin floating ribs, under her navel, downward. He pulls off her skinny jeans. He kisses her inner thighs. And he can feel her desire building. He removes her underwear. Taylor looks at her. Her breasts rise above her narrow rib cage. Her stomach declines to her hips. Her hips curve outward and inward. And the sight of her body rushes inside him.

He pulls her closer and holds her tighter and their kissing intensifies. She rolls on top of him and unzips his jeans. She pulls off his jeans, then his boxer briefs. Her eyes hold there, shift upward to his eyes, and return. She kisses his stomach and follows the two lines that veer inward, downward. She brushes her bangs away from her eyes and places both her hands there, touching and teasing, and her lips touch and tease, and in time he pulls her up to him, and turns her on her back and he takes her wrists again and brings them over her head and presses them into the couch, as they kiss, as skin presses skin, as she nibbles his lip, and her eyes blink and close, as he nears her and her torso arches, as she says, "Slowly, slowly," and he slows. She gasps and says, "Slowly," and holds her breath and gasps. He bites his lip, restraining himself, moving gently to let her know him, and she gasps again. In time, she knows him and he senses that and their bodies rise together, as they are together, as they move rhythmically, soon manically. And they lose themselves, as the light flickers off their bodies, as she pulls strands of hair frenetically, as he straightens his arms and digs his fists into the leather and arches his lower back into her, as her chest reddens and her voice rises, and she screams, as she digs her nails into his back.

XXV

"I like you so much more now," Cait says with girlish vim.

"Oh, do you?" He smirks.

She nods yes but looks away quickly, as if in a blink it hits her. She means that, but she means more than that. Taylor turns her on her back and they tease and touch and toy.

In time, as they lay together, his fingertip follows the decline of her torso, to her narrow waist, up along the slope of her hips. "You're giving me chills," she says.

"Sorry. I just love this C-curve of a woman's hips, when it's this dramatic. It's just so damn hot."

"Every woman has that."

"Not like this," he says. She presses her lips together, blushes, and lies back shyly on the blue cotton sheets. He asks, aware the words are corny but the meaning is not, "Do you know how beautiful you are?"

And her eyes narrow and she shrugs. She says nothing. She both knows and does not know. She knows men see her this way. But she only cares now how Taylor sees her. She looks back at him, sees his eyes, and knows.

Cait and Taylor drive along the highway. The scattered clouds glow blood orange. The sun slips from white sky to white land. And soon the sun is gone and the high sky is sapphire. Purples and blues gradate into a watery turquoise and yellow-fire horizon. Until the light is lost and night comes and only the headlights show the way, as Taylor holds the wheel and watches the road reach into the dark, and Cait looks over at him and sees him give a slight smile and she does not wonder why.

They awoke late that morning and missed the return flight. So they embraced the lapse. For once, they could have a slow day. They talked and were together again and fell back to sleep. After they awoke, she rose to make coffee, putting on one of his dress shirts, buttoning it twice in front. The shirt hung almost to her knees, over her naked body, and he watched her. She smelled the collar, smiled, and pulled the shirt closer.

They left the chalet by late afternoon. The drive passed quickly. They laughed about the stuffed-animal heads on the walls. They talked about Austen's *Pride and Prejudice.* Were those characters how we wished people to be or how people could be and sometimes are? Taylor drove with his left hand on the top of the wheel. Sometimes his right hand met hers. And they grew closer in the quiet.

As they enter Concord, New Hampshire, Cait pulls inside herself. The Republican debate is tonight. And with the hour, work returns to her mind. She is not ready to meet the thought. She knows these minutes, as if time is being etched. She cannot recall the last time she slept in. She thinks about the story she'll have to write tonight. And it hits her. She forgot about her phone. She finds it and turns it on.

XXVI

Hundreds of reporters buzz and blather, as they sit at long plastic tables inside a gymnasium, staring at the blank televisions, wide-eyed, with one eye on the clock, waiting for the camera to go live, because, as with all presidential debates, the media has traveled to the venue to only, like the public, watch the candidates on television. The politicians are a building away, in the college auditorium—where aides double-check the podiums, the airflow, the light.

Show time. "Debt Crisis." "Immigration crisis." "Jihadists." "Big government." "Defund the IRS." "We need a president who respects the limits of the federal government." "We need a president who can do more than get people angry or excited."

Taylor pays attention but also works on another story. The debate ends. Another *Current* reporter files the news story. Several tables away, Cait finishes the *Times* article, though she needs fresh quotes. She rushes to the spin room, where top campaign advisers gather after every debate and try to manipulate the media's interpretation of the event. It's not ironically named, which to Cait, seems ironic. The spinners stand beneath signs that brandish their candidate's name. Reporters and producers rush in and gather around those signs. The contender's viability is betrayed by the size of their media pack.

Reporters need quotes. And the spinners arrive armed with talking points, poll-tested words. Sometimes the pol's press shop selects reporters disposed to their spin. Ahead of time, the reporters and producers are told that the pol is coming herself. So these spinners choose the questioners, and with that choice hedge against hard questions. It's practice for White House hopefuls, perhaps a carrot to cooperate, to attain the White House. If the candidate they cover wins, they get the presidential beat, a sweatshop of a beat, but still a big beat. White House press conferences proceed in spin room form, only more scripted. If you choose the inquisitors, it makes for an easier inquisition. Sure, reporters huff and puff. Then they assume the role. Because some access is better than none. So the reporters do their work and, the spinners try to work the reporters. Arms go around journo shoulders. Scooplets are fed alongside groups of reporters. Minutes amass. Deadlines. Cait needs quotes. She shuffles from long shots to big shots and glides to the front of the circles, and gets away with it. She's too polite to be put off. Her colleagues remember the personable warmth and not the impersonal offense.

Taylor enters the room as Cait exits. They exchange a warm glance. Taylor watches reporters surround campaign surrogates. He waits until the strategists are alone and pulls several aside, asking questions, gathering material for future stories.

The debate concluded eleven minutes ago. Cait interlaces her quotes, speed-reads, and hits send. She exhales. Checks her phone and email. *Current*'s Luke Brennan wrote her. She remembers when the elevator doors opened and she saw him. Her stomach knots, again. *It can't be that. What did he see? What could he have seen?* They've never exchanged emails in the past. Girona's actions return to her. She recalls the way he made her feel, more than what he did to her. A blend of violation and anger flows through her. She stares at her email inbox, bites down on her lower lip, and double-clicks her mouse.

"Hi Cait. I hope this email finds you well. I've been working on something that I'd like to talk to you about. It can be on background. When are you back in Des Moines or D.C.? I can come to you. Please let me know. Thanks, Luke."

She deletes the email. Empties her trash. She doesn't want to think about it. She wonders where Taylor is. She wants to tell him. But she doesn't think she can. It's his colleague. All over again, she berates herself for letting it get that far with Girona. She thinks she should have been stronger. She tells herself, the great woman would never have let it come to that. It only makes her feel worse. She's embarrassed to tell Taylor. She wonders if she's making too much of Luke's email. *Maybe he wants to contact me about something else.* It could be a coincidence. But she knows the difference between wishful thinking and thinking.

Taylor has a scheduled appearance on BBC. He greets the producer, a witty woman who affirms America's infatuation with the British mind and manner. Until last November, when he went on the trail permanently, he was participating in these analytical segments every week. "Hiya," the BBC woman says.

Post punditry, Taylor returns to the plastic tables. He sees Cait twenty feet away, packing up. He sees her brush her bangs to the side. And she sees him. Something shifts in him. It is as if, in a blink, they are alone. Suddenly they are, in their minds. The clamor and chatter abate, until it is only the two of them, looking at each other. He thinks about the night before. He cannot believe how intensely he cares for her. But his certainty contains disquiet. At some point, she must choose.

She sees that look in him. But she's thinking about other things as well. She wishes she could tell him everything. She wishes it all could be simpler. She wishes Blake would just go away. He feels so far away. She tries to file Blake away. But for once, she can't think that way. At the moment she wants to put so many obstacles behind her, the thoughts stack inside her. *Could Luke have already figured out what happened? What could he be writing? How could he know? Is it possible he read the interview in the paper the next day, figured out what floor Girona was on, and put it all together? Are there security cameras in that hallway?* She gulps. Her mouth is dry. *What would Taylor think?* She looks at Taylor and finds a measure of resolve. *At least this is good. So good.*

She reminds herself to appreciate what's also going right in her life. She decides there, looking at him, as the past day comes over her, to break up with Blake. She tells herself that she can do this much right. But she dreads the confrontation. She wonders how her life became so complicated. She thought Blake was it. He was supposed to be it. She kept waiting to feel it. And now she finally does. For Taylor. And it frightens her. Because she now knows what it can feel like.

XXVII

January
Charleston, South Carolina

Taylor believes that time should not pass unmarked, that too much of life goes unmarked. Days blur to years and years to lifetimes. So he wants to recognize the day, if only in a small way. His thirtieth birthday is tomorrow. He is not in Playa del Carmen, as planned. He's in South Carolina. His bosses asked him to cancel the long weekend away. It was his eleventh month with *Current,* nearly all of it on the road, nearly every weekend a working weekend. It would have been his first vacation while working for them. It had never been that way for him before. He saw, at a young age, that if one did not do things now, they might never be done. So in his twenties, once he completed his post-college travels, he worked but still took at least three weeks a year and went somewhere foreign, to enjoy his youth and learn something of the world. That is, until now. Rick said what bosses say: "We need you. We'll make it up to you."

Taylor sees the future as if it were a Nebraska landscape, one of those forever highways where the horizon is an eternity away, yet visible, knowable, attainable. He sees weekends folding into workweeks and workweeks becoming a life. He knows the difference between having little free time and what's worth your time, the difference between busy and living. He is a New Yorker. He believes Manhattan is infested with the busier than thou. He told himself, long ago, that he would not be *that* guy. But like so many people who are years into their work, his job has grayed the principled distinctions he held yesterday—or what seems like yesterday. Still, he's trying. He wrestles with the idea—if not now, when? He imagines a few years ahead. They will again say, *The competition is catching up. We'll make it up to you.* And someday, maybe he will do his job his way, balance his work the right way. But to him, someday feels too abstract to trust.

Yet primary season is not suited to a break. He recognizes that. Initially, P&R approved the trip because it was brief, because he had been on overdrive for nearly a year. They changed their mind three days before he was to leave. And Taylor resents that. To him, the bigger issue is not the little trip. Yet he's resolved to roll with it and be an "adult." And the thought, the word "adult," rubs him all wrong. Because the context is compromise. But he knows that is the point of the word. Still, he'll do it his way. The moment he arrives at the airport, he decides to make the best of it. He walks to the car rental booth, passes on the usual midsize car, and rents a Mustang. He passes on lodging in centrally located Columbia, where the national media gathers. Instead, he drives to Charleston, locates the finest inn, and rents the finest suite. It is tantamount to an upscale apartment. He opens the oak shutters and large window and sees the water and smells the sea air. He plops down on the leather couch, rests his head against the rolled arm, looks around at the portraits of austere-looking men, and smiles, thinking, *Things could be worse.*

But it's not that easy for Taylor. His mind soon wanders into his angst. He thinks about how his work habits crept up on him and suddenly became him. He feels the erosion of his better self. He is reminded of the boy who became a young man and the young man who already let the boy go. His work still matters to him. He is not going to give up on his career. He thinks about his mortgage. His bills. He has fifteen years behind his career. In high school, he interned at a newspaper after school. He reported, photographed, served different editorial posts at his school paper, and became the editor. He climbed the same ladder in college. His college friends drank through their summers. He spent two summers working newspaper internships in Moscow, Idaho, and Milwaukee. He reported on rural meth labs. Covered odd Americana. He still recalls the animal carcass show in central Wisconsin. He worked the night cops' beat. He never forgot the trailer park double homicide.

He eventually earned his way back to New York. He worked at *Fortune* magazine over two winter breaks. He spent his last college summer interning at *Time.* After college, he worked at *The New York Observer*, the New York bureau of the *Financial Times,* and ABCnews.com, where he watched Mark Halperin produce the morning *Note*, a forbearer of *Scorecard,* of even *Current* and its kin, that set the political day, in its day, and demonstrated that political junkies' appetites were not only accelerating online, but also seeking a better fix. Taylor returned to newspapers after that, until *Current* crashed the old media club, and he applied. He thinks about all those years, the thousands of stories, how he's invested too much of himself to get this far, to throw it all away. This is when he should ascend to the top of his profession. He's not going to throw it away now. He decides not to fixate on the imperfections of his job. He will do what is required of him. That's what work is, he tells himself; it's work. And the thought kills him a little bit inside.

Yet he is beginning to learn to leave work at work. His job feels small beside his feelings for Cait. He has lived enough, seen enough to know that, in the long life, it's more important where one spends their nights than their days.

And if everything cannot be right, he'd choose to have this be right. It has been years since he felt this way. And now that he's there again, he wants to keep on, to know it sooner, further, more, for all the world is enlarged with Cait, and he wants more from it, to leap into the pulse of life and know it by its beat.

But he remains ambitious, a man, a New Yorker, an American. He cannot fully divorce his self-image from his job. *Current* is at the fore of journalism. If he is not with them, if he is not a journalist, if he is not succeeding, what kind of man is he?

Yet something has changed in him. He decides, without explicitly realizing it, that like so many of his generation, he owes his employer nothing. To him, most companies no longer honored the decent compacts of old. He has concluded, after years in this world, after years of watching his friends in other professions, particularly this one—as great reporters are told the future cannot afford them and given the pink slip—that corporations shredded their end of the social contract. They are not loyal to employees. Why should he be loyal to them? He believes that most executives see employees as another product that can be discarded or upgraded, that companies nurture the good resources as long as it's good for them, and once it's no longer good (enough) for them, they will unload you, because if people are products, only profit matters.

He believes the most dangerous employers are those that use such words as "team" and "mission" and "cause," as *Current*'s top dogs commonly do. They will ask you to sell out for the team. They will take from you, for the team, until you are taken. And the time will come, he knows, when the team no longer needs him or can afford him. And he fears that day will come when he is used up. So many reporters' numbers were coming up these days. Taylor does not want his number to come up when he can no longer lean into the future.

"Sometimes you have to make the best of things," Taylor says to Cait.

Cait nods pensively, as if the thought strikes a nerve. "I mean, yeah," she replies. "Still," she adds, looking around, "it's ridiculous that you got *Current* to pay for this place for two weeks. It's like twice the size of my apartment in the city."

"I'm going to have a fantastic expense report."

"Yes, you will." Cait walks over to Taylor. He sets down her bags. She reaches over his shoulders, clasps her fingers behind his head, tiptoes upward, and kisses him. "Happy birthday," she says.

"It's not until tomorrow."

"I know. I just wanted to be the first to say it to you."

They have not seen each other for four days. Constance Wallace won the New Hampshire primary Tuesday night. The media had its horse race. More readers for *Current* and kin. Political operatives had their marathon. Long campaigns are profitable campaigns.

Cait landed and checked into a nearby hotel. She wanted to keep her own room, to keep up appearances. Before he picked her up, Taylor went back to work. He wrote a story on the "Republican civil war." The national security wing versus the social conservative wing. It's true. The two leading Republican candidates personify two GOP pillars. But he is dramatizing the division. *Exaggerate and then walk back.* He's doing what he disfavors. And he knows it. Knows better. The GOP coalition is not strictly bifurcated. Social conservatives are as likely to keep a gun in the home as to attend church weekly. But it's what attracts readers. It's his job. And if it's what he does, he might as well do it well. Or so he tells himself.

"I missed you," she says, "so much. And guess what?"

"What?"

"I took a personal day tomorrow. I can be with you all day. We can celebrate your thirtieth properly."

He pulls her closer. "That's better than Playa del Carmen."

Taylor lifts her. She wraps her legs around his body. He takes her to the bed. And the day drifts away this way, as the ceiling fan spins overhead.

The old city loses all traces of twilight. Cait and Taylor sit inside a bar-restaurant. It has wood panels and small wooden tables and carries the faint odor of spilled beer and fried food. The husky waiter sets down two waters. He scratches his right sideburn chop and pulls the pen from behind his ear. He asks what they'll have. And Cait says to Taylor, "You choose."

"We'll have two dozen oysters. And Cait"—Taylor looks over at her—"what would you like to drink?"

"A mint julep."

"A mint julep it is. Do you have any wheat beer?"

"We have Blue Moon and Franziskaner."

"Franziskaner, fantastic. I'll have that." The waiter nods, notes, walks away. "So a mint julep, huh?" Taylor asks Cait. "I don't think anything should ever be mixed with bourbon except ice."

"When in Rome—" She smiles.

And so they talk to each other, draw closer to each other. The waiter returns. Sets down their drinks and two trays of oysters. Taylor asks if she likes lemon. She nods. He splashes the oysters with lemon and places the miniature fork next to Cait's bread plate. Cait sips her mint julep and cringes. "Oh, that's awful."

Taylor laughs and flags the waiter.

"I made a terrible mistake with my order," she tells the waiter. "The mint julep, I mean." The waiter melts with her smile. Cait asks for a Grey Goose soda.

"I'll be sure to get you the right drink this time," the waiter says. "I'll replace it."

"No, you can still charge us," she replies.

"I wouldn't dream of it," he says before returning to the bar.

"That's what I love about the South," Taylor says.

"They'll replace a drink in the city as well."

"Yeah, but in the city they won't make you feel like it's their fault."

"That's true. Some aspiring actress will glower at you," she cracks, picking up an oyster. "I wish dollar oysters tasted this good in the city."

The bar begins to fill. Cait asks Taylor if he wants the last oyster.

"No, no, it's yours," he replies and waves the waiter over.

She watches him order a third tray of oysters, and another round for them as he drinks his beer, and looks around, relishing the bar buzz. Her phone rings. She turns it on silent.

Blake has called her twice this evening. She told him she has tomorrow off. He said he might fly to Charleston. But Blake always says things like that. He never does things like that. Still, she doesn't want to encourage him or think of him. She has not seen him for a week and a half. It feels like longer to her. She wonders how she could have felt so close to Blake. She no longer jumps at his voice. No longer feigns laughter. She has stopped wondering, or caring, whether he will propose. And now he calls her more often. He suddenly wants to meet her mother. He finally brought her to meet his parents. *Of course, Cait thought, he's acting this way now. Now he wants to move forward.*

A squirrelly bartender tests the microphone onstage and sets songbooks on a bench nearby. Cait and Taylor talk as the eager ascend the stage for karaoke. A duet of young women first. Another girl solos after. Taylor steps outside to take a call from an editor. Cait watches the young and mid-twenties crowd. The few couples. The grouped singles. The girls focusing on each other, yet still peeking sideways, fingers combing through hair. They chat and dance and sing. The guys gather in smaller groups, only a few even sway to the music, as they hawk and gawk and toss back drinks. And Cait smiles. She thinks about this universal bar dance. Taylor returns. She asks him if everything is okay.

"Just the usual BS. So are you going to sing?"

"You first," she says.

"No way. I don't do karaoke."

"Oh, the best people for karaoke are the people who don't do karaoke."

Onstage, two college-age women rock the Dixie Chicks' "Not Ready to Make Nice."

"I like this song," he yells over the music.

"You like *this* song?"

"Yeah. It's sincere."

"You like country?"

"I don't discriminate."

"You should sing some, then."

"It's not for me."

"Let's make a bet," she says. "Loser sings."

He glances toward the back of the bar. "Okay, let's play darts."

She smirks confidently. "Done."

"Shit," he mutters.

She places a napkin over her glass and grabs her purse. As she stands, her long, black-beaded necklace drapes between her breasts and falls against her white tee. She steps toward the dart board. He watches her from behind, the way her jeans fit her firm figure. She turns back to him. "You coming?" she asks.

They walk to the board. He retrieves three darts and says, "Ladies first."

"Not this time. You chose the wager."

"Fair enough." He tosses three darts and hits the 17, the 3, smiles, and a high 19. He retrieves them and passes the darts to her.

"Warm up that voice," she says. She nails the green center, a bull's-eye, and the third dart narrowly misses the center and hits 18.

"Where'd you learn to do that?" he asks.

"I used to play with my dad a lot."

Taylor orders a whiskey. Cait approaches the bartender who is manning the stage. She tells him that they have to leave in ten minutes. In Cait's way, she convinces the bartender to call Taylor up next.

Minutes later, Taylor's onstage, singing Don McLean's "American Pie." He's fumbling lyrics and laughing between words. The song rises. His voice rises. And he leaps into the lyrics. He pulls the mic close, looks at Cait, and sings, " 'Can you teach me how to dance reeeal slow.' " She claps her hands and cheers real loud. And when the chorus comes, the bar joins in, and Cait sees what she loves in him, as he drinks his whiskey and sings passionately offfff-key.

An hour later, they stroll through the old streets of Charleston. They wander past flickering firelit lamps in doorways and cross under iron verandas. They pass galleries and antique shops and old brick buildings with iron rods protruding from their facades. An old man strolls alone. He says hello. The friendliness throws the New Yorkers off. There is an awkward pause until they do say hello. The man's skin is dotted with liver spots. His salt-and-pepper mustache has the texture of straw. His family goes back six generations in Charleston. He tells them to return in spring when the flowers bloom. Taylor says they will. Cait looks at Taylor. Taylor asks the man about the rods. The man explains, the rods were added to bolster buildings after the 7.3 earthquake in 1886. "It was the largest quake to ever shake the eastern United States," the man says. Cait asks if he'll take a picture of them. "It'd be my pleasure." She hands over her phone and explains how to use it. They stand under a streetlamp. Taylor puts his arm around her. She moves closer to him and places one hand on his stomach. And the man takes a single frame.

They thank him and say goodbye. They pass a large restaurant. Waiters gather silverware in cloth napkins and turn chairs over, placing them on the tabletops. It's almost midnight. The temperature bobs around sixty degrees. They come to a larger road. Lamplight reflects off old pink and yellow buildings. They meander along and soon pass a brick Revolutionary-era home with white stone trim.

"Charleston is the greatest small city in America," Taylor says.

"I think so."

They find their way to a butter-cream antebellum house that has two stories of wraparound porches. Cait imagines herself sipping a glass of chilled Sauvignon Blanc on the second floor, staring off, on a summer day long ago. Then she remembers what it took to support homes like this, the families with this, the many who were enslaved to sustain the privileged lifestyle of a few. And she no longer pines.

They let themselves get lost and walk down a cobblestone side street. Cait's high heels clap against the stone. They find a narrow pathway and arrive at a quiet corner. Two Colonial-era homes are divided by a walkway, which is blocked by an ornate wrought-iron gate. The town houses' shutters are closed. There's no light or interior noise or hint of occupancy. They hear the sound of babbling water. In the half-light, at the end of the alley, they see the faint silhouette of a sculpture of a woman.

"Let's climb over," Taylor says, "check it out."

"No way. I can just see the headline. *Times* reporter and *Current* reporter caught breaking into private garden."

"I don't think people live here. They look like offices." He points to copper signage on the walls.

Cait nods. "Well all right, then," she says with a shot of confidence. She takes off her blazer and removes her heels and hands them to him. "I'm glad I wore jeans."

At the middle of the gate, there's a horizontal iron bar. Taylor boosts her up. She steps on the bar, pulls herself up, and steps on top of one of the two stone pillars that border the gate. She hangs down and lands on the balls of her feet. Taylor passes her heels and jacket through the gate and follows her over. They laugh as mischievous children laugh. She places her hand to his mouth. Her eyes tell him to be quiet. And they are quiet. Cait remains barefoot. They patter to the back and enter a spacious courtyard. It has a fountain and a Hellenistic sculpture of a young woman. Cait says she'll meet him at the statue. "You go that way," she suggests. They take separate circular routes through the groomed walkway and exchange glances. Cait veers off and runs her toes through the damp grass. They meet on the other side. The statue is illuminated with yellow light. He takes Cait's hips in his hands. Her hands clasp over his shoulders. "Happy birthday," she whispers. He kisses her. And they feel like the only people alive.

In time, they sit on a bench in the garden. They are quiet in the night. He places his arm around her. She nuzzles into him. "I have always wanted a garden like this," she says. "Can we have one of these someday, Taylor, where I can sit with you when we're full of wrinkles?" And Taylor smiles.

XXVIII

Cait stretches out her waifish arms. She looks at Taylor, asleep, half covered in the late-morning light. She wants to wake him. She thinks about kissing him. But she lets him sleep in. She watches him breathe. He sleeps with his mouth cracked open. She finds him adorably vulnerable this way. She recalls the night before, blinks several times, and folds her lower lip under.

Cait remembers it's his birthday. She quietly rolls out of bed. She will make him a decadent breakfast, she decides, and they'll do whatever he wants after. She wants the day to be her treat.

Before the divorce, Cait's mother made a massive breakfast for her father on his birthday, and one year, her mother tried to plan a day for them, but something—Cait can't recall what—got in the way of their plans. Instead of the details, she recalls what these little disappointments did emotionally to her parents over time. Cait wants to avoid that fate. She tries, without realizing it, to do right what her parents did wrong, as if a child can correct her parents' mistakes.

Her phone is on the nightstand. She reaches for it out of habit. It's on silent. There are seven voice mail messages. *Two from Mom? Something's wrong.* She closes the bedroom door, tiptoes into the living room, and notices there are also text messages. She reads one from Blake: "Trying to reach u babe. B at your hotel at 12. Have a surprise 4 u." Her shoulders tense up. *That's forty-five minutes from now!* She doesn't bother to read the other texts. She listens to her voice mail. Skips two messages from Blake. "11:27 p.m. Cait, it's Mom, call me back tonight if you can." Next message from Blake. Skips it. "8:32 a.m. Hon, call me the moment you wake up." Blocked number. "10:46 a.m." Her mom whispers, "Caitriona Elizabeth, where are you? Jesus Christ. Blake's been trying your room. I'm calling you from the damn plane phone in the bathroom. It's supposed to be a surprise. But I'm on a private plane with his parents. He's flying all of us down to see you. We'll be at your hotel at noon. So wherever you are, make sure you are there by then. Oh, act surprised."

Her stomach drops. *Calm down. You have time. Jesus. What's going on? He wouldn't!* She's sweating scenarios. She has to get to the hotel. She's unsure how to leave Taylor. She doesn't have the heart to tell him right now, on his birthday. She doesn't think she can lie to his face. She picks at a cuticle on her left thumb and takes long breaths and decides. She finds hotel stationery and writes:

> Happy birthday, Taylor!! My editor wrote me. He needs me today at the last minute. I'm so sorry. You seem so at peace, asleep. I can't bear to wake you on your birthday, only to say I have to rush off. Please, please, forgive me. I'll call you in the midafternoon. By the way, last night was so beautiful.
>
> xoxo,
> Caitriona

Taylor awakens a half hour later. He reaches through the sheets for Cait, opens his eyes, and wonders where she is. He soon sees the note. It makes sense to him. *Current* has done this to him repeatedly. Taylor thinks about how he wants to stamp the day. He can see the clear sky from his window. He walks over to the window, opens it, and breathes in the warm ocean air. He decides that later, when Cait's done working, he'll rent a small boat for a few hours so they can enjoy the sunset on the Atlantic. Taylor calls down to the concierge to craft the day.

Cait ruffles her sheets. She wants it to look like a slept-in bed. She opens her laptop on the desk and places a DO NOT DISTURB sign on the door. She calls Blake and her mother. Leaves voice mails. She explains that she turned the ringer off to catch up on sleep. They only know the Cait before Taylor, when she had trouble sleeping. Her stomach remains unsettled.

She hopes Taylor's not angry or hurt. She wonders how she let it get to this point. She wishes she'd broken up with Blake on New Year's Eve. She thinks about how Blake disregards her, as he did that night, when she asked about "Auld Lang Syne." She frames his surprise visit within those terms. *He thinks only about himself.* Even when he thinks of her, she tells herself, he's thinking about what she should like rather than what she does like. *He never really asks about me.* She's doing this more. She dwells on the bad in Blake, to make it easier, to prepare herself to end it. She thinks again about New Year's and how she wished for Taylor that night.

But she shakes her head. *Get it together.* And she summons her strength. She reminds herself that their parents are coming too. She's still in this relationship. It's lasted more than three years. She should honor those years. She feels responsible for this mess. She wants to end it amicably. *I can't let it become a scene.* She admires how her mother handles drama. Her mother expects change in life, which diminishes the unease that comes with change. Cait always had a talent for social grace. She tells herself to just get through the day.

Knock, knock . . . knock.

"Surprise," Blake says at the door, placing his arms around her, pecking her on the lips. Her arms lay limply at her sides. She quickly shifts the kiss to a hug. She peeks over his shoulder and wonders where their parents are.

"What are you doing here, Blake?"

"Can't I surprise my girlfriend? You said you had the day off. I thought it would be romantic."

"Well, I mean, I do. It is. But I'm still doing a little work."

"Oh, babe," Blake says, "you work too much."

All he does is work.

"Can I come in already?"

"Yes, of course."

She steps to the side. He enters and turns toward her. She dodges his eyes and walks to her laptop. Cait stares at the monitor. She pretends to read. Her right hand presses down on the desk. She breathes in and out, in and out. Her eyes close and open with a pregnant pause. *You can do this.* She takes one last long breath and turns to him.

"Blake, can we talk?"

"Not now, babe. We have plans."

"What kind of plans?"

"It's a surprise."

"Blake, you can't always assume I'm free."

"You said you had the day off. Don't get into one of your moods, please. Hurry now. Oh, pack a nice dress that you can wear to dinner tonight. Today is casual."

She stands still.

"Please."

"How nice a dress?"

"A summer dress that's suitable for evening."

"It's January, Blake."

"It's summer here. I'm sure you have something. That's your territory."

"I might have something."

"That's my girl."

And the words slap Cait. She realizes she's still his girlfriend. *Technically.*

Blake relaxes in the cushy merlot armchair. He is a few inches over six feet. He has a long face, a narrow, sharp nose, long lashes, and small gray eyes with tiny cavities beneath. His blond hair has a quiff cut that's close at the sides but three inches thick on top and swept rightward. He crosses his legs. His hands rest clasped at his knee. His cotton shirtsleeves drape over his navy chino shorts. He wears no socks. His mid-top sneakers are white leather. Blake has always embraced the image of his family, his upbringing. He has irreverent boyhood friends. Some shift from one website venture to another. Others try to be actors, producers, directors, and musicians. Some simply party. They scoff at the money that funds their ability to scoff at money.

Blake never took his wealth for granted. Cait liked that about him. She liked that he spoke to his parents every week and that they were still married. She liked that he mocked a boyhood friend who was chauffeured to work every morning. Blake rides the subway in the morning. It's the fastest means of transportation during rush hour. He's in banking, a solid salesman. But he knew moneymen, often math men, who made far more. He saw the new stars of Wall Street all around him. The young ones, peers and prized rookies, often justified their jobs in societal terms. They said they wanted to earn enough to be philanthropic or help the free market function. Blake mocked them as "bankrolled-idealists," because, he said, if you remove the big money, they would move on. Once, Cait joined Blake for a work dinner with some blathering Silicon Valley guys who were illustrating the Web-world high art of spinning high checks into high ideals. Blake asked them what charity they were donating their stock options to. He didn't prove much of a salesman that night. See, Blake said, it *was* about money. Proudly.

Cait liked that about him too. Not the greed. The honesty. He was honest about himself, which she found rare in people. And there was a generous streak. A year ago, one of his best friends got fired; he secluded himself, became depressed, but wouldn't recognize it. Blake arranged a choice interview and called in a favor. His friend got the job. Blake never told his friend he helped him. Cait liked that most, partly because she found out only by accident. She once held on to these anecdotes. For all the times that Blake was cold or commanding or condescending, she thought, he also did things like that.

Yet she no longer can believe she ever clung to those things. She thinks about Taylor. What she feels with him. How she feels about him. She's contrasting the two men. Yet she doesn't want to mingle them. She wants it to be clean, past and future. She believes the past can be the past, if you let it pass.

She now fears what it will take to create that past. She'll have to tell Blake about Taylor. *Now? Must I now?* She feels inward dread, that human desire to delay the irreconcilable, the inevitable. Her parents come to mind. She wonders if her father also came. She's unable to recall the last time they were all together. She pictures them waiting for her somewhere in Charleston. *I can't keep them waiting.* She walks to her suitcase and searches for a suitable outfit. "No time to play dress-up, babe," Blake says, tapping his watch with the opposite index finger. She rolls her eyes. But says nothing. She selects a dress, grabs her pinstriped makeup bag, and rushes to the bathroom.

She closes the door and looks in the mirror. She cannot believe this is happening. She wanted the problem to sort itself out. In the back of her mind, she intended to keep on the campaign trail with Taylor, to not look back, to think of it as that, a long road, if you can go West in love. But she now understands that life's lines sometimes are circles.

At Charleston harbor, as they walk on the pier, Cait searches for her parents. She sees only two deckhands, across the white gangplank. She and Blake board the seventy-five-foot motor yacht. They descend stairs and pass through the lacquer interior, by cream-colored couches and glossy maple burl furniture upholstered in cream. A uniformed steward takes their bags. "You like it?" he asks. She nods yes. "Blake," she says, "I really have to talk to you." She wonders if this is the right time.

This is really nice. He rented this yacht. He flew in her parents. He's never done anything like this. She recognized that he had money when they first met. She's used to it. But she cannot recall when he last planned a day for them. He went to all this effort. She does not want to appear ungrateful.

"Babe," he says, "what's up?"

"I don't know—"

"Listen, I know—"

"No, wait. I do know. I mean, I don't know what you are going to say, but I need to talk to you. I should've said something to you back at the hotel."

"Whatever it is, can it wait?"

"Maybe not."

"Babe, I want to show you something. It can wait."

She nods.

She doesn't like who she becomes around him. She wants to leave that woman here. But she has always struggled with social resolve. She has never had to work at it. Cait was popular in school without being the mean girl. She was herself. And classmates gravitated to her. It was the opposite of her professional self. She paid those dues as a cub reporter. She wanted to prove that she could get there without her mother's name. She never applied to the *Journal* for that reason. She sought the *Times* and worked the internships, the small and medium-size papers, and arrived quickly. It was no small feat. But this is her private life. And here Cait struggles with the distance between want and will and how it defines a life.

Blake places his hands on hers. She neither holds his hands nor pulls back. He says, "Cait, I know I haven't been the perfect boyfriend. It's been crazy at work. I'm also not used to dating a girl who travels so much. I also know I kept you, as you once said, guessing. I'm sorry. That all ends today. You'll see, babe . . . Could you, please, try to be the girl back in the city during our first two years together, and think about our life there, and enjoy this day. I flew out here for a reason. Can you do that much?"

She surrenders. "Yes." And her mouth flattens and her shoulders with it. She welcomes this pliant feeling. She decides the hard move can wait. She tells herself, again, that they are already on the yacht. That her parents might arrive soon. The decision does not sit easy within her. But it's the easiest move. She'll take easy right now. She wants to survive the day without a scene. She tells herself it has been more than three years. *You can wait a few hours.*

Blake leads her above deck. They walk to the stern. Cait walks behind him.

"Sur-priiise!" the parents say.

Cait sees her mother and father. Together. Side by side. Actually side by side. Blake's parents too. Cait's eyes meet her mother's. And her mother knows. The way a mother knows. Something's wrong with this fairy tale.

XXIX

But how lovely fairy tales appear from afar. They flew in on a private jet. They relax on a private yacht. The chef prepares lunch in the galley. The uniformed waiter holds a silver tray with glasses of Pinot Grigio. Even the sky blends flawlessly into the ocean, one clean, bright blue, as if Blake handled that too.

Cait embraces her parents. Then Blake's parents, the Windoners. Cait exchanges one kiss on the cheek with Mrs. Windoner. She's overwhelmed. She reverts to her teen years in France and reaches for the second kiss. Mrs. Windoner pulls back. "We're Americans, dear. We only do one." And Cait replies, "Yes, of course." Erin Ellis thinks, *Jesus Christ.* Mr. Windoner says he's going to give her a "big American hug." Erin rolls her eyes. Mrs. Windoner sees Erin's eyes. Mrs. Windoner thinks, *New Yorkers.*

But it is not as bad as that. The flight went well. Blake's parents were fascinated by the famous war correspondent. Weren't you afraid? You're so brave. Really, the bullet holes are called rosebuds? And you can still see them on walls in Sarajevo? Erin regaled, as Erin does.

Blake's parents liked Cait's father too. He's a quiet and discerning man who teaches classics at Columbia. He must appreciate tradition and fine things. Ergo, them.

Cait texts Taylor from the restroom. She explains that she is swamped for the day, and so sorry. She'll make it up to him, promises to. She writes that he means everything to her. Cait sends it and walks back.

"A toast," Mr. Windoner says. "To Cait and Blake."

"Cait and Blake," Mr. Ellis says.

Glasses rise. Clink. Sips taken. Cait withholds eye contact. She likes to believe that a toast is only consummated with eye contact. So, in this tiny way, she rebels.

She soon raises her eyes. Her pressed lips turn up to express appreciation. She holds the stem of her wineglass in one hand, like her mother, pinching it between her thumb and her index and middle finger. Her other hand squeezes her phone as though it's a path back to Taylor.

The yacht makes its way to sea. They sit on teak deck chairs around a teak table. "You seem a little overwhelmed by all this, dear," Mrs. Windoner says to Cait. "Don't be. Enjoy the day." Cait nods politely. She sets down her phone. She's determined to betray no more of her thoughts. She crosses her legs. Sits up. Sips.

Mr. Windoner turns to Cait, "So you think Wallace can come back?"

"I don't really do that," she replies. "But the experts think she can."

"Don't really do what?" Mr. Windoner asks. "Don't give me that objective stuff. You reporters have opinions. I read them on the front page of your newspaper every day."

Erin Ellis thinks, *Jesus Christ.*

Mrs. Windoner says to Cait, "He only wants to know your opinion, dear."

"I think she can, yes."

"I hope so. I'm backing her one hundred percent. She's earned it. But I'd take anyone over a socialist like Girona."

"He's right about that," Blake says. "I'm sick of Girona trashing people for just wanting to make money."

Erin turns to Blake, "Is that how you and your coworkers interpret it?"

"Most of Wall Street does, yeah, and most are social libs."

"That again," Mr. Ellis interjects.

"What?" Blake asks.

"It's so popular today to say one is fiscally conservative but socially liberal. I hear that more often from my students. But I think it's more morally defensible to be socially conservative and fiscally liberal—that way you at least support services for the poor."

"It depends," Cait replies, "on whether . . . well, if your morals are personal or if you want the government to enforce them."

"Certainly," her father says. "But nevertheless."

"Yes, nevertheless . . . Blake," Erin says, "you were saying, what's the attitude of your colleagues?"

"Aaah, okay. I have a friend at Goldman who used to donate tons to Dems. He told me last week that"—Blake chuckles—"well, he said, if Girona was on fire he wouldn't piss on him to put it out."

Cait cringes. Mrs. Windoner eyes Blake. He stops laughing.

"You know what the dirty secret is of New York liberals?" Mr. Windoner asks.

"I'm sure you'll tell us," Erin says.

"In the city, programs for the poor are supported by the people whose incomes they call outrageous—"

Mr. Ellis interjects, "There's truth to that. But Wall Street is upset for other reasons."

"Why, then?" Mr. Windoner asks.

"They've been portrayed as capitalistic heroes since the Reagan era," Mr. Ellis says. "Now, the very thing they were glorified for is seen for what it is, a smarter form of gambling. Except, when they lose we all pay."

"It's not gambling," Mr. Windoner says. "It takes capital to build businesses."

"Dad," Blake says, "I must admit, that's not where the real money is made on the Street anymore. I mean, something like half of all trades are now between computers. That's all about automated software selling, on, say, bad news, beating another computer by a few milliseconds."

"And do you believe that benefits society?" Mr. Ellis asks.

"Not really," Blake replies. "To go with your gambling analogy, it actually allows high-frequency traders to know the winners, to seize the better prices before regular investors, by paying the exchanges and others for privileged access to data a fraction of a second faster."

"God, that makes Vegas look honest," Mr. Ellis says.

Blake shrugs. "But that's not everyone. VCs still provide capital for entrepreneurs. That's pure capitalism."

"I'm sure Girona has a problem with VCs too," Mr. Windoner says. "Of course, who knows what he thinks. The media is so soft on him."

"They don't even know him," Erin says. "It's not like when I was young. Presidential candidates are separated from the press, even those who travel with them."

"Is that true, Cait?" Mr. Windoner asks.

"Yeah," Cait says. "Wallace is a rare exception, comparably speaking."

"That's ironic, considering how much the media's in the bag for Girona—the *Journal* excluded. Erin, at least you worked for the last good paper."

"I also worked at the *Times* when I was young," Erin says.

"Sorry to hear that. The *Times* is the worst because it thinks it's the best."

"Meaning?"

"It thinks it's the paragon of journalism. Shoot, I'm sure liberals agree, because they don't see how biased it is."

"There's some bias, sure," Erin says. "But at least it strives for objectivity. I do think, flaws and all, it's a precious American institution."

"It's a dying *liberal* institution. Good riddance to all of it, all the liberal media."

"What do you want to replace them, Fox?" Erin asks.

"Well, talk about gambling. It wasn't Fox that reported that Ted Wallace gambles illegally, yet never published any proof of it."

"Too bad we can't all be more like Fox and convince viewers there's massive voter fraud to lower minority turnout, or that we found WMDs in Iraq to justify a war."

"Christ, will you people ever get over Iraq?"

"Can we please not talk about politics!" Cait shouts.

Everyone startles.

Erin says, "Of course. I'm sorry, hon."

Mrs. Windoner touches her husband's thigh.

Mr. Windoner says, "Yes, I'm sorry as well, Cait."

Blake laughs. His mother glares at him. Blake composes himself.

The waiter does not flinch. He's seven feet away. His hands are behind his back. Mr. Ellis looks his way and says, "Some more wine, please."

Mrs. Windoner says, "Me as well. And Cait's correct. You know what they say about discussing politics and religion. Cait, did I tell you how lovely you look today?"

"Thank you. And you as well."

"Yes, very much so," Erin adds.

Mrs. Windoner says to Erin, "Oh, so do you. You look so wonderfully continental."

What does that even mean? Erin thinks. "Thank you."

Mrs. Windoner has small deep-set blue eyes and a long thin nose. Her yellow blouse extends over her loose white linen pants. She wears matching yellow flats. Yellow gold hangs around her neck and drips off her ears. She wears a large black summer hat with a wide droopy brim. It shades her tight skin. And perhaps it's her skin, or the brittle hair beneath her hat. Or perhaps it's the heavy coral lipstick or the caked mascara. But Blake's mother has that anxious, fading feel about her, like someone who clings to the beauty she once was, to how people once saw her.

Erin's white blouse is tucked into her black cotton pants. A thin white-gold chain is around her neck. She remains in the shade. She wears black cork platform sandals. Periodically, she folds her right big toe over her second toe and presses down. She wants to pull Cait aside, ask what's wrong. Yet she remembers that Cait never appreciated her thinly veiled disapproval of Blake. Erin left Manhattan determined not to be that mother.

Cait looks at her mother and shifts her eyes right. Erin turns her hands up, as if to convey, *What should I do?*

"Cait," Erin says, "you want to go to the bow and see the view?"

"That sounds lovely," Cait replies.

"Oh, I'll join you," Mrs. Windoner says. "I'd love time with the girls."

Erin thinks, *Can't she take a hint?*

They excuse themselves and walk to the bow. Cait cannot say what she wishes to say. She taps her gray strappy sandal against the deck. The wind blows her gray coat back. Her white cotton sheath dress presses against her body, and her hair blows back with the wind, as does Erin's. Mrs. Windoner holds her hat. Cait grips the rope. Water breaks off the yacht. They take in the Atlantic's expanse. "I love it," Cait says, "when you can't tell where the ocean ends and the sky begins."

They are silent. And the pause extends with feelings unsaid. They return to the stern.

Mr. Windoner is talking. "That was an incredible Giants game."

"I remember it like yesterday, which is rare, because I barely remember yesterday," Mr. Ellis says. "McQuarters's interception was amazing. Now, that's football." And the dads energize. They do not make eye contact. But they lean into each other, clasping their wine, recalling the old game.

Mr. Windoner has thinning hair, once blond and now gray. He has a finely trimmed beard and a soft tan, with a long face and small bags under his gray eyes. Cait's dad has an Irish complexion. Wrinkles edge his eyes. There are creases on his forehead, emphasized with each furrow of his brow. He has a full head of sandy red hair, is clean-shaven, and tends to grab his wine more like a goblet than a glass.

Cait watches her mother sit down beside her father. It's the first time they have sat side by side in years. She thinks about how Blake made this happen. He knows what this means to her. *He does make life easier.* And she remembers his dependable nature. She knows that's partly his privilege. But she knew spoiled boys who were anything but reliable. And she looks at him and thinks, *It's nice to have things taken care of.* She looks around the yacht and thinks again, *This is nice.*

The afternoon fades this way. They drink lightly. Eat lightly. Take shelter in small talk. In the last hour of the day, they turn back to shore. Small waves splash off the boat. The sun nears the horizon. The distant land silhouettes black. The soft yellow sphere slides closer to the sea. A pink and orange line traces the wavelets and shows the path to port. Above the sun, a yellow fluorescence suffuses the sky. Below, the orange deepens, reddens, and gradates into dark clouds. Near the coast, sea gulls glide and chirp, as waves roll off the far shore. The water soon takes on a purple and pink shine, darker near land, glossier near them, until the ocean sleeps deep blue and the sun sinks into the land.

The yacht docks. Afterglow blends into dusk. Lamplight illuminates the wooden pier. Cait departs the boat and looks across the dock. There's a man standing on a small boat and turning a metallic crank. He's alone. She stops. Stares at him. And realizes it's him. *Taylor!* She thinks but does not move, does not blink. The others walk on. Questions fire through her. *Why's he here? How could he be here? What should I do? How could I do this to him?*

He rented the boat for them to sail. But Taylor read her text. Afterward, he went ahead anyway. He was determined to have his day.

Blake turns to Cait and calls to her, "C'mon, babe." She hears Blake but does not heed him. Blake persists loudly, "Cait." Taylor's head turns up.

Blake walks back to her. She feels Blake touching her lower back. She sees that Taylor sees. Their eyes meet. Her lower lip crinkles. Her eyes scream, *It's not what it looks like! I'm not where I want to be. Forgive me! I'm horrible, I know. I want to be with you.* But she does not move.

And Taylor does not move.

Cait takes one last long look at him. Taylor's body seems stuck in the sight of her. She looks at him, at her parents, at Blake, at Taylor again. She's paralyzed. And she does the only thing she can think to do. She turns her head down and walks away with her choice.

An hour later, a world later, Cait is in a new direction, the old direction, drifting. She's determined to push through the night, to finish it tonight, to make everything right. She frantically texts Taylor, apologizes, begs him to write her back. She tries to explain what happened. Two texts turn to five. She stops. No word from him. She exits the bathroom. Sees Mrs. Windoner. Cait pushes her pain deep. And so she will, in all her evening grace, perform. She will be more. She will hide all that is wrong. She hangs on to her determination to keep it together, to keep on, to be the vision people expect.

You know she's there by her echo. There is the material taste. The deep purple silk dress has black lace trim and is cinched at the waist with a skinny black belt. The dress drapes to her small knees, so easily, as if she is not trying. But she's trying so hard. How invisible that effort is. She walks with her shoulders back. She smiles that gracious smile. To the hostess. To the bartender. To the middle-aged couple who smile at her. She's unlike New York in that way. She not only knows what it is to be looked at, she looks back. And you no longer think she's beautiful. You feel beautiful.

But she does not feel beautiful. She walks through the onetime carriage house. She passes the chairs with floral patterns and the candlelit tables and the crimson wallpaper. She lets none of it inside her. She conveys what she thinks she must. She aches with regret. She thinks of Taylor. *On his birthday! How could I let this happen?* She wants to cry. But she finds her strength. Her mother's presence empowers her. And she pushes the pain deeper still. She thinks about the restaurant's name, Circa 1886. It feels like a cruel joke. She recalls the man who told them about the earthquake. She cannot believe that was last night. She wants to rewind the day, find Taylor, and run away. Cait feels outside of herself. It's as though she's floating beyond herself. She scarcely believes her motions. She's watching herself walk to the back of the restaurant. Toward Blake.

She takes it step by step. *Don't wallow in self-pity. This is your fault. Just get through the night. It's just a night. Just a dinner. You can fix this later.* Forward momentum. Polite nod by polite nod. Polite laugh by polite laugh. The food blurs by. Arugula salad with candied pecans. Roasted beets with duck confit. Seared scallops with shiitake mushrooms. The scallops are buttery and plump and have a crisp brown caramelized crust and a juicy tenderness inside. But she does not taste them. She tries the chilled lobster panna cotta. But it's as if she has lost her sense of smell. She's picturing Taylor on that boat. She's consumed by what happened. She is no longer considering what could happen. She thinks about how she turned away from Taylor. It hurts her to think of how that must have hurt him. The thought, however, provokes more resignation than resolve. She aches to tell her mother. And her mother senses that something is wrong. Their eyes meet. Cait flicks her eyes toward the restroom.

"If you'll excuse me, I'm going to the ladies' room," Cait says. She stands.

The men half stand.

"I'll join you," Erin says.

"I will as well," Mrs. Windoner says.

Cait feels that she can't get a break. And as they walk to the restroom, just as ignorance urges inaction, propriety propels its own motion.

Cait enters a stall. She checks her phone. No word from Taylor. The silence spurs anxiety. She takes a deep breath. She turns the steel knob. Deep breath. She walks out. Cait turns the faucet and watches the water pass over her hands and spiral into the drain. The three women stand by the mirror, small talk is said, nothing is said. What can be said? They return to the table. The main course awaits them. They drink white wine and eat their antelope loin and Carolina bass and black truffles with this and risotto with that. The anticipation is palpable. The course goes on. And dessert arrives.

Blake taps his glass with his fork. Ding. Ding. Cait tumbles inside herself. *Oh God.* She presses her teeth together, her lips together, her toes push into the ground.

"I want to thank Cait's parents for coming here with us. I would also like to thank you, Mother and Father, for being here as well and flying all of us down. I wanted us to be together today. I should've brought us together between Christmas and New Year's. I look forward, how should I say this, to many meals together not discussing politics." Polite laughter from all. Except Cait. Her lips remain locked. "It's like we're already family. And Cait"—Blake turns to her—"that's why I'm here, with our parents." He steps to her. Pulls out a small turquoise box. And kneels. He removes the white ribbon. The restaurant quiets. Everyone looks at her. Cait does not look at him, or the strangers, but to her mother. Her mother's eyes water. To her father, his mouth slamming closed to avoid tears. To Blake, on one knee, opening the box.

"Will you marry me, Cait?"

Breathing. Slow motion. Outside herself. The blur. *This is happening.* But it seems, to her, to be happening to someone else. And how lucky that girl looks. The handsome young man on one knee. The beautiful young woman. The large glimmering ring. What a pretty picture it makes. The diners gape. Strangers, parents, Blake waits. How it looks like fate. What was, for years, the desire of Cait. The room holds its breath. Split seconds aggregate. And the parents begin to wonder . . . *why is she pausing . . . is she in shock . . . Cait?* One woman rises. The other deflates. Cait glances at her parents, herself, swallows, musters a small voice, and drifts away.

". . . yes."

PART THREE

–

General Election, Continued

XXX

August
Washington, D.C.

"You know the *Times* reporter Cait Ellis?" Christian asks. Taylor's eyes stiffen. The Hilton bartender sets down their drinks. Christian gulps his second ginger ale as if he's trying to wash away the whiskey, but also the realization that three years of sobriety has just ended.

"Sure, I know her," Taylor says.

"Girona hit on her one night."

"What the fuck?" He forces himself to calm. "When?"

"How well do you know her?"

Taylor pauses. "I met her while I was covering Wallace. Hold on. What do you mean by 'hit on her?' When?"

"Around Christmas. In Iowa and—"

"And?"

"He made a pass at her during an interview. He told me he said she was pretty, and then immediately apologized. He said she ran away in a tizzy. But shit, I don't know what to believe."

"Why do you think the story's about her?"

"*Redline*'s editor told me the hotel and date. They match up. And knowing Joe, he may have done more."

Taylor stares down at his whiskey. He rubs his neck with his left hand and looks back at Christian. "What an asshole," Taylor says.

"I know it. Sometimes I wonder why I stick by him."

"Why do you?"

Christian shrugs. He tears at the cardboard coaster. "I've known Joe since law school. You know that old Washington jab—he has every quality of a dog but loyalty. I vowed that would never apply to me. But I don't know." Christian sighs. His leathery forehead compresses. "There's the Joe that can make a difference. And there's the Joe with women. I don't know why I thought the two could coexist, after Bill Clinton and everyone else."

"Yeah, well, Americans want presidents who are good family men."

"Why? After FDR, LBJ, JFK, Ike, Harding. Even Hamilton and Jefferson. They all had affairs. They were still great men."

"It was used against Jefferson," Taylor says.

"In the partisan press of his day, sure. But it was not considered public news for most of our history."

"A lot's changed."

"Sh*iii*t, obviously some things haven't."

"Everything has. The Internet alone. The media's desperate for content and clicks. People's lives became traceable online. But it also precedes all that. The sexual revolution. Women entering the White House press corps. You know all this."

"Sure, technology and values change. What I mean is, as our founding fathers understood, men's passions fundamentally do not—in every respect."

"Either way, if this gets out, it will dominate the news."

"So why didn't you report what you saw?" Christian asks.

"With Girona's wife in Iowa?"

"Yeah."

"It's just where I draw a line."

Christian continues to pick at his coaster. Shards litter the table like breadcrumbs. "Damn, I wish more people agreed."

"There is an argument for reporting it."

"For ratings."

"No. Girona framed himself as a family man. But I thought about that. All pols portray their family as the Beavers. Girona didn't oppose no-fault divorce. He didn't try to boot an opponent for having an affair. So it's not the equivalent of, say, a liberal who opposes public school vouchers but sends her own kids to private school."

Christian reaches into his pocket and pulls out the plastic container of antacid, pops another tablet, and chomps it. "You know what I keep thinking about? Fewer good men run today, partly because they don't want to surrender their privacy. And goddamn, do we really want only square or repressed people running our country? If there was more fucking around, more drinking, more horse trading, everyone would probably work together a helluva lot better."

Taylor smiles. "So excessive virtue becomes its own vice."

"Exactly."

"That's why practicing what you preach should be the benchmark."

"I wish. Don't ever underestimate a pol's ability to stand on a pedestal one day and lecture against that pedestal the next."

"It's like what Adlai Stevenson once said about Nixon."

"What's that?"

"Something like, Nixon is the kind of politician who'd cut down a redwood tree, then mount the stump for a speech on conservation."

"Nixon was always more like Washington than Washington ever wanted to acknowledge."

"That's what's starting to nauseate me about D.C."

Christian grimaces. "Don't become that sort."

"What sort?"

"One of those people who constantly bitch about how terrible it is in D.C. I've noticed a remarkable share keep living here, keep working here, and do little more than complain—if not worsen shit."

"So love it or leave it?"

"No. Listen, I'm not going to feed you crap about bettering it from the inside. But just don't continually scorn it and not do something about it, or leave it."

"I'm not continually." But then Taylor stops speaking and considers the point. "Anyway, this isn't germane. It's not black-and-white with Girona, regardless . . . wait though, about Cait Ellis—"

"Hold on. What's not black-and-white?"

"C'mon. Hypocrisy aside. D.C. bullshit aside. His wife's pregnant."

"Don't go there," Christian blurts back. "He can support his wife while she's pregnant—he always has, by the way, he loves her—and also have an affair. One is marriage. Standing by your spouse. The 'for worse' in 'for better and for worse.' And one is sex. They're different kinds of loyalty."

"I don't think you'll win over most women with that argument."

"I know. This is the shit that's only said in the company of men. I know this could ruin him. If it gets out, reporters will be hell-bent to find dirt on Joe. But Clinton survived it. Sure, today people forget how much the scandal aged and hurt him. But he outlasted the inquisition. And yes, it helped to be president at the time. But Joe basically is our nominee. Voters rally around their leader."

"If they must. It depends on the context."

Christian nods. "Damn. I know. It could be a shit storm. But if that happens, it'll be about more than framing your family as the Beavers."

"Meaning?"

"Meaning . . . shit, I'll tell you exactly what I mean." Christian rests his big elbows on the table. He pushes away the shredded coaster and rubs the hairy knuckles of his right fist into his left palm. "Here's this handsome, charming, rich, political superstar. And he's married to the everywoman. Sure, Sharon is pretty, but within norms. And she's a little overweight—which we polled and focus-grouped. Fat can humanize candidates and their spouses, if spun right. So here's this smart and sweet everywoman America loves. She grounded Joe, the way he's almost too good-looking, too charismatic. He is exactly the guy American women want to believe exists, especially within our base. The powerful and handsome man who does not stray, who stays with the first wife."

"He pushed that image."

"No." Christian slaps the table. "He didn't." Christian exhales and rubs the tabletop with his palm as if he's searching for friction. "Sorry. I've just been running over this in my mind too long. What I mean is . . . Joe didn't campaign as the romantic ideal or some feminist new man. Those images were projected onto him. That's why I'm worried it won't go like Clinton. We sensed from the outset that Bill was the conventional powerful man who chased tail. Joe was seen as better. I think if this gets out, most women will say they're offended because his infidelity occurred while his wife was pregnant. And that's real. But the anger will also stem from a sense of personal betrayal. Women thought he was the perfect man.

It's the goddamn romantic disappointment that could do him in."

Taylor hears Christian, but he can't stop thinking about Cait. He wants to know what transpired. How far did it go? Is *Redline* pressuring her too? But he dares not reveal how much he cares. So he talks on, waiting for a natural moment to shift back to her.

"But I guess the *why* ultimately doesn't matter," Christian adds. "I just don't know what I'm going to do."

"Listen," Taylor says, "this really could do Girona in. People will understand if you're done with him."

"No. You stick out your commitments. We still stand for admirable things."

"We? Don't fall down that D.C. rabbit hole. You're not your candidate."

"You know what I mean. He stands for admirable causes. Sure, if this comes out, we'll catch hell from all sides. Guys too. Male pundits will rush to criticize Joe. But they'll just be compensating. They're afraid to speak their minds around women. If they had his temptations and the balls to take risks and go after what they want—which, by the fucking way, partly explains why guys like Joe also succeed—most of these commentators would make similar mistakes. I don't know. Maybe that's simplistic. No, it's that simple. Balls are fucking balls, I guess. We just cannot say any of this out loud without the PC police going nuts and, i-fuckin'-ronically, stopping a free exchange of facts, of ideas."

"So it all comes back to hypocrisy."

Christian nods. "Shit, both sides do it. My side just pisses me off more because we claim to have open minds." Christian shakes his head. "Excuse me. I don't mean to rant. I've been thinking about this crap too long. It's maddening."

"The hypocrisy?"

"More like how we got here. I've consulted for lots of these guys over the years. The cheating risks everything, yet they can't help themselves. Sh*iii*t, I get it. Some of them come into their own late in life. They're unprepared for the temptations. But it'd be hard for most. I mean, how many older guys have hot chicks throwing themselves at them?"

"But Cait Ellis did not do that. If Girona hit on her, he crossed a big line."

"Maybe. *Redline* claims that something happened and . . . I don't know if they know more or are trying to gather something concrete." Christian presses his forehead into his palm. "You're probably right," he adds, tilting his head upward. "That doesn't take away from my larger point. But sure. This would be a mistake."

"It'd be a major fuckup," Taylor says. "If something happened, then he forced himself on her."

"Maybe."

"Cait Ellis has an impeccable reputation. If *Redline*'s right, he forced himself on her."

"She was really upset."

How upset? What the fuck did Girona do? Taylor drinks, swallows, focuses. "My point is, if he made an uninvited pass at her, anything like that, it's serious news."

"Hold on. You sure you don't know about Luke Brennan? Is this what he was chasing?" Christian asks.

"Even if I did, this conversation is unorthodox enough. I'm not going to start talking to you about what my colleagues are working on."

"Just remember, this is between *only* us."

"I know. I'm just saying, a consensual affair and sexual harassment are entirely different things. If Girona made an unwanted advance in that work dynamic, that's textbook harassment in any office. There should be a higher bar for workplace behavior when you're running for *the* office . . . Wait, where do you think this happened?"

"His hotel room."

"Were they alone?"

Christian nods.

Taylor shoots down the rest of his whiskey. "But why come to me? It's not because of Luke, is it? I hope you didn't expect me to leak shit about my coworkers?"

"No . . . so I've been straight with you. I need you now to be straight with me." Christian eyes Taylor. "I heard you had a thing with Cait Ellis."

Taylor does not flinch. "Who said that?"

"You know how people gossip on the trail. It's none of my business, I know. But I suspect my emails go to her SPAM. We spoke once. She's ignored my calls since. If you have, or had, a relationship with her, she trusts you. I need to know what really happened. Do you have a relationship with her? Did you ever?"

"No."

"You know what they say, don't bullshit a bullshitter." He scratches his neck. "I need help here. I know you're private. But I've seen you in past campaigns, going off with some babe."

Taylor wishes he could think of it as a fling. He has tried to forget Cait. It took months for him to accept what happened. He was already thrown by the random encounter, earlier in the week, with Cait's mother at Sofia's book party. Now this. He wants to leave and call Cait. He recalls that day at the Iowa diner. She asked what he would do if something unwanted occurred off the record. *I should've picked up on it.* He feels like an idiot. *But maybe she didn't want to talk about it. Still, why didn't she tell me? I could've been there for her.* He wonders if he misjudged what they had. Maybe I'm searching for an excuse to reach out to her.

"Taylor," Christian persists.

"No, I'm sorry, I can't help you. I never had anything with Cait Ellis."

XXXI

And just like that, she reenters the present tense of his life. Washington has cooled with the rain. Taylor ignores it. He exits the Hilton, combs his fingers through his hair, and tries to get his head around what Christian told him.

He's glad he did not confide in Christian. He had only told his best friend, Gabriel, about Cait. He spoke about it one night, months ago, when he was home. But not after that. He did not want his friends to have to listen to it. He thought about how countless women, countless men, for countless ages, have felt what he feels. He told himself that thinking about it was redundant, indulgent, or, worse, sentimental. Taylor is a product of his time. He's a natural romantic in an anti-romantic age, when "sentimental" became a slur, as hot turned cool, as cool turned disinterested, and passion became passé. He sees how the highbrow arbiters of culture esteem irony, matter-of-fact words, the sensible life, the sarcasm and satire that shield vulnerability, that stifle sincerity. He doesn't want to embrace those values. But few people are beyond the reach of their time. So he keeps it within him. In his mind, everyone has their problems, their excuses, their reason to break. And his are small. Journalism, at least the journalism he once practiced, reminds him of that. He thinks about how there are people with real problems. He feels no right to be this upset. He recalls a line from *The Grapes of Wrath*: "Anybody can break down; it takes a man not to."

What breaks is within him, not without, not the visible him. He leaped before he looked. Again. He never considered it could end so badly, so abruptly. He feels quixotic and ashamed. He's questioning his instincts for the first time in his adult life. Optimism to a fault, he concludes. He is, for all these reasons, impatient with himself. Yet there's a difference between how he thinks he should feel and how he feels. And the deeper thing often wins with him, eventually. However much he left her in the past, however foolish he feels, however much he demeans his feelings, they exist. He is these feelings. And he still loves her.

Yet as he walks, he realizes this incident is not about him. He is compelled to warn Cait. So he writes: "Hi Cait, I want to let you know about something. It regards an incident in Iowa. I'm writing as a friend. I'll explain. However you want to get in touch, you should. Contact me anytime."

He sends the email. It does not sit well with him. He believes she should be the one reaching out to him. She walked away from him. But he wants to be bigger than that. He notices a missed call from Luke. He thinks back to earlier that day and wonders if Luke has anything else on the woman from the book party, Saundra Winston, and whether her husband's firm is forming an unscrupulous relationship with Girona to fund NxtGen. He considers that the NxtGen story, if there is a story, will become meaningless if this scandal comes out. He wonders if Luke is still chasing this scandal, or something related. He calls Luke back. No answer. He remembers that the Republican operative, Jason, tried to reach him earlier. He decides to deal with him later. He thinks about how entangled he's become in the D.C. swap. He's exhausted by it. He trudges uphill to his apartment building and thinks about Ava, the ex-girlfriend he was with this morning in New York. He cannot expel her words from his mind. *You're becoming a bitter old man.* And the words hurt because they are true.

But he does not have the space inside himself to deal with that. His thoughts keep returning to Cait. He begins to wrestle, all over again, with why she chose Blake. He had wondered, though he was ashamed of the thought, whether Blake's wealth was a factor. He knew he might have framed her choice in the worst light to mitigate the rejection he felt. He is curious, still to this day, if she chose Blake partly out of passivity. He considers the power of the known choice. But that seems at odds with the woman he knew. Yet he appreciates that people are rarely one way in every way.

XXXII

Earlier That Day

Luke Brennan sits between stacks of manila folders. His chubby shoulders are tensed up to his earlobes. He feels a spasm of upper-back pain, reaches around his neck, and rubs his left trapezius, as he does unconsciously throughout the day. It was another world ago, while still at Ohio State, that he joined Wayne Barrett's army of summer interns. Barrett's a New York investigative journalism legend. In his first months at *Current*, Luke favored a Barrett axiom: There's no Democratic or Republican way to rob the public till; it's the robbing that counts. Yet Luke no longer speaks this way.

Luke's break came with the New York *Daily News*. He was twenty-six, a reporter in the city. He was working for the paper that inspired Superman's *Daily Planet.* Sure, the Daily News building was sold long ago. But few American newspapers could afford their towers anymore. The NYC dailies are luckier than most. New Yorkers have time to read on the subways, trains, ferries. In Manhattan, from Sixtieth Street down, on weekdays between 8:00 and 8:59 a.m., more than a thousand people arrive every six seconds by subway. Even then, before tablets and smartphones began replacing print on the train, public transportation could subsidize only so many reporters. The *Daily News* laid off Luke after seven months. He was one more victim of a 5 percent cut. Last in, first out, as union life goes.

After some hard years, he got a job with *The Washington Post* covering Northern Virginia schools. He called it "The education beat for the spoiled children of the WWT." That was his term for the "wealthy Washington tit"—top bureaucrats, lawyers, lobbyists, and the tax-subsidized industries, none more than defense contractors. A year in, he heard about *Current*, applied, and became one of *Current*'s investigative reporters. It was his dream job.

But those expectations feel foreign to him these days. He tells himself this is the way it is. He's an adult. Besides, aren't hard-news reporters supposed to be cynical?

So he tries to roll with it. There's a new conservative documentary premiering tomorrow. It skewers Joe Girona. Last night, Girona's campaign fed Peter Miller documents debunking the film's allegations. And as Peter waited for his flight out of Savannah this morning, he told Luke that he was too busy to do the story. Peter sent him the documents in separate emails. Peter rarely leaves an email thread to trace. He also regularly deletes sensitive emails from the server. Luke sensed that Girona was the source. He knew a dirt dump. "You can always smell a dump," Luke sometimes joked.

In a fresh email, Peter asked Luke, "Can you take this over?"

Luke replied, "I'm working a few stories."

He didn't trust Peter's motives. Peter made time for news. Maybe Peter didn't want his name on the article. All day, the conservative media has criticized Peter over the yacht story. Peter couldn't, so soon after, author this attack on a right-wing documentary and appear biased. Or so Luke assumed.

Peter replied, "Write it quickly. You'll be glad you did. The story will have legs."

"I can probably get to it later."

Fresh email. From, "Peter Miller." Subject, "Ding."

Arlington, Virginia. Girona's national headquarters could be mistaken for an Internet start-up. The leadership has glass offices that line one side. The remaining space is vast with minimalist furniture. Yet for all its size, it's cramped with hundreds of workers, mostly young diehards, eyes on their laptops, typing elbow to elbow, crowding the shiny maroon tables. Several young men pace the gray carpet, reading their phones and seemingly talking to themselves, as they use tiny single-ear headsets for calls. The foosball table is dusty, with campaign yard signs piled atop it. In the kitchen, a refrigerator carries a reminder to throw out old food. Empty Chinese food containers are stuffed into trashcans. Overhead, a banner reads WINNING THE DREAM.

Girona's communications director sits in his office and stares blankly at the banner, as he checks *Current* periodically. He refreshes the page. He's waiting for Peter's story to publish and discredit the documentary.

No one here knows about the potential sex scandal, not even the communications director. Christian, alone among the staff, ponders whether it will all fall apart. The campaign aides feel on top of the race and, accordingly, on top of the world, because this is their only world until Election Day. Girona's spokespeople intend to stay ahead. So they act as if it's any other day and fixate on winning the news day. Their goal is to preemptively dissuade mainstream reporters from discussing the documentary.

The documentary carries two incendiary charges. The first: "Girona socializes with drug lords." The source of this accusation is a small *Miami Herald* story published four years ago. Girona's brother-in-law invested in a land deal with a convicted drug trafficker. Neither Girona nor his wife was implicated in any malfeasance. The mainstream media decided it had nothing to do with Girona. The accusation also reinforced a negative stereotype of Latinos, so the national media avoided it. Wallace left it alone for the same reason. She put out word: do not push this story. She didn't want to win that way.

The other allegation, which is about the Mexican border, is based on an incident that happened seven years ago, in Minneapolis. Girona was on a panel with influential Latinos. It included a hard-news correspondent from MSNBC, a prominent Latino academic from Berkeley, and Girona. The discussion was broadcast on NPR. The documentary features this portion:

> Academic: It may be appropriate to see the Americas united into one nation.
>
> Host: I want to be sure that we understand you. People of all stripes are listening. You are all prominent Latinos. Do you all think we cannot be a moral nation and have borders?
>
> The MSNBC correspondent: This continent did not have borders once, not so long ago. Consider the ignorance out there. Most Americans who call Mexican immigrants illegals, don't even know that Mexico is in North America.
>
> Host: That aside, what I've heard here is 'bring down the border.' It's merger with Mexico. And that's fine?
>
> MSNBC correspondent: Oh my god, I can see the headline—three prominent Latino Americans declare that it should be a borderless country.

The recording captures the panelists laughing. It's unclear whether Girona is laughing. The diplomat knew when to be silent. But the documentary reports that Girona was laughing. At that point, he is heard saying, "I'm always open to ideas." The documentary's narrator follows: "What is Joe Girona open to? What is he not telling us? Girona may think it's funny to give up our nation's sovereignty. America takes in more legal immigrants than every other country combined. But like every successful nation, we also want to protect our borders. Does Girona? Is this why Girona says he's a 'citizen of the world?' Is Joe Girona yet another liberal who thinks patriotism is a joke?"

Cait Ellis sits with reporters in the back of an American Legion hall in Lexington, South Carolina. Wallace speaks her stump speak. Prosperity. Peace. Pork. Debt. Protect. Hard things. Hard calls.

Wallace wants to leave the yacht story behind her. So she decided to return to the trail. To move on. To campaign harder. She stands in a red pantsuit in front of a giant American flag, relaxed, as if she's more comfortable fighting than courting. "Today, the media and Democrats . . . but I repeat myself." Conservatives laugh. And she betrays the trace of a smirk. "The media is obsessed with silly stories about boats. But I have news for them. Americans have serious concerns. These are serious times. I will rise to the challenge. I hope you will stand with me."

Cait yawns. Checks her phone. She skims her email and a few political news feeds. At that moment, the documentary's publicist tweets "Exclusive, Joe Girona endorsed merging Mexico and US!" The publicist concluded the tweet with campaign hashtags, those commonly read by reporters. Cait notices the tweet. She glances left and right. Her colleagues must not see it. She has not covered Girona since that night at his hotel. She has compartmentalized what transpired. The distance has granted her emotional distance. She thinks this report is small-bore but also fair game. It occurs to her, this is what attracts Twitter followers. She can get more followers. Her editor asked her to do that. This feels tabloid to her. But she may be the first to see it. Seconds accumulate. It's not like she's reporting it. She retweets the news, forwarding it to her 14,233 followers.

One minute and thirty-four seconds later. Jason, the GOP operative, sits in his small D.C. office. There are no windows. A large file cabinet is behind him. Drawers list names such as Joe Girona and Miles Riley. Jason sees Cait's tweet. The biography on Cait's Twitter page describes her as a "National Political Correspondent, *The New York Times.*" Jason sees a way out. Talking heads are fixating on the yacht story. Give them something else to chew on. He sends Cait's tweet to *Drudge.*

Three minutes and forty-nine seconds later. *Drudge* posts a red headline: Times Reporter: Girona Endorsed Open Borders . . .

Twenty-three seconds later. Cait has received more than thirty emails. They cite *Drudge.* She goes to *Drudge.* And gasps. Both her hands are against her mouth. She wonders if she can reach Matt Drudge. She considers deleting the tweet.

One minute and thirty-one seconds later. Girona's communications director emails Cait. "Your tweet is a mistake.

That's not Girona laughing. The 'open to ideas' quote is from later during the panel; it was about something else. This documentary is bull! Fox saw it on *Drudge* and is re-reporting it as a *Times* report. You must stop this meme. Issue a retraction."

Cait hardens. No spokesperson can dictate what she "must" do. She replies: "See my bio's disclaimer. I note that neither the *Times* nor I endorse what I retweet."

Fourteen seconds later. Communications director replies: "No difference to *Drudge* and the public. You must correct."

Cait stops typing on her phone. She sees his point. She checks her phone. She now has 213 emails on the matter.

Three minutes and thirty-seven seconds later. Cait's editor calls Cait. Girona's communications director has already spoken with him.

Editor says, "Hi Cait."

"Hi. Hold on a sec."

Cait walks outside to take the call. Cars speed by. The sun highlights the cracks in the concrete. Across the street, kids rush out of a rusty minivan and enter a Dairy Queen. "Sorry. I'm back," she says.

"I'll get right to the point. Arlington called me. I saw *Drudge.* I think Girona's staff is right about this. We need to correct this thing on Twitter with, ah, a tweet."

"I cannot believe this BS. *Drudge* claims I'm reporting this. You know that's untrue. Did you see my bio's disclaimer?"

"But you're *our* reporter. You represent the *Times.* Your tweet could be construed as a *Times* report. We need you to retract this."

"This is absurd. You told me to tweet more."

"I know. Not like this, though . . . Cait, what would you advise if you were the editor here?"

Cait exhales. “A retraction.”

“Please take care of it.”

“Okay.”

Thirty-four seconds later. Back in her seat, Cait tweets: “My previous retweet was NOT an endorsement. I note in my Twitter biography that retweets never are.” A second tweet: “The report may be false as well.” Third tweet: “I apologize if I gave the impression I endorsed this report. It remains unsubstantiated to my knowledge.” Fourth tweet: “I apologize for any false story line I created. I hope *Drudge* will take down the link.”

Wallace speaks on. Cait stares blankly at her phone. Her hands fall to her lap. She's angry with herself. She knows better. She closes and reopens her eyes. She's never made a public journalism slip. She feels an impulse to call Taylor. She thinks he might know a way to reach Matt Drudge. *Current* is alleged, across D.C. media, to be uncommonly close to Drudge. She dearly would like to hear Taylor's voice. But she knows she cannot call him. She made her choice. She wonders whether this brief lapse in judgment will permanently sully her reputation. She checks *Drudge* again. The link is still up. She checks her phone again. There's an email from her mother. *Jesus, is the great woman on Twitter now too?* And then she gulps. She sees Taylor's email. Opens it. It's professional. There's no warmth. And that hurts her. But she's also stunned by what he wrote. She thought that incident was behind her. She does not know how Taylor could know what transpired between her and Girona. She wonders . . . *maybe Luke is still chasing the story. Could he have spoken to Taylor? Would Taylor have told Luke about our relationship? No. Oh God, it's so good to hear from him.*

Girona's communications director runs his fingers through his moppy-blond hair and closes his leaden eyes. *Drudge* rekindles his anxiety about representing a minority candidate. He worries that the documentary will stir lingering racism. He gave Peter the material to preempt the attack. But there's no story yet.

Peter's plane squeals against the runway. He was delayed an hour on the tarmac, but he was not allowed to use his phone. It infuriated him. How could he be on the ground, on earth, and out of touch? The plane taxis to its gate. Peter grabs his phone. He sees the barrage of emails from Girona's campaign. "When are you running your story?" "You said it would be up by now! We need to know ASAP, or we'll give it to someone else." "Should we be working with the *Post* or the *Times* on this?" Peter checks *Drudge.* He discerns what happened. Emails Luke: "Pls send me the story."

Luke types between those manila stacks. "I didn't have time."

Peter sends a new email. Subject: "CATASTROPHE." Body: "IT WOULD'VE BEEN A TINY INVESTMENT OF YOUR TIME, AND WELL WORTH IT. I hope you will reassess."

Luke hears the cleaning lady's vacuum. She's twenty paces away. That's all he hears. The printers are not warming up. This is Peter Miller. *Current*'s Olympian reporter. P&R's golden boy, or man. Luke thinks this is ludicrous. He has bigger stories to chase. And regardless, Rick agreed that he didn't have to write the article. Luke is unsure how to respond. He calls Taylor to see if he has anything new on the NxtGen story.

That way, Luke can describe to his editor what he worked on instead of Peter's story. No answer. He looks up and sees a *Fox News* report about the documentary. He checks *Drudge*. Cait's tweet is the headline. He scratches the back of his head. Clasps his hands. His sausage fingers intertwine. His arms stretch and straighten upward.

Ten minutes pass. Rick walks over, ducking his head abashedly, rubbing his blond buzz cut. "You need to do that story," he tells Luke.

"Dude, you said I didn't."

"I know." Rick's tone is calm and paternal. "But Peter called me. I guess Arlington is all over him."

"But you're the boss."

"Just do it."

"Why is Girona's office even on his case?"

Rick looks back at Luke skeptically. "Just do it. It's an easy lay-up."

Luke nods. He writes the article. The story's true. The documentary is a hit job based on false reports. But Luke doesn't want to be another propaganda instrument, another reporter who writes words like "exclusive," giving the air of a scoop but actually only reporting what a campaign wants reported. Most scoops derive from leaks, which serve another's agenda. But the good reporter verifies. Double sources. Filters. Luke usually does that. But the pressure is too much. The deadline too soon. He notes that the material came from a rival operative. But he did not fact-check it. He trusted Peter. Yet Peter, also short on time, expected Luke to verify the dirt. Luke's pushing a campaign's agenda. That's what annoys him. He feels more like a printer than a reporter.

Luke sends the story to his editors. Eight minutes later Peter writes an email to P&R, CC-ing Luke. Subject: "Great work." Body: "Luke did some great work tonight. He recognized a good story and he acted on it quickly. It will be big tomorrow. He really moved the ball forward! Great work, Luke!"

Luke's phone rings. It's Taylor, calling him back. But the incident's over. Luke doesn't want to talk about it anymore. He did his job. The next story needs writing. His last story defines him. There's a publishing metabolism. *Current* sped it up. It must be kept up. The beast must feed.

Luke has his reasons to keep it up. It's what his bosses demand. DCland wants to know the news first. *Current* wants to define in-the-know. Politics is an industry of information. But knowing the news sooner, in Washington, is more important than knowing it deeper.

And Luke needs the work. He has a mortgage, a young wife, a newborn. And there are upsides. Luke's on television. He's influential. He's a player. He's still writing takedowns. He does organic stories too. They're often uncooked. But there's meaty work. Sure, he chases some sensational news. But he tries to do hard news too. He has some liberty to do that work, or the promise of it. Promise is something. People grasp onto far less than real promise. He's still checking power, sometimes. He's not merely a butcher dealing in processed food. He hunts.

Luke's adrenaline still rises with the hunt. The meat tastes better when it's your kill. When it's deserved. He still wants *it.* He sees a scrum of reporters and wants in. He cuts in. He'll get the meat. The blood. The people must know! The people have a right to know! There remains a sense of mission. And maybe the hunts are rare. Maybe he often scavenges. Maybe some pursuits prostitute his ideals. Maybe the ceaseless deadlines, the constant critics, the public exposure of your mistakes, that your errors linger online like a bad day that never ends—maybe it leaves him perpetually anxious, often at his wit's end. Maybe the hard days mount and he works on fumes, reaching for energy drinks and pills, anything to get through the deadline, to survive the pressure—to win the minute, to tweet it first, to blog and broadcast and break news, to get the clicks or be cast aside. Because, he knows, beyond his felt cubicle, across the fluorescent-lit newsroom, on his boss's desk, is a résumé pile six inches high, old media refugees who ache to do his job, to be in the center of history as it happens, to turn the future around and turn off the television, unplug the Internet, restart the presses, and make newsmen matter once more.

So he will do the stories that must be done. He'll work those big bank hours, those big law hours, for middle-class pay. He'll sometimes place his byline above stories he's ashamed he wrote. He may even appear on cable news to compensate for the gap between his ideals and his reality, if only to feel significant in some respect. But at least he retains those ideals. He wants to fight the good fight. He aches for the noble takedown, to feel true to his principles once more. Sure, he is a dashed idealist. But at least his disappointment is for the *right* reasons. At least he retains his ideals. He still hopes to be the people's watchdog, to call out hypocrisy, to expose corruption. And how many of us can say that much about our lives?

XXXIII

Cait's plane descends along the river, past skyscrapers and bridges, as the sun reflects off towers, streaks the water, and the city feels balanced, at peace, like some mirage of the way it never was, or could be.

She has the day off. Her boss said she needed a break after the Twitter incident. The conventions begin Monday. She'll work hard enough, soon enough. So the *Times* assigned someone else to Wallace for a few days.

But she cannot relax. She has time to think about what's wrong. She picks at a cuticle on her finger, as she sits at her desk chair, Indian style, in a white cotton tank top and black leggings. Her hair is flat, undone. The window-mounted air conditioner roars on high. Her bedroom has rose-colored wicker furniture, a matching dresser, a nightstand. Some of her clothes are piled atop a blue fabric ottoman. There are discarded balls of paper on the floor beside her chair. She touches her cheek and struggles with how to write to Taylor. She wishes it could be simple. She feels unmoored—from yesterday's incident, from what Taylor wrote her, from being in touch with him again. She wants to see him. She can't bear to go online and read the criticism, how she's "another liberal media flack for Girona" or an "apologist who doesn't deserve her byline." She is still mad at herself for tweeting about the documentary, but she worries far more about what may come. She thought it was over. Luke pursued her. But she did not speak to him. If Taylor knows something, Luke must still be chasing the story. But she believes there's no chance Girona would say anything, nor Christian. There can be no story without a credible source. But the conclusion does not rest as easily as it arrives.

She impulsively texts Taylor: "Hi. Got your message. Thank u. So nice to hear from u."

Two minutes pass. No response.

"Can we tlk?" she asks.

"Sure."

That's it? Why isn't he writing more? At least he replied. At least he'll still talk to me. She texts back: "I know u wrote me for work reasons but I've missed u." She stares at her phone. Waiting. He replies: "Me too." Cait feels the dam break. Emotion overwhelms her. What they had. What she lost. What she kept herself from feeling since. But all she writes back is: ":)" Then she adds: "When can u tlk?"

"In a few mins."

"Great. I'll call on my landline."

"You're not with Wallace?"

"No, in the city." And she hesitates. Then texts: "Wish u were 2." She sees the words on her phone. She wishes she could reach in and pull them back.

"I saw what happened," he replies. "The Twitter thing. U ok?"

"More worried about the other thing."

And he writes back, "I can come into the city tomorrow."

"Really?!" And as seconds pass, and he does not reply, she can almost feel him regretting the words.

"Y," he texts.

"U sure?"

"I'm sure."

":)"

And anxiety accrues. She knows she shouldn't "need" him. She did not choose him seven months ago. Questions sprint through her head. *What can she say to him? How will it feel to see him? What does he know about Girona? What could he know? Why does he know anything about Iowa? Oh God, it will be so great to see him.* And memories overwhelm her, of their last day in Charleston. She recognizes that she was the first to walk away, but he was the last.

Cait did not sleep with Blake in Charleston. She has since, of course. But she would not then. She wanted to withhold something. They spent the day together after the engagement. Lunch and shopping and dinner. Blake flew back the following afternoon. She waved goodbye to him. His cab turned the corner. And she took out her phone and called Taylor, and this time he answered.

That same afternoon, Cait met Taylor at a Charleston pier. It was one of those places of bygone maritime commerce, once alive, later corroded, eventually abandoned, and recently resuscitated. Urban restoration is fashionable and lucrative these days. Defer property taxes a decade, fifteen-year abatements, just get the white folks back. Reverse their parents' migration from city to burb. White kid flight is urban bound, where they will cherish diversity even as they push out the black and brown. For the hipsters do come. Artists and posers. Then the gays. It became a real estate maxim: follow the gays. The creative professionals soon arrive. And, in time, yuppies. Staples spread with them. Liquor stores take down the bulletproof glass and stock Moët. Coffee shops open. Rows of glowing Apple icons. The first yoga studio appears. Fresh sushi. Organic grocers. Vegan brownies, Tofurky, and dried kale chips. Dank bars fade. Chic bars open. The remaining dank bars become cool. *This joint is like it once was, maaan.* Industrial lofts become luxury doorman lofts. More coffee shops. They serve fair-trade sustainable drip coffee. Jazz nights. French bistros. Mayonnaise with fries. Bikram. Cold-pressed juice. And then the apocalypse. Bugaboo! The strollers are coming. And the first children's boutique opens. So it's declared: the neighborhood is dead.

Hipsters migrate to trendier turf—read: more affordable—providing it's close enough to the urban pulse. And they gentrify another black or brown or Polish area. Claim it as their own. These black-clad colonists. These grim reapers of affordable housing. And the cycle recycles, as once more, bohemia beckons bankers. And naysayers graffiti: Yuppie scum! T-shirts read: "Your condo is ugly." Nostalgic purists rant. Oh, those good old days, of lower rents and more murders, of no gentrification but, sure, segregation. An ongoing NYC tale as yuppies streamed upward into Harlem, and it became a majority non-black neighborhood, and even the Anglos who wanted to be hip, who understood how white people can bleach, spread this way, over decades, into Soho, from the West to the East Village, down to the Lower East Side, into Williamsburg, and now Bushwick. As mantras proliferated: "Brooklyn is the new Manhattan." The hipster doth protest too much. So it went nationwide, into Cleveland's Flats, from Milwaukee's East Side to its Third Ward, westward, to remold even LA, where the Warehouse District was rebranded the Arts District. Really, it was worldwide. Tour the bygone

Communist bloc, from East Berlin to Tallinn, and see white-on-white gentrification, yet another trend Americans thought was about them. And how newcomers do embrace it. For even this corner of Charleston was reborn. The new pier stretched out over the river and tall marsh grass, and people did walk along the water and feel something fine.

Taylor wanted to be outside. She met him here, at the pier, on a mid-sixties winter day. Cait saw him at the edge of the walkway. As she neared him, she watched him. The breeze pushed his white linen shirt against his chest. The wind blew his hair back. And then she came close enough to make out his eyes. And they were hard.

Cait wore no ring. She didn't want Taylor to see it before she said it. Then she said it. He looked back at her in disbelief. His hardness fell away. Anger, incredulity, eddied in his glassy light blue eyes. He asked, raising his voice but not yelling, what was she doing? How could she say yes to a man she did not love? And she replied, He loves me. You never even said you loved me. And Taylor told her, I love you! And it took all of her will not to cry. Cait, he said, I'm here because I'm in love with you. You must know that. You don't need words to know that. And she said, No, Taylor, some things need to be said. Some things need words. You're a writer, for God's sake. And he understood. He said, Cait, I would've said it eventually. We're just beginning. He told her, I'm saying it now. And, come on, you never said it either. It doesn't mean it's not real. But, shit, now this. And he exhaled, adding, I guess I don't know what to think now. He asked her, Aren't you falling in love with me? And she hesitated and shook her head, but then she nodded yes and shrank. Her shoulders caved. Her lips pressed together in a pained and unyielding line. Her eyes grew heavy. She looked away. Turned back. Her eyes reddened. And she pleaded, I love you. I do. Nothing has changed! And Taylor replied, Everything has changed. You're engaged. Don't you know in life, you also say no when you say yes.

Taylor found her passivity infuriating, nauseating, and finally, like the last punch a man can take, debilitating. How could a woman who seemed so strong be so weak? So passive. He thought these things as she took his hand and, again, said she loved him. But she paused. The dam was rebuilt. And she let go of his hand. The other Cait took charge. She reached for her choreography. She explained. She and Blake had been together more than three years. They made sense together. Their families were there. Both my parents were brought together, she said. He made that happen. He makes things easier. She insisted, Taylor, you mean everything to me. But sometimes we don't marry the person we love most. And Taylor asked himself, Where did she get that line? Maybe, he thought, it was true for women who had to save families, some Austen novel, but how ironic was that, considering their offhand remarks a world ago in New Hampshire. The words felt true but contrived, if possible, that's how they felt to him, as if they came from someone else, some author who authentically felt these things, and she wielded those words to affirm her yes and her no. Taylor said, You don't have to do that. I know you love me. We are the authors of our own fate. And he damned passivity to the deep hell of misspent lives. He told her, You can marry who you love. This is the twenty-first fucking century. And he calmed his voice. And she replied, Who knows if you'll want to marry me. Blake's committed to me. Guys like you date girls for years and don't propose. I see it all the time in the city. She looked at him as if she felt her words were not sinking in. Taylor, I'm serious, I know too many women who have wasted their twenties on guys like you. And he responded, I get it. But I'm not *just* some guy. I'm here. I was all in. I *am* all in. I thought we had something rare. And real. We have something real.

And she felt like a woman without arms who falls into the ocean. She wanted to say she loved him, would still be with him, could still make them work, how she loves him now. And she said, Nothing's changed. Her voice raised. I'm in love with you, don't you know? He searched her red eyes. She was half crying. And then she found the strength. And her choreography returned and carried her. She said, I *did* love you.

Past tense came over them, parting them, like dirty gray shelf clouds. But he did not believe her. He said he still loves her. That she was making the mistake of her life. And when she was old, and life felt behind her, she would wish she chose him. He said there's time. But at some point it will be too late and there will not be time. He placed his hands on the top of her arms. His palms cupped her shoulders. And she stood there, wanting him to hold her. He moved strands of hair off her forehead. And her eyes flooded red. A tear rolled down her cheek. He wiped the tear away and kissed her. She became limp and closed her eyes and loved him all over again. He pulled back as she tilted in. She felt the last touch of his lips until they were gone, and there was only air and the absence of him. He said quietly, Whatever is right for you is right. He told her he loved her and he would not pressure her, but she should think about what she'll regret more. And he kissed her right cheek, her left, her forehead, aware of what each touch did to her, especially the last. He said, It does not need to end here, but I'm getting too old for lost causes. He brushed those wisps of her hair to the side once more. You have to decide, he said, what you want, and choose, because it's not what you want in life that counts, but what you do. And he withdrew his hand and with it went his touch and with his touch went him—as he walked away, wood plank by wood plank, as distance grew between them, as she stood motionless, watching him. And he did not look back.

She did not expect him to never look back. Taylor left the Wallace caravan after that day. She's longed to see him again. But she thought it was unfair to contact him unless she could be more to him. He was rarely on Facebook. She could go on Facebook and see what childhood friends in France ate for lunch. But not him. She has friends who posted photos of their pets on Instagram. But he was not on Instagram. She didn't think anyone needed to be this distant, these days. But he was like that. She still read all of his stories. She once saw him from afar at a debate. But he looked away. And Cait knew it had to be that way. She was a woman who honored her superego. She made her choice. She looked at him, felt regret, wished he would turn back. But he did not. So she thought she had to honor that. But the next day she missed him more. She found a website that records television news. She found segments of him and watched. She searched for his mood. But she only found him going on, talking politics. There was no sign of the inner man. And there she found emptiness. And in the emptiness was loss.

Today, she cannot imagine going through all that again. She cannot see him walk away again. She says these things to herself. She tells herself to stop thinking about him. To, instead, pay attention to why he wrote her. But if it were as easy as that, they never would have been what they were. Cait tells herself to deal with her career, to keep it professional with him, to remember why she chose Blake. She believes some choices are only honored if honored all the way.

Taylor never reached out to her after walking away. Nor did she reach out to him. She refused to be unrealistic. The more time that passed, the easier it was to tell herself that her choice was the only practical one. But now he's back. She cannot envision seeing him as a mere friend. And that scares her. She looks at her phone. Part of herself says, *Speak to him by phone, keep your distance, don't see him.* But, in a rare instance, she pushes away what she thinks is right and goes with what she feels is right.

XXXIV

At NBC's Washington headquarters, Taylor steps out of a black corporate town car. He has a scheduled appearance on MSNBC. In the lobby, he stands before the bulletproof glass. He gives his name to the security guard. A producer escorts him. The long hallway is decorated with posters of NBC shows. Taylor sits in the green room, thinking about how he'll soon see Cait in New York. He lounges back on the couch and smiles.

The makeup woman retrieves him. He sits before the vanity mirror. She places a paper bib around his neck. Powder is dabbed. He returns to the green room. Drinks a Coke. He moves to a studio. He's alone in the room. He stares at the camera. Someone checks his sound levels. One, three, five, seven . . . good. Producer says hello. Minutes pass. And he's live. He answers questions. Hears the anchor's voice in his ear. Talks to the inanimate camera. The segment lasts one minute and fifty-one seconds. Thank-yous are said. Earpiece out. He leaves. All that, for as little as that.

Forty-five minutes later, he arrives at Union Station and walks beneath the vast sunlit archway that is adorned with octagons of gold leaves. Trailblazing news blogger Mickey Kaus sits on a bench, bent over in a brown jacket, typing, ignoring the tides of commuters rushing past him.

Train to New York City. Taylor ascends the narrow stairwell into the yellow bowels of Penn Station. He's walking within the pale shadow of a once-majestic city entryway. It was demolished in the name of progress. Now there's merely progression. Escalator to street level. Exit. The city's vertigo brings him balance. It's familiar. Commuters' arms tight to their sides, swinging, pecking, walking their rush-hour walk. Honks. Yellow cabs shoving, spurting, whizzing. The sun splits towers. Humid August air. The squeal of trucks breaking. Manhattanites dashing for trains out of town. Taylor enjoys August weekends in the city. It's quiet. And now. Here. He savors all that is not quiet. The immensity. Intensity. It swells his veins. He'll have to go back. But he's here now. He's about to see Cait. He feels a sense of new beginnings. This is where people have always come to begin again. Because in this city, you can go home again.

Dark clouds crowd the sky. The wind gusts between towers, stirs leaves, slaps hats off New Yorkers. Rain shoots down like BB-gun pellets. Manhattanites dash beneath awnings. Umbrella salesmen appear. The rain stops. And the city carries on.

Taylor walks out from under the green awning at the NYU Starbucks. He enters Washington Square Park from the southeast corner. He walks over the walkway's hexagon stone tiles. Sunlight winks through the shale sky. The wind is calmer. The mugginess is gone. The sun breaks out. Clouds flee. Washington Square Park is damp and glossy with light.

Taylor looks for her near the white arch. They agreed to meet here. The rain delayed him. He's still eleven minutes early. He didn't want to appear eager. But she's been on his mind. He has not seen Cait, up close, for seven months. He saw her at one debate. Across the way. He looked and looked away. He did not want to let himself feel it all over again, to return to that place where he gave all of himself and she turned away. She would contact him if she wanted to see him. So he presumed. He was resolved to leave her in the past like that. He ached to look back at her that day on the Charleston pier, on so many days. But he refused to let himself.

Until now. He waits. He can hardly believe he's about to see her. There's a sense of contending tides of air tunneling between buildings, down Fifth Avenue, through the streets, and into the park, like small rivers feeding the sea. A man walks by holding a folded chessboard. "Brother, you look like jazz," the man says. Taylor nods. His eyes search for her in the crowd. They move with patient assurance. He begins to imagine how they'll spend the day. He leaps into images, like some movie montage that has yet to pass. *It'll be amazing to date her in the city, to take her out.* His memories of New Hampshire are spread wide into the future. He imagines waking up to her, holding her, making love to her. He smiles that slow smile and waits.

Nine minutes pass. No Cait. No word. The jazz fades.

Six minutes later. Cait texts: "Taylor, I'm so sorry! I cant come. Dont worry about Iowa. Ive got it under control. Thank u! I really wanted to c u. Truly. But I cant. I'm sorry!!" Cait follows up: "I thought I could. It's too hard. Forgive me. Please!! I'm awful. I know. I wish I could come. U r in my heart. Please know that."

And Taylor loses his wind.

He walks directionless for a half hour and finds himself in the East Village. He sees a Mexican joint he once frequented after bar time. But he's not hungry. He decides he can't be this way. When he arrived a few hours earlier, he stashed his bags at his friend Liam's place, unsure where he would spend the night. He decides to stay in the city. He wants to have a night. He will make this trip worth it. Cait will not get to him. He's been down that road. He will not let his expectations go so far afield all over again. He will not be that fool again. She did not show up. And he determines, walking up Avenue A, that he must let her handle her business and go her own way. She has Blake and her mother and the most powerful newspaper in the nation behind her—to the extent that any newspaper is powerful today. She'll be fine. So he tells himself to accept reality. Move on. After Charleston, after Washington Square Park, his belief in what could be with Cait feels antiquated beside her actions. He realizes that relationships can, and often do, end this way.

He calls Liam. "Can I crash with you tonight?"

"Thought you were with a girl."

"Never mind that. Let's party tonight."

"Sure, let me see what's going on. And of course, the Taylor Solomon suite is always open for you."

He returns to Liam's. Liam has plans for the day, but Taylor has plenty of work. He prefers to lose himself in his work. He returns to the Winston, Girona, and NxtGen story.

He looks up renewable fuel costs and calculates that NxtGen's biofuels are about $25 a gallon. The military's conventional fuel is about $3.50 a gallon. The watchdogs would notice that cost difference. The competition certainly would. The Pentagon's budget is larger than the next twenty most powerful militaries combined. But these days, even the American military could not ignore austerity.

Taylor gets in touch with an old acquaintance who, as a Senate aide, helped write a few defense authorization bills. They speak off the record. Taylor does not want Girona's people to get wind of his reporting. Taylor sets up the hypothetical: but wouldn't representatives from states such as West Virginia and Texas prove a serious obstacle? Yes, the aide agrees that coal and oil country will lobby against a new policy favoring green fuel. But the aide also notes that the more difficult obstacle would be the usual obstacle, partisanship. Just as Democrats were winning the new green dollars, Republicans remain reliant on oil and gas money. So GOP lawmakers would be a hard sell nationwide. Because, of course, all politics is not local.

After the conversation, Taylor considers the limits of presidential power. He wonders if it's a matter of policy rather than budgets. It hits him: the federal Renewable Fuel Standard mandates that gas and diesel include a small portion of biofuels. Taylor looks into the law. Congress sets the standard. But, among other loopholes, the Environmental Protection Agency determines the quotas for different types of biofuels to meet those goals. There may be leeway to shift demand from one type of green fuel to NxtGen's type. And that would be a matter of presidential power. But if it's about the standard, why is Clayton Winston's Republican partner on Girona's military policy group?

Day has become dusk. He closes his laptop, unsure whether he has made progress or gone in circles. But either way, he thinks, it's better than standing still and thinking about her. He checks his phone. Sees an old email from Christian.

He wonders if Luke is pursuing the story. If *Redline*, the tabloid Christian spoke of, really has a story. But he reminds himself that it's not his problem anymore. Cait can handle it herself. He knows the entire presidential race would turn upside down if something like this came out. He knows her life would too. But he tells himself, do your job and let what will happen, happen.

Liam returns home. He lays out the options for the evening. And Taylor remembers that being single also has its advantages.

XXXV

The taxi window contains the skyline at night. Checker-lit skyscrapers, neon billboards, green streetlights, red taillights, white headlights. The colors twist and curve and swirl in the yellow cab's dark glass, as the taxi races down Second Avenue beneath the charcoal sky.

Taylor sits shotgun. The taxi turns right at Twenty-Third Street. Gabriel, Liam, and another one of his old friends, John, are in the backseat. Taylor cracks the window open and, at the red light, hears strangers' conversations mingle into Manhattan's noise. The city pulse enlivens him. He wants to have a dawn night again, to rewind past Cait and Washington and relive the city of his twenties. If he cannot have her, he can at least have that.

They near the triangular Flatiron Building. "Guys," Liam says, "it's at best a second-tier show. That's why it's not in the tents. But it'll be fun."

"Who cares?" John says. "I'm down for any swimsuit show."

"Yeah," Liam says. "The designer's cool, young. She's beginning to get a little notice. Taylor, you've partied with her before."

Taylor is staring at the city.

"Taylor," Liam persists.

Taylor turns his head to his left. "What?"

Liam asks, "You remember Tina?"

"Who?"

"She's the designer for tonight's show. She's got a nice little body. You know, she wears those small Brit hats. We used to party with her at Double Seven. John, you were with us there, at least once."

"Oh yeeeah," John replies, "the Double Seven days. Was that the night when our favorite little starlet was all coked up and yelled at Gabriel for standing still?"

"When isn't that chick coked up?" Gabriel says.

"Give her some credit," Liam says. "She's not the usual type. She doesn't expect to be comped. She often pays for everyone at her table."

"Did she pay for our table that night?" John asks.

"Yeah," Liam says.

"Shit," John says, "I didn't know."

"Wait, what's this chick's label called—the designer?" Gabriel asks.

"Williamsburg something," Liam replies.

"We're going to Brooklyn?" John asks.

"Hell no. I wouldn't take you guys overseas for a show." Liam smirks. "That's just the label, or some shit."

"Why's she even doing a swimsuit show now?" Gabriel asks. "Isn't it off-season?"

"Who knows," Liam answers. "Maybe Tina wants to stand out, or go for the endless summer crowd."

"You mean people like you, Liam," Gabriel cracks.

"You know I don't go anywhere that doesn't have a Starbucks," Liam replies. "That's my marker of civilization. Luckily, some islands do."

"I find that joke incredibly sad," Taylor says.

They're inside a vast Chelsea art space. The black runway spans the white concrete floor. Taylor and his friends sit in the front row. Models in swimsuits file up and down. Kisses are blown at the runway's end. Big hair twirls. Hips thrust sideways. One wink. A mania of camera shutters. The models flirt with their power. Photographers swoon. Flashes bounce off bodies. And the fleeting is made timeless.

The crowd crams four rows. About 150 people. Mostly twenty- and thirty-somethings. Pretty people underdressed. Ugly people overdressed. Fashionistas examining. City cognoscenti brandishing disinterested expressions. Straight lips. Eyes listlessly shifting back and forth. Chins resting on palms. An indiscreet yawn. *I'm bored therefore I'm cool.*

The show ends. Liam says there's no after-party. Taylor suggests going backstage and inviting them to Liam's place. Liam's skeptical but obliges. Tina's petite, five feet one. Her naturally brown hair is bleached and pulled back. She wears a pint-size pink hat, pink eyeliner, and a puffy black dress with pink trim. She steps away from her clique. Greets Liam and Taylor. Air kisses. The models are mostly dressed. Taylor asks if there's an after-party. Tina says, "No, it totally slipped my mind." Taylor says, "You must have an after-party to mark the occasion. How about at Liam's loft?" Liam says, "That's a fantastic idea." Tina asks, "You sure you don't mind? It's so last-minute." Liam looks at Taylor. Taylor says, "Of course he doesn't mind." Liam asks if he should announce it. Taylor suggests that Tina do it. She does. Liam chats more with Tina. Taylor spends the next fifteen minutes talking to people, passing out the address, giving his cell number. Liam and Taylor return to the chairs. John asks, "You did what? No way they'll come." Taylor replies, "They'll come." Gabriel places his palms on Taylor's shoulder and says, "I knew there was a reason I missed you."

An hour later, Liam's hosting. Ten of Tina's clique. Eight models. Another dozen from the show. The crowd seems small inside the minimalist 3,400 square feet, one of the spoils of Liam's Internet start-up. John and Gabriel did a liquor run before guests arrived. The Killers' "Mr. Brightside" begins. Gabriel grabs a beer and pops the cap with his silver Zippo. He hands the bottle to Taylor and says, "Good to have you back." Taylor tips the beer his way.

Midnight passes. Taylor approaches a woman beside the kitchen island. She has an unopened bottle of Riesling in her hand. She's searching for a corkscrew. Taylor says "allow me" and pulls a corkscrew from a drawer. She hands him the bottle and says "ta." He introduces himself. So does she. Aasia has the precise bone structure of her work. Her eyes are big and dark. Her hair is black, straight, and shiny, and falls mid-back. Her casual gray blouse drapes over her small breasts and the waist of her black leggings. She wears black flats. Her feet are long and narrow. Taylor remembers her from the runway. She has a British accent. He suspects she went to an English school. He's trying to discern if she's Persian or Lebanese, perhaps part Indian. He can't place her. He pours her wine. She thanks him for hosting. "You're welcome," he replies, "but it's Liam's place." He explains where he lives. She says she's from Dubai and London. He asks, "Which do you prefer?" She says London. "Except when it's cold and rainy." "So Dubai then," he jokes. She smiles. "Oh," she says, "London's rather lovely in summer and early autumn." He says, "I like London in the rain. Not as much as Paris and Rome, but I do, very much. Old cities come alive in the rain." Her left hand touches her hip. "Why is that?" she asks. Taylor hesitates and replies, "I could say it's the way the rain washes over stone, especially at night, amid the amazing yellow light of cities like Paris. But really, the why doesn't matter. Does it?" And she nods.

They migrate to the game room and play foosball. The wine bottle rests on the windowsill. The window is cracked open. "It's not proper to spin the pegs like that," she says. He replies, "That's all I got is the spin. I'm actually not good at any bar games." Aasia asks, "What were you doing in uni?" "Drinking," Taylor quips. She half smiles. She asks if he liked the show. He replies, "Of course." Did he remember her from the show? He replies, "Of course." Her eyebrows rise as she asks, "What was I wearing?" Taylor recalls the runway and says, "There was that black bikini with a sarong that you took off at the end of the runway when you turned and toyed with the cameras. That was hot, by the way. And there was a multicolored one . . . with geometric patterns. I don't recall the others." Aasia says, "Not bad." She scores a goal. An elated squeal escapes her. Her smile blooms. He smiles, says, "Well done," and moves the peg to mark her lead. She sees the ashtray by the window. "Can we smoke in here?" she asks. "Indeed," he replies. "Bloody'el," she says, "a place in New York where you can actually smoke?" "You want one?" he asks. She replies, "I'd love a fag. But I don't have any with me."

Taylor walks over to the black Chinese liquor cabinet. He opens the doors and pulls out a pack of Liam's cigarettes and a nickel lighter. He walks over to the window. Hands her a cigarette. Their fingertips touch. She bows her head toward him. He lights her cigarette. She takes a drag, turns her head to the window, and exhales. "Ta," she says. "You want a drag?" Taylor says he's fine and sips his wine. She smokes and looks at him. He drinks and looks at her. And the silence teases them. "So is it difficult," he asks, "for you to get up in front of all those people in a bikini?" Aasia answers, "Not when I'm up there. I do lingerie too. There's not a great deal of difference. It's as if I'm at the beach. But it's a little awkward now." Taylor asks, "What is?" Aasia replies, "It's like you have already seen me nearly naked." He says, "No, not at all." "Still," she says, "since you have basically seen me in my underwear, it's only fair I get to see you in yours."

Taylor walks out of the guest room. He's barefoot and wearing last night's jeans and shirt. Liam's door remains closed. The kitchen island is littered with empty wine, vodka, and gin bottles, and at least a dozen half-full beer bottles. Wine and lowball glasses are scattered across the apartment. The air is stale with last night. Gabriel's on the stone veranda. He leans on the iron rail, slouched, smoking.

Taylor joins him. *"Qué pasa?"*

"*Nada,*" Gabriel replies, turning around.

"You crash here last night?"

"Yeah, on one of the couches." Gabriel takes a drag and exhales. Smoke clouds his face and fades. Their elbows rest on the wrought-iron rail. Below, a cab stops mid-block. Three cars bottleneck behind. Drivers slap their horns. Five cars pile. Drivers hold down their horns. The taxi pulls to the right. Cars edge past.

"Hey," Gabriel asks, "what happened to you last night? Liam got all pissed because you locked the game room. People had to come out here to smoke."

"Aasia happened."

"Aa—what?"

"That's her name."

"Niiice," Gabriel says. He takes another drag. "The brunette you were talking to?"

Taylor nods.

"Glad to see this Taylor again. She was ridiculously hot. She still here?"

"No. I walked her to a cab around dawn."

"You fuck her?" Gabriel asks.

"No. But it was memorable."

"What was?"

"We took turns undressing. Watched each other. It was like we were teenagers again."

"She probably was a teenager a few years ago. But she wouldn't hook up?"

"We had our fun."

"Niiice."

"What happened to you?" Taylor asks.

"Eh, I hooked up with Tina."

"Cool."

Gabriel shrugs. "She was something to do."

Gabriel takes a last drag, exhales; smoke curls and drifts away. He smothers the cigarette butt into the railing until the red tip goes black and ash scatters in the air. He flicks the cigarette out of his hand and watches it land in the middle of the road. "So you think you'll see that chick again?" he asks Taylor.

"She gave me her number. But I doubt it." Taylor yawns. "She lives mainly in Dubai, anyway."

"She's here now. I'd stay in touch with her, for sure."

"In other circumstances, maybe . . . She was something. Confident and—"

"And had the best ass on the runway."

"And that," Taylor smirks.

"Why not see her again? That's not like you."

Taylor stares off.

"Jesus, really?" Gabriel asks. "You're *still* hung up on that other chick? What's her name?"

"Caitriona."

"The one whose mom you ran into at that book party?"

"Yeah."

"Didn't she just stand you up?"

Taylor nods.

"Have you spoken to her since?" Gabriel asks.

"No. I should move on. I know."

"Aa-ya, whatever the fuck her name is, she's an ideal start. You have to forget that other chick."

"I want to. But, I don't know."

"Oh, Jesus. You're not still in love with her, are you?"

Taylor shakes his head. "Maybe . . . yeah, I think so. It's fucked-up. But I think so."

XXXVI

September
Milwaukee, Wisconsin

Constance Wallace watches her life replay on the mega screen. The biographical video flashes from prom queen to fighter pilot. Noise crushes the arena. She's six years out of high school. Her smirk is slight but assured. The video flashes forward to late spring 1999, to the A-10 Warthog she flew in Operation Allied Force, near Kosovo, to the day that changed her life. Tens of thousands become quiet.

Wallace specialized in destroying tanks and artillery. She had completed a mission. Then she saw them, a small company of U.S. ground forces pinned down. She was low on fuel. She still turned, flew low, and attacked enemy forces. Hit by ground fire, she circled back and destroyed the last two tanks. The ground unit was able to escape. She saved two dozen lives. But her plane was too damaged. The throttle was too hard to control. She ejected. She landed on jagged rocks, slid, and cut her back deeply. The plane's explosion was seen. She was taken prisoner. And shown on television. She became propaganda. Americans fell in love with her in three minutes of footage. Her captors screamed at her about the ills of America. They yelled demands into the camera. But she never flinched. She looked at them and showed no pain.

Three weeks later, with severe injuries to her back, Special Forces rescued her. The video shows her at the hospital, holding herself up on parallel bars. The crowd hears about those eight months. About her struggle to walk again. They learn how Constance Wallace came back.

But she never was the same. The sharp tick in her spine remains with her. She never wore high heels again. She has nightmares.

Network cameras break from the video, for a moment, to show Wallace now, watching these frames of her life. She presses her teeth together. She will not show one tear. She will never show how much it still hurts.

The video moves to her race for governor. The network cameras return to the biographical film. They miss the aide who walks over and whispers into Ted Wallace's ear. Ted whispers into her ear. The Wallaces rise. Enter the hallway. The nominee usually leaves early to prepare for her acceptance speech. But not this early.

Tomorrow morning, the *LA Times* will report that Wallace left Yale Law School for two reasons. The story is by the reporter who quizzed her on abortion so many months earlier in New Hampshire. One reason she left law school is known—her brother's death. The newspaper will report the other reason: the antiabortion Republican nominee had an abortion.

A man prepares to introduce her onstage. He is one of the soldiers she saved. Constance and Ted are backstage with Vince, inside a small, windowless office. And Vince asks her, "How the hell could you never tell me about this? You know the position this puts us in? The entire party?"

"I never expected it to come out," Constance replies.

Vince's mouth tightens and his cheeks contract as if he's sucking in his anger. He bursts, "These things always come out!" He exhales. His ruddy face is flustered. His brow is clammy with perspiration. He mumbles loud enough, as if he passive-aggressively wants her to hear, "I don't know how you could think this wouldn't come out." And his tone slackens still more. "Christ Almighty," he sighs.

Constance's arms are folded. Her back is erect. She stands between Vince and her husband. Her lips are an even line. Her dark amber eyes are withdrawn and offer the slightest hint of concern, yet even that appears contained. She reveals as little as that. Her chin is up. Her figure is steady to a surreal degree.

Ted rubs the back of his head. His short gray hair frizzes. "Vince," he asks, "how the hell did this reporter find out?"

"Best guess, Girona's staff."

"It doesn't matter now," Constance says. "Does it?"

"It sure as hell doesn't. It's out," Vince groans. He shakes his head. "Sonofabitch," he mutters. "How can I represent a candidate who had an abortion?" He looks up at her. "No one on that floor will ever see you the same way."

Ted steps up to Vince and darts his index finger into Vince's chest. "She's still the same woman!" His anger brays outward. And Vince stands slack-jawed.

Constance places her palm on her husband's shoulder. He steps back. "Vince," she says, "do you mean that?"

"No. No, I don't . . . I admire you just as much. But we are going to have a perception problem."

"I have to be proactive about this," Constance says. "I'll talk about it in the speech."

"Scoop the scoop," Vince says. "I like that."

"You sure that's the right move?" Ted asks. "What will you say?"

"I'll say I learned from my mistake. Perhaps . . . I'll say I did something I deeply regret. I don't want other women to know how much that hurts. Something like that."

"You can't put it that way," Vince says. "Independent women are not strongly pro-choice, otherwise they'd be Democrats. They are for some limitations. But they're not pro-life. You can't preach to them. You must maintain your broad appeal while using the third eye for your pro-life base."

"What the hell does that mean?" Ted asks.

"Suggest, but don't say." Wallace sighs. "I can't believe I've become this political."

"We do what we must to win," Vince says. "But don't kid yourself. The left will pummel you for this. The media too. They'll say you're pro-life except when it inconveniences you."

She nods.

"You sure you can wing this?" Vince asks.

She points upward. "Didn't you see that video before? I can wing anything." She winks.

"There's something else we can do," Vince says. "We've had some dirt on Girona for a little while now. We've been waiting for the right time to leak it."

"What is it?" she asks.

"Well, Girona's paternal grandfather comes from Girona, Spain. His grandfather's last name was not Girona as a boy. Girona, the city, as you may know, is right near the border with France."

They nod.

Vince continues, "It was ruled by France under Napoleon and other times in history, I guess."

"What are you getting at?" Ted asks.

"Girona's great-grandfather, on his dad's side, is French. His mother was born in Mexico. But as Girona has said, she comes from a small emigration of Italians to Mexico in the late nineteenth century."

"Jesus," Ted says. "Let me get this straight. Are you saying the first Hispanic nominee for president is actually just another white guy?"

Vince eases a guileful smile. "That's exactly what I'm saying."

"Why didn't you tell me about this before?" Constance asks.

"I figured we'd only use it if we must. You told me you didn't want to run that kind of campaign."

"I still don't."

"Constance," Ted says, "this is gold. It's gold! His entire pitch about change is linked to him being Hispanic. It's like finding out that your Mac is an IBM. He's been painting us as white plutocrats. And it turns out he's just another Anglo too."

"But he was still raised Hispanic," Vince says.

"We have to leak this," Ted urges.

"How could this not have come out before?" she asks.

"The media takes his biography at face value," Vince says. "It's the same thing with drugs. They've never delved into the fact that his pot smoking in high school was not a few times, like he says in his book, but constant during his senior year."

"I said you couldn't play that card."

"And we haven't," Vince responds.

"Well, I still don't think I want to play the race card either," Constance says. "If you win like that, America loses. I'll be remembered for doing the wrong thing at the right time."

"The right time? This is *your* time," Vince says. "Listen, first you win. You worry about your legacy after you win. George Bush senior used the Willie Horton ads in 1988. Today, pundits—even Democrats—refer to him as a statesman."

"He's right," Ted says. "Listen, Connie. Few people remember how you get somewhere in life, but everyone remembers where you end up."

"Exactly," Vince says.

"We'll talk about this after my speech," Constance says. "I can*not* think about this right now. So hold your fire. For God's sake, I have five minutes to figure this out. I never even told our daughter about this abortion. Now I have to tell America."

Constance Wallace walks onstage and holds her fist high. A photographer zooms in. He captures her glimmering ring, her clinched slender fingers. The symbolism burns the left. Firsts should come from the left. How can Republicans nominate this strong woman? How can a conservative personify progress?

Tonight she is determined to prove herself. She's the woman who, in pearls, killed the beast dead. She taps those archetypes. She's the prom queen who became a war hero. She's the high school hottie who won her school's girl wars. Miss America and Title Nine. Her white hair is combed back. She evokes understated elegance. She did not surrender her femininity to become a soldier. Her husband, for all his success in business, is the little man behind her big life. He holds his daughter's hand and gazes at his wife. Here is something to celebrate. She's antifeminism and feminism. Feminists watch. It's confusing for them. She's not their champion. But she proves that they won real fights.

Wallace feels the fight. She has been running against an idea, against a candidate named Hope. How can a politician overtake hope? She now sees that this cycle's change agent is flawed. She can be change too. Her campaign is in jeopardy. But she will see this through.

So she speaks of soldiering, of amorphous enemies, of why she warred and who she warred for, as she points to the convention floor. She talks of the "silent and good people who fight our wars." She will burn the left the old-fashioned way. She lauds small-town U.S.A. Sure, she's lived an extraordinary life. But she will lift up the small people. Sing that American song. Where little people are big people. She pledges to defend the good people against those who "mock our values." She will be the guardian of Americana. The *new* good old days.

"I'm a conservative because I believe there are some things worth conserving. The future cannot mean that we throw away all of our past." She talks family values. She tells an every-mother anecdote, how hard it is to work and parent. "And women especially know what I mean." So she praises mothers and the workingwomen "who keep their families going."

Super Mom is rocking the arena. She's a wife, a mother, a workingwoman, a warrior. This privileged hero is just like you. "But my husband had his work too. It was not perfect. My opponent portrays our family as a rich fairy tale. But the young woman you saw in the video, learning to walk again, she never felt her life was easy. Democrats love to talk about my money. My family has been blessed. But I'm not going to apologize for my family's success. They worked and bled for it. I bled for it. And so has this great nation. I'm not going to apologize for America's success, either."

And they cheer America's success.

"Now we can be better. There is no place in America for crony capitalism or racism or sexism. Our government, our laws, must not choose favorites. Every American deserves a fair shot at their ambitions. Yet, some politicians suggest you don't have a shot. They say you don't stand a chance. They say you all are victims."

Thousands boo and holler.

She raises her right palm and the crowd quiets. "Well, I don't see a nation of victims. I see the nation that paved the way for democracy in the modern world and sacrificed its countrymen to make the world safe for democracy. I see the nation that sparked modernity itself. The United States has pioneered everything from commercial electricity to the assembly line to genetic research. Americans have invented the airplane, the transistor, the microchip, the television, the microwave, the laser, and the personal computer. We brought cinema, jazz, and rock'n'roll to the world. In fact, the United States has earned hundreds more Nobel prizes than any other nation. After all, this is the country that carried humanity to the moon and connected the world with the Internet. And I'm here to say, to be continued. To. Be. Continued. The American epic has only begun."

The crowd chants: U.S.A., U.S.A., U.S.A.

"But, we will *not* inspire more success stories by bashing success. My opponent and I agree that hardworking Americans constitute our nation's backbone. But Mr. Ph.D. seems to have forgotten a key lesson of strong economies: you can't champion the workers and also condemn those who provide their jobs. Americans like Edison, Carnegie, Ford, Disney, Estée Lauder, Steve Jobs, and Bill Gates also made this country great. Walt Disney went bankrupt. He lifted himself up and created Disney. Ford's investors gave up on him. But Henry Ford came back, became a titan of industry, and created countless jobs. That's the America I want for all of us."

Her teleprompter stalls. But she does not. She was a hermit in her hotel room, preparing, lapping carpets. She worked with a speech coach. She recited her speech until her tongue was numb. She pushed through her infamous monotone. She was determined to prove she could be the star of the Big Show.

"That's also what's so wonderful about America. We may stumble. But we strive on. I've made mistakes. I'm not up here because I'm perfect. In fact, tonight, I want to confess one of those mistakes to you. I'm going to ask your forgiveness. I've never spoken of this before in public." The crowd hushes. Coughs are heard. The camera zooms in. "A long time ago, before I entered the Air Force, I left Yale Law School. As many know, my brother had died. I wanted to take up my family's legacy and serve our country. But I also had a trauma that year. I was young, foolish, and in love. I got pregnant."

Tens of thousands gasp.

"I had an abortion. It was one of the most traumatic periods of my life. I became depressed. I took that pain into the Air Force Academy. I was a little older than my classmates, but I was part of the first class to admit women and proud of it. Looking back now, I wish I had my child and entered after. I should have spoken about this before today. It's the one chapter of my life I could not talk about. I should have been able to. I should have understood that my supporters, and many Americans, would understand what happened. I am sorry for that. I know some of you might be angry with me for what I did. You might think less of me now. But this also has made me the woman I am today. Like all of us, the hard times helped prepare me for this day. After all, this is part of being human. We are not only our peaks. We are also our valleys. America, I stand before you *not* because I'm better. I stand here because I'll never stop working to be better, to make America better—and with the Lord of life's grace, we'll make America better. I've made mistakes, struggled in war, saved, and been saved. I've been injured and learned to walk again. I've always stood up again. Because I'm an American. And in America we don't define people by how they fall, but by how they rise up!"

She preaches on. Conservative churchgoers hear "Lord of *life*." They're reminded that she's pro-life. She's on their side now. The right side now. They watch her confess and speak of "grace." They feel her humility and original sin. She speaks of being "saved." Jesus died for her sins. She's a believer. She can know redemption too. She's proselytizing. Embodying their faith. Constance Wallace is still one of you.

"I will be a better president because of my mistakes. I didn't get this white hair for nothing. Trust me, there's a lot of wisdom behind these wrinkles." And they cheer her wrinkles. "I have the fortitude to make the hard calls. I'll strengthen the nation by balancing our books. Because I don't believe in passing the buck. America should not promise more handouts and ask our children to pay the bill." So she talks debt. Pledges to "put Uncle Sam on a diet." But she says she will also invest in education, new technology, and more research. "Because those investments pay dividends. They pay for a better future. And let me say it again, America remains the future. Ignore the naysayers. For no one ever succeeded by underestimating the U.S. of A."

Again they chant: U.S.A., U.S.A., U.S.A.

And with that fervor, she attacks. "My opponent will make government bigger. He'll increase our debt and give our children the check. He'll raise our taxes. He'll try to sweet-talk our enemies. He'll turn rich against poor and leave us more divided. I will make government smaller. I will lower our debt. I will lower our taxes. I will win peace through strength. I will unite us and make America stronger. Others may talk and talk, about change. But I've got the experience and the *real* strength to achieve it." So she emasculates the man better than any man can. Girona may talk a good fight, but he's never been in a real fight. He's another pansy silver-tongued liberal egghead. He spoke for a living. She fought for a living. It's said without being said. She's the only real man in this race.

Where did this woman come from? pundits ask themselves. Her monotone is gone. She has *it,* aplomb, the ability to jab with a smile. Float like a butterfly, sting like a bee. She can do Muhammad Ali. She can rouse. The crowd reacts like it's not pugilistic hyperbole. They're on their toes. So Wallace will own the role. She'll pound her foe. She'll be the red-blooded hero. "My opponent talks like he monopolizes change. Well, I've got news for him. Millions of women fought to see me on this stage. My opponent pledges to fix Washington. But he comes from Washington. He bickered in the Senate while I balanced budgets as an executive. Yes, I know, he says he'll fight for you. But if I may say so, only one candidate in this race has *actually* fought for you. And I'm only getting started. This nation is only getting started. Too many of us face hard times. But we are harder. We are strong. We persevere. We *will* persevere. Because we are Americans. God bless you. And God bless America."

The crowd erupts, screams, cheers. Lee Greenwood's "God Bless the USA" begins. Wallace gazes outward and smiles. Her family joins her onstage and as they embrace, the chorus plays and countless sing along. She faces the throng, holding her daughter's hand, standing above the tens of thousands, cheering her, and her countenance stiffens, except for her eyes, as she blinks back emotion.

Taylor takes one last look at Wallace and exits. He passes hot dog and popcorn stands and sprints up the escalator to make his scheduled appearance on BBC. He enters the packed skybox. BBC radiomen sit along a narrow table, on high barstools, wearing black headphones, speaking a fist away from their microphones. Taylor walks to the television teams in back, overlooking the floor. A producer sees him. Another man attaches the mic pack to his belt. The man weaves the earpiece under his suit jacket. Taylor is placed on deck. He sits in the high director's chair. Three, two . . . He's live. Taylor explains the sway of social issues in American politics. He talks of cultural populism and culture wars. He says that Wallace would have been better off publicly addressing the abortion years ago. Yet, he adds, from a strategic standpoint, she handled the report as well as possible. "Girona's media spinners are the best that can be hired on Madison Avenue. Yet they will struggle to respond to Wallace's confession."

Taylor returns to the big picture. He notes that many pundits say the culture wars are over. Taylor reminds viewers of historic fissures, from prohibition to school prayer to abortion, because "the issues change, but cultural differences endure." Though, he adds, "these issues do take on an exaggerated polarization because American politics is argued through a two-party lens." Soon he gets to today's bizzaro twist. Social conservatives are championing the working mother. And on Twitter, some feminists are criticizing Wallace as a mother. Many liberals see a Trojan horse. A woman can be at war with women. She is not progress to progressives. Polling shows that women have more polemical views of her than men do. Liberal websites are already overflowing with charges of hypocrisy on abortion. But, he explains, the left's new attacks will only further unite the right. American politics is tribal. Old saws true again. The enemy of my enemy is my friend. And the culture wars carry on. The Democratic spokeswoman emails Taylor while he is still on air: "Holy cow, the Republicans are playing hardball." You betcha.

Taylor ends his commentary by explaining that the race has settled into conventional formations. Dems wanted hope vs. past. They're getting change vs. change. Diplomat vs. warrior. D.C. has its drama. More viewers. More readers. More ads. More reason to focus editorial resources on the campaign. More polls to conduct. More competitive states, more consulting business. Whoever wins, the political class wins. Moneyyyy.

Taylor rides the escalator down. Republican delegates exit the arena. Tall Uncle Sam hats. Primary colors. There's a man dressed as Lincoln. The fading Republican establishment ebbs by. Delegates carry handheld American flags. There is a stream of suited men and women smiling, chirping, energized. They feel the buzzzzz. Wallace has given Republicans buzz. Democrats felt it the entire cycle. Now Republicans feel it too.

Taylor has to file quotes for a larger story. "She's just wonderful. She's one of us. She's just like me," says a lean blonde.

She wears a button with a picture of Rosie the Riveter: Strong Women for Wallace. The paraphernalia had been passed out beforehand. “I think liberals are intimidated by her,” the woman adds. “I forgive her for her abortion. We all make mistakes when we’re young. It’s the redemption that counts, as we become adults.” There’s a healthy melon of a woman, fleshy faced, wide-eyed, with big brunette helmet hair. “I love her! She’s a strong Christian woman,” the woman perks. She holds her rail-thin preteen daughter’s hand. The daughter says, “Wallace is realeee cool.” There’s a tall man with salty black hair, a prickly beard, a long orange face, taut skin. His tie is red. His suit is gray. His slacks bunch at the top of his brown cowboy boots. “We needed someone who could take Girona down a few notches.” What do you think about the fact that she had an abortion? “We’re all sinners. What matters is that she’s born again with Christ. Shoooot, she’s fighting for life now. And boy oh boy,” he adds, shaking his head with pride, “that lady can fight. I just love her.” Republicans are not walking out. They’re floating out.

XXXVII

Libations. Nightly celebration. Open-bar exploitation. The high must be maintained. Political conventions are partisan pep rallies. And parties. Each tribe's heavyweights schmooze, spill over, mill about—former presidents, past nominees, senators, top strategists. And those faithful troops. Reporters can shoot fish in a barrel. That's the journalistic value. Work sources, conduct interviews. But that's all still sideshow.

Welcome to the Big Show's half-time show. The drinks are on the house. Thank you companies, interest groups, lobbyists. The big munificent money. Quid pro quo, of course. Sponsors receive access. But the pol can listen and not do. Pols have free will. Let them have their fun. The money need not corrupt the pols. The pols need not corrupt the journos. You purists. Let the flacks and hacks have that much. Let the grunts mingle with the flyboys. There's Karl Rove! "Our rock stars aren't like your rock stars," goes an old Intel ad. And there are real stars. It's like the White House Correspondents' Dinner. The Demidork photographed beside Oprah, Steven Spielberg, George Clooney, Matt Damon, Ben Affleck, Natalie Portman, Spike Lee . . . The Republidork photographed beside Clint Eastwood or Stephen Baldwin or Jessica Simpson. Republicans will take what stars they can get, as long as stars attend. And people see. D.C. hangs with the popular kids. Post it on Facebook. Tweet it. Instagram the pic. And curate that cool. My two-dimensional life rocks! Check out my friends and followers. Sure, they're virtual. But I have followers. Seee. I am cool!

"America's politics would now be also America's favorite movie, America's first soap opera, America's best-seller," wrote Norman Mailer of Kennedy's budding Camelot. Years later, with deaths done, Mailer wrote of that mystique, "The Kennedys had seemed magical because they were a little better than they should have been, and so gave promise of making America a little better than it ought to be."

Americans like their presidents a little better than they ought to be, or are. DCland dearly believes in that mystique. They work to become it. For it all must be worth it. Mailer foresaw the soap opera. But not even he imagined that the Big Show would expand beyond the stars. That the private would become public. And everyone would be, potentially, both actor and cameraman—as every phone became a lens, as everything became fit to broadcast online at anytime. Because there would be no more fade-outs.

As the world turns. New party. Same scene. Taylor arrives at the Republican Google- *Vanity Fair* party. It's at a modern art museum. A *TMZ* reporter chases Fred Thompson. *Redline* and *People* reporters record the notable guests. The political press does too. Red carpets blend. And fans wait. They hope for the candidate herself, for signatures, to meet her. She may not be Esperanza. But loyalists love her. One woman holds a copy of *People* magazine. The headline: Constance Wallace Reveals Why She Fell for Her VP. Another fan holds the magazine *Garden & Gun*. On the cover, Wallace is pictured before her vegetable garden, holding her shotgun, embodying Republican America.

Taylor gives his name. Bouncer checks the clipboard. Taylor enters. Minimalist decor. He weaves to the bar. Red light brushes white walls. Modern art consigned to background.

Trays of hors d'oeuvres glide past. Public servants nosh on caviar blinis.

GOP underlings inch toward one couch. It's Henry Kissinger chatting with a founder of YouTube. OMG! It's him. Really him. Excuse me. Ex-cuuuse me. Elbow aside. Dart forward. Maintain that dignified expression. Harrumph. There's a line. Fine, I'll wait. For him.

Kissinger oozes into the wall, relaxing, his rotund belly pushing out of his blazer, his blue tie resting atop. The Wizard of Oz is jolly tonight. This is his kingdom. Kissinger once said "Power is the ultimate aphrodisiac." Oh, how the political scenesters do swoon.

Democrats have Hollywood. But the GOP has Nashville. Country star John Rich chomps a cigar beneath his black cowboy hat. He sports a red tie. His lapel is adorned with a flag pin. Wallace's daughter flutters about with girlish glee. Taylor sees Owen. Owen is a top GOP strategist of yesteryear. He is portly and pale, and his hair makes him look like a sheepdog. Owen bumps into former New York senator Al D'Amato and says hello. Owen passes the *Times*'s Gail Collins, Jill Abramson, and Joe Lelyveld of *The New York Review of Books.* Oh yes, conservative activists, Republican players cocktail with the enemy. Pundits, pols, journos—the circus folk are chummy. Owen tips his glass to the media mega minds. He knows everyone. Owen greets Taylor. "Taylor Solomon. Shit, man, how are you? It's been a helluva night, huh?"

Taylor says hello and asks, "How do you think she handled the abortion news? Word is, they found out it was going to break tomorrow morning."

"It was a damn good recovery. The *LA Times* posted the story just now."

Taylor nods.

"Even for the *LA Times*," Owen says, "it's messed up. I mean, that they would publish that piece the day after her big speech. Could they act any more partisan? It would've served as a huge buzz kill for us. So hell yes, I'm glad Wallace got out in front of it."

"It may keep you guys in the action."

"What I wouldn't kill for some action. Two decades ago, there would've been less of you guys here and more escorts."

Taylor smiles at the candor.

"Now don't get me wrong," Owen adds, smacking Taylor's back, "I never partook." And Owen bumps along, ho-ho-hoing to himself.

Current's Philip Larson chats with two of the smartest observers of American politics, Ron Brownstein and Charlie Cook, as well as Wallace's top adviser, Vince, and GOP strategist Steve Schmidt. Taylor glances at his boss and nods. Philip nods back. Taylor's phone vibrates. A colleague wants help getting inside with a girl. But this isn't a choice lounge in Meatpacking. Taylor has no pull here. This is a festival for the moneyed interests, available stars, political players, *Meet the Press* guests. The talking heads merge and mingle. This is a private event. But this too is a made-by-television event.

Taylor chats with Jason, the wunderkind RNC operative. They rarely see each other in person. "Dude," Jason says. "Wasn't Wallace amazing tonight? She fucking saved her campaign."

"Whatever the impact, whatever one's politics, it was impressive."

"Damn right. And we've still got an ace up our sleeve. Potentially, a real game changer too."

Taylor asks what it is.

Jason replies, "I was actually going to give some of it to you before—the ace, I mean. But now that the Dems tried this bullshit to kill our campaign in such a public way, I'm under orders to hold my fire."

"You can't mention a potential game changer and leave it at that."

"Listen, my bad. But I have orders." Jason's stare swings sideways. "Holy shit, there's Kissinger. He's my idol. I gotta meet him."

Taylor notes the greeters circling Kissinger. "Take your time, you'll meet him."

"Yeah, you're right. Dude!" He hits Taylor's arm. "That's Rosario Dawson!"

Taylor asks who that is. Jason looks at him in disbelief. "C'mon, you know her," Jason says. "She's the hottie from movies like *25th Hour.*" Taylor nods, now recognizing her, as Jason continues, "Dude, I'd like to nail her."

"Half this party probably agrees. But don't forget those family values." Taylor winks.

"Fuck you."

Taylor smirks and says, "Relax. I'm kidding. Happy hunting. But I think you'll have better luck with Kissinger."

Taylor drinks and thinks about the story Jason has in his pocket. He suspects it's something newsworthy. Still, he doesn't care enough to do the dance, to attain dirt on the operative's terms, to suck up to suck-ups, or do the barter some of his colleagues favor—give me a scooplet and I'll give you your puff piece. So Taylor downs his whiskey and excuses himself.

⚜ ⚜ ⚜

Vince sees Taylor walk away from Jason. He walks over and tells Jason to follow him. They enter an office. Vince shuts the door. "What's up?" Jason asks. Vince does not respond. He looks around the office. Sees a small radio. He turns it up. Fifties rock plays. He steps a half foot from Jason. Speaks below the music. So only Jason hears.

"Time to use the file on Girona's ethnicity."

Jason grins.

"Here's the play," Vince says. "Make a copy of all the records, everything, including the old Spanish birth records from that church in Girona. Pick one reporter who you trust will honor your terms. Maybe at *Current* or the *Post*, even Drudge himself. Just be sure it's someone the mainstream media cannot ignore. Tell the reporter, if he wants the material it must be published at about one p.m. tomorrow and it cannot be traced to you or the RNC. Be sure there is no hint of this campaign's involvement."

"Of course," Jason replies.

"Remember, I want to let the media have time to devour the news on Constance. That way, the abortion story will feel like old news when this comes out."

"Smart."

"Just don't screw this up. The media will cover this abortion thing wall to wall. Dems are already going ballistic. I don't even know why the hell you're here and not working."

"It's nomination night. Did you see Rosario Dawson's here?"

"Are you fucking kidding me?" Vince barks. "This is battle stations. Get back to your hotel room and get to work. You can have fun after the damn campaign."

Jason nods.

"Dems are going to seize on this abortion to cut into her outreach to women. So this must go right."

Jason nods.

"Hopefully, this hurts him enough," Vince adds. "I don't want to touch that other shit. Constance would kill me."

"But she doesn't have to know," Jason says. "You can't pull a punch like that in a campaign. What would Atwater or Rove do?"

"This is *my* show." Vince scratches his ruddy check. "Listen, I hear you. We may circle back to it, if we must. For now, focus on this ammunition."

"He'll look as white as me when this is over."

"That's impossible. But that's the attitude. So get your mind off women and get that folder in the right hands."

Jason nods, rushes out, and passes Taylor.

Taylor finishes his whiskey rocks at the bar. He doesn't notice Jason darting past. Taylor orders another drink and cocktails on. He migrates up another level. There, in a white corner, is Cait. And she's with Blake.

Cait's eyes pop. Her mouth gapes. Her lips are novocained. The color leaves her cheeks. Her hand clamps down on her cream clutch. Her eyes remain fixed on Taylor. Mr. Windoner placed Cait and Blake on the list. Blake's father is a Trailblazer, the title for someone who raises more than $250,000 for the Wallace campaign.

Taylor sees her shock. He recognizes the man by her side. He considers walking away and not making a scene. He could spare Cait that. But Blake sees Cait's expression, looks at Taylor, at Cait, glares back at Taylor. Cait's still frozen. She jerks her body up, closes her mouth, vaguely shakes her head, breathing. She looks at Blake. It's too late for nonchalant. Taylor walks over. Instinct takes hold. He's buzzed, but not drunk. He's not all id. He turns sideways to slide between two circles and approaches them.

Taylor: shoulders back, not eyeing them, carving through the crowd, almost there, in a black two-button suit that's tailored to him, a slim black tie, indigo shirt, staring at Cait, sipping his whiskey.

Blake: his expression austere, his blond hair combed back, clean part on the left, his gray eyes lost in the low light. He's holding a beer in his right hand. He wears a traditional navy suit with a red tie. His jacket is buttoned. The cuffs of his crisp white shirt show. He's rocking Ronald Reagan cuff links. The Gipper is pictured on each.

Cait: now rigid, in a cream knit skirt to her knees, a matching jacket with cream piping at the lapel and the slit of her skirt. It fits her figure and the evening, alluring and elegant. But she's off-kilter. She can't believe Taylor's approaching them. She searches for shock in Taylor, anger, pain, something. But he's casual. She looks only at him. But she cannot read him.

"Hello, Cait," Taylor says.

"Hello, Taylor." Cait's tone is barely audible.

"Is this your fiancé?" Taylor asks.

"Yes."

Blake shoots his hand forward. They shake. Taylor notices that Blake's trying to be firm. "Blake Windoner. And you are?"

"Taylor."

"How do you two know each other?" Blake asks him.

"I'm a reporter."

"For who?"

"*Current.*"

"What's that?"

"Blake, you know it," Cait says. "They sponsored several debates. It's that new political website everyone reads."

Blake glances at her with a mix of curiosity and irritation, as if he's wondering why she's defending him. "Right. I've caught it through *Drudge*," Blake says. "I didn't know they were letting reporters in here."

"I'm a reporter," Cait says.

"But babe, you're with me."

"Well," Taylor says, "they asked me to come to balance out the tools." Taylor deadeyes Blake.

Blake hears the insult and says, "By tool you mean?"

"Don't worry about it."

"So how exactly do you two know each other?" Blake asks Taylor.

"Debates and such. Everyone knows Cait. You have a famous fiancée." "Do I?" Blake takes two deep gulps of his beer. He looks down at Cait. She's now stone-faced. He studies her, as though a lingering suspicion has surfaced. He eyeballs Taylor again. "Where are you from?" he asks Taylor.

"New York. But I live in D.C. now."

"Where in New York?"

"The city."

"Not an outer borough?"

"Who cares which borough," Cait says.

Blake looks down at her in every way.

Cait continues, "You're acting like a snob, Blake."

"It's okay," Taylor says. "I'm sure he's not acting."

Cait glares at Taylor.

Taylor sees her stare and understands. He tells himself to relax. He maintains his focus on Blake.

Blake thrusts his left arm forward to shove Taylor. Taylor shoots sideways. Dodges. Blake's momentum carries him forward. He stumbles and drops his beer.

"Blake!" Cait says. "What are you doing?"

There's a puddle of beer on the floor.

Blake straightens up. He wipes beer off his blazer. Checks his cuff links. Most people don't notice over the music, the bunched and buzzed bodies, the cocktail clatter.

Blake turns to Taylor. Blake's eyes tighten with anger.

Cait picks up Blake's beer glass. She sets it on a cocktail table. "Blake, please calm down," she says.

Taylor downs his whiskey and sets his glass on the table. He notices that Blake's watch is on his left wrist. He remembers that his beer was in his right hand. He knows Blake is right-handed.

Blake's face clenches. Taylor subtly shifts his right foot back, and places his weight on it, to be sure he has his balance, to be sure he can shoot forward if he must. He breathes and says, "Why don't you chill a bit?"

"Fuck you. I do what I want."

Blake swings a right hook. But before his arm outstretches, Taylor shoots forward. Cait yells, "Blake!" Taylor's left forearm is pointed upward and blocks Blake's forearm mid-motion, as Taylor's right forearm hits against Blake's sternum, halting his momentum, and Taylor instantly slides his left hand along Blake's arm and slaps him in the back of the head, to distract him, to get him to lift his chin, as Taylor rapidly slides his right hand up Blake's chest and grips his throat. Taylor's palm presses Blake's Adam's apple. He holds his windpipe firmly but carefully, his fingertips pushing inward and pulling slightly outward, cutting off Blake's air to the degree he knows is safe. Blake's punching arm goes limp. Taylor sees him slacken. Taylor holds his throat, chest to chest, near enough to smell the beer on his breath.

And in the split seconds that seem like minutes, Cait yells, "Taylor! Let him go." Taylor looks at her, at Blake's compliant state, and lets go. Taylor steps back, realizing he went too far, realizing a technique he had practiced hundreds of times was not for this context, was too severe for this context. And these thoughts rush through him as Blake bends over, coughing. Blake stands up, rubs his throat, coughs again, and fixes his hair.

"I'm sorry, Cait," Taylor says. "I let that get out of hand. I should go."

Cait's mouth hints at opening but nothing comes out. She stares at Taylor. She glances at Blake and looks back at Taylor. Taylor turns his back and walks out. Cait's eyes follow him through the crowd. She's irritated with him, faults him, but she also wants to run after him. Instead, she only watches him. He is lost in the crowd.

It lasted less than a minute. But Taylor knows word can quickly spread. He doesn't want to make more of a scene. He walks to the escalator. Descends to the lobby and exits. There's one protestor in the cold night. She's middle-aged, strawberry-faced, hefty, layered in pink clothing. She holds a sign that reads STOP WALLACE THE WARMONGER. A laminate hangs around her neck. It reads MAKE OUT, NOT WAR. Taylor passes her. He admires her doggedness as he flags a taxi. "Where to?" the cabbie asks. "Any bar away from the convention," Taylor replies. He rests back against the seat. He should have let Blake's slights go. He should not have walked over in the first place. But he regrets nothing. He feels his adrenaline pulse. He smiles. Stares out the window. City lights shine off the glass. His expression straightens. It occurs to him. He had the moment. But Blake still has her.

XXXVIII

Jason's face is clenched with anticipation. The hour nears one p.m. The lead headline, everywhere, is Wallace's abortion. The coverage of Wallace's speech is secondary. The abortion debate dominates drive-time radio, Twitter, the comments below online political stories. Partisan spinners spar on cable. "She's a hypocrite." "Her abortion turned her against abortion." "How typical. Isn't she the one who promises to make the hard calls?" The pundit consensus is? She handled the news as well as possible. "But how well can any politician manage this curveball?" John King asks on CNN. "We'll be right back to discuss whether this is a game changer?" Cue commercial.

Polls were scheduled to gauge the public's immediate reaction to Wallace's speech. Some pollsters added a last-minute question. Predictably, Americans were split. About half thought less of Wallace because of the abortion. About half said it didn't change their mind. The adversary of my adversary is my hero.

The hour hits one p.m. *The Washington Post* has the scoop. *Drudge* sirens it. Tweets multiply. Two minutes later, Fox flashes a breaking news headline, REPORT: JOE GIRONA IS NOT HISPANIC. Bloomberg News pounces. *Current* reports it. CNN follows. Rush Limbaugh reads the news live to his listeners. NBC dispatches its Paris correspondent to Girona, Spain. *Huffington Post* links to the news but the banner headline remains WALLACE'S HYPOCRISY. Univision and Telemundo interrupt their broadcasts. An MSNBC regular questions the story on air, asks if the coverage itself is racist. Pundits universally ponder, how will this impact Girona's Hispanic support? BBC attempts to explain why, in America, someone who is Caucasian can be seen as another race because he identifies with a Spanish-speaking culture. Stateside, cable news begins to debate what this means. What constitutes Hispanic? He speaks Spanish and identifies as Latino. America has long classified white Latinos as Latinos. Others say, but he's white. He looks white. He has those gray-blue eyes. He comes from French and Italian ancestors. It continues this way. Back and forth, across the news-scape. One quake replaces the other. And the media storm goes on.

At the southeast corner of Central Park, on the thirty-sixth floor of Time Warner's towers of glass, inside the Mandarin hotel, Joe Girona sits at the head of a long conference table. The sunlight reflects off the table's sheen and catches his light eyes. His black hair is parted pristinely, his black suit is pressed pristinely. He casually twirls a pencil in his hand as he speaks. Sixty wealthy donors listen to him, amid panoramic views of the Hudson River and Central Park. They eat Wagyu beef tenderloin with smoked potato purée or butter-poached lobster with white corn grits and kaffir lime emulsion. Each contributed $50,000 to be here. Proceeds will fund the Friends of the American Dream, a liberal advocacy group that is aligned with Girona's campaign. Yet, however well funded, the group's leaders did not foresee its acronym, or the fun conservatives would have with it.

Girona leaves tomorrow for a trip through swing states, from Colorado to Ohio to Florida. The following week, he's scheduled to return to the city for the last day of the convention. There, in climactic fashion, he plans to make his way through the city and accept his party's nomination at Madison Square Garden.

Today's schedule concerns money. He will discreetly tour the convention floor. He'll also sprint through three New York fund-raisers. His staff believed that the GOP convention would open wealthy liberal wallets. One week of right-wing attacks rallies the left wing, and vice versa. Girona has already raised record sums, but he recently insisted on much more. And few knew why.

Girona refused to betray why. He focused on the good news. The Wallace headline feels like a gift. He is impressed with how she handled it, as one political athlete admires another. But he thinks this story is too large to contain with mere talk—at least her talk.

Democratic mega-donor Saundra Winston organized today's lunch. Her circle is seated, a squadron of suits, mostly white, early forties to mid-seventies, a little more male than female. Girona lacks the vast financial sector support of past Democrats. His rhetoric during the primary explains why. Back then, CNBC ran a special report asking "Is Joe Girona a socialist?"

Today, privately, Girona speaks more like the reasonable man holding back the rabble. He still promises the public that he will "stop the moneyed interests who corrupt our democracy." But to this group, that sounds like the gun lobby or the bad guys who don't deserve to sit beside them at the Metropolitan Opera's opening night. Still, some here do hail from finance. They expect tax loopholes to be closed, if he wins, if he can work with Republicans in Congress. These donors are willing to pay more in taxes. They have a progressive worldview, providing Girona will not upend their world. How much is just words? Is he really a radical populist or was that primary politics?

A man in a blue pinstripe suit, with brown curly hair, leans on the table with one arm and pulls out a piece of paper from his breast pocket. He reads a quote Girona said six months ago in Ohio: " 'The superrich get rich off our sweat. And trust me, these supposed masters of the universe are actually thin-skinned bullies who can't take the truth. Wall Street preaches free enterprise until they need Main Street's help. And when companies fall and innumerable livelihoods are lost, as towns and cities empty like ghost towns and American dreams die, these war profiteers move on to the next profit, the next town, like locusts.' "

The man stops reading, sits up, and adds, "Senator, in this city, the top one percent of earners pay over forty percent of the city's income taxes. They fund the social safety nets. About half of my earned income goes to federal, state, and city taxes. Now, I wouldn't be a Democrat if I minded doing my part. Affluent Americans have more to lose from instability, which would come with small government. But who *exactly* are you comparing to war profiteers and locusts?"

"It was a rhetorical flourish."

But the questioner's stare does not stray. Girona knows he must offer more. He knows they support him because of the environment, gay rights, abortion rights, because they do believe the government should provide more help for poor people. But Saundra has warned him. His past rhetoric led some attendees to vote for Miles Riley in the primary. Girona expects their vote in the general election. But he wants their dollars too. Still, this crowd expects to be courted. The big money is accustomed to future presidents flattering them. So he shall flatter.

Yet behind those gray-blue eyes, Girona's confidence has limits. Christian forecasted a storm. Girona is less anxious than he was last week. No news is good news, or so they say. He knows Christian is on it. Still, the possibility lurks. Thus Girona raises every dollar he can. His private life could still burst across the Internet. Campaign upheaval would follow. He'll need large cash reserves to fund an advertising fight. He's like a man preparing for a great storm that no one else foresees, that even he scarcely believes is coming.

But still he gathers his resources. So he answers the suit. "Listen, I'm glad you asked this question. I understand your concern. I will implement *responsible* reforms, but only with all *your* critical input. The reforms *we* decide upon are meant to improve our economy. They will make the markets more efficient and avoid upheaval. We have to do something. Out there," he says, pointing to the wall of windows, as if showing the way beyond the skyscrapers, over New Jersey, to the vast wilderness beyond, "the nation, left and right, is boiling with anger over Wall Street, corporate heartlessness, and a sense of unfairness. Trust me, it simmers even when the GDP is good. It's awakened every time corporate America reports record profits while countless Americans are forced to work more for less or are bled in innumerable small ways, such as by excessive bank fees. I know you understand their frustration. You want to give back. That's why you're willing to pay more in taxes, as you noted. You *care*. But if we don't win, if we don't enact some reforms, the rage could boil over someday. I don't want that. I want healthy and stable markets. But I can't steward that stability, I can't win, I can't fight back against the right-wing attacks without you. Indeed, I can't fight for the issues we care about, like climate change and equal rights, without support from all of you."

As a woman begins to ask a question, a young aide whispers in Girona's ear. Girona breaks the pencil in his hand. The donors hear it snap. See it snap. See his cool snap. Girona apologizes. He excuses himself. Saundra Winston's eyebrows rise.

Girona walks to a private room with two aides in tow. The news is not anything he foresaw. But he knows far worse could be reported about his personal life. That possibility offers perspective. He asks the young aide when this story broke. The aide says eleven minutes ago. "Why didn't you get me?" The aide explains that he thought it was best to wait until Girona finished his comments. "I figured the money should also get in a question or two," he adds. Girona walks to the window. He looks down onto the park, the sea of plush trees, the manicured lawns and lake, this massive rectangle of green encased by skyscrapers. He taps the divot in his top lip. A forty-something aide asks him, "Did you know that your father's side was originally French?" Girona still faces the park. His gaze retracts inward. "How's this being covered in the Hispanic media?" he asks. "I can*not* lose Univision." The young aide says he will check on it. "Are we sure it's true?" he asks. The aide replies, "It comes from *The Washington Post.* Who knows who fed it to them, but I guess they confirmed birth records." The forty-something aide asks, "What should we do?" The aides hang on his silence. Girona cracks his knuckles and turns around. "You know, there's that expression," Girona says, "it's not what happens to campaigns, it's how you deal with it." The aides nod. "So let's deal with it," Girona adds. He tells them to organize a call "with the circle," his closest four advisers, as well as a separate call with Christian. "I want to thank these donors first and apologize to Saundra. Then the calls. But I know what to do."

And so he does it. Thirty-seven minutes later he stands at street level. Reporters scramble. Cameras click. A mass of microphones collects before him. They corner him. Some kneel down, settling into configuration, like a bygone military formation, some standing, ready to fire volleys, knees to pavement, pressing their microphones forward like pikes. Secret Service agents push back. Reporters push harder, maintain their ranks. Cameramen shove competitors with their shoulders. An eager and pretty female producer, carrying a microphone, sweetly asks one videographer to let her in. He won't. She tries again. He won't. She yells, "Excuuuse me, you jerk." "Fuck you, lady," he responds, remaining in place. She looks at him in astonishment. "This is business, not a bar," he barks, refusing to move aside, his eye never straying from the viewfinder. The ranks thicken, lines condensing, as sweat drips in the hot sun. All eyes are on the target before them. A wiry young man holding a CNN microphone tries to burrow into the scrum. A photographer elbows him in the stomach. He falls to the ground, drops his microphone, and gets stepped on by another photographer. He stands, grabs his mic, pushes forward, and bumps into Taylor.

Earlier that day, Taylor had flown in from the GOP convention in Milwaukee to New York. Most of the national media did, in preparation for the Democratic convention. He came to the Time Warner Center to see the chaos. The hive was told that Girona might make a statement. *Current* wants a big think article from Taylor on the politics of racial identity. He came to the presser to gather string for his story, the contextual color outside the television frame. And Taylor watches reporters now. They shove and jostle for position like too many commuters packing a subway car. The media corners Girona against the building. Reporters scream questions. Camera flashes fire. The man is aware he's dinner for the horde. But he does not sweat.

Girona's eyes are calm and his chin is up. He smiles his preternatural smile. Questions ricochet off him as if they are only sound. Taylor imagines the talking points to come. And to him, it all seems to slow and reveal itself, as if the feeding frenzy has a script and this is another scene in the same show.

Taylor makes his way outside the pack. He wonders why he came. A hundred reporters, cameramen, newshounds encircle the candidate. Horns honk. News trucks are obstructing traffic. Taylor stands outside the gaggle, watching.

Three, two . . . action. "I only have a few minutes. I will make my statement and then I'll take a few questions." Girona clears his throat and looks into the cameras. "For hundreds of years, this nation has been a melting pot for immigrant waves. I always thought that my father's side of the family came from Spain, which, by the way, they did. But it looks like they came from France before they lived in Spain. My mother was born and raised in Mexico, like her parents. But as I wrote in my biography, her grandparents were Italian immigrants, like millions of Americans. I was raised with the Hispanic culture that weaned both of my parents. I identify deeply with Hispanic culture. Spanish was my first language. But it turns out that like much of this nation, I descend largely from southern Europeans. I am another story of America's glorious melting pot. Am I ashamed of that? No. I'm proud of it. I'm proud to be one more American story. This is *our* story. It's who we are." Watch him spin that newsflash. Look, Medio Joe is also an Average Joe. He descends from southern Europeans too. Italians like you. The Rorschach enlarges. It doesn't merely reflect the better you. He's more like you, and you and you and sure, you too. He's all of us. He's U.S. "What are the words on the United States seal? It reads '*e pluribus unum.*' Roughly translated, out of many comes one. I'm proud to be a part of that great one, part of the quilt of cultures that constitutes our glorious United States . . . I'll now take a few questions."

Reporters yell and shout and shove. Cable news broadcasts the scene live. Girona calls on a familiar face amid the swarm, a reporter from his traveling pack. And the reporter asks, "But strictly speaking, Senator, if I may put it this way, do you think the public should still consider you the first Latino nominee for president?"

"The word you chose is interesting. Latino derives from Latin, which may derive from Latium, a country in ancient Italy. Latin, in the vernacular of that age, is the mother of the European Romance languages, which are spoken in Spain, France, and Italy. So yes, I—"

"But Senator, Senator. Sen-a-tor!" a *Daily News* man—sweaty black hair, tie unable to reach over his belly—interrupts and stares Girona down.

Girona's taken aback. The national journo, who asked the first question, glares at the *Daily News* reporter. Girona's used to a degree of deference. The D.C. regulars respect an unspoken propriety. But this is not the usual gaggle. It's not another local press pack that reveres a candidate. No, it's a hungrier sort. A hardened sort. This is the New York City press. And they smell blood.

Girona hesitates. The *Daily News* man pounces, "C'mon. That Latin stuff may work in a classroom. But when you say Hispanic or Latino on these streets, people think of Latin America, or at least Spain. Aren't you really yet another white man running for president, and no less or more white than Constance Wallace?"

"I am not going to let anyone tell me I should be ashamed of my Latino upbringing." Girona eyeballs the white male newsman because he knows that to rally loyalists in politics, sometimes the best offense is to take offense.

The newsman looks down at his notepad. And the jujitsu seminar continues. Because just as smoothly, Girona pivots, calms, and his voice soothes. He looks past the reporter and into the cameras. "I am proud of my deep bond with Hispanics. That bond is as strong as ever. I care profoundly for Hispanic American culture, more than words can ever express. And today I've learned that I also have stronger roots across southern Europe. I'm no less proud of that. As I said, that's the beauty of this grand nation. You asked me what I am? I'll tell you. I am who I was yesterday. I'm an American."

Reporters blare. Girona excuses himself and strides past Taylor. As Taylor's phone buzzes, he watches the whiplashed herd rush the pol. And the feeding frenzy grows. Two presidential nominees are bloodied. Pundits are debating abortion and race. It's an American media feast.

Girona steps into a black SUV. He looks back once, smiles, and waves to the reporters as if they're an adoring crowd. Security closes the door. Cop lights flash. Police block traffic and lead the way out. Girona's SUV speeds off with them. Staff and Secret Service vehicles follow. The media buses are left behind. Aides insist that was an accident.

Inside Girona's vehicle, the older aide tells him, "I can't believe you did that from the hip. I've never seen such a brilliant recovery. The jackals didn't know what hit them. It was like the prey suddenly became the predator." "It's true, Senator, wow, just wow," the young aide says. "Seriously, it was magnificent."

Girona ignores them. He feels relief. He checks his phone. Reads an email from Christian, "Well done. Remember what they say, the dogs bark, but the carnival moves on." Girona nods. He sees a message from Saundra Winston: "Everyone up here understood. I just watched the press conference. You were fantastic! So it looks like there are no problems. We're ALL still behind you. So ignore the media and focus on the convention next week. Nothing's changed. We all look forward to celebrating your nomination soon, Saundra."

Girona looks up and grins.

XXXIX

Back in New York, Cait feels a peculiar blend of anticipation and exhaustion. She thinks of what has drained her and what could follow. She has lunch plans with her father today, near his office at Columbia University. She has not spent meaningful time with him in months. But she received the news alert about Girona. It's her job to know what's happening. She's also curious. She plops down on her couch, turns on the TV, and watches Girona step before the media.

The past week was hard on Cait. But after last night, work feels like the easy part. Once Taylor walked away, Cait's night fell apart. Blake wanted answers at the party. She was mortified. Her professional world looked on. They left the museum, took a cab back to his hotel, and it got worse.

She cried. Broke down. Finally, she admitted it. She told him that Taylor should not matter now because she chose Blake. But Blake demanded details. She hesitated. He yelled, Tell me everything! And she cried. Then she told. Blake hit the wall with his fist. She screamed. He apologized. She cried. He apologized. She told him she hadn't seen Taylor since then, not until that night. Blake looked at her as if he couldn't detect lie from truth. She repeated, I chose you. But then she looked up at him and wondered why.

She thought about that day at the dock. She walked away from Taylor. She thought about the pier. Taylor walked away from her. And she let him go. She recalled Washington Square Park. She wanted to meet him there, but something stopped her. What kept stopping her? And as her thoughts strayed, she remembered what Taylor said to her. "It's not what you want in life that counts, but what you do." And everything hit her in a new way. She listened to Blake rant. But she thought about Taylor. She pictured him walking away at the party. And she stood still. She keeps standing still. She never does what she hopes with him. She didn't even want to let herself hope for that. Not anymore. And in that instant she somehow crossed over and found herself someplace else. She looked at Blake through her tears. And the words left her like one long exhale. I can't do this anymore. Blake heard her. But he seemed to think he misheard her. He calmed instantly and asked, You can't do what? And she whispered back, Us. He said, You can't mean that. But she nodded. And he knew, Cait did mean that. That's when impulse took hold of her. She slid the ring off her finger.

Blake would not take the ring. He stood over her, shaking his head, his gray eyes wide and red. He said, You can't. She did not blink. He added, I gave you that ring because I love you, it's yours, we're supposed to be together. He took her hand. She took hold of his wrist with her other hand and separated them. She placed the ring in his palm. He held it, open palmed. Then he threw it against the wall. He yelled, You slut! The ring ricocheted and fell onto the carpet. But no one reached for it. He glared at her. She stared at him, more stunned than upset. He told her, You'll regret this. And she nodded. Then she walked out. And for the first time in a long time, she felt no sense of regret.

The next day, this morning, she awoke at the hotel room the *Times* had booked for her. And it wasn't easy to think about last night. But oddly, she thought, it wasn't awful either. She feels as if she's been running against the wind for the past year and only now realizes it, because the resistance is gone. This morning, Blake reached out to her by text and email. Apologies were written. He called twice. He begged to see her in the first message. But as she began to listen to the second message, she heard a hint of anger. So she pushed a button and it was gone. She boarded her plane back to the city. And it was not Blake she thought about.

The coming week should allow her some rest and perspective. She had worked at least thirteen hours a day at the GOP convention. But Wallace will be off the radar during the Democratic convention. Nevertheless, her editors brought her home. They wanted their best political reporters in the city. This is the home turf of the *Times*. Still, she considered, her editors might want to keep her on a tighter leash since the Twitter incident. But a top editor spoke to her. He said, sure, there's a lesson to be learned but we all make mistakes. He went on to say that this was not a serious incident. Later, adding, Your best stories are ahead of you. And that's all it took, six minutes of encouragement from someone with stature.

She's happy to be home now, though she can't help but think of Taylor. Of course, he will also be at the Democratic convention. She wonders how to handle that. But the week ahead will allow her to figure things out. The subject is Girona. And her beat is Wallace. She is only expected to assist. She'll have time to sort her life.

So like everyone else, she watches the story on television. She waits for the press conference to begin, glancing periodically at her phone. She thinks about Taylor. Then it begins. Girona opens his mouth. And she's captivated. She does not think of the far worse story. Time has passed. If someone had the story, it would have run by now, or so she tells herself. Whatever the reason, she feels pleasure. She would not admit it, but she wants to see Girona squirm.

She leans forward. She hears him say how he's "proud to be one more American story." Reporters fire questions. He is collected. Yet again, he turns disadvantage into advantage. "I am not going to let anyone tell me I should be ashamed of my Latino upbringing." And she can't believe it. He's going to sail through this too.

She watches Girona exit the gaggle of reporters. And there's Taylor. He's on the television. Girona passes him. And Taylor's gone. She wants to call MSNBC and tell them to pan the camera left. She checks Fox and CNN. The pundits are already post-gaming. Impulsively, she texts Taylor: "Just saw u on TV. Can we tlk?"

She didn't expect to reach out to him this way, or this soon. But it's done. She bites her lower lip. Waits for a response. She texts again: "Im so sorry for everything. Truly sorry. Pls, let's tlk. Ive things to tell u."

"Hi," he texts.

"Hi. Thx for responding."

"Ur welcome."

"Can we tlk?"

There is a pause. She waits. But then he texts: "Sure."

"When?"

"Have to file a story. Call u in 20 mins."

"Thank u."

Taylor calls eighteen minutes later. Says, "Hello."

"Hi," Cait says.

Taylor's silent.

"I can't believe you're in the city," she says.

"Yeah, because of the Dem convention."

"No, I know . . . just . . . can I see you?"

She hears him breathe.

"Cait"—and she notices how he says her name—"we know how that went last time. How it always goes."

"It won't be like that. That's why I called. I want to talk to you. But I'd much rather do it in person. I mean, you're in town . . . can I see you? Please."

"I don't know."

"I want to talk about last night. About everything."

"You sure you're ready?"

"I am, yes."

"Today?"

"Yeah. I have to run up to Columbia to see my dad. Any chance you can meet me up there after?"

He pauses, as if after everything, after Charleston, after Washington Square Park, after the convention party, he wants to say no to her.

She holds her breath, biting her lip, waiting, waiting.

"Okay, Cait. Meet me outside St. John the Divine at four."

XL

The cathedral is neo-gothic and massive, and yet with its spires, its arches, its hand-carved grandeur, it seems misplaced beside the concrete buildings, the traffic, the sidewalk-casual New Yorkers. But if one approaches it from the right direction—west along the street, as Taylor walks now, passing beneath the slouching trees, until the view opens up and the cathedral seems to consume the city block—there is only the majestic, and it not only fits, but for Taylor, reminds him of a part of the city he has always loved, like a long-cherished friend seen again. And there too, standing alone atop the stone steps, resting against the great bronze doors, is Cait. Taylor crosses the street. He is too far away to notice Cait's anxious eyes, how her left hand squeezes her thigh, how her purse's black leather strap crosses between her breasts and over her tight pink tee and oversize black blazer. He ascends step by step. And sees. She's wearing his blazer.

It's the blazer from the night they first kissed. He remembers placing it over her shoulders in New Hampshire. She sees that he sees. Her nervousness shifts to joy. She smiles widely and high and her eyes are large with anticipation. He reaches the last step and grits his teeth. He wonders what it means. He presses his hope down. He's afraid to hope that much. He nears her. Stands a pace away from her. His eyes search hers. And she nods. *Yes. Yes. Yes.* He notices her hand. No ring. He asks, "Really?" She answers, "Really." And he picks her up, holds her close, and kisses her.

He sets her down and small, elated laughs escape them. He sees those hazel eyes, and her tears build, but do not fall. "What happened?" he asks.

"A lot, after you left the party. But . . . is it okay if I don't get into it right now?"

"Of course. I only care that you're here."

"It took me a long time to find my way back here."

"You're here now. That's all that matters."

Their lips touch again and intensify by the touch. Taylor feels a great beginning shoot through him. He lets go of the disappointment as easy as that, because what's in front of him is what he has waited for, and he's not going to question that. He's never been one to question that.

He asks if she's ever gone inside the cathedral. She shakes her head no. He takes her hand and leads her in. "It's one of my favorite places in the city," he says. They walk beneath the dim expanse of limestone pillars. Candles hang by cast-iron chains. He says it's the largest cathedral in the Western Hemisphere. "Tourists visit St. Pat's. Even most New Yorkers never come here," he says. "But this is the true jewel." He guides her down the right aisle. They walk past altars. The sun filters through stained glass. They pass the high pulpit and the grand organ that shakes the world on Sunday mornings. They walk up the opposite aisle. There's a preaching post overhead, carved in stone. They reach Taylor's favorite place, Poets' Corner. Dark granite rectangles line the floor and walls. They're cold to the touch and carry engraved inscriptions. It's immortality in two-by-three slats. Inscribed, the range of their lives and a glimpse into their words. And in their words is them. Robert Frost: "I had a lovers quarrel with the world." Ralph Waldo

Emerson: "Give me truths; for I am weary of the surfaces." Henry David Thoreau: "Be it life or death, we crave only reality." And Fitzgerald's line closing *Gatsby*: "So we beat on, boats against the current, borne back ceaselessly into the past."

"This place reminds me of all there is to life," Taylor says. " 'To live deep and suck out all the marrow of life,' as Thoreau put it. But I haven't been here in a few years. I think, well, I didn't want to face this part of myself. It was easier that way."

Cait looks up at him and says, "Taylor, I'm so sorry about everything."

"I know."

"Thank you for being patient."

"You're worth waiting for. I knew, right away, you were worth it."

She tiptoes up to him. And they meet each other there. He pulls her close. Closer. His arms wrap around her. And she never wants him to let her go.

Clouds roll over the sun. Gray light fills the Hungarian coffee shop. The café is a few blocks from the cathedral. It smells of espresso and fresh bread. Students crowd inside. Cait and Taylor sit beside the front window, on the same side of the table. They share a slice of carrot cake. She eats most of the frosting. He eats most of the cake. They speak inches from each other. Taylor tells her that he ran into her mother last month at a book party. "I know," she says. "She called me after. The media world is too small." "It is," he says. Cait says, "The great woman said you were 'rather thoughtful.' That's high praise for her." Taylor smiles and says, "I was surprised she recognized me." "I sent her that picture from Charleston," Cait explains. "Yeah, she mentioned that," he replies. Taylor asks if she knew everything that happened between them. Cait replies, "She knew enough. And she had opinions about Blake. But I think my years of yelling at her to back off, well, it finally led her to do that."

Taylor looks across the table at a scruffy young man. His eyes are fixated on his computer. His ears are covered with big black headphones. Taylor quietly asks Cait about Girona. She sips her espresso, sets down the little porcelain cup, and explains what happened. Why she did not write about it. Cait skips over the details of where Girona's hand was, how she felt. Taylor notices the residual angst in her eyes. But she speaks unemotionally. He wonders whether that is borne of resignation or indifference, or something else.

Taylor tells her what he saw in the hotel that day. Why he did not write about it. They speak in private whispers. He asks her whether *Redline* knows what happened between her and Girona. She shakes her head no. Her face cringes with nervousness. She thought Luke was the one looking into it. She asks if Luke said anything to him. He tells her that Luke asked for his help around New Year's, but he maintained a poker face. She says Luke tried to reach her around that time. She twitches her lips sideways as she asks about *Redline.* Taylor feels no obligation to keep Christian's confidence beside his feelings for her. So he tells her.

"You think *Redline* knows?" she asks.

"They may have only heard a rumor. They may be bluffing to get more. Otherwise, they would've run it." He adds that she can talk to Christian.

"I feel weird doing that. It's like I'd be colluding with them to cover it up."

"Yeah, that's probably the right instinct. I feel the same way about what I saw." He touches her hand and reiterates, "Nothing has come out. So it's likely nothing will."

She nods, and her eyes grow diffident with thought. "I don't want to think about this anymore," she says. "It accomplishes nothing. And this is a good day. Can we talk about something else?"

"Sure."

"Thanks . . . so how's work been?" she asks.

"Can we talk about anything else?"

"Oh—"

He smiles. "I'm joking. It's fine."

"We don't have to."

"Really, it's fine. I do have to face up to it."

"To what?"

"I think"—Taylor pauses and sips his coffee—"I think I'm going the wrong way."

"In what sense?"

He presses his palms together and looks at his hands. He unclasps them. And his eyes meet Cait's. "I'm beginning to think I'm not going anywhere I want to end up. Self-expectations are a bitch, right? But we don't choose our ambitions."

She searches for him between his words. But he says no more. He only finishes his espresso and savors the sugar at the bottom.

Later, they stroll downtown. They find their way to Central Park and follow a dirt path. Sunset nears. Day edges to night. Clouds part. Orange streaks the sky. Twilight comes over the city. Manhattan is polished with life. The cityscape glows over the tree line. And their world is luminescent.

They cross the width of the park and reach the north side of the Metropolitan Museum. They pass a wall of glass, and in it, they see themselves. Thick clouds return. A dark dusk comes. The wind stirs. The trees undress. Leaves twist in the air. Raindrops fall. They dash over to Fifth Avenue. And the hard rain comes. The Met's tourists scatter. People run, huddle beneath scaffolding. Umbrella salesmen emerge. Taxis shine yellow. Thunder rumbles. A red streetlight saturates. White headlights glow smoky. Water bathes buildings. Raindrops pop off the pavement and crack like glitter in the evening light. The water gathers, streams at the edges of the street. And the gutters swallow the rain.

Taylor takes her hand. They run and smile and laugh, as they cross the street and find shelter beneath a blue awning. A river of umbrellas passes. The street shimmers with city light. Taylor pulls Cait close and kisses her. The rain pours on.

In time, they find a taxi. He opens the door. She races inside. He leaps in after. They're drenched and laughing. Taylor kisses her again. The cabbie waits for them to tell him a destination. Horns honk. The white-bearded driver looks at the young couple in the rearview mirror and smiles. He waves the taxis past with his left hand. The driver does not rush them. He knows they have the rest of their lives to be rushed, and how quickly it does go by with the rush.

They become aware of themselves. Taylor apologizes. He does not want to take Cait to Liam's. It feels wrong to him. Cait tells the driver the address of her apartment. They plan to go to a late dinner in the area. But they arrive and do not leave.

And so time is lost, as they make up for lost time.

With the evening, they lay quiet and together and listen to the rain, as drops drum against metal and slide off the window air conditioner. The other window, nearest to them, is cracked open and a damp breeze passes through. Cait nudges between his arm and his chest and falls asleep first. She awakens at one point, looks up at him, and closes her eyes. The hour nears four. Taylor wakes to voices outside. He kisses the top of her head. She nestles into him. And the rain patters on.

They awake the next morning. The hour nears ten. The rain has long passed. "I sleep so well with you," she says with a yawn. She rises to make coffee. The covers slip off her body and diffuse sunlight bathes her cheekbones, her breasts, her narrow waist, the curve of her hips. He leaps out of bed and lifts her and tosses her onto the bed. She lands on her back and smiles impishly. He rises on top of her. Kisses her. She kisses him harder. He takes all of her and she lets herself be taken.

Afterward, they stare up at the ceiling. Taylor's eyes open and reclose and open. He's falling asleep. Cait lays docile. Her hair is disheveled. In time, she turns to him and asks, "Will you let me get coffee this time?" And he smiles and she smiles. She rises to her feet. He watches the light grace her body all over again, and she looks back at him, pushing her bangs to the side, shyly folding her lower lip under, and she is now, to him, as she ever was, beautiful.

Taylor hears the coffee grinder. Cait asks, from the kitchen, over the noise, if he has to work today.

"No. I'm not on the VP stuff. I just have to do a little research later and jump over to Fox for a quick hit."

"On what?" she asks, as the coffee drips and the smell fills the apartment.

"Just based on my story. Abortion and race politics. Then I'm all yours. What about you?"

"A little work, yeah. It seems like *Current*'s not riding you as much."

"They're disorganized with the new staff. They're also taking freelancers now, for the new mag section. It's easier to sneak in breathers lately."

She returns with two ceramic mugs glazed earthy greens and browns. "I hope they remain disorganized," she says. She hands one mug to him. He takes it and sits up against her headboard and drinks. She looks at him. Steam rises from her coffee. "Can we talk about the convention, about what happened?"

He nods.

"I don't know. Blake was a jerk at that party, but you were kind of a jerk too."

"I know."

"Just know, I'm not with you because you did that to him."

"Whatever—you loved that."

She rolls her eyes, nudges him, and says "maybe." His hands move up her legs. "Wait, Taylor." And he does. "I want to be serious for a moment. Let me explain." She sits beside him in bed and places her hand on his. "I want to explain. It's hard for me. You say all these things. I'm supposed to be the one who's good at this stuff. But it's hard for me."

"Okay."

"It's because of what happened after you left. I wanted to leave with you. I kept wanting to leave with you. I realized that everything that kept me with him was in my head and everything that made me want you was . . . well . . . from someplace more."

He nods.

"I thought about what you said back in Charleston," she continues. "That it's not what you want in life that counts, but what you do. I always thought I wanted a guy like him. But it was you. It just took me a while to realize it. Maybe I always knew, and I tried to ignore it." She looks at him, recalling what he told her at Poets' Corner. "Did you really always know?"

"Know what?"

"About us."

"Since I saw you navigating the snow in red heels."

"Really?"

"Not completely. It was after I told you that I worked for *Current.* You rolled your eyes at the bar. It was love at first eye roll."

"Stop. Don't joke."

"All right," he says. "It was when I first saw you, but also that entire night. When I talked about returning to Paris, you didn't roll your eyes. You weren't just another cynical New Yorker. Your eyes took on this beautiful weight. You said you would like that. And I just knew, I knew then, I wanted to take you there."

And she gives the smile that begins more quickly than it ends.

XLI

Cincinnati, Ohio

"Girona is near—get this—Paris," Jason says.

"There's a Paris, Ohio?" Vince asks.

"You bet. It's no Paris, Texas, let me tell you. It's near Canton. Girona's making a quick stop somewhere around there. He's doing some Americana crap. He'll probably turn stone to ice cream and bless a few babies. After that, his schedule says he'll stop at a vacant factory for a quick speech in Akron, where I'm sure he'll pledge to lead Chinese factories back to the Heartland."

"You mean the Promised Land."

"Exactly. Tonight, he hits Cleveland for his rock star revival."

"I can't believe he has Mellencamp and Lady Gaga," Vince says.

"I wish Constance would let us use Kid Rock."

"She deplores his music, even his name."

"Why?"

"She thinks his name is emblematic of a culture that doesn't want to become adults or take responsibility for their lives. Or something like that. You know, typical Constance. Actually, that's why I needed to talk to you. But again, it can't get back to anyone, especially her."

"What, you want me to see if Kid Rock will perform for us?"

"Jason, are you a fucking idiot?"

Vince sits in a back office at Wallace's Ohio headquarters. He's unshaven. A cigarette rests behind his ear. He stuffs Pad

Thai into his mouth with chopsticks while speaking to Jason over a landline. Outside the door, the office could be mistaken for a customer-care call center. Pastel clothes and pastel people. Pleated khakis. Hundreds of people work their call lists. Vince flew to Ohio to survey the state's staff and oversee the response to Girona's big event.

"Sorry," Jason replies.

"It's fine," Vince says. "But listen up. What we're about to do, it's serious shit."

Meanwhile, in New York City, the Democratic convention is under way. It's day one. And this evening, as Girona rallies in Ohio, state delegates will officially nominate him. It can last hours. The networks don't cover the nomination roll call anymore. It's scripted, predictable. Girona wants to appear beyond the script, beyond party politics, beyond the city, too. He will not look too Manhattan, too liberal. So he heartlands.

And sets fire to the land. Girona seems like a man rewound. He's ahead in the polls by a few points. Still, he campaigns like the insurgent of old, as if it's the previous year and Miles Riley remains the front-runner. But Girona has won the primary. He did not even select Riley as his VP. As Cait and Taylor reunited, Girona chose a young female governor to reinforce his Esperanza, his change, his "new Washington" message. He also hoped to mitigate Wallace's appeal to persuadable women. Riley is old Washington. He did win big southern and midwestern states in the primary. Girona took California, however, Riley's home state. The veteran had to accept his limits. The nomination would not be his. So Riley suspended his campaign. Still, most pundits, even Riley himself, thought Girona would select him as his running mate. After all, the very qualities Girona criticized Riley for in the primary—six-term senator, finance power broker, that old-man demeanor—might prove beneficial. It may take native knowledge to revitalize the swamp. But Girona doubled down on the theme that has taken him this far.

And he has come so far, only to return full circle and find his fire again. Perhaps it was the campaign upheaval. Perhaps he feels like a man who escaped the storm. But his inner populist has returned. He's gliding from fire to water once more. Pledging, "I will stand up for the invisible America. I will fight elites who corrupt our democracy." He's onstage with leading Latino activists. He pledges, "No one will divide us anymore." And so this man, who came from so little and became so much, preaches the great populist ballad—where the common is cherished, where good people are assured of their goodness and elites are scorned for compromising that goodness—even as Democratic delegates gather in the mecca of elitism to nominate him to lead the world's most powerful nation. There is some disappointment—in the D.C. establishment, among Wall Street Democrats—that he's firebranding again. That he ignored Riley. But he excites most delegates. They love to feel that fire. It makes them feel young. It reminds them of why they're Democrats. Girona is right. They always want to believe again. So Girona will heighten that emotion. He will delay his attendance at the convention and escalate the suspense. No winning campaign is without stagecraft. And Girona appreciates that better than any contender since Reagan. So he will be that image. He will embody their ideals. Because, he intuitively understands that in politics, if you win their hearts, their minds will follow.

Vince wants to break their hearts. If that's what it takes. Because maybe Constance Wallace will not do all that it takes. But he will. He thought of what Wallace's husband said about H. W. Bush and the Willie Horton ads. How easily dirt washes away. He called his old friend from past campaigns, Owen, the veteran GOP strategist. And Owen put it plainly, "History celebrates winners. Everything else—good intentions, causes, should-have-beens—they're just appendixes. And who the hell reads the appendix to anything?"

This is what Vince recalls, his conversation with Owen, as he speaks with Jason.

"What are we about to do?" Jason asks.

"Huh?"

"You said we're about to do some serious shit."

"Sorry, yeah," Vince replies. "So I was watching Fox the other night. Someone said that this news has damaged Girona's lofty image. That it could tamp down Dem turnout. I think that's right. It's not being written yet. But we chinked Hope's armor. This idea of him as the dream, and all that's baked into that—the first Latino nominee, the miraculous orator, the people's champion—I think his mystique is vulnerable for the first time. He's human again."

"So let's treat this like a fight," Jason says. "Let's pound his ass while he's stunned."

"That's what I'm getting at. Time to continue that conversation. I've talked to a few and reconsidered. You were right. You either play for keeps or you don't play."

"Hell, yeah!"

"We started this with the race thing. Let's finish it." Vince clears his throat. "Be sure the news comes out sometime soon. I'll leave the when to you. We need it to steal the thunder from the Dem convention. I want to do to them what they tried to do to us. I know they fed that abortion crap to the *LA Times*, or some Dem did. That damn yacht story too. Dems have been dehumanizing us as cold elitists. I never thought they could do that with her war story. But I guess even heroism is fickle. Or, rather, the media is fickle."

"So let's give them a new story. Every cycle, reporters wish for the crazy old days, those volatile conventions. Right?"

"Right."

"So let's give them what they want."

"We'll see if it's what they want," Vince says. "It depends on whether they love him or the story more. They have not had to choose yet. The race story was small-bore compared to this. But at some point the mainstream media always has to choose, at least those not expressly partisan. We'll just force that choice a lot sooner than it usually comes for a Democrat."

"We could just sidestep them—go for the conservative media."

"No. I want disengaged moderates. We need authoritative voices—those who are above the cross fire—to write Girona's obit. Someone like Peter Miller or Dan Balz, someone who can quickly mainstream it. I want the morning shows on it, drive-time radio, Jon Stewart, the late-night comics. I don't just want people arguing about it on Facebook. I want your aunt in Omaha asking you about it."

"Okay."

"But it must be done right. You did well last time. But this is the real shit."

"Because of how we found out?"

"No, huh . . . how did you find out? Wait, you're on a landline too, right?" Vince asks.

"Sure."

"How then?" Vince persists.

"A reporter began feeling around about it. He was guarded with me, so I knew something was up. Once I caught on, I had some folks followed, messages . . . well, attained. The media is always on the candidate. Instead, I focused on who might come to him. You know what I mean."

"Not really."

"I mean—"

"It's probably best that I don't know."

"Suit yourself."

"Just make sure that reporter doesn't realize he triggered the shit storm. You can use reporters, but they never want to feel used."

"Like a lot of women I know."

"Stop that crap. Listen, I know you think you know. But once we go here, there's no going back. Dems will have everything to lose. It'll be war. Constance cannot know we leaked it. No one can. The leak cannot be traced back to the GOP—"

"Vince, I know the playbook by now."

"Don't tell me that. Show me."

"I will."

John Cougar Mellencamp sings, “Used to daydream, in that small town. Another boring romantic, that’s me.” Mellencamp is spotlit, strumming his guitar, belting the lyrics before an American flag. Red, white, and blue balloons scatter the stage. Overheard, a sign reads BELIEVE AGAIN.

Thirty thousand Ohioans swell and sway and sing along. Joe Girona stands backstage, across the platform from Christian. Girona watches Mellencamp play. He feels the romance rise within him. He cracks his knuckles. He is eager to walk onto that stage. Excluding Christian, Girona’s senior staff and family are all back in New York, at the convention. But even as Democrats begin to nominate him, he’d rather be here and feel this rock’n’roll, this sense of possibility, this massive crowd that believes in him. He looks out into the darkness and feels limitless. He thinks about where he’s come from, the obstacles he’s overcome, the pride his grandfather would feel this night. He considers the mistakes that should’ve ruined him. He feels like a man given a second chance to be great. He wants to rise to the vision of him. And as Mellencamp sings “Boy, you’re gonna be president” and the crowd roars, his eyes dampen, because it’s almost too much to be true. For destiny must feel something like this.

In Manhattan, on the convention floor, a sea of delegates cheers and revels and screams with pride. State by state, alphabetically, Democrats declare Girona their nominee. And a man moves nearer to the presidency.

"On behalf of the great state of Arkansas, the home of the little place called Hope that gave America Bill Clinton, I am proud tonight to support a new generation of hope, and unite behind Senator Joseph Esperanza Girona, and elect him the next president of the United States of America."

The party secretary, presiding atop the dais, says, "Thank you, Arkansas. Thank you. Arkansas casts forty-seven votes for Joseph Girona." And the crowd cheers. "California. California, you have four hundred and forty-one votes. How do you cast them?"

"Madam Chairman." Thomas Fuller speaks over the applause.

Taylor is four yards away from Thomas, who heads the California delegation. Taylor recalls Sofia's book party. How buzzed Thomas was. How he bickered with Saundra Winston. And Taylor can't believe that the party was only weeks ago.

Cait sits among rows of reporters, working on her laptop.

Thomas continues. "The great state of California, home to the most diverse and talented people, the most dynamic economy . . ." As he speaks, a wave of delegate heads look down at their phones. Thomas does not notice. ". . . home to the world's greatest high-tech and entertainment industry, and . . ." The wave builds from hundreds to thousands. A tide of chins drop. Eyes fixate downward. The arena becomes eerily silent. Thomas pauses. He asks a colleague what's going on. He's told. And his eyes widen.

For there it is, in big red font, atop *Drudge*: Exclusive: Girona Cheated on Wife in Hotel.

Cait sits back in her seat, staring blankly at her laptop monitor, numb. Taylor weaves his way out of the crowd, toward the press box, searching for Cait. Delegates flick through their phones. Quiet ebbs to chatter, questions, anxiety. Inside a skybox, overlooking the convention floor, Saundra Winston reads her phone, looks downward on the mass of delegates, and closes her eyes. The Democratic secretary calls for order. She asks Thomas to continue. Thomas ignores her. He huddles with three colleagues. They cover their mouths like football coaches who fear the opposition can read lips. Thomas returns to the microphone and requests an intermission.

The secretary doesn't know what to do. She looks over at Nancy Pelosi. Pelosi looks at Thomas Fuller. Fuller whispers into Miles Riley's ear. Michael Dukakis intertwines his fingers behind his head and walks over to John Kerry. Kerry gulps. Party mandarins form an impromptu conference on the floor. Two Rules Committee members step in. More talk. Girona's representatives furiously wave their arms. Word is sent. Reporters pour onto the floor. Some journos lack floor passes, but they push past security to corner the delegates, to get the story. They finally have a convention story.

The secretary pounds the gavel with her hammer. "Order. Order! We will have order!" A recess is announced. Girona loyalists scream at the dais. Amid the cacophony, some delegates press their palms against their ears; others stand there like directionless buoys, as waves of people rush past them.

Cait places her laptop in her bag. Taylor pushes through the crowd, looking for her. Saundra Winston exits the skybox. Miles Riley shoos reporters away. Thomas Fuller speaks with Joe Biden and the head of the New York delegation. Meanwhile, forty-two blocks uptown, at her apartment in the city, Erin Ellis watches television in her living room, as the network interrupts its regularly scheduled programming.

Christian looks like leather gone wan. In minutes, 452 messages amass in his inbox—emails, news alerts, Twitter feeds. He goes to the source of the news. Sees the flashing siren. The red headline.

Mellencamp sings on. Mobile phone light spreads across the darkness. The crowd becomes visible gradually, as countless faces fixate on their tiny monitors. A stagehand walks over to Mellencamp and tells him. Mellencamp plays on. Christian clicks on the headline and reads the report:

> ****World Exclusive****
> ****Must Credit DRUDGE REPORT****
>
> **Joe Girona had an affair with a yet-unnamed woman as recently as the primary, according to an authoritative source. THE DRUDGE REPORT has learned that there is evidence of at least one tryst, "sexual in nature," in an Iowa hotel room around Christmastime.**
>
> **Mrs. Girona, who won the public's heart after speaking about her difficult experience with IVF on *Oprah*, WAS PREGNANT with their second child at the time of the affair. The extent of the relationship with**

the mistress remains unknown. Girona's campaign may be compromised.

Apparently, there have been backroom whispers among a small group of Democratic insiders over whether Girona has a mistress. A source says several media outlets have been looking into the scandal but either chose not to report it or failed to get the story, reported first on DRUDGE REPORT.

The shocking news comes as Democrats nominate Girona in New York City.

Developing . . .

Christian looks across the stage. Girona's gone. He checks the AP's Twitter feed. Skims headlines. The nomination roll call was stopped at California. Delegates have left the convention floor. Christian feels as if his world has been inverted. The old basset hound's face sags. Then he tells himself to focus on the job before him. And duty orientates him. He emails his candidate and his colleagues at the convention. Reads more news. Girona finally messages him. They plan to meet in five minutes. Christian wants to know everything in advance. He wants to collect himself. It's not the news that unnerves him. It's what may still come. That goddamn word "Developing . . ."

Thousands flood the arena hallway. Cait and Taylor stand inside a doorway. "The report probably has nothing to do with you," Taylor says to her. "*Drudge* used the word 'mistress.' You weren't a mistress."

Her eyes peek leftward. Strangers speed by. No one is listening. She looks back at him and whispers, "But what if there's a misunderstanding? What if Girona told someone what happened with me was consensual, to cover himself? You said you heard his wife freaking out about some email or text about an Iowa hotel. What if they got hold of that? *Drudge* mentioned other media. What if he knows that Luke was, or is, looking into it? You said Christian asked about *Redline*. Why would a tabloid hold back any news this sensational?"

"I don't know."

"More must be coming. This is a nightmare." She blinks. Breathes. Tries to keep her composure. She peeks sideways again. Still only strangers.

"We'll figure this out together," Taylor says. "But step back for a moment. If *Drudge* had any hint of this involving a *Times* reporter, he'd be all over it. He hit you about an inane Twitter post. He'd be sirening the *Times* aspect alone."

"Yeah." Cait hesitates. Picks at her cuticle. "But he wrote 'developing.' What if they're slowly feeding this stuff to *Drudge* to keep the media hungry?"

"More may be reported. But that doesn't mean it's about you, or that he'll name you."

"But he wrote 'developing.' Jesus."

"I know."

"I mean . . . I mean, he could be about to name me. I can't stay here to find out. This place is swarming with reporters."

"Let's go then." Taylor takes her hand. He cuts their way through the crowd. Peter Miller sprints by. They exit Madison Square Garden. Taylor notices Thomas Fuller walking out with several delegates. He sees Saundra Winston entering her black town car. He leads Cait across the street. Finds a taxi. He tells the driver Cait's address. Erin calls Cait. Cait looks at her phone and answers.

Taylor checks his phone. The avalanche is under way. The news tops media worldwide. Scooplets proliferate. "Girona missing. Aides can't find their candidate." "Source: delegates 'considering options.' " News websites are so desperate for original content that they turn no information into news. Girona Institutes Media Blackout leads CNN's website. Peter Miller tweets: "Democratic superdelegates meet in secret. See *Current* for story." *Drudge*, *Huffington Post*, and *Reddit* link to the *Current* story. *Slate*'s John Dickerson tweets: "Based on the most recent rules, superDs could shift nomination to Riley. Race was close enough. Riley only 'suspended' his campaign." A *Huffington Post* reporter rebuts with a tweet: "A superD shift would be extreme, undemocratic. Girona won the most primary votes. Dems are the party that says every vote should count." The same tweeter follows up a minute later: "Riley quoted in '68 paper supporting rules changes that will 'return primary to the people.' " Veterans see what's afoot. No reporter could know that fact off-the-cuff. Girona's press shop must be feeding content to *Huffington Post.* Naturally, Girona's staff wants to kill the possibility, however remote, that he could somehow still lose the nomination. A *Times* blogger follows. He echoes *Huffington Post.* The *Times* authority mainstreams the Twitter debate. And conventional wisdom gels.

Taylor is tempted to back up Dickerson. Dickerson's doing his job. He's not reporting what should be done. He's reporting what could be done. The Democratic nomination rules were changed in 1968 to disempower party bosses and diversify the nomination process. But four years later, George McGovern won only one state. Then came Jimmy Carter, hardly a formidable candidate himself. So Democratic veterans decided that they needed to retain some power to assure pragmatism. Democrats did not want to be trounced again. They gave special status to leaders, those who fought the long fight, pols from Harry Reid to power brokers such as Thomas Fuller. These unpledged delegates, known as superdelegates, cemented Walter Mondale's 1984 bid. Of course, Reagan decimated Mondale after that. But the winds were too strong for any Democrat that year. Taylor thinks of these things. But writes nothing. Judges recuse themselves from cases that compromise their objectivity, or they should. He decides he must do the same. He must stick with his decision. But he's one of *Current*'s four senior political writers. His editors know he's close to some Girona bigwigs. He wonders how long it will take them to realize he's not contributing.

The sensational news soon overwhelms all else. Sex. Power. Sex. Power. Who's the woman? When? Where in Iowa? How often? What does the mistress look like? Insiders tweet sourceless speculation. Newt Gingrich goes on Fox and says, "I'm told this is very serious. It feels like Donna Rice on steroids." Gary Hart's second chance, his serious prospect at the 1988 nomination, sank after the media reported his affair with Donna Rice. But that was early in the primary. This is nomination day. After Gingrich speculates, Fox anchor Shepard Smith reminds viewers, "So far this is solely conjecture. There has been no evidence put forward, as of yet. *Fox News* has not confirmed these reports." Still, conservative sharks smell that blood. Townhall.com headlines: Lewinsky Part II? *Drudge* links. Lucianne.com devotes its homepage to the scandal. Republican officials are oddly silent. A *Current* news alert explains why: "Wallace asks campaign and RNC staff to offer no comment until more facts are known." An influential union, SEIU, puts out a press release reaffirming its support for Girona. MSNBC discusses the report's timing more than the report. One of its anchors, Rachel Maddow, posits, "This looks like a Republican hit job to me. And I must say, a questionably racist one, to attack the first Hispanic nominee with unsubstantiated accusations of an affair. Or at least someone perceived as the first Latino nominee." *Drudge* posts a red headline in the upper left: Where Is Girona??? It links to a live C-Span feed of the Ohio rally. Mellencamp is no longer singing. Soon, some networks offer a split screen of the same shot. Viewers see an empty stage.

In the taxi, Cait tells her mom over the phone, "I understand. I won't do anything without running it by you." Cait listens and nods. She adds, "I love you too." Taylor reads an email from P&R to the staff: "This is the ballgame. So if you have no assignment yet, think about how you can contribute. Let's get the story! Let's own this news!" Cait puts her phone inside her bag. Peter replies-all to P&R's email: "Tick-tock!" Taylor clicks off his phone. Looks at Cait. She grips the seat cushion with one hand and stares off. City lights blur by. Taylor puts his hand on hers. He wishes he knew what to do. But he only feels anger in that instant. Peter's email flashes through his mind. *Tick tock.*

⚜ ⚜ ⚜

Joe Girona screams at Christian, "Of course I called her! She won't pick up."

"Calm down," Christian replies. He leans against the dressing room door.

Girona sits before a vanity mirror and stares at his hands.

"Most wives wouldn't talk to their spouse in this . . . situation," Christian continues. "Give her time. We'll do this without her. But we can't do anything if you don't calm down."

Girona nods. His gaze retreats inward. Soon he stands, kicks aside a plastic bin, and stares at his shoe, which reflects the room's incandescent light. He takes a few steps and begins pacing. He stops and turns to Christian and cracks his knuckles. "You can't spin a turd, right?"

"Right."

"So we'll handle this like Wallace. Only better," Girona says. "Pundits always say it's the cover-up that kills. That's what they said about Nixon. What really hurt Bill? He lied. So if it's the cover-up, I'll come clean."

"I don't think that's a good idea. I don't care what they say. I've thought about this every day for too long. Affairs are different, especially here, especially when it concerns the presidency. And your wife's pregnancy is no small thing either. People see you as this ideal family man. The public's sympathy will not be with you, to say the least."

"You don't believe this sensational crap should matter."

"It doesn't matter what I believe. It only matters what voters believe. You know that."

"No. I've heard for years, every time another politician gets caught with a mistress, pundits say the guy should just come clean. I'll do that. I'll tell the truth."

"I just don't know, Joe. You've got more guts than you could hang on a fence. It'd be brave to confess and all. That may help you come back later on, like in some shitty little Democratic House seat. Sure, if a Democratic electorate has to choose between you and some Republican, they'll select you. But you have to appeal to the entire public right now." Christian's droopy cheeks inflate and deflate. "And listen, in my experience, the more people involved in any conversation the less honest the conversation becomes."

Girona shrugs.

"Listen to me. There's a reason many smart men before you have not been candid," Christian says, eyeballing his friend. "People may request honesty, but on some explosive topics they can't tolerate the entire truth. And let's not forget, you screwed up here. So for you, right now, every damn word counts. The entire nation will join this conversation. They will deconstruct every word you say. The media, especially."

"Precisely. I can take control of the situation. Americans believe in second chances. It worked for Wallace. She's not in my league."

"But Wallace's abortion happened decades—"

Girona puts up his right index finger. "I've made my decision. The media probably knows everything already, or soon will. It's better if it comes from me. I'll give them nothing left to report. That'll gut the story."

"I just don't know."

"I do know. And don't sweat the press. I've always handled them, haven't I?"

Christian blinks but he has no words.

"Tell the circle," Girona says. "Before delegates panic, I'll cut this off at the pass."

Christian furrows his leathery brow. Perhaps his friend can do this too. Yet he worries. Is he witnessing one more great man who believes too much in his greatness? But this is Joe. He can wield a crowd like no other. Christian can't recall a time when his friend failed to spin his way out. And Christian has dedicated everything to him. He loves him like a brother. He never thought his friend, the diplomat, could become a superstar. He's been surprised before. He was awed when he realized that Joe was like the orators of old. He searched so long for a Democrat with some Huey Long, some William Jennings Bryan, someone with a visceral connection to the workingman who could rouse the masses but also manage the modern Big Show. And after so long, it was his friend, all along. When he realized it way back when, an old saying occurred to him: "Here's a horse that can be ridden for distance." And he had to do a double take—it really was Joe up there, over there, captivating people this way. Now they've gone the distance, almost. They're so close. He thinks about the candidate his friend's become, the icon he's become, how well Joe handled the race story. *Maybe he can handle this too. If anyone can, he can.*

XLII

The yellow cab glides beneath green lights, past electric buildings, and nears Cait's apartment. The driver turns on the radio. A city news station, 1010 WINS, is broadcasting its traffic update. Then it reports, "We've gotten the two-minute warning. Girona is on his way out."

"Girona's doing a presser," Taylor blurts. Cait's face tenses. Taylor looks at the meter and drops the cash in the front seat. The cab reaches her apartment. They rush upstairs. Turn on the television. It's already tuned to CNN. The media sit, hungry, waiting. Pundits are pre-gaming.

Taylor checks his phone. He reads the latest report: "Girona to come clean." Taylor's throat becomes parched. He shows Cait the headline. She places her head in her hands. Taylor takes her hands gently, lowers them, and says, "It's probably not about you. Why would he admit that? It's sexual harassment."

"He may lie. He may say it was consensual. We talked about this. I can't trust him in any way. I mean, what if it's my word versus his? People will wonder, if I had nothing to hide, why'd I hide it? I just . . . I just can't believe this is happening." Her eyes flush red.

Inside a hotel conference room, Thomas Fuller stands among hundreds of superdelegates. No aides are present. The superdelegates stop talking. They stare at the live broadcast. The televisions frame an empty podium, with a nest of microphones bundled atop the lectern. Not far from the hotel, uptown, Erin Ellis bites down on her fist and waits. A few avenues away, next to Central Park, Saundra Winston sits in her apartment. She too watches the television. Her maid pretends to dust an antique settee five paces back. Winston holds her vodka rocks with both hands and tilts toward the TV. At Madison Square Garden, the Democratic faithful gather again on the floor. The mega screen broadcasts MSNBC's live feed. The press box is rife with speculation. Luke waits with his laptop, transfixed, ready to jump off any news. He wonders if he was right all along.

Down the Atlantic coast, 863 miles south in Savannah, inside their mansion's TV room, Constance Wallace sits with her husband on a deep, plush couch. Their feet no longer rest on the ottoman. The projection television shows the empty podium on the large white screen. The room's lights are dimmed. The punditry, the surround sound, is muted. Wallace reads news feeds on her phone and glances upward with her eyes wide.

In D.C., beside old metal filing cabinets and a small television, Jason sits in his cluttered office and grins.

Vince stands at the center of Wallace's Ohio headquarters. The call center stops. People stare up at the televisions. Vince's mouth remains rigid. He is on the edge of a smile. But he hesitates. He will not assume the outcome. He has never faced a politician as gifted as Girona. He used to feel this way about the Bulls in the 1980s. He never liked any Chicago team, but he disliked the Bulls in particular. Back then, if the Bulls were down by a basket with only a few seconds left, he was never confident. Because the team had *him.* And there was always something about Jordan that was not quite mortal.

Cait bites the inside of her cheek. She presses her feet into the ground. Taylor takes her hand, looks at her, and wishes he could do something, anything, to help, as he turns up the TV's volume. Joe Girona hurries to the microphones.

Shutters fire. Flashes ricochet off of him. Girona's eyes are downcast. He coughs into his right fist and scratches behind his left ear. His gaze rises. And he sees the circus. But his eyes are detached. He looks at everyone and sees no one. There's no assured smile.

"In my career, I've fought for progressive causes. Above all, I've tried to stand up for the forgotten Americans. I've spoken up for the middle class, for the working class. But I've made my own mistakes as well. Today, I want to address a private and serious failing."

Girona clears his throat and continues. "As some reported today, I made a mistake last year. I violated a solemn vow and my wife's faith in me. I regret that with all my heart. I will regret it for the rest of my life. I hurt my wife. I hurt my family. I hurt all of you. I violated my obligations to my family. And perhaps, though I cannot know how all my supporters feel, I violated their belief in me. I am so profoundly sorry for that. And let me say to my supporters, to my party, to America, what I have said to my family; I am responsible for my actions. This is *my* mistake alone." He coughs into his fist. Camera shutters shuffle. Flashes flicker off his skin. He blinks several times and scratches the top of his left ear.

"Now, I don't know exactly what has been reported. But I would like to take this opportunity to tell the entire story. I'm sure a lot of fabrications will be written. I'm sure there will be many exaggerations. But I think it's important to disregard the sensationalism and clear the air. I think it's important that I talk straight to you. Because it's the public I care about, not the tabloid media. And . . . well, during the campaign, I spent too much time away from my family. I did not think enough about my personal conduct. I became . . . I made a grave mistake with another woman." He coughs into his fist. "She and I, well, I guess it's being reported, or is about to be. Regardless, I want to be frank with all of you . . ."

In New York, Cait watches and clenches her jaw. Taylor closes his fist.

Flashes fire. Shutters click manically. Girona breathes and continues, "She and I . . . Saundra Winston and I had . . ."

Cait's mouth drops. Taylor's mouth drops.

Saundra Winston drops her glass. The vodka spills across her rug. Her maid flees to the kitchen.

Erin Ellis stops biting her fist.

Christian, standing to the side, off camera, closes his eyes.

At the convention, thousands stare upward at the mega screen. Transfixed.

Luke's eyebrows rise. He begins searching for his files on Winston's campaign contributions.

Memories race through Taylor's mind . . . The book party. Saundra Winston glaring at Thomas. How she defended Girona and said, "He's *not* just another pol." Mrs. Girona storming into Christian's Iowa office. She mentioned Iowa and a hotel. The night Girona hit on Cait, Girona's biggest fund-raisers were in town, which likely included Saundra

Winston. He thinks about the millions in contributions. He realizes that the donations may not have concerned currying political favor. She may have simply convinced her powerful husband to help her paramour. He recalls seeing Saundra hurry into her town car half an hour ago. *That's why she rushed out.* He looks over at Cait. Her eyes are fixed on the television.

Girona speaks on, defends Winston. He says she is a "dedicated American who engaged in politics as a private citizen." He asks the media not to bother her. He reiterates, "It's my fault alone. I'm the one in the public eye, not her, or her family. Please remember that." He coughs into his fist. "And—and I am the one who should've known better. There are"—Girona's voice becomes guttural and his shoulders rise and the veins in his neck show—"there are moral absolutes. There are consequences if you violate them." Flashes pulse off him. He pauses, blinks, glances around the room, nods downward, looks at the cameras, and adds, "Today is one of those consequences."

So he shall face the consequences. He gives the pro forma political apology. His words echo fallen men before him, after him, always. It's a very American ritual. The disgraced pol receives his scarlet letter. Live on television. Inside America's town square, the man must be shamed.

On the convention floor, thousands watch their candidate confess. Heads shake. Some whisper to one another. Eyes narrow. Questions linger within long stares.

Was Christian right?

Will liberals forget that they share Girona's cause? He is the populist candidate. Ostensibly their candidate. Girona used his platform to speak for the invisible class. But infidelity eclipses, and the bond can get lost in that dark. For the adulterer is outed. Soon ostracized? How can he be a progressive champion yet act so regressive? How could I have ever thought he was so handsome? I can't believe I wore a pin that read GIRONA IS SEXY. He fooled me, us, U.S. He humiliated his wife. He betrayed her. Betrayed U.S. He cheated on the everywoman. The idealized husband looms like a great athlete who wasted his potential. Is he the dreamy man in the marriage announcements? Mr. Right gone wrong. The expectations embitter the disappointment. Even some loyalists begin to think, The scum did this to his wife. While she was pregnant! While she was suffering through IVF! God, he's *that* guy. What's with assholes and their infidelity?

Americans watch nationwide. There is immeasurable sympathy for his family. His wife. Whatever your values, his poor wife. To see your husband, your spouse, talk about cheating on you live on national television. "Breaking News" ticks below.

It's never happened quite like this before. But the public has, in that broader sense, been here so many times before. So. Many. Times.

And they'll be here again. This is America. The philandering pol must be shunned. What follows varies. Who is the alternative? Partisans will rarely throw away all their principles for one principle. Some men survive. Some recover on the smaller stage. Because partisans consider the alternative. But these men confess their shame. They re-conform to the monogamy compact. Most stay out of the spotlight long enough to prove repentant. Can Girona recover in real time and on the main stage? Democrats still, technically, have a choice. Must the adulterer be expelled from the arena? He was never a man in his arena. It's their arena. And citizens make the rules. That's democracy.

The perennial debate already dominates Twitter and kin. For the people shall judge.

Some liberals have reached a verdict. Don't tell us not to judge. Judging feels good. And he deserves it. But you espouse tolerance? Not in these cases. You know, you liberals don't seem so libertine. I notice your high marriage rates, the conservative way you wish girls dressed, your belief in strict monogamy. U.S. liberals are social conservatives in an American way, even if they dare not say.

The religious right will say. They're preaching. The fallen man teaches us to live upright. Liberal behavior proves we're right. But judge not, lest ye be judged—right? You've overlooked sins to protect your cause. For every Bill Clinton there's a Newt Gingrich. And who's the greater hypocrite? While having an affair, Gingrich supported Clinton's impeachment. And Gingrich is *still* standing on that values soapbox. What does the Bible say about casting the first stone?

Feminists are torn, again. They once accepted Oval Office behavior that they condemn in other offices. Must they stomach Girona too? Supreme Court nominees do not depend on him, yet. He's not their president, yet. They hate the notion of standing by your man. He's a fake new man. A traitor. Yes, we believe in sexual tolerance if it liberates women or gays. But strong women do not tolerate piggish men, promiscuous men. She must leave him. Right? Or is that left?

Of course, the id can overcome all. Biology is destiny. So we've heard. But men say they want monogamy too. If only we could conduct an experiment and isolate a random population of humans with similar biology? Oh yes, gay men. See gay male clubs for details. It's not a gay thing. It's a guy thing. But hetero men date women. Thus fidelity's flaws. That's the power of our instincts. Generally. Of course generally. What do you think generalizations are? The exceptions are not the point. This behavior, in part, exemplifies the larger point. Biology. Successful men are competitive men. Competiveness and risky behavior correlate with high testosterone. Success raises testosterone. And testosterone enhances risk taking and libido. Groan. Sexuality is sooo sexist.

Because it's society's fault. I believe in the concept of gender, not sex. Men and women are basically the same. Really? Fine, worldwide, men swoon over the universal waist-to-hip ratio. But women like handsome too, though most will take their pinups with plot. And yes, women, in their unique way, are attracted to powerful men—strong men, rich men, celebrated men, celebrities. Watch girls scream over boy bands. Society. Female models earn far more than male models. Society. Female lust is open to a wider range of arousal, but male lust is monomaniac amid the visual. Society. Yes, I see the data. Many more men cheat. But haven't you heard me? Society! Sure, I believe in evolution and climate change. Just don't give me the unfiltered science of sex. Never mind hormones. But the sexes' neural circuitry even differs. Whatever. I have faith in the outliers. I only read those who keep the faith. It's not nature if you don't nurture the conclusion. Keep your evolutionary biology to yourself, you pig.

Yes, you, pig. Should your woman leave you if you fail at work? Stark sexual economics goes both ways. But they need not. Times have changed. Some things can change. We are our nature and our nurture. Diet and distress can impact our genes for generations. But from survival to sex, our instincts developed over eons. Human nature is on geologic time. Modernity is a speck in our species' time.

Fine, but we all compromise sometimes. We women do, every day. And be honest, most of us like the differences between men and women—love them, in fact, how we complement each other and all that. So please, manhood is no excuse. You men say, "I do," too. This is female-male marriage. There are terms. You agreed to society's terms. Monogamy can be hard for women too. Okay, we have different biology. Testosterone enhances libido. And sure, I don't know what you're feeling. But grow up. Socialize with grown-ups. And manage your libido. We are mammals. You may especially be an animal. But we are also modern humans. We constructed culture from our better nature. Culture restrains our primal nature. But nurture failed to restrain Girona's nature. Then learn from him. Because society expects more of him—and you. Welcome to adulthood. So bridle those instincts. Men, be gentle men. You mean feminize? I mean modernize. Recognize. Civilize.

After all, this is American civilization. Even our liberals conserve social rules. And look at what happens if you break the rules. You lose. Girona's losing. He's humiliated. Dishonored. He could lose everything.

Libertines, do you believe in the people or not? Power to the people! Or only when it suits you? The people denounce Girona's infidelity. Don't be so Western European. So tolerant. Don't most Americans want family men, or women, as their figureheads? Isn't that our deal? Watch the press enforce the deal. They're the people's values police. Cuff the cheater. Bring him before us. The scandalized pol must endure his perp walk.

But tribalism can outweigh all. Americans disapproved of Bill Clinton's affair *and* his impeachment. American prudishness has limits. But partisanship defended those limits. Liberals weren't going to side with the opposition. Besides, in politics, what's more American than choosing the lesser of two evils?

And Girona knows that. He relies on it. He ignores the culture warriors. He worries about what Americans don't tune out. He feels them watching him. Now. This is his one chance. Can he pull a Clinton? He is not his party's nominee, yet. He recognizes his challenge. He broke a moral contract. He has lived in the South. Will he know his Gospel again? The preachers who weaned him are like ghosts beside him, whispering: reap what you sow, Joseph Esperanza Girona.

But he is Esperanza. He has hope. And talent. So much talent. He will fight. He utilizes sex scandal PR 101. This man is the true showman. He's facing the media firing squad. He's suffering public humiliation. For he knows that's what the adulterous pol must do.

So he checks the boxes. He stands alone onstage. He is being a man and taking it. He evokes contrition. Solemnity. Confesses. Apologizes. He takes responsibility. He promises to seek forgiveness. But can a politician who wants to retain great power check that last box? Can he pledge therapy?

Therapy. Girona can take responsibility but evade it. He's not the archetypal powerful man with that ego, those male appetites, the opportunities and opportunism—that most male variety of selfishness and shortsightedness. He has an illness. Wink-wink, men. It's the fallen man's modern path to redemption. Illness can be cured. It wasn't Girona. Or his nature. Or the sin of his success. Not even egocentrism. It was the illness. The illness cheated on his wife.

Girona won't go that far. He refuses to look too weak. Weakness invites enemies. He wants it all, still. He can't yield, seek therapy, and climb this high again. He knows few get a second chance at the Big Show. He's too close to surrender. He was about to be nominated. He can still have it. Believes it. Believes in himself. He feels that he's on firmer ground. His voice is steadying. He sounds sincere. He's no longer coughing into his fist. He speaks confidently into the camera. He believes some men can beat back the storm.

"We are more than the tabloids who spread gossip and dirt." Girona's voice rises as if he's onstage. "My campaign has been a long journey. We've come this far because we believe in something. My severe mistake does not undercut that belief. We believe America can be more just, more fair. We believe everybody deserves the same pay for the same work. We believe in equal rights, in privacy, and personal rights." Are you listening feminists? Oh how he suggests it. He still supports abortion rights. Fair pay. He wouldn't dare use female as an adjective. See, he's still with you. He's still the only real women's candidate in this race.

"We believe America is only as strong as its middle class," he continues. "I have always fought for that. We need to continue that fight. Otherwise, Constance Wallace's idea of change will come to pass. She wants rich people to pay lower taxes and you to pay more for retirement. She judges a nation's success by the yachting class. I believe only in waves that lift all boats. And I'm not going to stop believing. I'm *not* going to stop fighting. Sensationalism will *not* steal my fight. Republicans can throw what they want at me, at us. We're going to fight on. Our cause is too large for petty politics." He eyeballs reporters. "No matter how much the media fixates on the small things,

I will fight for the big things. Lest anyone forget, we have big problems. I'm going to become president and solve them. I remain no less dedicated to the cause. I'm not Martin Luther King. But I do *not* believe King's perfect cause was sullied by his failure to be the perfect husband. I have fought all my life for his dream. Many of you have as well. Throughout this campaign, I've spoken a great deal about the dream. I urge you to not let this distraction deter your belief. As my opponent said last week, 'I'm *not* up here because I'm perfect.' I'm flawed. But I've never lied to America. I've meant every word I've said. I believe someone has to stand up for the invisible America. I've never said I'm a man without flaws, without problems. I've spoken about America's problems. I've fought elites. I've fought to help more people realize the American dream. I've fought for that dream. And it can be done. I've made an awful mistake. But, to paraphrase Ted Kennedy, the dream does go on, and the cause does endure. And no matter what, I intend to see that cause through . . . Okay, I'll answer a few questions."

Cait watches with distant eyes.

Questions come. Reporters bombard him. How could you? When she was pregnant, on IVF! Do you know what it's like to take those hormone shots? How many affairs have you had? What do you mean "small thing"? Do you think infidelity is a "small thing"? You may not have lied, but you acted like the perfect husband. Is the affair really over between you and Saundra Winston? *Current*'s Luke Brennan just reported that Mrs. Winston gave millions of dollars to your campaign; do you have any response; are you going to return that money? If you stay in the race, aren't you risking Democrats' chances of winning? If you remain a candidate, won't it be awful for your family? How could you do this to your wife? You know you're in the public eye. Did you really think you'd get away with it? Did you think at all? Why do you men never think? One woman, behind the reporters, screams, "Shame!"

Girona creases his forehead. "It was a mistake," he confesses. "It's over. And no, there were no others. I've been in love with the same woman for all of my adult life, my wife. And I always will be. That never changed, never will." He says he will look into giving back the Winston contributions. He says marital fidelity "is not a small matter." He did not mean that. "But I also believe the public cares about how I'll act as president, not whether I've been perfect in my personal life. And let me tell you, I'm going to make them proud as president."

Reporters hit back. One asks, "I heard *Times* columnist David Brooks speaking a few minutes ago on PBS. Brooks pointed out that Americans see the presidency as personal. He spoke of our nation's puritan history. But he also contrasted England's prime minister and queen with us. The president is our head of government *and* our head of state. Isn't he right? Don't Americans have certain moral expectations of our head of state? Isn't character not only about how you act in public but also in private?"

"Character is also about facing one's critics, looking them in the eye, and owning up to your mistakes. Character is not only about who we've been; it's also about who we try to become. It's not only the mistakes that brought us low. It's how we fight to come back. It's why we fight, and what we fight for. The mothers who are paid too little and work too hard, the dishwashers who don't earn a living wage, the teachers who go unsung, they all know I fight for them." He looks at the camera. "And let me say to the hardworking Americans out there, those who know hard times, if you stand by me, I'll never stop standing up for you. I'll never stop fighting for you. For once, you *will* have a president who really does fight for you."

He keeps at it. Echoes those bygone men, again. Sure he's doing what escaped lesser men. His shoulders are now pulled back and he stares forward, unbowed.

Reporters scream questions. He's compelled to explain more. "I focused too much on my public life and let my private life go terribly astray." The line flows too fluidly, as if canned. He hints at his assured smile. Shifts back quickly. Evokes solemnity. Nods contritely. Check. "One thing is for sure, this will never happen again. And with God's help, we'll come out of this stronger. We shall finish the fight."

Cait saw the smile. Clicks the remote. The television goes black. "I can't suffer this bullshit anymore," she says. "God, he has an answer for everything. Will he actually talk his way out of this too?"

XLIII

In midtown Manhattan, inside the hotel conference room, superdelegates watch Joe Girona on television. Girona walks away from the microphones. Reporters scream questions at him as if there's any chance he'll turn around and take more. Someone mutes the sound. A woman murmurs "asshole." One man shakes his head in silence. But most of the power brokers are already talking and, however dispirited, passing options back and forth. Thomas Fuller leaves the conference room, closes the door behind him, and calls Saundra Winston.

"Hello," she says.

"Saundra, thanks for picking up. It's Thomas."

"I know. That's why I answered."

"Thank you. I do need to speak with you."

"Okay."

He hears her sniffle. "You okay?"

"What do you think? Clayton is on his way home. I have yet to speak to Joe. So, amid that hell, what is it, Thomas?"

"I just left most of the superdelegates. I need to meet with a few key figures, my delegation, and then go back into that room. Afterward, I go back on the floor. So decisions must be made. I must know what's true and if anything else could come."

"It's all true."

"Jesus Christ!" He turns around, faces the door, and covers his mouth. "Sorry. But you mean, at Sofia's book party, you had the temerity to scold me for discussing rumors when you were the damn mistress all along?"

"It wasn't like that," she cries. "I didn't want you talking about him like that in front of others. I didn't want to risk Joe's future, or that of the Democrats. I didn't want to risk Clayton's business. I didn't want to expose us. I didn't want any of this. Oh my God, my mother saw that . . . You know, that coward didn't even have the decency to call me first and tell me he was going to do this . . . I hope he gets what's coming to him."

"He may, sooner rather than later."

"Pardon?"

"We're considering options."

She clears her throat. "What options?"

"People are asking Miles Riley if he still wants it. Miles said he doesn't want it under these circumstances. But the delegates know him far better than Joe. Hell, he's been around forever. I think if he's nominated, he'll accept. He can always say it's for the good of the party, for the good of the country, all that. Saundra, you there?"

". . . I'm here."

"I'm sorry to bother you. But I must cover my bases. As you can tell, things are up in the air. There's no telling whether everyone will agree one way or another. But many superdelegates are fuming. They can't believe he'd jeopardize the party's chances this way, that they're reliving this nightmare, only worse."

"I'm sure he has his supporters."

"Sure. Some delegates are afraid of appearing to undermine the popular will. We're conducting a flash poll to assess the public's response to Joe's presser. However, before I see the results, I need to be certain of every angle."

"Meaning?"

"Any other . . . controversial facts to come."

"I don't know. I'm looking outside my window. The doorman is already fighting off reporters. I've just been outed as the other woman live on national television. So I might not be in the best state to recollect details."

"Please think for a moment. Is there anything else I need to know?"

"Maybe. I don't know. I'm sorry. I have to go." She hangs up.

Cait and Taylor return to Madison Square Garden. They enter the arena floor, exchange a knowing glance, and go their separate ways. The nomination vote is expected to soon proceed. *TMZ* and *Redline* are already reporting from the Winstons' apartment building. The networks are still not broadcasting their regular programming. Rumors are rampant on Twitter, on television, everywhere. Confusion reigns.

A young and serious woman walks up to Taylor. "Are you Taylor Solomon?"

Taylor nods.

"Thomas Fuller would like to speak with you. Would you come with me?"

Taylor follows her into a passageway.

"Evening, Taylor," Thomas says as his aide walks away.

"Busy night?" Taylor replies.

"You've no idea."

"So how's this story going to end?"

"That's what I want to tell you. We conducted a flash poll to gauge the response to Girona's presser. We sampled fourteen hundred registered voters."

"Damn, that must've been expensive."

"Well, costly moment."

"True. What'd you find?"

"If I give it to you, will *Current* publish right away?"

"Oh, I see."

"What?"

"Either it's good for Girona, and you want to affirm why delegates stand by him, or it's bad for Girona, and you want to nominate another and make it look like the democratic move by citing the poll."

"Which do you think it is?"

"The latter."

"Bingo. Can you get it up?"

Taylor feels a pang of self-loathing. Because he knows the answer. The question is not can he get the story up. It's when. This is his job. This is real news. "I feel like a starving prostitute asked whether I'll take your money. So sure, even though you're using me, it's hard currency."

"Damn right it's hard currency. Seriously, though, I need to be certain. You can get this up quickly?"

"Yes. What'd you find?"

Thomas takes out his phone and forwards the results to Taylor. "I just sent it to you. I'm going on that floor in about a half hour. Can this be up in fifteen to twenty minutes?"

"My editors will want it to be. What's the headline?"

"Notably, most respondents had actually already heard the news. But we did tell them what happened, if they had not. You can look at the wording. I know you will. It's solid."

"And the headline?"

"Girona's favorability dropped from 61 to 34 percent. Our last poll, same methodology, had Joe ahead of Wallace in the head-to-head 51 to 48. This poll places Wallace ahead of Joe 52 to 43. She's never been above 50 the entire campaign. Girona's dropped 14 points with moderate women alone."

"Wow. But that drop may lessen in the coming days, after anger subsides and people recall their politics."

"I'm skeptical of that, under his circumstances. The public will have a lot to swallow. His wife's IVF. The donations your colleague Luke reported. Joe was the new hope. He now looks like the worst sort of old-time pol."

"What are the superdelegates saying?"

"People are debating what's better. It's either a candidate who is incredibly compromised or a new horse this late in the race. We know if we drop him, many Hispanic groups and some unions will be angry. But the recent news about his background has weakened that bond. Some of the populist tweeters and bloggers will be up in arms. But that dog is all bark and no bite."

"Miles Riley isn't exactly a new horse. Political junkies know him."

"Precisely."

"Still, there must have been pushback. Girona won the most delegates. I can't imagine that people are not nervous about a bunch of party barons overturning that."

"But Miles won the popular vote in the Texas primary and still lost the state. Remember, Miles won the vote there narrowly, but due to proportional representation, Joe won more delegates in the state."

"Because Girona won the state's caucus."

"You got it. And he won the caucus because, outside Iowa, only activists show up at caucuses. That put him over the top in the delegate count. So Joe subverted the popular will in Texas. And . . . as one senator pointed out, we have superdelegates and caucuses for a reason."

"So how are you going to do this? Can you really move all the superdelegates one way?"

"No. But I don't need to. It may be a matter of nudging. And that I can do. There are enough people leaning that way. I think. Remember, Miles retains his delegates. So it's already close."

"But you pledged yourself to Girona."

"That's not binding. Events change. We must too. You know your Machiavelli?"

"Don't we all."

" 'The promise given was a necessity of the past. The word broken is a necessity of the present.' "

"That was meant for princes, if you will, not the royal court."

"Well, this is a republic. Sometimes the court is the prince," Thomas replies with a wink, and walks away.

Taylor sits down. People race by. He takes out his laptop, plugs in his aircard, and writes. But he doesn't merely report the poll. He quotes the conversation, the politicking, the Machiavelli. Taylor realizes that Thomas presumed their conversation was off the record, based on their casual friendship and D.C. journalism norms. But Thomas didn't say as much. Taylor knows that Thomas chose him because he felt he could trust him and, of course, because he works for *Current.* But Taylor goes with his impulse. He decides the lede is not the poll, but the motive for it and the events that may follow it. Taylor realizes that Thomas will be furious. He will burn a powerful source and other bridges with him. But no part of Taylor cares about that. Not anymore. He wants to report what's real and be done with it. So he writes the 437-word scooplet and presses send.

The party secretary pounds the gavel. She tries to quiet the chatter of tens of thousands. Thomas Fuller stands at the entrance of the arena floor. His assistant shows him her phone, the headline, the angle Taylor took. *Drudge* has already linked. Twitter is spreading. And the networks are piling on. Thomas mumbles, "That fucking asshole." He realizes his surroundings and calms. "Fine. It doesn't change anything," he continues. "He's only reporting something a few minutes before it happens. Only the media cares about that crap. At least the poll is out there."

"But," she replies, "he has you even quoting Machiavelli. You sound like LBJ on Ritalin. I mean, we should do something. He describes you like some D.C. cliché."

Thomas pauses, looks ahead at the crowd, and grins.

The assistant asks, "What is it?"

"It may be cliché, but work with people long enough, and you realize clichés are clichés because they're true." He looks ahead at his fellow delegates. "The thing is, when Joe won, I felt weaker than I had in a long time. And now"—his belly juts outward with his inhale—"I've never been stronger. Some in the party may hate me, considering what I'm about to do. Hell, some in my delegation already do. But they respect me again. Maybe some even fear me a bit. And I don't have to know my Machiavelli to realize that's real power."

His assistant shakes her head and watches Thomas enter the crowd. And if image were all, it would be as if nothing had changed. But it's past midnight. Beyond the television lens, the arena's upper decks have filled. Tension weighs down the air. And there is Thomas. The ocean of Democrats parts. He approaches the microphone.

"Madam Chairman, this has been a long night," he says. "We have agonized over what to do in light of this heart-wrenching news. But this is not a personal matter. This is a matter of what's best for our great nation. We have to decide what's best for America, not for any one candidate or party. Some of us have made promises to support Joe Girona. I have, personally. But in my view, a wise man changes his mind when new events require it. The California primary vote was close. And as I've said, the delegation has just convened. Many unpledged delegates decided to exercise their responsibility to do what is best for the nation and the party. In that vein, the California delegation casts 209 votes for Senator Joe Girona and 232 votes for the next president of the United States, Senator Miles Riley."

Tens of thousand gasp. And the dominoes fall.

At 1:53 a.m., in the dressing room, Joe Girona turns off the television. It's over. He has lost the nomination. The delegate count was close. But losing is losing. Christian watches Girona and reaches for his antacid. The tablets rattle out of the container and land in his thick, clammy palms. He tosses them into his mouth and chomps them. His stare never strays from Girona.

The small creased bags under Girona's eyes have enlarged and become sallow half circles. His crow's-feet seem to have expanded at the outer corners of his eyes. And in those eyes, in that sunken posture, is a man extinguished and the knowledge of what almost was.

Christian does not know what to say. The metallic ceiling vent rattles. Girona shakes his head, as if reproaching himself. He stands and leaves the room.

Girona walks down the empty hallway, past folded aluminum chairs and cardboard boxes of buttons wrapped in plastic. The blue buttons have a picture of his arm held high and they read OUR NOMINEE, OUR TIME. They were to be passed out tonight, after he was officially nominated. He can't look at them. He thought he did the right thing. He came clean. He thought it was the best tactic. He explained himself. It worked in the past, for him. It worked for Wallace. But this was not the action of youth, when everyone is allowed a measure of mistakes, whatever one deems a mistake. It was infidelity exposed live on national television, and it concerned the presidency, when voters still had a choice. America adores his wife. The details infuriate too many. Democratic anxiety rose with a surge of shock, of betrayal, of fury, and pure strategic insecurity. Some delegates decided they had a better chance of winning without him. Others wanted to punish him. Many had both motives on their mind. Even those who voted for him, if they did speak, cited unity, blamed the "Republican attack machine" for the "same old dirty politics." Few defended him. Girona still can't digest that. Countless delegates once begged him to campaign with them, once praised him in public and stroked his ego in private. They have disappeared. *They disappeared.* Girona now realizes, no man can survive some storms.

But he can still feel *it.* He was so close. Minutes away. The nomination was almost his. He led Wallace in the polls. He was on his way. The Oval Office. His hands on the Resolute desk. Convention long shots won a political eon ago, in a world of black-and-white photographs and bearded men. Conventions were now formalities. Scripted shows. Everyone said so. It was supposed to be his. Was. Almost. These words stalk him. Worse yet, he did it to himself, like so many men before him. He thinks of those politicians. He knew better and still did it. *How could I be so stupid?* He can't grasp how he let himself make the same mistake. But he realizes, none of them probably could either, afterward. Then he thinks about how much more he lost. The presidency. And reality burns. He tries to ignore such thoughts. He could not even look at Christian as he walked out. Christian invested all of himself in him. His staff has given up opportunities, birthdays, their children's recitals. Years for nothing. Girona feels rotten for that. Since it became official, he hasn't said a word to anyone. And, no matter how inappropriate, the only person he wants to confide in is his wife. But for the first time since they met twenty-four years ago, his closest confidante will not be there for him. His wife will not return his calls.

Girona walks onto the stage. The crowd is gone. Countless balloons, bearing his name, are popped. The lights are on. But there is no one out there.

There is no one out there. He cannot conceive it. He can still see them. He can still feel that endless crowd. *I'm so good. I would've been so good. How could they have chosen that Wall Street Democrat over me? I would've done so much damn good.* He still wants it. Still tastes it. *I deserve it.* He can still see Mellencamp onstage. "Boy, you're gonna be president" rings in his head. Yet the anthem has become an elegy, a swan song echoing what might have been. If he hadn't been careless with his star, if he was the man they believed in, if his mistakes had never been reported . . . if . . . If . . . IF. He wants to yell. He wants to speak to millions. He wants to tell his supporters he'll fight back, he'll fight on, that all is not lost. But there is no one out there.

He cannot stand to recognize that, to look up and see his signs discarded in the seats, to see that empty arena. He can hardly eye the present itself. He can't fathom the future. But somewhere inside himself, he knows. He must walk off this stage. He must live with being shamed off the American stage. He must learn what it's like to lose the fire. He will no longer feel that buzz. The crowd. The masses' adoration. He will suffer the silence, alone in his wedding-cake house, haunted by *ifs.*

XLIV

By Thursday night, as Miles Riley thanks his fellow Democrats and God blesses America and greets his family onstage amid deafening applause, the convention ends. And the race carries on. Because no actor is too big for this show. And it always does go on.

Cait worked hard all week long. She covered the new nominee. Interviewed delegates every day. And kept her head down. She spent her nights with Taylor, and it was as she hoped it would be.

She closes her laptop. Balloons descend onto the convention floor. The Riley family waves to the crowd. And the blue tribe roars. It's as if Joe Girona never was.

As if. The scandal fills headlines. Democrats try to move on. But convention machinations cannot compete with sex and the misfortunes of the fortunate. Schadenfreude is plentiful. Christian saw this whirlwind coming. Redemption is American. But puritanism is too. And this regarded the nation's top role, the leading man, the head of state. There are second acts in American politics. Someday, Girona might have that chance. But he clearly sought his chance too soon. Today, the Gallup poll reported that Girona's "favorable" rating—the metric for judging whether Americans like someone—has plummeted more than any other politician since Gallup first asked the question in 1992.

Luke Brennan is working on the reach of that drama. He huddles over his laptop, two rows above Cait at the convention, stabbing keys with those sausage fingers. She has ignored his emails for months, and twice this past week. She packs her bag, stands, and steps to the stairs. There's Luke, with that lineman's quickness, blocking her. "Cait," he says, "I'm sorry to hassle you. I really do need to speak with you in private." She replies, "I can't. Sorry. My editor is expecting me." And before he can respond, she slips past him, ascends the stairs, and texts Taylor: "Do u knw what Luke's working on?!"

Cait walks a few blocks, finds a cab, and arrives home. Taylor is sitting on her stoop, waiting. And she's grateful for that. She exits the cab. He takes her bag and puts an arm around her. "Let's head upstairs," he says.

On their way up, she asks about Luke. He says they should speak about it inside, "but it's not clearly bad." And "clearly" hangs on her thoughts. Her phone rings. She clicks her mother to voice mail.

They enter and drop their bags. Taylor pours her a glass of Pinot Blanc and pops the cap off a beer bottle. She asks, "Should I be sitting?" He enters her living room and says, "I don't know yet." He hands her the wine. She pinches the glass stem and sits. She looks up at Taylor. He sets his beer on the coffee table without drinking. He paces and palms his fist. "What is it?" she asks.

"Luke is working on a story related to Girona. I could tell that by the morning lineup. I wrote him. He's not getting back to me. Still, Philip and Rick are definitely distracted. So yeah, something doesn't feel right. Damn, I just don't know what they'll do."

She grips the cushion with her left hand. "I can't believe it. After all that. Now?"

Taylor looks at her and calms. He squats in front of her, takes her left hand in his, and says, "Maybe it's time to call Luke back."

Cait curls herself into a ball and hugs her knees.

Taylor places a hand on her foot, brushes her bangs away from her eyes, and says, "You can do this. If it concerns that night, we may still be able to contain things. Remember, at worst, you did nothing wrong."

She looks up. "I didn't report it."

"I think a lot of people will sympathize with why."

"Not the media. Not the right. Conservatives will say the *Times* was covering up for Girona."

"It won't get that far. You probably can still bluff your way out of this. I doubt Luke has the story nailed down." Her phone rings. "Do you want to see who that is?" Taylor asks.

Cait nods.

Taylor sees and passes her the phone. Cait looks at the screen. She downs her wine and places the empty glass on the coffee table. "Hi, Mom."

"Cait!"

"Mom, calm down."

"I've been trying to reach you. I left you a voice mail."

"What's going on?"

"Philip Larson called me. He's *Current*'s editor."

"I know who he is. He was at the *Times*."

"Oh yes. I forgot he'd stayed there long after I left for the *Journal*."

"Why'd he call you?"

"Because you won't call them back. Maybe they're trying to give you the benefit of the doubt."

"Ummm."

"Cait, I know I told you to let this go. I don't think you can now. You have to call him back."

"Did he give you any details?"

"He wouldn't. But he said it's urgent. They're on deadline. I asked what it's about. He said he doesn't think it's appropriate to go into details with me. He seems to want to give you a chance to confirm or deny . . . something. He said you should call him back, directly."

"He didn't say what that 'something' is?"

"No, but it feels like someone's talking."

"Oh my God."

"Hon, you have to call him back. Speak off the record at first. You may still be able to kill the story if they only have one source."

Cait exhales and considers her options. "Taylor thinks I should call him back too."

"Taylor's there?"

"Yeah."

"Listen, I have to ask, is there any chance he would've said anything to anyone at his paper about what happened?"

"No!"

"Sorry, I had to ask. I'm sorry . . . Hon, are you there?"

"How could you ask me that?"

"I'm sorry. I shouldn't have. I'm glad he's with you. Maybe he can help you kill the story."

"I don't want to put him in any more of an awkward position."

"I can see that. Hold on. Let me call Philip back. I jumped off the phone with him to call you. But I can push him or call in a favor. I'll end this once and for all."

"I'm not having my mother handle this. I'm not a child."

"I know. But—"

"Mom, I'll look worse, even guilty, if you call him and try to fix this. I don't want to put you in that position either. I have to handle this myself."

"Meaning?"

"I'll call Philip back."

"Are you up for it?"

"I think so."

"Call when you *know* so. You need to be calm and cogent. You must work him like a prosecutor."

"I know."

"Hon, let me talk to him first. There can't be any mistakes like that Twitter incident."

"Mom! Forget that stupid Twitter thing. That has nothing to do with this. Jes-us."

"Okay."

"This is my problem."

"It's *our* problem. And I think it's best if I call first and—"

"Mom, why would he listen to you? I don't care what history you two share. He's not going to kill a major story for that. This is *Current*."

"He may be calling because he's not confident in the story. He'll listen to me."

"Please spare me the great woman routine."

"Caitriona Elizabeth. I'm trying to help."

Cait's anxiety shifts to frustration. The tension with her mother is familiar. It leaves her more clearheaded. "I know, Mom. But you're not helping. This is something I have to solve on my own."

"But—"

"Mom."

"This isn't the time for you to assert your independence."

"Actually, it's exactly the time. I know how to handle this."

"How? We should rehearse the call. What's your plan? How—"

"Mom."

"Yes."

"I got this."

Erin pauses. "Okay," she says.

"I'll call you after."

"Okay."

"Bye, Mom."

Cait moves her thumb to end the call. She hears her mother yell, "Cait, wait!" Cait puts the phone back to her ear.

"What?"

"I want to say . . . good luck. You *can* do this. No matter what, I'm proud of you."

And Cait closes and reopens her eyes. "Thank you. I love you."

"I love you too, hon. Call me after."

"Bye."

Cait sets the phone down on the couch. "I'm going to call Philip," she tells Taylor. She squints nervously and asks, "What if he only wants a confirmation or a denial and they already have the story?"

"If they had the story, after trying so hard to contact you, they'd likely just go ahead with it. They'd report that you didn't respond to attempts to reach you. I think they're fishing."

"The great woman thinks that too. But Luke saw me that night with his own eyes."

"That's circumstantial. Your mom may be right. Do you know Philip?"

"I briefly worked under him at the *Times*. But I don't know him that well."

"Well, he's not really what you would expect. I mean, shit, he's still the man behind *Current*. But he's ponderous too. He's actually conflicted about *Current*'s impact, unlike Rick or Peter. He's the one who pushed the new magazine section. If they have only one source, play into the fact that *Current*'s not a tabloid, but a top tier, substantial, and responsible news source. Emphasize the responsibility."

"Maybe . . . no one there knows we're together?"

"No. Regardless, it wouldn't matter to them. Not if they have the story."

"If he says they have the story, maybe I should just tell the truth? I could also write it for the *Times*. That's better than someone else reporting it."

"Don't do that," Taylor blurts. His eyes trail off. He stands, paces, and turns around.

"What?" she asks.

"I've got an idea. If he's fishing, bluff. But if he says they are going ahead, offer to make a trade."

"I have nothing to trade."

"But I do," Taylor says.

"No way."

"It's the least bad option."

"I can't let you do that."

"Well, if he says he's going ahead with it, yet you still sense doubt in his voice, pass me the phone. He'll be in shock. I'll get him off guard. Say I need to talk, between us only, off the record. He'll respect those terms. I'll tell him what I saw. I'll tell him how Christian tried to steer me. I'll offer to write a first-person on why I did not report it. That would receive tons of traffic."

"He'd likely fire you. And they'd probably publish another story on why they did."

"It's okay."

"That's not okay."

"I've been thinking about leaving them for the past year."

"I know. But you just had that scoop about the convention vote. They must've loved that."

"I know. But I still was a mouthpiece for superdelegates, to give them cover for the vote. I reported more than Thomas wanted. But it still served his purpose. It's like, either way, I'm being spun by someone."

"You're being too hard on yourself."

"Never mind that. Let's worry about the problem before us."

"Well, this is not a solution. You can't be rash about something this big."

She's still on the couch. He kneels before her. "I'm not being rash. I've been sweating *Current* for far too long. This is as good a time as any to do something about it. No, it's better. It pisses me off that they'd even consider this story."

"Most would."

"I don't know."

"If you were to tell Philip, *Current* might just report both stories. He may see your offer as confirmation and report on me, then fire you."

"Well, he'll only know about me off the record. So he won't have that story. And my story is a sure thing. There's no fear of a *Times* libel suit, like with you. Like you said, people would love a story of me embodying some mainstream media cover-up."

"Don't even say that. You didn't do that. You just don't think a pol's marriage is news unless he's made marriage a public policy issue. I mean, it would really bother me if my dad ran for office and reporters saw that as carte blanche, alone, to run an autopsy on my parents' marriage and divorce."

"They can frame it however they want, if they kill the story about you."

"Taylor, I'm not letting you do that. Your reputation will be destroyed. Our reputations are all we have in this business. Conservatives will forget you're one of the few reporters who covered Girona critically. They'll decimate you. And the media will trash you too."

"Some will."

"Taylor—"

"Conservatives who would go after me will do far worse to you. You're with the *Times*. You'll have to get into details about what he did, all that. It will get messy, and that mess will follow your future."

She cups her hands in front of her face. Taylor takes her hands and brings them down to her knees. He looks at her and brushes her bangs to the side. "It might not come to this," he says, "but I'm the ace up your sleeve if it does. It just makes sense. Better me than you. I've been thinking about leaving it all, anyway."

"I don't know."

"Please, let me do this for you."

Taylor's fingertips touch hers. And she nods.

She retrieves her bag. She prepares to record the conversation. "Okay," she says, "here goes." Taylor tells her, "You'll rock." And she twinges her lips rightward.

"Philip Larson."

"Philip, it's Cait."

"Cait"—he yawns—"glad you got back to me."

"Sorry about that. I didn't think Luke was contacting me for anything important."

"You didn't?"

"No. So what is so important that you reached out to my mom?"

"Okay, I'll get right to it. Luke has a source claiming you and Joe Girona were intimate."

"What?"

"The source was, how should I say, well placed in the campaign."

"That's absurd."

"Cait, is that for the record?"

"I have no comment for the record right now. I don't even know what you're talking about. So let's speak off the record, and maybe you can clue me in."

"That's fine." He yawns again.

"Is this a bad time?"

"No, no," he says. "I'm just tired from the conventions."

"So what is this now?"

Philip lays out the facts. How on this night, at about this time, Luke was told by the source that Cait and Joe Girona were intimate. Philip adds, "That was how he phrased it, 'intimate.' "

"He?"

"Yeah. Okay, that's all I'm telling you about the source. We confirmed you were in the hotel that night. Girona's schedule had you interviewing him in his suite at about the same time the source says."

"I interviewed Girona that night. The story was published soon after. Everyone saw that. Did Luke ever consider that the source knew the schedule too? And nothing happened. And second, no one was in the room when I interviewed Girona but Girona and myself. So how could he know anything, regardless?"

"The source says he was told by Girona and Christian Ulster shortly after you were with him. Luke couldn't get through to Christian. I spoke to him, and he offered no comment. But he didn't deny it."

"Are you kidding? That's all BS. And c'mon. You were my boss once. 'No comment' is not a confirmation. Take me out of this for a second. Consider it journalistically. Luke has one highly flawed source relying on hearsay. You never would've let that trash run at the *Times*, especially without a second source."

"Depends. And you're the subject here, not me."

"I'm sorry, Philip. I'm just taken aback by all this. I'm trying to look at this objectively. God, I wonder who made this up? I guess it could be a misunderstanding. It's just crazy."

"Luke also says he saw you after that interview. He describes you as extremely upset."

"That had nothing to do with work or Girona. Frankly, it's not anyone's business why I was upset . . . a lot's been going on in my life." She hesitates. "I just broke off my engagement for goodness' sake."

"Oh, I didn't know that. I'm sorry to hear that."

"Don't be. Just don't do this to me. How could you even consider something so circumstantial?"

"Circumstantial evidence can accrue. The source is very close to Girona. He says Girona spoke to him about it. Cait, listen, I understand why you don't want this to get out. But unless you tell us your side of the story, people will presume the worst."

"I'm telling you, honestly, your source is wrong."

"But you would say that, wouldn't you?"

Cait looks at Taylor. He mouths, You can do this. And she inhales and exhales and says, "Philip, one reporter to another, you know this source is flawed. That's why you haven't reported this BS yet."

He yawns. "Sure, we'd like a tighter story. We'd like a source that witnessed what he says. But sometimes all you need are the aftershocks to know there's been an earthquake."

"Not in this case. Please, this would kill my career. No one will take me seriously. And my denials will mean nothing. You know that. The tabloids will pile on me. I've busted my butt to get this far. Please don't take that away from me. Not over some baseless story."

"It's not personal. It's about the story."

"The story could not be more personal. So please, with all due respect, don't use that line. Don't say it's not personal."

"Cait, was your night with Girona a onetime thing?"

"There was no night with Girona. It was an interview."

She can hear Philip breathe into the phone. "Cait, perhaps he made a pass at you and you rebuffed him? If you are innocent here, we'll report that."

"Nothing happened."

"We already have enough. We can attribute it to an unconfirmed source."

"I can't believe you'd run a story with one source. Just for readership, really . . . you'd show such reckless disregard for the truth, act so maliciously, and destroy my career?"

"Don't use First Amendment legalese with me. I've been doing this too long."

"Of course, if you publish this story, I'll sue you for libel. The *Times* lawyers will sue *Current* for libel. You know that."

"People usually threaten me with the lawyers first," he chuckles. "Cait, you're not going to scare me. And frankly, I think reporters who go on television, who do punditry, put themselves in the spotlight. So I don't even think you could make a plausible libel case, like a civilian can. And if there were a case, the truth would come out."

"Philip, please—"

"Listen, Cait, we have a source who was very close to Girona. We have Luke witnessing you upset on Girona's floor. It was right after you were in Girona's room. We couldn't get the hallway security footage. But if this goes to court, we'll subpoena it. You'll also have to testify."

Cait's shoulders tense up. She breathes. "So what? I'll be proven right. And c'mon, the court costs will far outweigh the ad dollars you'll make from publishing this lie."

"Hell, I know your bosses. The *Times* may not want to litigate it. They may wager you did it."

"Oh, not after they hear this conversation."

"Oh, Cait. That was unnecessary. This is off the record. You shouldn't be recording us."

"I can still play it for my editors. If you hit me with this lie, I don't care about some off-the-record BS. It will come out in court. And I have you admitting the story is flawed."

"Jesus, you're lucky I'm so tired and off my game. No story is airtight. It's strong enough to run."

"Please, Philip, step back. You really think I'm crazy enough to risk my career by making out with some presidential candidate? It's absurd. And, however reckless he was, Girona was not crazy enough to hit on a *Times* reporter."

"I don't know about that. My job constantly reminds me about men's idiocy when it comes to sex."

"C'mon, I knew you once. You are one of the most respected journalists in Washington. These are basic ethics. *Current* is changing a lot about the political media. But Philip, do you really want to change this too? There is a basic code."

"Nothing is black-and-white anymore. There's too much competition. You know that. And Cait, frankly, I don't have time to be esoteric right now. Neither do you."

"I'm not trying to be esoteric. Please . . . I mean, if you do this, what separates *Current* from the tabloids or the big gossip websites like *Gawker, TMZ,* and *Redline*?"

He groans.

"Remember when you were a young reporter," she continues. "You'd be destroying my career with lies to get clicks. Please do the right thing here. Your source is lying, or has been misled."

"Are you actually telling me the truth?"

"Yes. Listen, I know it's tempting to believe the source in light of recent events. But Luke's been misinformed. It doesn't matter if the report is false. It will destroy my future. You know what a story like this can do to a young woman . . . Do you have daughters?"

"One."

"Imagine her in my position."

And she listens to him breathe.

"I still think you're bullshitting me, Cait. But . . . well, of course, I also don't like the idea of ruining a promising young journalist's career."

He hesitates. Cait bites her lower lip.

"Here's the deal," he continues. "I'll tell Luke to dig some more. We'll hold the story for now. For now. But you better think long and hard about whether you want to tell the truth or let the story come out as we have it. Right now, you look like a mistress. But you're right. I would like more evidence. So no promises, but I'll hold it."

"Thank you."

"For now."

"I know. I appreciate it. You're doing the right thing. I never thought I'd say this, but thank God for sensible editors."

"If we get more evidence, it's running."

"I'm not worried about that. There's nothing to find. Still, I appreciate you reaching out to me to clear this up."

"Yeah, yeah."

"Get some sleep, Philip. And thank you, again, for your integrity. I'm grateful. Bye."

"Bye, Cait."

Cait hits the end key on her phone. She drops the phone on her bed. "Eeeeh!" she squeals, tossing her arms around Taylor. "You're in the clear?" he asks. With her chin on his shoulder, she nods and pulls away. But the question tempers her excitement. "I think so, yeah. He said they'd hold the story and only run it with more evidence. But what evidence could they get? Girona and Christian are not going to admit to it."

"I can contact Christian. I'll make sure of it. But I think you're right."

She leans back on the couch and runs her fingers through her hair. "Jesus, what a week," she exhales. "I need a drink." "You deserve more than one," Taylor says. He gets the bottle and refills her glass. She drinks. He takes a swig of his beer. "God," he sighs, "I still owe them a story tonight." She listens and watches him over her wine. "By the way," she says, "thanks again for what you offered to do for me before."

"What?"

"You know, what you were willing to say to Philip."

"Oh, yeah. It was nothing."

"You offered to ruin your reputation to save mine. That's not nothing."

XLV

The morning sun slides above the cityscape, streaks the buildings, and brightens Cait's apartment. Taylor wakes and looks at Cait, at the curve of her body, as she sleeps on her side. He cannot imagine returning to Washington. He does not want to go backward in any respect. He has slept only five hours. Yet he feels a restless wakefulness. He quietly gets up, walks into the living room, and checks his phone.

Last night, after Cait spoke with Philip, Taylor worked. *Current* is preparing a series on the presidential debates. The debates begin next week, which is sooner than most years. The vice presidential debate will take place the following week. Taylor already filed his story highlighting the past presidential debates that mattered and what made them matter. He also owed *Current* copy on the VP debates. His editors wanted the series completed early to allow time to prepare art and graphics, amid the busy post-convention days. He had studied the polling before and after every debate. So he reread his notes last night and wrote the article while Cait slept. His angle: VP debates do not impact the presidential race.

And now Rick's response arrives in his inbox. "We can't run this. Get us something else." Taylor realizes he should have known better. The story showed that a major political event didn't matter. How could *Current* pre-game, cover, and post-game an event that didn't actually matter?

And that editorial tension matters to him. The conversation reignites memories. He recalls his New Year's Eve phone call with Rick. Taylor said that Girona likely had, before the first vote, secured enough support from critical demographics to win the primary. Thus, all the campaign events, all those minute-by-minute battles to "own the hour," to win the news day, would likely not decide this nominee, if any. Rick said that angle would undermine too many *Current* articles. So Taylor let it go. *And look at what did upend the primary—this rare, this real-life soap opera.* He thinks about the billions of dollars spent on consultants, on advertising, on campaigning, of how little of it matters in the way it's meant to matter. He recalls pitching the series about the industry invested in partisanship. Rick dismissed it. And Taylor let it be dismissed. Again. Then, Taylor reminds himself, he contributes to that industry. He sometimes hypes the business, the campaign. And that's the rub. His conciliations have become him. As online journalism reached adolescence, he decided that if he could not have time or leeway to investigate, to report deeply, he could at least offer perspective. He could call out the bullshit. The Internet led to record amounts of content, but he believed the cost was depth, as if online journalism thought in lateral terms rather than vertical. But he found himself rarely striking his ideal balance, sobering hyperbole with facts and historical perspective, while retaining the human story. Sure, Taylor pushed back. Sometimes. But he ultimately went with it. It was his job. He could hardly stop the momentum alone, or so he told himself. After all, it's never easy to confront your delusions. Our delusions can sustain us. But everything that cracks eventually breaks.

Yesterday's impulse returns to him. He remembers the conclusions he reached when he acted on instinct. He stares out the living room window as the city brightens with the dawn, and he reminds himself, we are not what we believe, but what we do. He knows it's hard to leave a profession when you're failing. And yet, he thinks, it's even harder to walk away when work is flawed but still gainful. For the first time, he recognizes how difficult it is, after you put so much of yourself into something, to walk away from the good enough.

And it occurs to him, he asked Cait to do that with Blake. He considers what he must do. He thinks about what Cait's mother said to him at the book party. Erin Ellis refused to write for a lifestyle section and became a great correspondent. He recalls the painting that night, the accountant who tried something else and, along the way, became something more. He realizes that far more fail than succeed. He may not have a talent for something else. But he has always believed what he once read somewhere—we regret the things we do not do more than the things we do.

He thinks about the fifteen years he put into his career. The side newspaper jobs in high school and college. The five internships. The near decade since, as he climbed up the journalism ladder. He thinks about September 11th, of all things. He gazes downtown and recalls how the ground shook as the towers collapsed, and what he saw and felt. He wonders if his choice to race down there as an aspiring reporter, to witness and interview, was for nothing. *Was it all for nothing?* The three campaigns, all the research he did on presidential politics for his book, for nothing? He realizes he should have known better. He'd read books about journalism. Did he ignore veterans' disappointment because he thought he was special? Was he really another young man who needed to learn the lesson for himself? Even *Boys on the Bus*—a book that largely glorified campaign journalism in a time when media thrived—carried a telling quote from a reporter: "Pretty soon the realization hits that there *isn't* any good stuff, and there isn't gonna *be* any good stuff. Nobody's getting anything that you're not getting, and if they are, it's just more of the same bullshit."

The same bullshit. The VP story feels like the same bullshit. Taylor knew that his professional issues were modest. He faced no epic journalism test. He never encountered the grand investigative story. But almost no one ever does. This is real life, for most reporters. His compromises are small. But they have amassed to something too large for him to ignore. He remembers a line from Hemingway's *Old Man and the Sea.* "Anyone can be a fisherman in May." Autumn and winter test fishermen. The water is colder, stormier, and there are less fish. Life's choices feel this way to him. And perhaps becoming a man is this way. He has always agreed with Mailer and Hemingway here, that manhood is not given, but earned. He must be true to himself. But he does not want to only concern himself with his passions. He must make some real money soon. He'll want a family in the next decade. He is young enough for these thoughts to remain abstract, but he's old enough to know that the abstract, in a blink, becomes real. Still, he realizes his restlessness would not abate if he won the lottery. His expectations lay in the markers of a life that are worth a life, at least what he believes is worth his life.

He remembers what he told Gabriel at that book party: *I need to go after something worth failing at.* It's time he follows through on his beliefs. If we must choose our battles, we must be willing to make a choice at some point. He must be willing to fight at some point, however humble those fights are, because choices about one's career can feel like a fight. He remembers the Girona media gaggle. Girona took questions about his Latino lineage. Yet, while reporters closed in, Taylor stepped out of the pack. He knows Peter or Rick or Luke would have pushed in. But he stopped respecting the hunt a long time ago.

He is not Luke. Luke relishes the reporter's life. Luke and Taylor came to journalism, like so many, because of a book that became a movie that became a calling, *All the President's Men.* But there is only one Watergate. There are few sources like Deep Throat, who come to reporters, who are that connected, who have real news to tell. And the bitter realization of that sets in. If you seek journalism's great white whale and never get it, it eventually gets you.

It gets inside you. So it's supposed to go for the young and ambitious. They seek distant horizons. Some distance is traveled. And there they find themselves, adults, on the real terrain of life. And it's hard. That's when they are told to grow up. That's when realism should set in. That's where the negotiating of life is supposed to begin. The young and hungry are told to carry a canteen of compromise. But not everyone sees the same trade-offs. Or settles the same on similar terrain. Two young men may stand close, work the same work, and seem to seek the same thing. But they do not arrive with identical trials, responsibilities, burdens, constitutions, values, and dreams. They once saw a similar horizon. But it seemed similar only from afar.

Because today, when Taylor stands amid the media pack as the pol is encircled, he feels more like the prey. It's as if he's always playing a part in a film he wants to walk out on. He is tired of feeling driven by outside events. He sees the candidate, ahead of the horde, and feels interchangeable, even parasitic, as if, at best, he would gain a story because of another man's fall. It seems, to him, that he's always chasing drama, newsmakers, doers, that he's covering quotes and not news—nay, covering talking points or spin, and not news. If this is political news, the news world around him, why not enter the other side of life and make news? Make something. He feels that he's been covering life and not living it, not to the degree he expects of himself. He wants to produce something he prides, however humble. He needs to feel proud of himself again. He was once so passionate, in every way. It took meeting Cait to begin to feel that again. He hopes to be that man again. Renewed hope has unsettled him. He spends most of his week working. Most of his life working. He knows that some people have no choice. But he still has a choice. He wants to be able to meet his twenty-year-old self and look him in the eye and say, *I followed through.*

Because Ava's words linger—*you're becoming a bitter old man.* He wonders how true that is. His work no longer feels worth most of his days, his energy, his pride. He doesn't feel that it's a good living. He doesn't feel that he's living. He feels that he's dying inside, one practical decision at a time.

He would not say any of this aloud, however. It feels too arrogant to say. Too self-indulgent to say, or even feel. He thinks his life is too small to feel this much. Who is he to want more? Who is he to think this way? But the answers have festered for too long. And we do not choose what festers within us, or how it compels us.

For water boils over. And angst scalds.

After all that, it's like that. He emails Philip and Rick. He asks if they are still at their hotel in the city. "Can you spare fifteen minutes to meet with me this morning? It's important."

He goes to the refrigerator, pulls out the ice tray, snaps a few cubes loose, and savors a glass of cold water. He checks his phone and reads Philip's reply: "Sure. Meet us here at 8:30."

The hotel's business center is wood-paneled and small and empty. Philip and Rick sit in the two computer chairs. Taylor leans against a printer. "We've only got a few minutes," Rick says. "Luke's flipping out about his story."

"What's the story?" Taylor asks.

"You know it," Rick replies. "He said you wouldn't help him with it."

"I gave him Christian Ulster's contact info."

"But you have the relationship. He's your source."

"I did what I could."

"Meaning what?"

"The story's topic is not my thing."

"It's your job. Peter is right. You only think about yourself. It's like the other week on BBC, when you dissed Girona's press people."

"What?"

"Yeah, we heard about that. Girona's spokesman called Peter. He filled us in. They were furious."

"So what?"

"You called their spokesmen 'spinners' and 'the best that can be hired on Madison Avenue,' " Rick says.

"But that's literally true."

"It was a poor choice of words. And Girona's shop told Peter that it changed their relationship with you."

"That's immaterial."

"It's part of your job to maintain a relationship with the campaigns."

"Not with the spinners. I never went to Girona's sophists for stories. They're not real sources. And even if I did burn them, so what . . . I find it troubling that Peter, a fellow reporter, contacts my editor to bitch on a campaign's behalf."

"That's not the point," Rick says.

Rick rubs his buzzed blond scalp and squints his small brown eyes. He sits on Philip's right. Both men wear white shirts. Philip listens, leaning back, his chin resting on his chest, his fingers clasped behind his head, his elbows splayed outward.

"This is not constructive," Philip says.

Taylor realizes the conversation has veered off course. "Listen, I'm sorry I reacted that way. But it's difficult to hear someone accuse you of only thinking about yourself when you live your job most days. I wasn't putting myself first. But I have put myself last, too often, while working here."

"Bullshit," Rick blurts. "You're widely read. You're on TV. You're paid well."

"By journalism standards, I'm paid well. I do the TV hits as part of my job. Punditry is not a fringe benefit. And what's the use of my stories being read if they systematically make mountains of molehills, if I'm not proud of them?"

"Get off your soapbox," Rick says. "You sound like a wiseass blogger."

"I don't know about that," Philip says. "But I would like to see you put more time into your copy."

"That's fair. I could reread it more. I'm, perhaps, too eager to put it behind me."

"And what's with the VP story you filed last night?" Rick asks.

"It's what the facts showed."

"We do not need stories telling readers not to read us."

"Rick, I also got you that story on the convention vote this week."

"That's true," Philip says. "That earned us huge traffic. But you did it with a relationship you had. That's what we would've liked to have seen with Luke's story."

"And what's next?" Rick asks. "Sure, that was a great dunk. But you were hired to be a scorer. Yes, analysis too. But above all, we need you scoring like that all the time. Do you get me?"

"All too well."

"Then prove it. Be a team player. Help Luke. Get us something on this affair. Set aside your damn principles and do your job."

Taylor grimaces but says nothing.

"Okay, okay. No one is saying set aside anything," Philip says. "Hold on. Taylor, this does not need to turn into your annual review."

Taylor realizes it. He's digressing into the past. Arguing with Rick again. And for what? Why does he have this compulsion to defend his job performance? What could they change to suit him? They have different objectives. "You're right. What's done is done," Taylor acknowledges. "I shouldn't have gotten into all that. There's no need to relitigate the past."

"I agree," Philip says. "And we *both* appreciate your work."

Rick shrugs.

"Thank you," Taylor says. "I'll get to the point." He takes a long breath. "Listen, this isn't working. My heart's not in it. It hasn't been for a long time. I don't even think I want to be a reporter anymore. How about you let me work out of New York for the rest of the campaign, when I'm not on the trail. Pay me until the end of November. I'll finish the campaign and write the copy you need. And I'll quietly exit come December as you're transitioning into your post-campaign dynamic. That should work smoothly for all of us."

Philip's and Rick's eyes meet. Philip's stare swings back to Taylor. "I thought you might be coming to this," Philip says. "We figured that might be why you asked for this meeting. You've certainly hinted at your dissatisfaction, off and on . . . Listen, I don't think you should quit journalism. I'd like you to stay with us, but only as the guy who's all in. So if you really want out, we can do that stuff if you finish the campaign, if that's what you *really* want."

"It's what I want."

Taylor returns to Cait's apartment. She's on the couch reading. She took the Friday off. He sits beside her on the arm of the couch. "I got a little scared when I woke up and you weren't here," she tells him.

"I emailed you. I hope you don't mind that I took a set of keys."

"Of course not. And I saw your email." She sets down her book. "So how'd it go?"

"I quit."

"You did?"

He nods.

Her fingertips touch his hand. "Good for you." She sits up. "I'm proud of you."

He hesitates, as if still swallowing the notion that he quit. "I'm finishing the campaign," he says. "Who knows after? I'll put my apartment on the market. But I can move back to the city now. I'll figure it out here."

"Really?"

He nods. She jumps up and throws her arms around him. And he holds her. She leans back against his arms, shaking her head in disbelief, and says, "It's perfect."

"It is," he says, almost too quietly to hear.

Midday blends into afternoon. They sit in Cait's kitchen, at her counter, on white stools. She wears his button-down shirt. They drink wheat beer and munch salty popcorn and talk. They make plans to go out tonight, like any other couple. And the normalcy of it unnerves her. She looks at him and can hardly believe it. Here they are. She finds it surreal. Blake's over. She's with Taylor. He's returning to the city. And the Girona ordeal feels behind her. She wonders if life can really work out this way.

XLVI

They stand up in a dark theater. Credits. Cait looks over at Taylor. He's keeping to himself. They walk the row, the aisle, out the doors. A couple is in front of them. The man says, "It was bullshit. All that, to just walk on a wire. I get it. It's a rush. So call it skydiving, already. Who the fuck would risk their life for that?" The woman nods. "A crazy man with no responsibilities," she adds. Cait looks over at Taylor. He pushes the glass doors open. Fresh air. The sound of cars bumping off uneven road. Dispersed horns. Taylor stands at the curb to hail a cab. He turns back to Cait and asks, "Did you hear the couple ahead of us?"

She nods yes. "Fuck that," he says. "That was amazing. I can't believe I didn't see this until now. I'm glad they're reshowing it." Cait says, "Yeah, it's part of a festival of documentaries about New York." "Man, that guy's amazing," Taylor says. She replies, "Wouldn't you just love to have him over for dinner." Taylor says, "Exactly! That was one of the most beautiful documentaries I've ever seen." He exhales. Traffic speeds by. "I just loved the bold simplicity of that dream," he goes on. "The discipline. It was so pure. It was not a movie. It was a metaphor. You don't even have to know what the dream is. Just that it's unprecedented, pure, extraordinary, slightly mad. And that it took immense discipline to get there, and so much skill. That's what only film can capture. There's something about seeing the life in him, hearing him talk, seeing his emotion that's essential to understanding what he did—and him. If we could all only live that way. I love that line at the end: 'To see every day, every year, every idea, as a true challenge, and then you are going to live your life on a tightrope.' " And Cait listens. Watches him. Taylor talks without eye contact. He speaks to her but also to himself. He's trying to discern why he loved the documentary. "That you must," Taylor adds, " 'refuse your own success.' I was just thinking about that concept. God, that guy is alive."

Taylor sees an open taxi and waves. "Anyway," he mutters. The cab slows, edges to the curb, stops. He opens the door. Cait slides in. He follows, closes the door, and tells the driver, "Bank and Waverly."

They enter the packed barroom of the Waverly Inn. Taylor gives his name. The hostess seats them. They eat tuna tartare and short ribs and goat cheese with beets. It's not the same modest inn that Taylor once enjoyed. He used to come here before it was purchased and remodeled. He would drink by the fire with friends and argue the world. But he admires some of the renovations, especially the mural that spans the dining room, with its mingled caricatures of famed New Yorkers.

"There's Walt Whitman. That's Anaïs Nin. That's Norman Mailer at the pond, of course painted as the narcissist." Taylor eyes the caricatures he names.

"Why is Truman Capote a butterfly?" Cait asks. "Or is he a fairy?"

"That would be lame."

"It would."

They sit beneath the wood-beam ceiling. Taylor gazes at the mural. He tilts back on the wood chair. His eyes return to Cait. Her lacy black dress rises along her leg. She pulls it down. "Every time you do that, it drives me a little crazy," he says.

She does it again.

"Now you're being cruel."

"Okay, I'll stop."

"No, don't stop."

She smiles and looks at him. "I'm glad we went out." She glances at the mural. "I like it here. It fits the area."

"Did you ever go to Chumley's, just south of here?" he asks.

"Sure. The great woman actually loved it there. You know, behind all her poise, she's a secret romantic."

"I know a few others like that."

Cait nods. "I realize it more every day, how I'm like her. We're having brunch tomorrow. You should join us."

"I don't want to intrude on mother-daughter time. I have plenty of time to get to know her."

"You'll like her. She used to tell me stories about this area too. You know, living in the Village in her early twenties. She thinks her Village was the heyday."

"Well, for most New Yorkers the city's best when they lived it most. I think, when people mourn a period of the city, they're usually mourning the loss of their youth. Although the Village and Chumley's probably were better in your mom's day."

"In its last years, it did get fratty around six o'clock. But it still was special . . . It's sad about the fire."

"Yeah. I used to go there on Saturday afternoons and sit at that one table by the street window. It had this little stream of dusty light. God, I remember looking around and thinking that Steinbeck and e. e. Cummings and Fitzgerald all came here. And with their books lining the walls, it was inspiring."

"Taylor," Cait says, "I like that you're not such a secret romantic."

After dinner, they walk down West Eleventh Street. Taylor asks whether she's still thinking about the Girona scandal. Cait says she's trying not to. That tonight, she doesn't want to. But then she talks about it. He was about to tell her about his conversation with *Current*'s editors. That Luke's still pushing the story. Yet as she speaks, he realizes she's not thinking about what could happen. She's talking about what happened. And he doesn't want to worry her more. Her eyes are already downcast, as she recalls the night and, for the first time, tells him what happened in detail. She speaks in the third person. She's reporting on herself. Until she says, "I just froze. I can't believe I did nothing, at first. I was so ashamed of that for so long." It's why she rushed out of Iowa. But before she left, she says, it meant the world to her to be able to just talk in the diner. "Grilled cheese has always been my comfort food." And, for reasons Taylor does not understand, he loves her more for that.

After that, she says nothing more of it. So they leave it behind them. They pass the green awning of a little French bistro, Tartine, and turn right on West Fourth and she places her arm in his, as they cross over the cobblestones of West Twelfth, and pass Corner Bistro's neon sign and stroll, a short while after, into a small eighties bar named Automatic Slim's. Inside, Queen and David Bowie's "Under Pressure" plays. Taylor asks what she wants to drink. She tells him. He cannot hear her. She yells "vodka soda." He orders four. "It's too hard to get a drink here," he says, "we need to stock up." They make their way toward a window. Pat Benatar's "We Belong" begins. Cait squeezes his hand and says "I love this song," and turns to him and sings there's "no turning back" and kisses him. They drink and dance and touch. Def Leppard's "Pour Some Sugar on Me" whips the bar up. Cait and Taylor sing the chorus with strangers. One guy, wearing a popped-collar polo shirt, hints a headbang. They take their drinks in hand. Madonna's "Like a Prayer" starts. Cait jumps. Most of the girls enliven at once. Cait hands him her drink. He retreats against the wall. She joins the girls around her. They sing, "everyone must stand alone, I hear you call my name," and they sing every word loud, as their bodies bounce and dance. Cait turns to Taylor, takes his hand, and tries to pull him out to dance. He shakes his head no but smiles. She jumps to him, kisses him once, and lets go, returning to a circle of girls. Their heads tilt back and they sing on. Cait twirls at the center of them. And Taylor watches her, smiling.

The people dance and ricochet off one another in the tight space. Later, as Toto's "Africa" plays, Taylor says in her ear, "This is one of those pop songs that makes no sense to me at all, but I still like it." She replies "absolutely," as if there's no disputing it. Taylor finds his way to the front. The floor is slippery from spilled drinks. He rests against the sticky bar and orders another round. The drunkenness is energetic. Later, when Bon Jovi's "Livin' on a Prayer" plays and the first words of the chorus come, the bartender turns the music down and the crowd belts the lyrics.

As the hour nears four, Alphaville's "Forever Young" plays. Easiness comes over the room. Taylor stands with Cait near the same window. His eyes are large and his smile has a fresh immensity to it. Cait cannot know it's his old immensity. She did not know him years before. But she sees him now. He hears the words "do you really want to live forever" and he nods a firm and subtle yes, as if only for himself. And she understands.

They leave at bar time. "Let's go somewhere else," Taylor says. Cait pauses and says, "I know where!" She lifts her hand, and a taxi stops. They cross town as they kiss, as his hand glides up her dress in the backseat. "Behave," she says, gently pushing his hand down her leg. He gives a boyish smirk. She has the taxi stop outside her apartment to pick up a bottle of wine. Taylor offers, runs upstairs, and returns.

The taxi sails uptown on a tide of green lights. They're dropped off at a dead end in midtown's far east side. Cait leads Taylor down steps to a small scenic point. It's a few feet above the East River. They hear waves lapping against the land. The city night is a distant whirr. Cait sits on the bench and rubs her feet. Taylor realizes that he forgot a corkscrew. "Nooo," she says, hinting a frown. Taylor smirks and says, "Oh, we're not beaten yet." He unwraps the neck of the bottle, takes off one of his boots, and places the bottom of the bottle inside his boot. He stumbles, laughing, as his alcohol catches up with him. "What are you doing?" she asks. He gives that same slight smirk. Then he bangs the boot heel against the stone wall. The pressure pushes the cork outward. He pulls out the remainder of the cork and hands her the bottle.

"Not bad," she says.

They sit on the bench and pass the wine between them, as they talk and drink and take in the last minutes of the night. The lit bridges leave a trail of shadowy white dots along the river. "This is a great spot," he says.

"See, you're not the only one who has places."

"I like seeing your places. I've always loved that sign." Taylor points to the Pepsi-Cola sign across the water in Queens. It's large and old and neon red.

"I wonder if something was once there," she says.

"There was a bottling plant there, once, I think. I'm glad they never got rid of the sign. Although, imagine what it's like to see it from the Queens side."

Cait concentrates her stare and says, "I guess, aloC-ispeP."

Daybreak. A neon sapphire glosses the sky. Taylor stares ahead. "You know, the Spanish call this the *madrugada.* The blue hour. God," he says with an exhale, "I love this time. The world feels so vital, and I don't know, everything seems possible." Cait looks at Taylor and brightens at the edges of her eyes. Orange striations come over the horizon. The bridges profile dark. The hum of traffic rises with the city. The sky becomes purple and blue and blends into the pink, sunlit edge. And the water reflects the sky.

XLVII

Taylor watches Cait's eyes flutter. Her body lies still. He looks at the clock and pushes strands of her hair behind her ear. She yawns and wakes. He tells her the time. She's late for brunch with her mother. Taylor watches her rise, as the light graces her hips and small back, as she puts on her bra and clips it, clasp by clasp, and he wishes he had a camera to freeze this image forever. She puts on black leggings, a long black T-shirt, a belt, and little pink sneakers. She turns on her ringer. Checks her email. And gasps. Her lips are shaped like an O. She reads her phone. Stands still. And Taylor leaps up, sensing it without her saying a word.

Current ran the story.

GIRONA'S OTHER MISTRESS? the headline reads.

The article begins: "Disgraced presidential candidate Joseph Girona likely had more than one mistress, according to two sources close to Girona. The sources claim that on at least one occasion at an Iowa hotel, the former Democratic front-runner was 'intimate' with *New York Times* reporter Cait Ellis . . ."

Cait stares into space.

Taylor reads on. The article lays out Luke's version of events. It reports that Cait offered "no comment."

"Who the hell could that second source be?" Taylor asks. "God, those fucking assholes."

Cait continues to stare into space.

Taylor realizes that she needs him to remain collected. He checks his phone. He sees a missed call from Christian. He checks Cait's phone. Her mother called three times. He tells her that. She says nothing. He urges her to call her mother back. To still see her. He says anything is better than thinking about this. He explains that Luke is probably still in the city, at his hotel. Taylor says he'll figure out what happened. He'll correct the report. "You may need to speak to Luke now," he says. "But let me talk to Christian and Luke first."

She nods.

Downstairs, the doorman suggests that they exit from the side door. A media pack has already gathered outside. They agree. Cait puts on her sunglasses, and like that, the reporter becomes the news.

Taylor's cab speeds toward midtown. He calls Christian back. And Christian explains. He thinks the first source was Girona's bodyman. He believes the second source was Girona's wife. "Luke somehow got hold of her. Hell, she probably *wanted* to speak to Luke." But Girona's wife won't speak to Christian. She blames him for enabling the infidelity.

Taylor asks him to do the right thing now. Christian hesitates. "I understand your loyalty," Taylor says. "It's admirable in today's Washington. But there are limits. There *must* be limits." And Christian is silent. Taylor continues, "Cait did nothing wrong. Yet this will ruin her career if she looks like another mistress. The story makes her look like some stereotype of the female reporter who hooks up with the pol to get the story. She's not that woman. Give her a fighting chance, a chance to explain why she did not report it."

Christian exhales and agrees. He'll speak to Luke on background. He'll confirm that Girona made a pass that night, but Cait rebuffed him.

Taylor texts Cait: "Christian will speak to Luke on background and tell the truth. I'm about to speak to Luke. A correction is in the works. We'll get through this. I love u."

Taylor arrives at the midtown hotel where most of the *Current* staff stayed for the convention. It's where he resigned the day before. *God, only yesterday.* He takes the elevator up to Luke's room. And knocks on room 403.

As Cait arrives at a café-restaurant on the Upper East Side, she reads Taylor's text. She opens and closes her eyes. It's not great news. But it's better news. And she looks up. Outside, through the door's smudged window, she sees her mother.

She steps out and they embrace. Cait leans into her mother and her mother's arms feel like home. "It's going to be okay, hon," Erin says. "We'll straighten this out." Cait nods, holding back her tears. She shows her mother Taylor's text. "Good," Erin says. "You'll look a lot better when the truth comes out. I think we should come clean now. You'll write something explaining why you did not report it. I think you're right, a lot of women will support you."

Cait nods. She looks around and sees normalcy. Four outdoor tables. Tablecloths checkered red and white. The awning above them is red and green. The restaurant is crowded inside. The Manhattan side street is quiet. It's Indian summer. A jogger passes them. A couple walks across the street with a massive stroller and a small dog. A young black woman helps an old white woman. The old woman inches along on her walker and looks at them. Cait looks away.

"It's on *Drudge, HuffPo, Redline,* CNN, everywhere," Cait says. "I can't even look at Twitter. My doorman said reporters are camped outside my building."

"It will get better. Taylor's seeing to that. Do you want to go back to my apartment?" Erin asks.

Cait looks around. "No. It's nice and quiet out here. I could use something in my stomach. But it's too crowded in there. Can we just sit here?"

Cait's phone rings. She recognizes the number. It's her editor.

Room 403. Luke answers the door. Taylor shoves him five feet back. Luke's body thuds against the plaster wall.

"What the fuck!" Luke yells.

"What are you doing writing that crap?" Taylor demands.

"What crap?"

"You know what. On Cait Ellis."

"You knew I was working on that." Luke's arms hang at his sides. Taylor holds Luke's collar, pinning him against the wall.

"I didn't think you would go ahead with it, publish her name," Taylor says.

"Who is Cait Ellis to you?"

Taylor sees Luke's confusion. He looks at his own flushed fingers, gripping the white cotton of Luke's shirt. And he realizes that his personal feelings are distorting his judgment.

Taylor lets go. He walks to the window and faces the cityscape, but his focus drifts inward. Luke seems unconcerned with the ruffles in his shirt, the button that popped off. He only watches Taylor.

"Are you with Cait Ellis?" Luke asks.

Taylor looks out the window, and the city goes on, indifferent. He turns around and nods.

"Since when?" Luke asks.

"It was off and on. We had a thing during the primary, but then separated. We got back together after the GOP convention."

"Jesus. How together?"

"Very much together."

"Shit . . . I'm sorry. I'm really sorry. But . . . but it was about the story. I tried to get her to talk to me. I didn't mean her any harm."

"What you meant is beside the point. It did harm."

"I treated her as fairly as anyone else."

Taylor thinks about that. Luke saw a story and acted. Most reporters would do the same. He reminds himself of these things as Luke shuts the door. Taylor decides to focus on the problem before Cait, not his own feelings. He explains to Luke what he got wrong and arranges for Luke to speak with Christian. Christian tells Luke the truth, on the condition he's described only as a source close to Girona. As they speak, Taylor calls Cait.

Cait says she's with her mother. Her editors want to meet with her Sunday evening and decide a course of action. After that, they say, they'll put out a statement. She explains this to Taylor with a hint of resignation about her, and it hurts him, to hear that fatalism in her voice.

He tells her that she will look "much better, publicly, I mean" before that meeting. He tells her that Christian is speaking to Luke right now and confirming what really happened. "I think you should speak to Luke too and tell him the truth. It's better than what's out there now."

She hesitates, but agrees.

Taylor sees Luke hang up with Christian, so he passes the phone to him. Luke takes notes as if it's just another story.

Nine minutes later, the conversation ends. And Taylor asks, "Was Girona's wife the second source?" "You know I can't say," Luke replies. Taylor explains that she never knew what happened. Luke asks how he knows that. And Taylor looks at him with stern eyes and says, "I just know." Luke nods. Luke calls Girona's wife. She does not answer. He calls Girona's bodyman, who answers. Luke explains what has transpired. And Taylor hears the bodyman say, "It could've gone down that way. That would explain why Girona was so paranoid about what occurred. You know, why he insisted that Christian speak to her."

Luke hangs up a few minutes later. He says he's going to correct the story. Taylor watches Luke's fingers stab the black keys. He reports the true story, citing new sources, and sends it. He calls Philip and explains everything. Philip tells the copydesk to update the story. Philip sees the phone number. He asks why Luke's calling on Taylor's phone. Luke explains and passes the phone to Taylor.

Philip asks, "You don't think you should've told us more? Perhaps, why you did not want to involve yourself in this story?"

"No, it was private."

"I wish you would've."

"It wasn't just about her. It was all of it." And Taylor sighs. "I don't want to be part of this shit . . . any of it." He hesitates.

Months of questions, of professional self-loathing, of indecision flash through him, as if conclusions were reached, and he need only let his mind go where his gut has already arrived.

"Listen, I'm done."

"I know."

"No, I'm done. I can't return to work on Monday as if nothing's changed. Forget all that about staying on until the end of November. I quit. I'm sorry not to give notice. But I'm just done."

Taylor hangs up.

Luke's mouth is agape. "You can't quit because of this."

"Can I sit down?" Taylor asks.

"Of course."

Taylor sits in the faux leather armchair. He breathes long breaths. Luke stares at him. And Taylor tells him, "I didn't quit only because of this story. I actually resigned yesterday. But I was going to stay with them through the campaign."

"Really?"

"Yeah."

"Still, maybe that was better. Don't abruptly quit over this shit. It's just a story."

Taylor looks at him. Luke blinks and acknowledges that it's not just a story to Taylor. And a pregnant silence fills the room until Taylor asks, "You ever feel like you're so busy doing your job that you no longer think about *why* you once wanted to do this job?"

"I try not to think about that sort of shit. It's not helpful."

"Yeah."

"But really, I tried to get this story right."

"Enough about intentions. You're not a child. The fact is, you wrote tabloid copy on suspect sourcing, and that story threatened Cait's reputation, her livelihood."

Luke nods contritely.

Taylor looks at Luke, breathes, and lets some anger go. "Still, I know you asked her for her side. My gripe is not solely with you. I'm just done with it all. And really, I think, I've been done for a long time."

"What else are you going to do?"

"I don't know. Maybe write another book. Just something different."

"It's never that easy."

"I don't expect easy. I'm just sick of being ashamed of my work, of the dysfunctional circus, all of it, you know? And that has to be enough. Right now, leaving has to be enough."

"But don't quit like this. You'll never get a reference. P&R could blackball you to every editor. I've seen Rick spread bullshit about people who pissed him off."

Taylor shrugs. "I just don't care anymore."

"Dude, be careful. That sounds like the headstrong conviction of youth. That shit can quickly take you a bridge too far."

"I don't care."

"You should care. You will care. I mean . . . I know you think you don't care about being on TV or having your stories drive the news. But if you leave, it will get real quiet for you, real quick. I've seen it happen to some good reporters who take retirement packages too early. They think they'll do something else. But soon they miss the game. They miss the respect that comes with being a player."

"Fuck this game. I never wanted to be a player like this."

"Okay, okay. I just don't want you acting impulsively. You've worked your way up to get here, just like me. It's crazy to give that up. You still don't have to. I mean, damn, if you do, you'll never get this far in another profession again."

"The thing is, what's the use of going far in the wrong direction?"

"That's greener-grass bullshit."

"Maybe. But maybe not. I mean, if I don't try, surely not. Right?"

"I guess. But it still feels like a mistake."

"I never said it was an easy call." Taylor rises, walks toward the television, and opens the cabinet door beneath. "Do you mind if I grab something from your minibar?" he asks.

"Of course not."

Taylor pulls out a small bottle of Johnnie Walker Black. He chugs it down. He sets the empty bottle on the desk and grabs another.

"Fuuuck." Luke exhales as he sits on the bed. "I'm sorry if I had any part in this. But why would you give this job up for nothing?"

"It's not for nothing."

"I meant, for nothing better, like another job."

"I know what you meant." Taylor drinks and looks at Luke. "You ever heard of a reporter named Russell Baker?"

"No."

"He was a Timesman in the sixties and for a long time after. I read his memoir a few years ago. There was this one story about Scotty Reston."

"Who's that?"

"He was the Peter Miller of his time, though even more influential. Reston was the *Times* star in Washington when the *Times* still set the agenda. So anyway, there was this scene where Baker recounts going to lunch with Reston in D.C. Before they went inside, two cars collided down the street. So Reston, the most powerful man in D.C. media, immediately runs down the street like some hungry cub reporter. And Baker just marvels. The *Times* didn't exactly cover Washington traffic. And men like Reston certainly didn't."

Luke rests his forearms on his thighs.

"I now better understand why Baker marveled," Taylor continues. "In any line of work, it's always something to watch someone who doesn't have anything to prove keep at his trade, and therefore prove everything."

Luke nods.

"Reston was not perfect. He was too close to some people in power, including JFK, like Miller and others today. But Reston was great at the craft. I must admit, issues aside, like Miller too. So Reston was a big deal. But he didn't feel too big to check out the everyday story. He knew it might matter to someone. Or maybe it was just because it was news. And that's what reporters do. They chase news."

Taylor looks at Luke and continues, "What counts is, he ran after it. I was once like that. But somewhere along the way I stopped respecting what I was chasing, and why I wrote about it. And I don't want to go back. But you'll always be like Reston. I wish it didn't include this shit. You could've handled this story better, even if you believe who's fucking who is news." Taylor shakes his head and adds, "But I also recognize that some things in politics do matter, and I'm glad there are still guys like you out there who'll always run after the good stories too."

XLVIII

Cait sees that the story has been updated. Yet there's too much pain around the words to read them. She hands the phone to her mother. And Erin reads the story aloud.

Afterward, Erin looks up at Cait. At least the truth is out. The truth is difficult. But it's better than what was out. Erin warns her daughter, "You still could lose your job. The *Times* will be accused of covering it up. They'll get a lot of heat, though your motives were good. They may offer you a package and insist you resign. I mean, they're regularly offering retirement packages anyway these days. But . . . it may also be okay. Just be prepared for the worst." Cait nods. Erin adds, "Do you want me to talk to them? I know a lot of them."

"No, Mom. I can handle it."

"They may let you shift to perhaps an arts beat. If you want that."

Cait fiddles with her fork. "I don't really know what I want. But I don't see how I can stay on the campaign."

"That's probably for the best."

Cait's eyes redden.

Erin puts her hand on Cait's. "Hon, I know this is an awful day. But I promise, you'll come out of this stronger. In a couple of years this will seem like a setback on the way to something better."

Cait nods.

"And some things are going right in your life. It sounds like what you have with Taylor is truly special."

Cait hints at a smile.

"That's better," Erin says. She wants to change the subject to that smile. She asks about Taylor. Cait does not respond at first. She eats a little more. Erin waits. Cait is quiet. Erin mentions him again and in time, Cait lets it out slowly. She speaks of the cathedral and the previous night.

"You know," Cait continues, "before we watched the sunrise, we went to this eighties bar in the West Village. It was one of those bars where people sing along. And just before we left, he mouthed a few lyrics to this song "Forever Young." And, I don't know, it feels somehow cheesy to say. He was just reveling in it. You know how they always say Italians have this joy for life. He has that, so much." And Erin smiles Cait's smile. "So you're right," Cait adds, "things with him are really good. I'm just stunned by today. I mean, I never actually thought it would come out."

"I know, hon. Things just go this way sometimes."

"Please don't say this happened for a reason."

"No, I despise that saying. Things don't happen for a reason. But we can give reason to the things that happen to us in life."

Cait blinks. And Erin knows she understands.

The waiter returns and clears the table. Erin asks for the check and pays the bill and the waiter leaves. Cait rubs her fingertips against the checkered tablecloth, seemingly lost in thought. Erin watches her and quietly says, "I'm proud of you."

Cait looks back at her mother. "For what?"

"You were right to not let me call Philip back or call your office. I'm proud that you had the strength to leave Blake. You'll get through everything else. You should take pride in how you've managed these past few weeks."

Cait half smiles.

And Erin's eyes dampen. Because here's her daughter. Fighting back. Holding strong. Steadying. She did what Erin hoped. She left him. How dearly she wanted her to leave Blake. She was always unsure about him. But initially, when he proposed, she was overwhelmed by the sight of it. The man on one knee. Before her own daughter. To see this moment in person. But it never felt right to her. She could not say it. She tried to hold back. She knows children must live their own lives. And sometimes parents must watch their children relive their mistakes, or make their own mistakes. She's seen too much of life to fixate on today's events. She knows what matters in the long life. And here is her girl now, having broken out, with a man she loves. Erin feels this profound sense of a circle realized. Because the child she had, this girl who came from her, this baby that was once the size of her forearm, is now a young woman, her own woman, a strong woman, and in love. Erin decides she did all right. Maybe she worked hard. Maybe she disappeared for months on a story. Maybe she risked her life sometimes, risked leaving her daughter without a mother. But here they are, eating together. And her child is grown and, no matter what happens, a great reporter in her own right, an independent woman telling her about the hard times but also about the man she loves. And though Erin has known the feelings, the experiences, it feels new to her. For it's her daughter, living it.

A photographer runs up to them. Begins shooting.

Cait covers her face.

"What the hell are you doing?" Erin demands.

"I'm with *Redline*. I just need a few pictures."

Erin tosses her water on him.

"What the fuck?" the paparazzo says.

She stands, takes Cait's hand, and says, "Let's get out of here."

They walk away and turn down Lexington. Erin looks for other photographers. None. Cait wears her sunglasses and looks down. She never expected anyone to recognize her uptown. She's never been news before. The paparazzo returns. They pass the crowded traffic on Eighty-Sixth Street. Another photographer arrives. The paparazzi run ahead of them. Block them. Shoot a series of frames. "Don't you have something better to do?" Erin yells.

"Lady, your friend's all over the Web now," one bites back.

"Are you kidding me?" Erin puts her arm around Cait's waist and hurries her along. "Let's cross here and go somewhere they can't follow," Erin says. "I'll call us a car." Cait nods, as they begin to cross the street.

Horn. Screeching. Flash of yellow. Erin tosses Cait back to the curb. A taxi skids leftward. Thud. Erin flies six feet. Lands on her back. Her head snaps against the cement. Strangers scream. Cait screams, "Mom!" She runs to her. Erin's unconscious. The driver grips his wheel. Strangers gasp. The paparazzi run away. A man calls 911 on his cell phone. A thin old woman holds her hands at her mouth. A crowd gathers. Erin lies still. Her silver hair dampens red. Cait cries spastically. Heaves. Her hands tremble. She kneels over her mother. Erin's unconscious. Cait has her hands near her head. But she trembles. Hesitates. Should she touch her? What should she do? She does not want to move her head. Cait squeezes her hand. "Mom. Mom. Mom," crying, "Stay with me! Oh Mom, please. Please! God!" Cait turns to the crowd. Screams, "Did someone call 911?" The man who did nods, holds his glasses, wipes away the tears under his eyes. The thin old woman walks over to Cait. She places her hands on Cait's shoulders. Sirens. Flashing lights. Cop car. Fire trucks. Ambulance. Paramedics. A female cop pulls Cait back and hugs her. Cait's gasping. Paramedics run to Erin. They move a board under her. Blocks stabilize her head. She's lifted. A small red puddle remains on the street.

The cop tells Cait, "Calm down, and you can go with her." Cait tries not to hyperventilate. She enters the ambulance and holds her mother's hand. "Hold on, Mom. I'm here. I'm here." A medic separates them. Cait sits, biting her fist. The medic checks Erin's vitals. A small black flashlight is waved in her eyes. Her shirt is cut off with scissors. Sensors are taped to her. The monitor blips. The red line seems to trace a mountain range. Heartbeat. The ambulance slows. Traffic. Sirens deepen. A graffitied white delivery truck bangs its horn. The blue Nissan ahead nudges into parked cars. The truck follows. Ambulance stutters forward. Green light. Traffic spreads into the cross street. The ambulance accelerates. Three blocks go fast. Traffic. They slow. The ambulance wails its low siren. Cait takes her mother's hand. "Mom, stay with me. I love you. Stay with me. You're going to be okay. I love you so much." Cars split. The ambulance accelerates. There's a clear lane. "We're almost there." Sailing. Slowing. Turning. Breaks. The driver door opens. The back doors fling open. Erin's still unconscious. Cait squeezes her hand. "Mom," she cries. "I love you. I love you. Stay with me." *Beeeeeeeep.* A medic yanks Cait back. Cait cries, "Mom! Wake up!" Another medic places a mask over Erin's mouth. Squeezes a pump. Paramedics rush Erin inside.

An orderly sits Cait down. The chair is cold and white and plastic. The waiting room is cold and white and sterile. The overhead fluorescent light tints yellow. Strangers surround Cait. She looks at the round black-and-white clock on the wall. The second hand ticks. Mascara trails down Cait's cheeks. She wipes her face. Sniffles. She takes out her phone and calls her father. It's difficult for her to say it. Her words choke out. But she gets it out. Her father says, "I'll be right there." He hangs up. Cait calls Taylor. She explains. Taylor says he'll be right there. Cait hears rustling, white noise. She realizes he must have put his phone in his pocket and forgot to hang up. She sets down the phone. But does not hang up. A nurse walks toward Cait. Cait looks up. Her mother's condition? The nurse passes her. Cait sees the clock. The second hand ticks.

Taylor arrives at the emergency room. He sees strangers. Strangers. Strangers. Cait. She's weeping in a man's arms. Taylor walks to them. He senses that the man's her father. Taylor stands a pace away and catches his breath. Cait opens her eyes. She looks at Taylor, unable to stop crying. Their eyes meet. And Taylor knows.

XLIX

The orderly pulls the sheet back. Erin Ellis is still. Her chest does not rise. Her eyelids do not blink. Her lips retain pink. But her skin is whiter, duskier, a little waxen. Cait steps to her mother, but keeps a pace away. Her father walks bedside. Cait shakes her head, and tears press her eyes. It doesn't make sense to her. She was just with her. *How can she be gone? Like that. We were just together. How can she be gone? What am I supposed to do without her? How am I supposed to know what to do without her?* Cait does not touch her mother. She stares in disbelief. She can't get her head around it. Her mother cannot be dead.

Her father's legs give out. He collapses to his knees. He grips his ex-wife's left hand. It's not cold. But there's no warmth. He calls out to her. Again and again. As if he can wake her. As if she can hear him. As if it matters. As if naming the dead is more urgent than naming the living.

Cait stands over him. She's never seen her father cry.

Taylor waits in the ER. He thinks about his mother. He imagines Cait decades from now. She's talking with their daughter. And she's hit by a car. The randomness stuns him. He knows these things happen all the time. But to Cait's mother. After everything else. In front of Cait. He shivers. He remembers talking about a car accident with Luke. He chides himself for being glib. It feels unreal to him. Again, he reminds himself, these things happen every day. But still. Now. To Cait. It feels too close to be real.

Taylor wakes at his parents' apartment. He slept in his boyhood bedroom. There are old CDs on the nightstand, Pearl Jam and N.W.A. and Radiohead. Trophies on shelves. There's a photo of him with his thirteen-year-old crew of guys. None smile. They're trying so hard to be hard. There are photos of high school friends, dances, and prom. The image of Taylor in his first tuxedo, his hair overly gelled. There's a black-and-white newspaper photo of Taylor dribbling a soccer ball in a tournament. His fist is clenched, as he pushes back another player. The veins in his boyish-thin forearms show. Taylor stands above the image. He stretches up, pushes his hair back, and stares out the window. Predawn blue light brushes across Riverside Park.

He thinks about Cait. He wants to call her, but it's too early. He hopes she was able to sleep. He feels compelled to do something. To help her. His mother walks into his room. He tells her he wants to do something for Cait. Her hand graces his right arm and she explains, "Cait doesn't need you to *do* anything for her right now. Just be there for her."

L

And the mourners come. The obituary was read. E. F. Ellis, Veteran Correspondent, Dies at 59. There were other stories in the days that followed. Police questioned the photographers but released them. The tabloid media hounded Joe Girona, but stayed away from Cait. The first presidential debate took place. Cait didn't watch. She heard that Constance Wallace now had a secure lead in the latest polls. And she didn't give it a second thought. None of that seemed important anymore.

In the days after, some of Erin's old friends reached out to Cait. They read the obituary. Older readers recognized her mother's name in the news. Erin Ellis never was on television. She never attended a junket. She was rarely at the backslapping correspondents' dinners. She was not even a gender in her byline. She was the reporter in faraway places, who covered the news of faraway places. During war, during upheaval, she was on the front page every day. When it ended, she vanished. There would be a sporadic story from Lyon or Riga, a travel journal article, little narratives from the world on newsprint, stories that stay with you like ink on your fingertips. Did you read that charming story from Bratislava in today's paper? Then something else broke in the world. She went. You read her name again every day. And that was enough to know. Something's wrong in a faraway place.

People here admired her that way. But also in respects particular to the woman they knew. They have personal memories. And they carry those memories inside the dim church. They file in pew by pew. A cough echoes. Heels clank. Heads are down. Some mourners avoid eye contact. They fixate on the floor—the worn patina, the antique granite slabs that vary from dark blue to black, the mortar that has darkened with time. Others glance around. See familiar faces. Strangers. Black attire. And ahead, they see the casket. It's difficult to conceive. The life led. That she's suddenly dead. Erin Fiona Ellis is in a box.

The day is gray. It's Thursday morning. Cait organized her mother's funeral. It kept her distracted. Cait didn't want days of ritual. She asked for one ceremony. The priest would not deny a grieving daughter that.

Hundreds gather inside. *Wall Street Journal* graybeards, retired colleagues, competitors. Cait's bosses are present. They tried to reach her when they heard the news, but she ignored them. And they understood. There's a pack of war correspondents. The correspondents feel closer to one another than to their media outlet. They saw each other more. They share what lived around the stories. The most famous American war photographer, of the old *Time,* sits down, keeps to himself, but people who know him see him, and in him they see something they hold dear, something fading, even ghostly in the cranelike thin strength, in his veiny, taut neck and hands. Marc Andrews arrives. His eyes are fixed on the casket. He rubs his white bushy beard. Taylor recalls him. Marc too is of the old *Time.* Taylor met Marc when he was an intern at *Time.* Marc had been *Life* magazine's war correspondent. *Life* folded. Marc went to *Time.* And, in time, *Time* told Marc, before 9/11, "We don't cover wars anymore." And Marc was eased quietly into the good night. The modest retirement package. The cursory thank-you. A toast. Now please disappear. But Marc did not retire. He was seen years later in sub-Saharan Africa, working as a stringer for CNN. More mourners arrive. Taylor watches them. The withering newspaperwomen and newspapermen. He spots their worn suits. Most of them never saw themselves as journalists. They were reporters, tradesmen, not professionals. They are fossils of a bygone time, when words were worked and edited and copyedited and reedited. And stories were perfected as much as they could be in a day's time. Because words were printed on paper and worth the cost.

Stories of Erin Ellis's journalism, of her life, run through her colleagues' minds. She survived three weeks on the water in her bathtub. She was assaulted. Twice. She became proficient in Krav Maga after that. She knew the whistle of bullets as they fly within inches of your head. There are personal recollections. She disliked Merlot. It bothered her when writers romanticized typewriters. She thought it was akin to romanticizing the horse and buggy. She loved the song "The Weight." She thought *On the Waterfront* was the greatest, most quintessential American film. It annoyed her when a person argued that chocolate was good for you. "Stop thinking up excuses. Enjoy enjoying," she would say when the subject came up vis-à-vis chocolate, wine, or sex. Few people know every detail. But they know pieces and they carry those pieces inside.

There are now more than eighty retired reporters in the church. They all know how she won the Pulitzer. She wrote a series about one family during the Kosovo war. The father and two sons died in battle. The teenage daughter died by an errant bullet. The mother remained, alone. And E. F. Ellis reported how the mother channeled her grief and sought to end the war. This is what they recall of Erin Ellis. And yet here she is. Not in the world. She's in a box. It feels too pedestrian to be true. How could this remarkable woman die crossing the street? Gone at fifty-nine. Many feel their middle age, their twilight, their mortality. These are people who really dodged bullets. They have trained themselves to be dispassionate. But mortality sinks in, and stone cracks.

One accident, not in war, but off a curb, and it could be any of them. And to die like that. To be hit by a car, fleeing a gossip website's photographer. It feels as if the fates mocked her in the worst way. Everyone heard, she tossed her daughter away from the car. She was like that. They've seen far worse. War carries coincidental and cruel ironies. Fact is stranger than fiction, they say. But still, for this to happen this way, and to Erin Ellis. She was one of them. She was so alive. If it can be Erin, it can be anyone. Two sixty-something men enter in crisp U.S. Marines dress blues. They find a pew in back. The church is full. Her former colleagues collect together. Other reporters gather in groups. They seemingly need to be near each other. Perhaps something else is dying here too. Erin Ellis is dead. But an era goes with her. It's not the end. But it's a signpost. She was one of them. Generations of print reporters. And that too should be mourned.

But do not say that to Cait. She has no room for metaphors. Her mother is dead. Cait stares at the coffin. Taylor watches Cait. She sits in the front row, beside her father, with her family. Taylor's behind her. Able to reach her. But he does not. She's not crying. She's upright. Shoulders back. Chin straight. Eyes ahead.

The bier, holding Erin's body, points toward the altar. Her feet face the front. Rosary beads are in her hands. Cait cannot look at her. She doesn't want to recall any more death. She's already seen her mother that way. She wants to remember her the other way. Alive.

A crucifix is attached to the interior of the casket's white lid. The priest wears white vestments. The altar boys wear white over black. A woman sings. The congregation stands. Cait hears the word "hallelujah." She cringes. The congregation soon sits. And words are said. Revelation 21:4 is read: " 'And God shall wipe away all tears from their eyes; and there shall be no more death, neither sorrow, nor crying, neither shall there be any more pain: for the former things are passed away.' " More readings come. The priest says that Erin Fiona Ellis's "true destination is eternal life." Cait hopes. But it's hard for her to hear. To believe. *She should be here. With me. She just came back to me.* Cait feels fury. Her eyes narrow. Her head shakes. She wants to keep it together. She bends down and places her head in her hands. Taylor reaches over and touches her left shoulder. She sits up and leans her head against his hand.

There is a hymn. Catholics rise to take communion. They file to the priest. Thin wafers melt in mouths. In time, the priest sprinkles holy water on Erin Ellis's body. And soon the casket is closed. A white pall is placed over it. The priest says it is a reminder of baptism. Spasms of tears are heard.

The priest requested no eulogies. The Catholic Church traditionally favors homily, brief hopeful words that carry a religious subtext. But this is a city church. It has come to terms with the erosion of faith. Cait stood her ground. Her father would speak his way. She was his wife. The mother of his girl. Cait would speak her way. Erin was her mother. And the priest would not deny a grieving daughter that.

Mr. Ellis stands before the church. He wears a black suit, black tie. He clears his throat. His pale complexion has crossed over into wan. He's hardly slept. He runs his fingers through his sandy red hair. He looks at the coffin and coughs. And the cough echoes in the silence. Then he begins casually, speaking of his ex-wife, how they met, where they were when they realized she was pregnant. He recalls her early days in journalism, her ambition, her ability to keep it together, to be strong, to survive. And he shakes his head. He says, "despite her amazing achievements," Erin had the "noblest possible death." She died saving her daughter. His eyes seem to push outward. Tears slip down his cheeks. Cait looks up at him. "Erin pushed Cait out of the way. She protected her baby. They could've . . . they could've both died. For all that she did with her life, that's her greatest accomplishment. She brought Cait into this world and she kept her here."

Mr. Ellis looks down at Cait and composes himself. He says that Erin and Cait had a book club in Cait's early teen years. It was only for them. "Wherever Erin was, she read those books and stayed in touch." He says they mostly read the Brontës and Jane Austen. And so this man, who teaches classics, chooses Emily Brontë's words, but makes them his own:

> There is not room for Death,
> Nor atom that her might could render void:
> Thou—thou art Being and Breath,
> And what thou art may never be destroyed.

In time, the pallbearers lift the casket. And the bells toll. A smaller procession drives out of the city. Cait stares blankly out the window. She sits with her father. Cait sees the concrete highway, signs, buildings, nothing.

Black iron gates open. They park. The procession makes its way graveside. The leaves are beginning to change. The day is still gray. Mourners pass gravestones. The ground is damp. Dirt collects on black shoes.

Graveside. People sit in black wooden chairs. The highway hums in the distance. The priest skims a page in his black Bible. Taylor stands off to the side, watching people, waiting. She sees him. Her lips press together and crinkle. Something breaks within her. It's seeing him there. All week, he has been there for her. She wants to collapse into him. She wants to feel none of this pain. She wants to remain numb. She's trying not to cry. She walks to him and hugs him as if something could be lost if she lets go. He holds her. She rests her head against his chest. And she weeps. People continue to arrive. And she weeps.

Cait loosens her arms and tries to gather herself. Taylor turns her chin up to him and says to her, "You can do this. I love you so much. You can do this." She nods and looks up at him. He's still holding her. She folds her head back into his chest. "Caitriona," he whispers, "I know she had so much life left. But what a life she lived. Don't remember her death today. Remember her life. Think about Poets' Corner. She lived that life. Celebrate that." And Cait nods.

The mourners wait in their seats. The priest begins. More words are said. The priest intones, "I am the Resurrection and the Life." Cait stares at the coffin. Taylor regrets what he said. He realizes that he cannot understand what she's going through.

Cait feels the break of nature. And words cannot mend that.

"Thy servant departed, that she may not receive in punishment the requital of her deeds who in desire did keep Thy will."

Cait's rage returns. Her nails dig into her palm. She glares at the priest. *Punishment, what punishment? This is the punishment.* She has heard too many words. About the afterlife. About her mother's ongoing life. People have told her that her mother is in a better place. *This is where she should be. This place. She's gone.* She wants to grab the priest. Shake him. Her mother is gone. Admit it! Force him to say it. She is dead.

Psalm 23:4 is read: " 'Even though I walk through the valley of the shadow of death, I will fear no evil, for you are with me; your rod and your staff, they comfort me.' "

Cait stands to give her eulogy. Forty-four people sit in silence. Cait takes small, slow steps. She touches the casket. She looks at it and breathes. People watch her. She turns around. The peaks of her cheeks are not flush. Her pixie hair is flat. She wears black: sunglasses, pantsuit, blouse, heels. Black.

Cait takes off her sunglasses. The skin beneath her eyes is puffy. She's unsure where to place her glasses. Her father stands. She hands them to him. He takes her hand for an instant. She inhales.

"Thank you all for coming. We really appreciate it. I appreciate it." Her shoulders arch, but then she exhales and her shoulders rest. "For years, I referred to my mother as 'the great woman.' I thought I did that to escape her shadow. But I now think I was always chasing my mother. When I was eleven, I ditched class and hopped into a taxi and followed her to the airport. She never knew that. And as most of you know, I followed her professionally too." Cait shakes her head and stiffens. "A lot has happened in recent weeks. A lot of lies have been written. Things have been misunderstood. But that seems so small now, doesn't it?" She takes a long breath. "And yet, my mom knew that right away. As it happened, she knew what ultimately mattered. God, it took me so long to understand her. Many children, I suspect, struggle in a parent's shadow. There are all these books and movies about sons who have great fathers. They describe how those boys fight their fathers' legacies and struggle with the pressure. I cannot think of one about daughters who have great mothers. And I know all mothers are great. Yet my mom accomplished some remarkable things in her life. I want to honor that. But I cannot find a movie about that. I think it's the same with those boys and their fathers, but different too. Many of those boys seem angry. I was never angry at my mother. I was hurt when she went away on those stories. I worried. But I was also so proud of her. I bragged about her to my friends. When she returned, when I was a little girl, I would give her the silent treatment. But I knew. I always knew. I knew everything was possible because of her."

The mourners listen intently. Some women nod. Others wipe their eyes.

"I find it hard to believe that she's dead. I try to forget how she died. During that meal, shortly before it happened, we were talking about a lot of stuff. And she listened. She always listened. I was so happy to have her back in my life. When she returned to the city, I felt like we had decades left . . . It's hard to think about that. I feel like I was only just getting to know her, as an adult." Cait's hands tremble. She closes them. A tear traces her right cheek. She wipes it away. "Someone I love very much told me, only last week, a line by Henry David Thoreau.

That we must suck the marrow out of life. My mom did that. I realize I should celebrate that today. We all should. But it's hard for me. I can't believe she'll never see me get married or have children . . . I keep thinking about that . . . I don't know how to do that stuff without her." Words stall and start, and Cait breathes deeply and gathers. "I thought I could do everything without her. Now, I don't know how to do anything without her. For God's sake, I wanted to call my mom this week and ask how I should eulogize her." Cait lets out a single, sad laugh. She covers her mouth briefly and then goes on. "I know mothers die. But it feels too soon. I know we should celebrate her life. But it feels too soon." Her eyes saturate red. *You can do this,* she tells herself. *Breathe.* And she breathes.

"This week, I thought a lot about what to say. I wanted to find the perfect poem to convey what I feel. All week I looked at people living their lives in the city. I wanted to grab them and shake them and ask how they can be so happy. How could they go on with their lives this way? But that's absurd. They didn't know her. It reminded me of this W. H. Auden poem. But I felt that was, well, done. People recite Auden at funerals. How silly is that? I was worried about sounding trite at my mom's funeral. I could hear my mom telling me to be original." And there is sympathetic laughter. "Yet I kept feeling those words: 'Stop all the clocks, cut off the telephone.' I want all of the city to hear her bell toll. To mourn my mother. My mother, in Auden's words, really was 'my North, my South, my East and West. My working week and my Sunday rest. My noon, my midnight, my talk, my song.' " And Mr. Ellis mouths the words with his daughter. "In a way, I thought that would 'last forever, I was wrong.' " Tears run down Cait's cheeks. She wipes them away. "Mom, you gave me direction. You looked out for me until the very end. I'll never forget you. None of us will."

Cait sits down. She leans forward and hides her face in her hands. Her father puts his arm around her, kisses the top of her head, and whispers to his daughter, "Your mother would be so proud of you."

After Erin Ellis was lowered into the ground. After all the words had been said. After respect was paid to the dead. Cait sits. Guests leave. Cait still sits, alone. Taylor walks over to her and sits with her but says no words. She stares at the plot of soil. Mr. Ellis thanks guests for coming. The couple sits alone among the rows of empty chairs. The day remains gray. Trees are beginning to change colors. The smell of wet grass lingers in the air. Taylor leans toward Cait and whispers, "I shouldn't have said that before. You should mourn her in your time. There is no right amount of time . . . We will celebrate her life after that."

Cait nods and sniffles. "No, you're right. I want to think about her life. It's hard, though."

"I can't even imagine."

"So you really think she lived a life like those people, in the cathedral?"

Taylor looks at her and nods.

"I know," Cait says. "I just wish I had her longer. I just want her . . . I just want her back." And she spasms with tears and her hands open and close with her words. She sniffles and Taylor wipes her tears and brushes her bangs to the side. "I keep picturing her on the street," she adds. "I can't get it out of my head. I'm trying. I want to so badly. But I just can't."

Mr. Ellis walks over to them. Taylor stands and shakes his hand. "Thank you for coming, Taylor," Mr. Ellis says. "I appreciate you being there for Cait." Taylor nods. Cait watches them. Her father continues, "Would you like to ride back with us?"

The black hearse drives along the highway. Cait wears her sunglasses. She holds Taylor's hand but looks out the window, saying nothing the entire drive. But she never lets go of his hand.

They return with dusk. Cait wants to go for a walk. They find their way back to the park. She shivers. Taylor removes his blazer and places it over her shoulders. "It's starting to get dark earlier," he says. Cait nods. She's not spoken for an hour.

They walk uptown along the park's stone wall. They're quiet together. Until Cait says, "You know, at that last brunch with my mom, I was so upset at first. I could not see anything beyond the BS online about me. But at some point, we got to us. And I could just tell, you know, how happy that made her. Amid all that was going on, she cared more about that."

Taylor listens as they walk.

Cait looks at him and says, "Thank you for being there for me, for not giving up on me, or us."

"You don't have to thank me. I never had a choice."

"But you did."

"I didn't. Once you realize you have what we do, and how rare that is, you can't give up on it." He leaps up a step. She follows him. He stands in front of the Metropolitan Museum's high pillars. He tosses his arms wide, bends back, looks up at the smoky sky, and breathes deep. He turns to her. "Like you said, there's been so much bullshit lately. Yet it all seems so petty now—the gossip, the horse race, my work. And your mom knew that. She reminds me of why I had to leave all that behind. You know, when I met her at that book party, she told me about how she quit her job to go to Asia. So I said, 'It clearly worked out.' And she replied, 'I worked it out.' I'll never forget how she said that. People always say it's the small stuff that counts. Someone nears death, and they talk about the little things, like when we take our first steps. There's truth to that. But, you know what your mother's life says to me?"

"What?"

"Don't stop going after the big things too. I mean, even if it doesn't work out, at least you won't have regrets. At least you won't be stuck with what-ifs." He walks up a couple more steps and she watches him. "I felt that way only a few years ago. But I lost it. They say you should never stop trying. But I think we all stop trying at some point in our lives. That's human. They really should say, it's never too late to start trying for the life you want. And . . . I don't know. Well, I guess, what we have, it helped me realize that again. It brought me back, in a way."

"You brought you back."

"But what we have . . . it reminded me of what I once demanded from life."

"Taylor, it's not always going to be this way for us. Things won't always be perfect between us."

"I know that."

"How can you be sure we won't fall out of love? People do, every day."

"Sometimes they don't. We tend to forget those people, these days."

"You think we're those people?"

"I do. But I also think we don't have to worry about it. People focus too much on what can go wrong in life, rather than on what can go right."

She looks at him. Her lips shift leftward. "I love that you think about what can go right," she says. "I keep thinking about what you said to me. 'It's not what we want in life that counts. It's what we do.' I keep coming back to it. I don't know. Maybe because I believe it. Or because it's you. It's so you, Taylor. But it also makes me proud of my mom. She did so much. You're right. She had that kind of life."

"She did. And we will too."

Cait nods. She looks up at Taylor. The night is quiet. They stand alone on the white museum steps. "You can't let that go."

"What?" he asks.

"What you've found again in yourself . . . I don't know. I guess you're not only defined by what you do but also by what you believe is worth doing. And in the end, the only person you must answer to is yourself."

Taylor nods.

"You've rediscovered that part of yourself," she continues. "Don't let it go. I love that part of you that showed me Poets' Corner. The man who loves life and isn't afraid to say so, who wants more, who has let himself feel that again. You can't lose that. You just can't. Not ever."

"I won't."

"You promise?"

"I promise."

Her lower lip folds under. As Cait does. He brushes her bangs to the side. As Taylor does.

Cait looks up at him. "Am I asking too much?"

"I would rather you ask too much," he replies, "than too little."

"From you or from life?"

"Both."

Acknowledgments

I would like to thank my agent, Matthew Carnicelli, for believing in this novel and seeing that the unconventional road would take us to the best place; Maxine Bartow for her copyediting skill, advice, and support; Joslyn Pine for her sharp proofreading eye and encouragement; cover designer Jim Tierney for being so open to input and for translating that input into art; and Brian Mitchell for his production assistance and professionalism.

I am also grateful to several readers of the novel's first draft: Lara Schweller, Amy Merrick, and Jacob Margolies. Your time was most generous. Your counsel was most welcome.

I would *not* like to thank Bill Gates and the makers of Microsoft Word. Because of your computer bug, you turned my entire novel into asterisks.

I *would* like to thank my wife, Jessie Kuhn, for her actions supporting me the day I lost my novel and throughout. You are everything one could hope for.

Photograph by
Minush Krasniqi

David Paul Kuhn is a writer and political analyst living in New York City. He has held senior writing positions across the political-media landscape, from *Politico* to *RealClearPolitics* to CBSnews.com. He has also written for *The Wall Street Journal, The Atlantic, The Washington Post Magazine, The Los Angeles Times, The New Republic,* among other publications, and regularly appeared on networks ranging from BBC to Fox News. As the Macmillan Speakers Bureau described him, "David Paul Kuhn is an expert analyst of presidential and gender politics." He is also the author of *The Neglected Voter,* which General Wes Clark called "a brilliantly insightful analysis of American politics."

Kuhn has covered four presidential campaigns and politics from Washington to the United Nations, and has driven the width of the United States for CBS News documenting Americans' lives and outlooks. He has reported on events from the epicenter of the collapse of the World Trade Center to North Korean backroom nuclear negotiations. Early in his career, he reported on the United States for the Tokyo-based *Yomiuri Shimbun,* the world's most widely circulated newspaper.

Kuhn can be reached at DPK4Media@Gmail.com.